Also by M. A. Bennett

S.T.A.G.S.

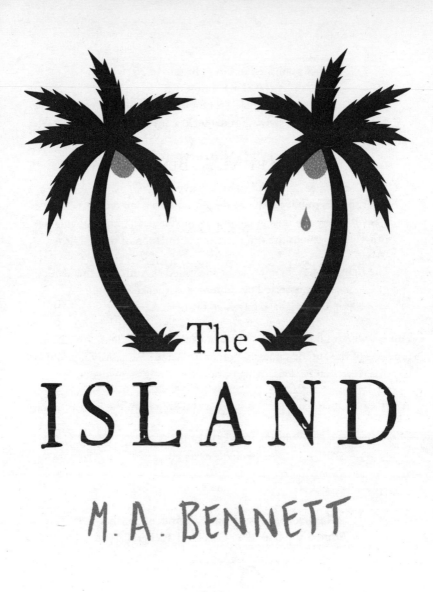

The
ISLAND

M. A. BENNETT

HOT
KEY
BOOKS

First published in Great Britain in 2018 by
HOT KEY BOOKS
80–81 Wimpole St, London W1G 9RE
www.hotkeybooks.com

A CIP catalogue record for this book is available from the British Library.

ISBN: 978-1-4714-0753-6
also available as an ebook

1

This book is typeset using Atomik ePublisher
Printed and bound by Clays Ltd, Elcograf S.p.A

Hot Key Books is an imprint of Bonnier Zaffre Ltd,
a Bonnier Publishing company
www.bonnierpublishing.com

To Sacha,
who used to be a Nowhere Man
and is now a Somewhere Man

'No man is an island entire of itself . . .'
John Donne

The People on the Island

Lincoln Selkirk: A Nerd

Flora Altounyan: An Emo

Sebastian Loam: A Jock

Miranda Pencroft: A Gorgeous Girl

Ralph Turk: A Delinquent

Jun Am Li: A High Achiever

Gilbert Egan: A Dork

DISC ONE

Ode to Joy

Ludwig van Beethoven (1785)

Prologue

The first thing I remember about the island is opening my eyes and seeing nothing but sand, up really close like it was under a microscope. It sounds stupid but I didn't realise until that moment that sand up close just looks like a bunch of tiny rocks all stacked together like that crumbly brown sugar you have in England. My head, on the side that I was lying, felt as though it had been squished flat, like my skull had morphed from an English football shape to an American football shape.

I blinked and tried to focus. Something was rushing towards my face. It was warm salt water. It splashed into my mouth, making me gag, then rushed away again as quickly as it had come. Then a few seconds later it was back, and this time it brought something with it. I put out a hand that didn't seem to belong to me and caught at the spidery black shape, bringing it closer to my face. It was my £4 pair of glasses from Tiger, still intact.

I sat up, and my head throbbed once, hard. I washed my glasses in the sea and out of habit I put them on, the water from the lenses falling down my face like tears. It was so hot the tears dried almost at once. I wiggled my jaw. It hurt. Then

5

I explored the teeth on the right side of my face with my tongue. They felt a bit wobbly, but there were no gaps, just the sharp edge of the tooth that had been cracked where I'd been punched in games. My mom had been hounding me to get it fixed for weeks, but I hadn't gotten around to it. I guess now it would have to wait a helluva lot longer.

I looked down at the rest of me. I didn't seem to have any injuries. My skinny white arms were all right, and my skinny white legs seemed OK too. I had no mirror so I couldn't check my football head, but I looked down my shirt and my torso seemed good too – its usual puny, concave self, with about as many hairs as Homer Simpson's head – pathetic for a sixteen-year-old, but good. The white shirt and khaki shorts that I'd worn on the plane were a bit scrubbed and ripped, and somehow I'd managed to lose my sneakers – my long white feet were bare. But all things considered I was in pretty good shape for someone who'd just fallen from the sky.

I looked around me. I was on a classic, SpongeBob SquarePants island, with palm trees, and green sea, and blue sky. A golden sun was burning down from overhead – I'd never been so hot in my life, not even back in Palo Alto. I could hear my own breathing inside of my head, and outside of my head I could hear the sound of the tide washing in and out. The island was breathing too.

There was a sudden, delicious breeze and another sound was added to the mix: this sort of whispering of the wind in the palm trees. The big glossy leaves were wagging about, above these huge green coconuts dangling in pairs below them. Inland beyond the palm trees was a jungly wilderness, and a high

6

green hill. Of course, I didn't know right then that I was on an island, but it sure as hell looked like one. Behind me there was a long scar in the sand as if I'd been pushed or dragged along the beach as I'd landed. Far along the beach were scattered white somethings, which I figured must be bits of the light aircraft my class and I had taken off in.

I got up from the beach slowly, spitting sand, my legs wobbling like a new foal's. My eyes, nose and mouth were full of sand. I blinked and hawked and spat. The right side of my head, the squashed side, hurt like hell. But I didn't care. I turned around on the beach, three-sixty degrees, and peered as far as I could to the horizon. There was not a soul to be seen. Just me.

I should've been frightened at that point. But I wasn't. No, sir. I did a little victory dance, flapping my hands at the sky like those tube dudes you see at gas stations, the ones with the air blowing through them. With my sandy throat I sang a few shaky bars of 'Ode to Joy'. The fact that it was the tune to our school song couldn't ruin it for me any more.

My classmates were dead. All dead. And *that* was a cause for celebration.

My mom had been right.

The geek had inherited the earth.

DISC TWO

Nowhere Man – The Beetles

John Lennon, Paul McCartney (1965)

THREE YEARS EARLIER

1

Desert Island Discs

My kind – the lesser spotted geek – have our stereotypes to conform to. We like words (I can quote Star Wars verbatim). We like numbers (I can quote Pi to hundreds of places). And we are as happy as a pig in shit when words and numbers intersect (I like that there are 39 Steps, or 101 Dalmatians, or that the Count of Monte Cristo was known as Prisoner 34.) We like computers. We like Marvel and DC. We can build stuff, but we can't talk to people. We can make anything you like except friends. We like girls but we can't get 'em. And what we don't do, what we *absolutely* don't do, is Sports. Or as my new school called them, Games.

Games to me were always video games. Video games would've been OK. Like most of my kind I'm a pretty serious gamer. (*Fortnite. Uncharted IV. Link's Awakening.* And my old-school favourite, *Myst.*) Sure, some of them can get pretty violent. But it's all virtual, so it's all harmless.

11

What happened at my school were not games.

They were serious.

I'd managed to avoid games lessons until I was thirteen for the very good reason that I'd avoided school itself. Ever since we'd moved to England when I was just a little kid, I'd been home-schooled and I loved it. I was born on the West Coast of America. My parents were academics who taught in this hippy college where people wore tie-dye and sandals and collected crystals. Then the academic parents both got research posts at Oxford University in England, and we moved to Oxford.

We'd all had to make an adjustment moving to England. My folks look like they walked straight out of the seventies without getting changed. My dad has big hair and a beard, and aviator glasses, and wears nylon shirts that crackle when you hug him. My mom has waist-length hair, and wears floor-length skirts. At the University of Palo Alto (their old university) they were known as Paul and Marilyn, even by their students. I don't think I ever saw either of them wearing any shoes other than sandals. At Oxford they were known as Professor P. Selkirk and Professor M. Selkirk and they had to wear actual shoes. But they didn't seem to care. They loved all the history and old colleges and stuff, and they were working on this ground-breaking new Behavioural Science project that got them really pumped. And as for me, they thought the transition from my West Coast American freewheeling elementary school which basically taught finger-painting and not much else, to a buttoned-up British primary school in a very academic town like Oxford would be a bit tough, so they decided to teach me themselves.

Because I was home-schooled I didn't really know any other kids until I was thirteen. Sure, I went to the birthday parties of the kids of my parents' colleagues, but I made no lasting friendships. For one thing, academia is this kinda transitory life and people are always buzzing around the world taking up different fellowships and the Chair of This or the Reader of That. So the kids I got to know were only in Oxford for, like, two seconds. For another, I felt like I didn't need anybody but my folks. I had a great time being taught by them. They were attached to a box-fresh, modern faculty called the Institute of Behavioural Science, and also to this incredibly old, incredibly beautiful college called Trinity. But there was always someone at home, and that someone would teach me.

They taught me science – of course – and math and English, and even some Latin because it was, said my dad, the language of science. They taught me politics, which I was always interested in from Day One, because of my name. I'd known all my life that I was named after President Lincoln but weirdly it wasn't till we'd moved to England that I asked my parents why *him*.

'He's my favourite president,' Mom had said.

'And sometimes if you're named after someone you emulate them,' added Dad. They often talked in turn like that – they were a real double act, not just at work but at home too. 'It's called nominative determinism.' My parents never dumbed things down, even when I was little. They just expected me to keep up.

I said: 'You mean you want me to be shot in a theatre at the age of fifty-four?'

They laughed at that. 'No, silly,' said my mom. 'I was thinking more of how he *lived*, not how he *died*. He was an ethical leader, with a strong moral compass. He abolished slavery, you know.'

I did know. 'I think the slavery thing has been done, Mom. I can't exactly abolish it *again*.'

'There are still slaves in some places, son,' said my dad. 'And what your mom means is that you could be president one day.'

'But we live in England now.'

'Doesn't matter,' said Dad. 'Lots of presidents came to Oxford. John Quincy Adams. JFK. Bill Clinton. The only thing that matters, Link, is that you were born in America. You're welcome by the way.'

My parents always called me Link. Nothing to do with *Zelda*, if that's what you're thinking. For the longest time I thought it was short for Lincoln but dad said no, it was because they could never find me at mealtimes because I was always playing those games, or finding the prime numbers on a chessboard, or building a model airplane or something. There was always this empty chair at the dinner table, so one of them would sigh, throw down their napkin and come and find me. And that's why they called me 'the Missing Link'. It always cracked them up but it took me *years* to get the joke.

That was the great thing about being home-schooled. There was no structure. If I was inventing something in the garden they'd just leave me to it, until it was too dark for me to see what I was doing. Or if I was really into a book I was reading they'd just let me finish it, until hunger pangs clawed at my stomach and pulled me out of the story. Then there would be great days when we were all at home and my mom and dad would just decide at breakfast that we'd ditch schoolwork for the whole day and go off on some trip. These trips were always educational but they sure were fun for a nerd like me. We'd go off to London on the train and spend the days in the brown and dust-smelling Natural History Museum, dwarfed by dinosaur skeletons, or go to Stratford-upon-Avon and feed the swans and then go see a play at the Royal Shakespeare Theatre. In fact, thinking about it, my parents sure took me to a lot of plays considering I was named after a president who was shot in a theatre, even plays that were too old for me. I can still remember the first play I ever went to in England. I must've only been around eight. It was about this butler, who is a total slave to this hoity-toity upper-class English family, and him and the family get marooned on a desert island, and on the island everything flips and he is the boss, and they are his slaves. My parents sold it to me by saying it was by the same guy who wrote *Peter Pan*. I was much too young to really get it, but I was Hooked. No pun intended.

After our happy days of lessons or trips, there would be happy evenings at home. We lived in a red-brick, Victorian house in a pretty nice neighbourhood in Oxford which was, for reasons no one ever explained to me, called Jericho. We'd sit around the table in our warm kitchen after dinner, listening to the washing machine coming into land, and the same show playing on the radio. My parents' favourite thing about England was the BBC, and their favourite thing about the BBC was BBC Radio 4, and their favourite thing about Radio 4 was *Desert Island Discs*. It's presented by this chick with a really soft (Scottish?) voice, and what she does is she gets all these famous people to choose their eight favourite pieces of music, and she asks them why they've chosen them, and then she plays them on the show. I don't mean shitty celebrities like the Kardashians, I mean like really amazing actors and scientists and politicians and stuff. The subjects also get to choose one book. You already get given the Bible and *The Complete Works of Shakespeare*, so there's no point wasting your book choice on those. Finally you get one luxury like a piano or a hot tub or something. It sounds like a crazy show but it is kinda cool. Apparently it's been running for like a million years and it's had awesome people on it like Stephen Hawking. (They even April-Fooled everyone in 1963 by doing a whole show on this guy who was totally fake. They made up this dude called Sir Harry Whitlohn, who was supposed to be a mountaineer, and they had him voiced by an actor who bragged about his expeditions and chose all his music and everything. Everyone totally bought it.) The idea of the show is that the music choices of the person tell you more about what the person is really like than the interview bits they do in between the tracks. I really liked it because I've never felt like a child of my time musically. For me all the latest music is totally linked with social media (ya know, people like old Taylor Swift hawking her wares on Instagram) and social media means *fear* for me for reasons which will become clear later. But *Desert Island Discs* introduced me to old music, the kind of music my parents liked. The kind of music that was actually a disc, made of vinyl, and not a download, or a stream, or an mp-whatever. That kind was safe. And I dug it.

So I had all kinds of lessons, and in the evenings I'd listen to *Desert Island Discs*, or be in my bedroom gaming, but one thing I never, ever had to do was play actual *games*. No Phys Ed. No sports. Not so much as a star jump. And then I turned thirteen and all that changed when it was decided that I had to go to school, because that's when the rest of the kids in England would be choosing their options for GCSEs and starting the two-year courses that led up to the exams. I was outpacing my parents in some subjects, not science (of course) but other things. My folks didn't exactly press me to their bosoms and say *My boy, you are a genius. We can teach you nothing more.* But that's kinda what they *meant*. I needed subject teachers, teachers who were experts in their field. I needed to follow the curriculum, and have a more serious education than just a few hours here and there. And, most of all, according to my folks, I needed to be 'socialised'. My parents use lots of Behavioural Science jargon, and what they meant by that was that I needed to know other kids. 'You're an only child, honey,' my mom would say. 'Heck, we'd keep you with us forever if we could, just the three of us. But you need to mix with kids your own age.' Then my dad said something that would keep coming back to me. 'No man is an island.'

So they found this prestigious private school – ironically, on an island – where they gave assisted places to the kids of dons (professors of the University like my mom and dad). And that's how I ended up, at the age of thirteen, in the living hell that was Osney School.

2

The Games Nazi

And of course, one of my very first lessons at Osney had to be games. I found myself standing, just before noon on my first morning, in the middle of the Great Court at Osney School, freezing my ass off, dressed in nothing but my games kit.

The material of this kit was good quality but thin as paper. It was only September but it felt like it was below zero. I'd never been so cold in my life. The Osney School games kit consisted of navy-blue shorts and a navy tee with the school badge on the right breast. The school crest was a little tree, like an oak tree, on an island, with these three lines underneath to symbolise water I guess. This was because the school was on a sort of island called Osney in the middle of the river.

The only comfort this games kit gave me (because it sure as hell wasn't warmth) was that I looked just like everybody else. I hoped that if I could hide in this crowd of kids dressed exactly the same as me, maybe I could get through the class without making a giant fool of myself. I knew that at Osney School they wouldn't be playing any of the sports I would've failed at back home, like basketball or baseball; there'd be a whole raft of new sports for me to fail at. Worse still, Osney was a school for boys *and* girls, so half the crowd around me was female. This was not good news. My potential for humiliation always rises exponentially when there are girls around. So I shivered, and hid, and tried not to be too conspicuous.

Of course, I didn't look *exactly* like everyone else. My hair was badly cut, as always, by me. My parents don't believe in haircuts and I have longish, brownish hair, but whenever the front bits get in my eyes I just hack them off with nail scissors, usually much too short so I don't have to do it for a while, and that, I know, gave me a weird surprised look. My mom always goes on about how handsome I am but I automatically discount that – moms are programmed to think their offspring are beautiful. On the plus side I had pretty clear skin for a thirteen-year-old (lesser spotted, you see). Also I was wearing a new pair of glasses, my pride and joy, which cost three hundred pounds. That morning I doubted the wisdom of wearing them for games (no one else had glasses on) but I didn't have a locker yet and I didn't really want to leave them anywhere, they were too precious. My parents had bought the glasses for me as a kind of bribe when they announced that I'd be going to school for the first time. They were a bit too big for my face but they had black glossy frames and crystal bright lenses and they said **Tom Ford** along one arm in discreet silver type. I wasn't even upset about going to school – little did I know, huh? – but I accepted the glasses anyway because I thought they were pretty cool. I'm not actually too short-sighted, but I like wearing glasses. They are the insignia of my people.

So it was through the new glasses that I gazed at my surroundings. Osney School looked exactly like an Oxford college, which it kinda was. It even looked like a smaller version of the college (Trinity) which my parents were attached to. Right now I was in the central bit – the Great Court, which was a big square of green grass in the middle of the school. Around four sides of the grass and paving stones were these long low buildings from the days of Olde Englande, all beautiful, all slightly different, making up this huge 'quad'. Osney School was a pretty expensive day school, and looked it. There was no way I would've been there except for the fact that it had connections with the University.

As we all waited, and shivered, this dude walked out into the court in an Osney sweatshirt and track pants (lucky guy – no shivering in short pants for him). He did this exaggerated little jog out into the middle of the grass just to prove he was sporty as hell. He wore a whistle round his neck on a ribbon like an Olympic gold medal. In my whole time at Osney I never once saw him use it. The whistle for him was like my glasses for me. Unnecessary, but his defining insignia. This was Mr Llewellyn, the games teacher.

He was a huge guy, with thinning sandy hair and piercing blue eyes. As if to make up for the hair he'd lost on his head he'd grown this big sandy wartime moustache. He looked at us all like we were roaches on his pizza. I tried to shrink back behind the others, but he spotted me at once, and looked at me like he'd won something.

'Ah! I see we have a new student joining us today,' he said, pointing at me with a big hotdog finger. 'Step forward, boy. What's your name?'

So much for staying under the radar. I stepped forward, teeth chattering. 'I'm Lincoln Selkirk.'

'I'm Lincoln Selkirk, *sir*.' He sniffed and his moustache took a leap. 'Bit of an odd name.'

'I was named after Abraham Lincoln, the sixteenth president of the United States.'

I could see that Mr Llewellyn didn't really care that I was named after Abraham Lincoln, or that he was the sixteenth president of the United States. That was too much information for old Llewellyn. I was to learn that he was only really interested, like most people at Osney, in games. If Lincoln had been a soccer player – sorry, football – then maybe.

'Well, we don't need to concern ourselves with your first name here, however outlandish,' said Mr Llewellyn. 'Here you're just Selkirk.'

'Yessir.'

'American, are you, Selkirk?'

This was the first time I'd ever been asked that question, so I had to think about it. What was I? I'd been in England since I was seven, but I'd been *born* in America, so I guessed that tipped things.

'Yessir.'

'Hmmm. Probably never played any proper sports then, I'll bet.'

That sentence told me everything I needed to know about Mr Llewellyn. He was a Games Nazi. If Mr Llewellyn was on *Desert Island Discs* he would choose tracks like 'Chariots of Fire' and 'Escape to Victory' and 'Eye of the Tiger'. His book would be

21

one of those books that aren't real books but are called *1001 Sporting Facts* or something, those books that are designed for people to read while they're taking a shit. His luxury would be his phony little whistle.

'Well, Selkirk, in that case I think it's only fair that we should show you how we do things in Oxford. What do you think?' He had this very upper-class accent, like the World War II pilot he resembled. 'Well?' he asked his class. 'Should we show our American cousin how we do things at Osney?'

Now I'll tell you a bit of trivia. The play President Abraham Lincoln was watching when he was shot (aged fifty-four) was called *Our American Cousin*. I remember thinking at the time that Mr Llewellyn accidentally saying this exact title had to be a very bad omen for my first day. Turned out I was right.

'Selkirk, you are about to become part of a great Oxford sporting tradition. Like all new Osney students, you will be required to take part in the Osney Dash, a race around Osney Great Court.' He waved his arm in a sweeping arc, taking in the four sides of the court, including the kind of chapel bit in the middle with a clock and a bell tower. The clock had a blue face (like most of the kids by now) and gold numbers. The gold hands stood at five minutes to twelve. 'I will give you a pacemaker – a student to run with you – but the race is not between you and him, but between you and the bells.' He pointed the hotdog finger at the clock. 'It is nearly noon. The idea is that you will complete the circuit before the bells strike twelve.'

I looked around the vast courtyard. It was immense. 'Starting now?' I asked.

The class tittered.

'No,' said Mr Llewellyn. 'You can't begin until the sound of the first chime.'

This was a nightmare. Not only would I be at the centre of attention, exactly where I didn't want to be, but I knew just how slow I was at running. 'Excuse me. You want me to run all the way round this court in twelve seconds?'

'No,' said Mr Llewellyn patiently. 'There are four quarter strikes before the hour begins to chime. That's at least another ten seconds. You begin at the sound of the first bell of the first quarter.'

I think I knew what he meant. The quarters were the four *bing bong bing bong* bits before the hour strikes. But even with those, I figured it was impossible.

'You're *kidding*.'

'Don't be insolent, boy,' said Mr Llewellyn. 'It's perfectly straightforward. It's even possible to complete the circuit *before* the first chime of the hour, a distinction known as the "Quarters". Loam here is the only Quarters boy in a century.'

This enormous kid stepped forward – as wide as he was tall.

'Most students complete the dash somewhere between five o'clock and ten,' Mr Llewellyn went on. 'Their position in the chimes allows me to assess their probable sporting prowess.' He spoke to the giant kid, in quite a different voice from the one he'd used to me. 'Loam, you'll be the pacemaker. See if you can beat your record, eh?'

'Sir.'

'Selkirk; this is Loam.'

23

The giant put out his hand. Not sure what to do I sort of nodded at him.

'Shake hands, Selkirk,' barked Mr Llewellyn. 'You're in England now, not the colonies. We are civilised here.'

I took the giant kid's paw, and he damn near crushed my hand to death.

And that's how I met Sebastian Loam.

3

The Sockdologiser

If Sebastian Loam was on *Desert Island Discs* he would choose songs that people sing at English ball games, like 'Jerusalem', or 'Swing Low, Sweet Chariot'. In the Venn diagram of *Desert Island Discs* his choices would have a lot of crossover with Mr Llewellyn's. Sebastian Loam *might* be able to think of eight tracks, but he probably wouldn't be able to think of a single book, and his luxury would definitely be a ball of some kind. In the States we'd call him a jock.

Even at thirteen Sebastian Loam was huge, and broad with it. (I'm not short myself but at that point in my life I was skinny as a straw. If I wrapped my first finger and my thumb round my wrist they, like, overlapped. Loam, as he was known, was the best sportsman in the school. He rowed, he played cricket, he played rugby, he played football. In the US jocks are tolerated, laughed at as simple souls, strong but not too clever. The problem with old Loam was that he was mean as a whip *and* great at sport. He was a good-looking sonofabitch too. A triple threat. At Osney Loam was a king because, oddly for a school in such a prestigious university town, sports (or games) were far more important than academic achievement. Even the terms at Osney were given sporting names instead of semester numbers. Autumn term was the Rugby Term, spring term was the Cricket Term, and the summer term was simply called Rowers. I was to learn later that Loam was literally the King of the School, as there was this bizarre annual ceremony called 'Toppers' in which the most achieving sportsman of the year was crowned 'King' with the lid of this big silver trophy. The most achieving sportsman was always Sebastian Loam, so he won Toppers every year. There was this Osney legend about his entry interview with the Head (Principal). (The head teacher of the school was also Mr Llewellyn. Go figure. Typical Osney to elevate the games teacher over everybody else.) The story goes that Mr Llewellyn didn't ask Loam any questions but just took a book from the shelves and threw it straight at Loam when he wasn't looking. Loam caught it one-handed and Mr Llewellyn said: 'We need a good fly half. You're in.'

Old Llewellyn's faith was justified. Loam won *everything* for the school. He was a natural sportsman, and carried Osney to victory in every competition in Oxfordshire and beyond. The whole school was silver-lined with trophies. In the States you could win trophies for science competitions or spelling bees, but there was no hardware at Osney for anything but games. Even the teachers treated Loam like a hero. He had about a million followers on Instagram and was always posting photos of his muscles or his trophies or him meeting David Beckham and crap like that. Of course I didn't know any of that stuff on that first day. I just saw this big kid with dark hair, and this small kid standing behind him carrying a bag like a hotel porter. (This was Loam's shadow, Egan. His first name is Gilbert but he shortens it to Gil. If Egan was on *Desert Island Discs* he'd choose exactly the same tracks as Loam. Egan was Loam's bitch.)

Mr Llewellyn did his little jog to the piece of the paving stones opposite this archway under the clock tower. 'This line, Selkirk –' he scrubbed his enormous sneaker across an ancient stone drain set into the paving stones – 'is the start and the finish line. Line up, you two.'

Loam stood toes up to the stone line, jiggling about like a boxer. He was doing that warm-up thing athletes do, pulling his arms across his body and his knees up to his chest, shaking out his shoulders and waving his head from side to side. I reluctantly walked forward. Many times in my life I've wanted the ground to open up and swallow me. But unfortunately I knew enough about geology to realise that just wasn't going to happen. Maybe in California I might have hoped for the San Andreas Fault to come to my rescue, but here in England I was on solid ground and would have to endure the attention. All those eyes I didn't want to look at me were looking at me, and the mouths that I didn't want to whisper were whispering. I knew what they were saying because. Weird hair. Weird body. Weird glasses. *Geek*.

I just stood there at the starting line, heart hammering, my eyes on the big golden hand of the clock crawling upward to noon.

The crowd of kids suddenly went silent.

Loam suddenly fell absolutely still by my side.

High Noon, I thought.

This dumb English contest had suddenly taken on an American significance. Loam and I were the gunfighters, albeit that we stood side by side instead of face to face. But I knew, right there and then, that I was dead.

In that last millisecond before the bell started to chime I stopped looking at the golden hand and looked dead ahead at the course I was to run. But then something else golden caught my eye.

She'd obviously just made a tiny movement, like shifting from one foot to the other, or moving slightly so she could see better, and I turned my head to look at her. She had this golden hair, tied up in a high ponytail. Bits of baby hair, almost white blonde, were escaping from the ponytail and curling round her perfect face. She had clear pale skin, and cheekbones touched with pink like magnolia blossom. She had full pink lips and one of those tiny noses, and these blue eyes the colour of which I'd never seen before, but I was to see again three years later in a cloudless sky above a desert island. I didn't have time to wonder what this goddess would choose for her Desert Island Discs because then the bell in the tower began to strike, and I began to run.

I knew I was never going to win but I was not prepared for just how fast Loam would be. He streaked ahead of me along the pavings like some superhero, kicking up chippings into my face. He should've been wearing a cape. By the time the first quarter had rung, he'd completed one side of the square. I could hear the rest of the class cheering Loam on from the middle of the grass, chanting his name. No one chanted mine.

I really can't run. I'm very much an indoors kind of cat. When I wasn't having lessons from Mom and Dad I spent most of my time in my room, reading, gaming, inventing things; the geek curriculum.

By the time I'd got to the end of the first side of the square I had a crippling stitch and had to do this half-hop, half-walk thing. That lost me a lot of time. Then I jogged for a bit, the stitch like needles in my side, my lungs bursting. Three quarters had rung before I'd completed two sides of the square. As the fourth quarter rang Loam crossed the finish line to rapturous cheers. And after that there was just this eerie silence as the stony-faced class watched me jogging and limping pathetically home. I reached the fourth side of the square as the first chime of the hour struck.

ONE. Suddenly it was hugely important that I complete the circuit before the chimes struck twelve. They were all watching. Loam. The Games Nazi. And, suddenly more important than all, the goddess. I tried to urge my poor legs to go a bit faster. **TWO**. The cobbles swam before my eyes. I couldn't pass out now. **THREE**. It was going to be all right. I'd make it by seven, maybe eight. **FOUR**. I stumbled and tripped, in my unaccustomed new sneakers, throwing out my hands to save myself. The gravel bit into my palms. **FIVE**. I was on my hands and knees, head down, breathing hard. **SIX**. I scrambled up, palms stinging, kneecaps bleeding. **SEVEN**. I began to walk. **EIGHT**. I began to jog. **NINE**. I began to run but – **TEN** – it was no good, I was no more than halfway by the time **ELEVEN** struck. I lengthened my stride and summoned every bit of my puny strength, but the bell had struck **TWELVE** and the chime had fully died away before I got back to the starting line.

I doubled over, my hands on my knees, my breath burning and coming in dry heaves. I thought I was going to make matters infinitely worse by puking right in front of everyone, but instead I just collapsed right there on the hallowed grass of Osney Great Court, looking up at the clear blue sky and breathing hard. The huge shadow of Mr Llewellyn fell over me.

'Twelve,' he almost spat, with half wonder, half disgust. '*Twelve*. We haven't had a twelve for *years*.' Then he gave this little speech that I didn't understand at all. 'Not enough meat on you for a fly half. Not fast enough for a winger. Can't rely on you to sprint between the wickets. Too puny to pull at stroke. Too tall for a cox.' But then he finished with something I understood very well. 'You're no use to me at all, are you, Selkirk?' He turned and strode away, talking to the class at large as he walked. 'Let's get out to the playing fields then – there's still time for a spot of rugby. We've wasted enough time here already.'

Feeling less than worthless, I wobbled to my feet and followed him. I felt like something had gone badly wrong. I wanted to protest, to say there'd been some sort of horrible mistake. I'd fallen – surely I could have a do-over? I couldn't see Loam, I couldn't see the goddess, I couldn't see anything apart from red spots in front of my eyes.

We all clattered through the archway under the clock tower to the green fields beyond, but under the darkness of its shadow, Loam's massive paw descended on my shoulder. 'Where d'you think you're going, Selkirk?'

'To the –' I pointed – 'playing fields?'

He shook his head. 'Not yet.'

My eyes were adjusting to the darkness of the archway after the bright day. What I saw was not encouraging. Loam and a little knot of his cronies, faces looming from the darkness, all looking mean as hell. Loam turned to the smaller kid carrying the bag, who was still dogging his footsteps. 'What was your Dash time, Egan?'

'Eleven o'clock, Loam.'

'All right,' said Loam. He grabbed the massive sports bag from Egan's hand and held it high in front of my face. Then he dropped it on the toes of my new sneakers. It hurt.

'Congratulations, Selkirk,' he said. 'This is what you won.'

I didn't understand what was happening. 'But I lost,' I said.

'Egan here used to be the slowest. Now it's you.' He turned to the small kid again. 'What do you say, Egan? We're Englishmen, we have manners.'

'Thank you for this year, Loam.'

'You're welcome, Egan.' He turned back to me. 'Now, Selkirk, you are my new slave. You had slaves in America, didn't you? You understand the concept? I have rugby club after school. You'll bring that bag to the changing room. As it's your first day I'll go easy on you. That's all you have to do today. Tomorrow I'll tell you your other duties.'

I'm not a tough guy. I cry very easily. I get what I call my Wi-Fi forehead – a series of three lines radiating up my forehead, small to big. I could feel the lines gathering now, and usually when I get the Wi-Fi forehead there's no going back, tears inevitably follow. But I knew I couldn't cry in front of Loam.

I stared hard at the kit bag at my feet. It was enormous – you could have gotten a small child inside it. 'What am I supposed to do with it until after school?'

'Carry it round with you.'

Just then I had a premonition that if I touched the bag – if I just so much as wrapped my fingers round those tough sports handles – that it was over for me, and this kid would be on me for the rest of my natural life. That other kid, Egan, had obviously been carrying Loam's shit for a year. A *year*.

I had to stand up for myself. 'No.' I said.

Loam contemplated me for a second. Then he put out his hand and took my glasses off my nose. He calmly snapped them in half, and threw the pieces over his shoulder. For a moment I couldn't actually believe what had happened. I was so shocked I couldn't speak or move.

Fortunately my glasses are mostly for show – I didn't have to go feeling around on my hand and knees like Velma on *Scooby Doo*, but I was angry, so angry about my beautiful glasses, that I lost my shit. I searched my mind for the worst word I could think of. A word that could kill.

'You . . . you . . . **Sockdologiser**!' I screamed in his face.

This stopped Loam in his tracks, just for a second. Then he started to laugh, and of course all his cronies started to laugh too. 'Is that the best you've got?' he said. He pointed to the bag, and his voice changed. 'Pick it up,' he said through his teeth. He glared at me, unblinking. I knew there was a chance he would hit me. And I knew if he did, it would hurt. I started to feel sick again, this time with fear.

What happened next was not very admirable. I dropped my

eyes first, knelt as if I was Loam's subject and gathered the handles in my hand. He turned on his heel and walked away, followed by his gang.

Suddenly I found that my knees wouldn't let me get up again. I sat back hard against the wall, in the shadows, the back of my head connecting with the cold stone. I sat there for I don't know how long, still clutching the handles of Loam's sports bag. The legs of all the kids who were behind us went past me, oblivious. Box-fresh new sneakers like mine, blue Osney sports socks with white bands, bare legs, blue shorts. And then a pair of legs stopped in front of me. A girl's legs, shapely and long. I looked up, hoping for a moment I was going to see the goddess. But no. The legs belonged to this plumpish, prettyish girl with pink and purple hair. She had a bunch of studs in both ears, and there was a tattoo of the ace of spades on her pale right wrist.

She sort of slid down the wall until her butt was on the floor and she was sitting next to me. Her blue shorts rode up her thighs.

'*Sockdologisor?*' she said

I couldn't really look at her because we were sitting side by side. Instead I fixed my eyes on her legs where they were humped next to mine. I could see very fine gold hairs sticking up on her knees from the cold. I said to her knees: 'Abraham Lincoln was watching a play when he was assassinated. It was a comedy, and John Wilkes Booth, Lincoln's killer, went every night for a week to identify what was the biggest laugh in the play. On the night of the assassination he waited for the laugh. It came when the main character accused another character of being a "Sockdologiser". The audience laughed their asses off, and under the cover of all the noise Booth jumped out of his seat and shot Lincoln dead.'

'Not exactly a hilarious word.' She had a very cut-glass English accent. It didn't really go with the hair.

'It killed that night,' I said. 'Literally.'

'What was the play about?'

It struck me then. 'It's about an American guy who comes to England and doesn't fit in.'

She didn't say anything for a while after that. Then she took my grazed hand and put something in it. Two somethings. My new glasses, neatly snapped in two.

'Sorry about your specs,' she said. It was the one kind thing anyone ever said to me at Osney School. But then the girl with the pink and purple hair got to her feet and left me alone under the archway. I was to learn, a lot later, that this girl was called Flora Altounyan. If Flora was on *Desert Island Discs* she would choose obscure Death Metal tracks with names like 'Those Who Have Lost the Right to Exist'. Her book would probably be *Dracula* and her luxury would probably be a tame black rat or a human skull or something. Flora was the only one who I was even vaguely sorry to see go down with the plane. Not that she was a friend, she wasn't, but she was the only one at Osney who wasn't shitty to me.

4

The Nowhere Man

I carried Loam's bag around school all that first day. At 3.30 p.m. I left it in the changing rooms, and then walked home, my legs still aching from the Osney Dash. As soon as the front door closed behind me I did cry at last.

My mom hugged me and breathed in my hair, not just to tell me it needed washing like she usually did, but the way she used to when I was a little boy. She said to my hair, and this I particularly remember: 'Don't worry, Link. The geek shall inherit the earth.'

At first I didn't understand what she meant. She told me to run and find out. (My mom was really big on the whole 'run and find out' idea. So was my dad. I guess it was an academic thing.) My mom told me to go look in the Bible at Matthew 5:5. Normally I would've googled it but it felt sorta weird googling the Bible, so I thought I'd look at the actual book. I knew we'd have a copy on the bookshelves. (Our house is full of books. I'm talking *every* wall. It's like a goddamn library.)

I got the Bible down and looked up the reference. The Bible doesn't have chapters and numbers like normal books but is a whole mess of different little books within one big volume. These little books are mostly called after people, and they have chapters and verses in. This is what I read in Matthew, Chapter 5 verse 5:

Blessed are the meek: for they shall inherit the earth.

It didn't say 'geek' at all, but 'meek'. That meant my mom was making what she called *a play on words*. It was something Shakespeare did a lot, apparently, and we went to a LOT of Shakespeare plays, being so near Stratford, so I got what she was going for with the whole geek/meek thing. I was still all blubbery and sniffling and some of my boogers fell on the Bible and I sort of looked up as if God was watching me. My parents were behavioural scientists (which means that they studied humans and the reasons they did what they did). Like a lot of scientists they didn't have any religion, and so neither did I, but I was pretty sure it was disrespectful to drip boogers on the Bible. I sort of scrubbed the drips away with the scratchy wool sleeve of my brand-new Osney School blazer. They left a smear over the word 'meek'. It could've actually said 'geek' at that point, cos you couldn't see the **m** any more. I shut the Good Book and wandered into the kitchen.

I opened the fridge out of habit but I couldn't face any food so I took out a can of soda that I didn't really want. The radio was on and *Desert Island Discs* was playing, as it always seemed to be. There was a Beatles song playing which was a pretty safe bet, as they are the most chosen band in the whole history of the show. This one was 'Nowhere Man'. I didn't know the song very well, but that day I sat at the table just listening to the words. The lyrics seemed to be all about me – a real Nowhere Man. I watched the can of soda without opening it. The can had condensation on the sides and it all started to collect together to make big droplets, and the droplets ran down the can. We both cried together and I didn't move until the song was over.

Then I dried my eyes and thought about what my mom had said. I think I knew what she was getting at. She hadn't been making a joke to laugh at me, but to comfort me. She meant that I didn't have any power now, when I was a Nowhere Man, but it wouldn't always be that way.

At the time it didn't work. I mean, I loved my mom, and I loved that she had tried to comfort me, but when you're being bullied a bit of clever wordplay doesn't mean shit.

Now, on the island, it meant everything.

5

The Boy Island

It was actually John Donne, not my dad, who said:
    'No man is an island, entire of itself.'
    I say:
    If John Donne said that, then John Donne didn't know shit about English schools.

And he should've. He really should've. John Donne went to Oxford University at the age of eleven. *Eleven.* You're not telling me he just fitted in on Day One. After all, he was the son of a Welsh ironmonger. Probably had weird clothes and a weird halfway accent like mine. I'll bet he had some shitty experiences which helped him become such an awesome poet later. Maybe they just weren't as shitty as mine.

Every weekday morning I crossed the drawbridge onto Osney Island, this weird kingdom where only games mattered. That little bit of the river that surrounded the island was a daily Rubicon for me, and when I crossed it I became a different person, a drone, a slave. An island, entire of myself.

I'd walk through the iron gates, braced like a soldier, expecting the horrors of conflict which had become everyday. Even the towers and mismatched ancient roofs of this mini city, so ancient, so English, didn't lift my heart. I'd tread the passageways, zombie numb, reflections of my face distorted in the bright metal trophies branded with other people's names. I knew those trophies pretty well, because it was part of my lot to polish them. I also had to wax the Toppers board, with its gilt inlaid names of Sportsman of the Year going all the way back to Georgian times. I had to do strange things to sports equipment, things which had unfamiliar names: waxing, piling, seasoning. I had to wear in new boots that weren't my size until my feet bled. I watched team buses drive off daily with a strange mixture of regret and relief; a combination of FOMO and joy at a couple of hours without orders. Then the coaches would come back and my work would start again with the return of my chief persecutor, Sebastian Loam.

For I quickly came to realise that, unbelievably, your position in Osney School society was determined by your time in the Osney Dash. Imagine if your results at one sports day defined you for the rest of your school life. Not just one sports day, but one *race*. You got to do the Dash once, and it defined you all the way up the school. No do-overs. Mr Llewellyn said you don't get to try life again, so why the Osney Dash? As there were no other Twelves in the school, I was in a company of one.

The strict hierarchy extended itself to every aspect of life at the school. There was a choir for Ones and Twos only. A chess club for Threes. A debating society for Fours and above. There was zip for Twelves. I was the last to be picked for teams, the last to be called in the register (yes, we were listed by our Dash times, nothing so conventional as, ya know, the *alphabet*). I was even the last in the queue for lunch.

Although there were no other Twelves (I guess everyone else had managed to at least stay on their feet for the minute or so of the Osney Dash) there were Elevens; and I thought that they might represent some hope for me. They were all slightly quirky, slightly oddball. Flora, the chick who had consoled me about my glasses, was an Eleven. But after that single conversation she would just give me small tight smiles in the corridor, as I was carrying Loam's kit bag. Sorta halffriendly, halfpity. I would take them though. I collected those half-smiles, cos enough halves made some whole ones.

Flora was the only person at Osney School who was known by her first name. Everyone else was strictly second name only, like they were playing some televised sport. Maybe Flora was an exception because with her pink hair and her ace-of-spades tattoo she was different than the rest, or maybe because her name – Altounyan – was such a ballache to pronounce. Flora hung out with the same two friends ALL the TIME. This chick called Smith and this dude called Fry. Flora, Smith and Fry. They sounded like a folk band from the seventies – the kind of band my mom would choose for *Desert Island Discs*, the kind who did trippy songs about Remembering What the Dormouse Said. To begin with I thought those three had friend potential. Flora had already been nice to me, Smith was the only one who came anywhere near my marks in math class, and Fry, I was sure, was a gamer – I could smell one a mile off. But Flora, Smith and Fry had their own little trifecta, and no interest at all in me.

I tried to reach out to Egan, Loam's ex-bitch. I thought he might like the company of a fellow lowlife, or might have some empathy for the guy who was his successor. But he blew me off too. He seemed to have some weird loyalty to Loam, as if Loam still had some sorta hold on him. Egan wouldn't hear a word against his ex-boss, and was damn near as lousy to me as Loam was himself. It was as if Egan couldn't bring himself to ally himself with me, because that would identify him as my kind, a loser. Instead he ran after the winners like a little dog.

You might be thinking at this point: *Hold* on a minute. This Dash thing is actually quite fair. It might be what you call a meritocracy: if you can run fast, you're at the top of the heap. That's got nothing to do with money. It's to do with being good or bad at games.

Not so. Osney School was fee-paying, and it had a countrywide reputation as an ace sports school. Every single person I knew at Osney, except for the dons' kids like me, had gone to an expensive prep school that drilled the little pupils relentlessly in their sports skills. Every kid was tutored to get into Osney by ex-Olympic athletes and world champions and shit. So if you're thinking some kid from the mean streets could just get in and run right past the rich kids, you'd be wrong. The whole system was rigged.

So I, Selkirk, was the lowest of the low, my own little island. But that didn't mean I was ignored. Oh no. When I was doing the Osney Dash I never heard my name once, not one peep of support from the bleachers. Now it was *all* I heard. Because I was a Twelve, every number above me, even the lowly Elevens, could boss me around. *Selkirk, do this. Selkirk, do that.*

I couldn't protest. The sheer weight of the triangle of numbers above me, like the biggest pyramid of cheerleaders ever, meant there was nothing I could do. I couldn't exactly start a rebellion. There was no one to start a rebellion with. The Elevens, mostly Emos like Flora, were a bunch of stoners who were the least active activists I'd ever seen. They weren't about to start a revolution. And at the top of the pyramid, waving his pom-poms, Sebastian Loam, the Sockdologiser, the only student who'd run the Osney Dash in the Quarters. His Quarters status gave him absolute power. And he had absolute power over me.

Why I Didn't Exactly Weep When I Thought All My Classmates Were Dead

Loam had it made in the shade. Everyone wanted to be his friend. You know that thing people always say about James Bond? That guys want to be him and girls want to be with him? That was Loam. Even the teachers loved him, in spite of the fact he was thick as shit and flunking every class. Loam brought home the precious silverware and that was all that mattered at Osney.

He didn't act alone. It would have been easier to defy him if he had. He had a little cohort of Ones around him, his Best Supporting Actors. During my three dramatic years at the school, I became familiar with the cast of characters in Osney's sick little play.

The goddess that I'd seen on the day of the Osney Dash was Pencroft, first name Miranda. Osney didn't have cheerleaders, but if they had she'd have been bang on the top of the pyramid too. She was beautiful, and when she walked down the corridor with all her buddies in her wake it always looked like she had a wind machine on her. There should've been music playing too – maybe something from the Miranda Pencroft playlist. (If Pencroft was on *Desert Island Discs*, she'd choose Taylor Swift, Ariana Grande and Justin Bieber). Miranda was a swimmer and her prowess in the pool had given her this ridiculous body: long strong limbs, amazing legs, and hair that was almost silver blonde from the chlorine. She always smelled of swimming pools, and for the rest of my life that smell gave me a feeling of sick, fearful excitement. Miranda Pencroft was like the Little Mermaid, not the cutesy red-haired Disney one, but the one from the original Hans Christian Andersen story. Pencroft was her in the part of the book when she went on shore and was allowed to walk on the earth as the most beautiful girl in the world, a girl who could capture a prince just with her looks, even though she was mute. (I think in the story she had to have her tongue cut out to get legs for a day – those old fairy tales were pretty dark.) Pencroft was just as hot, and just as silent, as the Little Mermaid. She never looked at me, although I looked at her all the time. I couldn't help it. She might have been a One in the Dash but she was a stone-cold Ten in the looks department. She never talked to me either, but that didn't mean she didn't bully me. Pencroft's weapon of choice was social media, and with that she damn near pushed me over the edge.

Pencroft's best friend was Jun Am Li. Li had waist-length black hair which she wore in a thick braid when she was participating

44

in her two passions, tennis and violin. She was a prodigy at both. If Li was on *Desert Island Discs* she'd choose Mozart violin concertos, those ones that begin with a K. Li had the worst case of resting bitch face that I've ever seen. She looked hostile even when she wasn't trying to be; but most of the time, Li *was* trying to be hostile, so that worked out just fine. Li was mega-protective of her bestie, Miranda Pencroft, and her hostility to me was born out of the fact that she caught me, *once*, staring at her. 'What are you looking at, you perv?' she'd asked, all fierce eyes and pointing violin fingers. I was, at that very moment, having my Little Mermaid thought about Pencroft but I couldn't exactly say that. So I said, 'Nothin'.'

She got right in my face. 'Better not,' she said. 'She's WAY out of your league.' Like I needed to be told.

Loam's BFF was Turk, a brilliant natural footballer. Turk thought he was a real Roadman, and he was lucky in his second name because it fitted that image perfectly. I happened to know though, from picking up prescriptions for him, that his first name was Ralph and he was just as rich as the other kids. Turk had this dumb haircut which was almost shaved up the sides and long on top. He probably thought it gave him *edge*. He wore this Adidas pouch on a long strap strung across his body, presumably to hold all his 'drugs'. He also made that really annoying noise with his mouth, that one called *kissing your teeth*, a sucking little 'street' noise which punctuated everything he said. He called everyone *bruv*, or *cuz*, or *fam*, and it was rumoured that he dealt drugs, even when I first knew him, and he was thirteen then. Apparently he hung out on the dodgy estates far from the dreaming spires of Oxford, places like Blackbird Leys in the grimy suburbs. I didn't really buy what he was selling – not the drugs, the image. Sure, he talked a good game in chemistry, the only subject he was any good at, and he seemed to know a lot about chemicals and drugs paraphernalia. In the science lab he acted like he was cooking up meth in his basement like some kind of Breaking Badass. But I privately thought that if Turk saw an actual drug he would run a mile. If Turk was on *Desert Island Discs* he would choose Grime artists from the 'streets', like Lethal Bizzle or Wretch 32. But he was a total fake. In actuality, his prescriptions told me, he lived very near me in middle-class Jericho, his parents were perfectly respectable, and he probably played Ed Sheeran and Coldplay at home. But because everyone thought Turk was tough, he ruled the school alongside Loam. Turk's tortures were chemical – something I learned the hard way.

7

Blucozade

It must have been in the dining hall that Turk spiked me that day. A long, oak-panelled room, with a raised platform at one end with a 'High Table' and all the teachers, in their inevitable sports kit, sitting under walls hung with equally inevitable trophies and rosettes. My usual company at lunch was the one portrait in the whole room, which was a massive canvas of George III, founder of the school, hanging over the door, facing the high table and the big window. I knew, appropriately, exactly three things about George III.

1/ He founded Osney School.

2/ He lost the US for the English Crown in the American War of Independence.

3/ He went mad.

You couldn't really see the mad thing in the portrait. Obviously old George was still managing to keep it together at that point without letting on that he was a total fruitloop. In fact he had an air of entitlement and authority about him, of

47

superiority to everybody else. He reminded me of Loam, i.e. he looked like a dick.

Anyway I always ate my crappy, protein-based lunch – lots of meat and eggs at Osney – on my own at the end of the table, under the eye of my ol' pal Mad George. But that day was different. Turk, in his habitual football kit, slid his tray up next to mine, ('What up, my G?') and bounced onto the bench beside me. He upset my drink in the process and righted it again, saying, 'My bad.' After that I could swear my sports drink was a bit gritty, but it was already coloured such an improbable radioactive blue it was really difficult to tell if there was anything in it.

The cramps came on in games. When else? I didn't know shit could go as runny as pee until the pain doubled me up halfway across the rugby field and I saw the horrifying trail of brown liquid running down my leg. I had to run behind a tree as my ass exploded. I took off my shorts and had to use my underwear to clean up. Throwing my offending jockeys in a bush I put the shorts back on. I had to hobble back to school with my legs pressed together, noticing as I ran Turk having to lean on a rugby post, doubled up too. Not with diarrhoea but with laughter.

There was no disguising what had happened. It wasn't just the streaks on my legs that gave me away but the smell. I spent the rest of the afternoon in the can, as whatever Turk had given me turned me inside out. You can guess what the name-calling focused on after that – shit-for-brains, Pampers etc. Let me tell you I got tired of seeing the poo emoji.

It was a pretty crude joke, the old laxative Lucozade, but

Turk was cleverer than that. He had all the words. Loam wasn't articulate – he was a brute, a mouth-breather and a knuckle-dragger. But Turk, with his ever-flowing stream of street slang, always had new things to call me. Every day. Some words were familiar: *nerd, geek, loser*. Some I didn't understand at all: *lemon, donut, melt*. One of them, *faggot*, I understood very well. Quite a skill, you've gotta admit, to be a girl-stalking pervert (according to Li) and a faggot (according to Turk) at the same time.

Gil Egan, for some reason, leaped on this suggestion of Turk's that I was gay. I wouldn't mind, except I wasn't. It would've been funny, except it wasn't. It would have been laughable, but I didn't laugh. Egan's systematic campaign of misplaced homophobia pretty much ground me down more than anything else. He would never lose an opportunity to go after me about my boyfriends. Even worse, he constructed this fantasy that I had a crush on Mr Errington, my math teacher. Sure, I liked Mr Errington fine, but not in *that* way. I liked him principally because we could talk about math.

I'd come in to math one day, straight after a particularly brutal lunch hour, with my Wi-Fi forehead. I swear Mr Errington could see me trying not to cry. He eyed me, then he eyed my tormentors, Turk, Loam, Egan, Pencroft and Li, filing in behind me. He gave everyone a page from our workbook to do and let the class settle. Then he came over to me. He crouched beside my desk and put a hand on my shoulder, I thought he was going to ask me what was wrong and I dreaded it, I absolutely *dreaded* it, because I swear if he'd asked me that – if he uttered just one kind word – I knew I would break down and cry and things would be even worse for me.

49

But he didn't ask me anything. He just said: 'Hey, Selkirk. Did you know that there's a really easy way to remember the beginning of Pi? You just remember the phrase: "How I wish I could recollect Pi easily today."'

I sniffed. 'How does that help?'

'Look.' He wrote down the words in a column, and then the numbers next to them.

How	3
I	1
Wish	4
I	1
Could	5
Recollect	9
Pi	2
Easily	6
Today	5

'*Cool.*' He knew I liked quirky word-and-number stuff like that because we'd talked about it before. I looked at him, and he looked at me kindly and smiled until his eyes sorta crinkled at the corners. That one little trick, told to me like I was a human being, using my name instead of referring to me as a saddo, a wimp or a weeb, made him my hero.

But Egan saw and jumped all over it. 'I spotted Mr Errington giving you the eye,' he said, straight after the lesson, whispering in my ear like a bad conscience. 'Are you gay for him? Because *he's* gay, you know.'

I didn't know. Nor did I care. But Egan made me feel like

I couldn't even talk to Mr Errington any more, because if I did, I would see Egan out of the corner of my eye, laughing and whispering behind his hand. There was clearly no getting off my own personal, desolate, island.

8

The Reestablishment of Slavery

Twelves (that meant me) had to do stuff for everybody. But Loam was always the worst slave driver.

He literally had me carry all his stuff from class to class. I could still describe that bag of sports kit to you: as long as a coffin and just as heavy, navy waterproof material, red racing stripe, discreet Nike tick, rough Velcro handles. I would feel things shifting inside it, according to the day of the week and the season of the year: cricket bats, shin pads, tennis rackets. Things would push out the sides of it so you could see their shapes like an alien birth: football studs, running spikes poking out to graze my shins as I walked. My hands were rubbed raw by those handles, my shoulders ached from the straps, my back was permanently bowed. I swear I stooped for three years under that goddamn bag.

And that wasn't the full extent of my slavery. If Loam wanted a Bubble Tea at lunch, I had to go get it. If he needed his stinky, cheese-smelling socks or cricket pads washing, or even worse, his support underwear, there was I, in the kit room at break, scrubbing away.

Sometimes, for no reason, when he passed me in the corridors, he'd lift my glasses off my nose, and snap them in two. As I wasn't really short-sighted – just a minus-one – I didn't really need the glasses at all. But I kept buying them, because they were a buffer zone between him and me. I'd always react as if I was really devastated, but I didn't care. When I ran out of pairs, I'd buy more. My plan was that if Loam broke my glasses, maybe he wouldn't break *me*. I was afraid of him, you see. I was a coward. I didn't want him to hit me, and I thought the glasses stopped him. The thought of his hitting me made me physically sick.

After my glasses got broken a second time I stopped bothering to get nice ones. My parents bummed pretty hard about the first pair – the expensive pair – when I told them I'd stepped on them by mistake. The replacements were pretty nice ones from Specsavers for about a hundred quid. When Loam dropped *them* into the river I didn't even tell my folks. I went down the High (Oxford doesn't have a high street, but a High. Don't ask . . .) and found this crazy little shop called Tiger. It sells all kinds of brightly coloured shit and, among it all, reading glasses for four pounds. I bought a whole rack of identical plain black newsreader glasses. I figured I was gonna need them.

And I did.

So my parents never knew about the third pair of glasses, or the fifth, or the sixth. They were close enough in style to the replacement pair they'd bought for them not to notice. For a couple of behavioural scientists they sure seemed oblivious to what was going on at Osney. But you can't blame them really. I got good at hiding it.

After that first day I never cried again, and although I'd sometimes catch my mom eyeing me in that half-beady, half-affectionate way she had, I managed to convince them that all was well. They were so happy in Oxford, so happy in their work, that I didn't want to rock the boat. I suppose I could have pleaded with them to take me out and put me in another school because I was being bullied. But I couldn't imagine myself saying the words. I guess I felt ashamed, like they would think less of me if I told them that I was the whole school's monkey butler.

And there was something else too. Home was my precious haven, a house full of love, the soothing tones of Radio 4 with the calm poetry of the shipping forecast and the lovely strains of the *Desert Island Discs* theme tune. Home was where I would fantasise about being a castaway, being on my own on an island far away from all my classmates. It was where I could disappear into my room, and shoot all the bad guys on *Overwatch*, pretending they were Loam, and drift away onto the island of *Myst*, and float around on my wind wing as Link in *Zelda*. Then I'd be called to dinner, where there were no screens but there were my parents, slightly nutty, adoring, intelligent. At dinner we'd talk about cool science stuff like Pavlov's dogs or Schrödinger's cat and their eyes behind their glasses would sparkle with conversation and animation. We'd eat the delicious food that, like everything else about us, was a weird hybrid of American and English. I wasn't the last in the queue here, but the first. I was the apple of their eye, no longer a Twelve but a Number One Son. It was the only place I felt the most important, not the least. Home was my escape from slavery and oppression. I didn't want to bring Loam and his cronies there, didn't want to even utter their names, didn't want to let them into my haven. I wondered how many other bullied kids do this, ensure that their parents don't even know their tormentors' names.

But I was never totally safe, even at home. Not in my bedroom, late at night. There the phone took over; social media, or rather, anti-social media. Loam and Li and Turk and Egan and Pencroft entered my sanctuary in the shape of the beeps and whooshes and tings of Instagram, Snapchat, email, text. Lots of different multimedia ways for their insults to enter my citadel like arrows. Little symbols that looked innocent, the cute little emojis, white 'like me' hearts and little green bubbles of text. How can something as benevolent as a smiley face make you feel sick? How can a tiny speech bubble no bigger than a thumbnail make your heart leap into your throat? Or a little baby ghost make you want to cry? I'll tell you how. When they are laughing at a well-crafted insult that Miranda Pencroft has made about you. When they 'love' a dumb photo that's been posted up of you in your underwear in the changing room. When that bubble of text calls you gay, or sad, or gross, or tells you, on one memorable occasion, that you are 'too ugly to live'. I began to fear my own phone, to dread the little noises it uttered. Why I didn't just get rid of it I don't know. I wanted, so much, to smash its glossy face in, but it had some hold over me, cool and confident in its expense, holding in its nickel belly more technology than the Apollo moon missions. So it sat, inviolable on my bedside table, a malign black rectangle. Sometimes it would buzz just as I was going to sleep and then the sick fear would douse me, and my churning stomach acid would keep me awake till the early hours, when the sky outside my window turned headache grey.

9

Toppers

I'm telling all this in a casual, overview way, because there were three years of this crap. But of course every single incident hurt, and every day I got my Wi-Fi forehead at school with the effort of not crying, and most nights I did cry in my room, looking at my passive-aggressive phone until it stopped pinging around midnight when even trolls have to sleep. But if I listed everything that happened in super-fine detail you'd stop reading pretty quickly. It would be a total downer. And this bit is only really a prologue to the real story of what happened on the island.

By the end of my first year I'd had enough, and had decided to go to Mr Errington. As is the case for most kids who are bullied, lessons themselves were my safe haven. Ask any kid who's getting it tough at school and he or she will tell you that when you're in class, under the eye of the teacher, you feel safe. There is where I blossomed. There I lived. There my beloved science, my beloved math and my beloved literature, were a comfort to me. The teachers – with the exception of the vile Mr Llewellyn – were the only people at Osney School who liked me. I had that sick feeling as the clock hands crept round to break or lunchtime that I didn't want the lesson to end. At Osney, you weren't allowed to hide in the library or the classroom – the teachers were such Fresh Air Freaks that they chased you out of the passageways of silverware.

Nerds don't do Fresh Air. We like the closed curtains and artificial light of our bedrooms, and the friendly hum of a computer processor emanating from the tower of our PCs. I hated Fresh Air, because Fresh Air meant Loam and his cronies coming after me. Until I got to the island, that is. Then I learned to like Fresh Air just fine.

Teachers-wise, I'd formed a good relationship with Mr Adamson in science, Miss Hardy in English literature, and especially with my 'boyfriend' Mr Errington in math. They were all academically pretty strong, but I probably knew as much as they did, because all the teachers were primarily recruited for sport. Miss Hardy used to play tennis professionally; Mr Adamson was a sports scientist who designed training regimes for footballers and Mr Errington boxed, so I reckoned that he was the one to stand up to Loam. In class you could see the teachers were relieved when they called on me, or I put my hand up, because they knew they'd be getting a right answer from someone who was engaged with their subject, a little island in the sea of bored, uninterested, un-academic students just waiting for the next games lesson. Every time they shared a fact with me, like Mr Errington had done about Pi, or we shared a little joke that went above everyone else's heads,

I stored it up. Although teachers were the nearest things to friends I had in the school, I didn't fool myself. I was nothing to them – just a kid who was good at their subject. No one made a big deal of me, or tried to draw me out. They were offhand, these compliments and jokes, but these fragments of interaction were the only respectful exchanges I'd gotten at Osney. And that's why, after the horrors of Sports Day, I decided to talk to Mr Errington.

Sports Day was not something we'd had in the States. The worst sporting humiliation I suffered over there was striking out in Little League, never hitting or catching one single baseball. But I was too young then to really care, and Little League was just for fun. At my first Osney School Sports Day I was old enough to care very much indeed, and as with all games at Osney, it was deadly serious. Sports Day in any school, if you are not a sporty kid, is torture. It is a day designed to highlight your failings in public, with maximum humiliation because the whole school is watching.

We all trooped over the drawbridge to the vast sports fields – no using the local park for Osney; they had their own running track, playing fields, pool, you name it. I was only in one event – I was allowed to compete in the Elevens' relay, one of the very last events of the day, and in between running errands for Loam and his cronies, I felt sick to my stomach all day with the waiting. Of course I dropped the baton, and of course the whole school chanted my name, and even the Elevens looked at me like I was dirt. By the end of Sports Day I'd had enough. I resolved to talk to Mr Errington the very next day. I couldn't handle another school year like I'd just had. Not another term, week, or day.

Just one problem. The day after Sports Day, the last day of term, was Toppers. And so I witnessed, just before summer vacation, the wonder of the Toppers ceremony.

Toppers could not be more different from Sports Day. We were not on the playing fields, but in the Great Court, at the heart of the school itself, where I'd done the infamous Osney Dash on my first day. We were not in our sports kit, but in our 'dress uniform' worn for special occasions, which consisted of a black tailcoat instead of a blazer, a bottle-green waistcoat, and – wait for it – a top hat, just like Mr Peanut wears. I shit you not.

We all stood around in a huge, neat square, straight as soldiers. There were no Harry-Potter-esque houses at Osney; we all just stood in our numbers. I was next to the Elevens, who all, even old Flora, studiously ignored me because I'd dropped the baton the previous day. I could see Loam, bigger and broader than all the other kids, even though, remember, at this point he was nowhere near the oldest in the school. His little clique of Ones – Li, Pencroft, Turk – stood around him, Turk spoiling the line by wearing his topper right on the back of his head so it wouldn't flatten his stupid hair. The teachers stood around us in their academic gowns, and I could see, at the corner of the quad, Mr Errington, my New Hope, standing with Mr Adamson and Miss Hardy, his own particular clique. I looked around at all the kids in top hats and tailcoats in the warm summer sun and the ancient stone of the quad behind them, and thought: *This is batshit crazy*. I felt like I'd gone down a wormhole in the space/time continuum and flipped back to the nineteenth century.

And it was about to get even more surreal. Mr Lake, the music teacher, stepped forward, gown billowing, and sang a single note. This was our cue to sing the 'Toppers Song', which had been written by an ex-pupil in eighteen-sixty-something who went on to become some army general during the Boer War. They didn't really give much of a crap about music at Osney, a fact that annoyed Li, being a violin prodigy, but for the past week we'd been practising this dumbass song, to the tune of Beethoven's 'Ode to Joy', so when Mr Lake started us off we were word perfect:

When you're th'eleventh man and there are six runs to
get
When there's a score to draw and you're not even yet
When there's a furlong to run and your steed is tired
Or a duel to fight and your last shot's fired
When the whistle's raised and almost blown
Or you're out in front and on your own
Remember you're made of Osney stuff
Where only your best is good enough

Run on, run on, you're an Osney man
Run on, run on, run as fast as you can
If your goals are wealth and fame
There's a game to play, so play the game!

Run on, run on, through the quad of life
Run on, run on, through joy and strife
If your goals are wealth and fame
There's a game to play, so play the game!

This song made me feel physically sick. First of all, who rhymes *life* and *strife*? It's like some cheeseball like Bryan Adams rhyming *ocean* and *emotion*. (Bryan Adams would definitely figure on my dad's Desert Island Discs. Mine: not so much.) But what made me feel sicker than the rhyming structure was the sentiment. Like games were everything, like everything was a game, and you could live your whole life as an 'Osney Man'. I had a flash forward to the rest of Loam's life – some sporty university, maybe a sporting career, then – God help us all – politics, living his whole life like he was doing the Osney Dash. There was nothing in the song about caring for others, or being a good leader, or watching out for the little guy. It was all about winning. It was the anthem of fricking Charlie Sheen.

Song over, things got even more nuts. Mr Llewellyn, head of the whole school, head of games and the original Sports Nazi, stepped forward. He was holding this enormous silver trophy. I knew what it was. It was the All-Rounder trophy, the ultimate glittering prize of Osney School, and everyone treated it like it was the Holy fricking Grail or something. Anyway old Llewellyn brought it forward as gingerly as if it was a nuclear warhead, then walked to the middle of the quad. He set the trophy on the ground, on a pale stone circle in the centre of the lawn. Then he took off the lid of the trophy and held it high, where it caught the sun.

Then he called, in his bellowy voice: 'Who is an Osney Man?'

The school chorused: 'I am an Osney Man!'

Without knowing why, I tipped forward on my toes and looked down the line at Flora, her pink and purple hair flicking up under her top hat. She should've looked ridiculous but instead she looked kinda steampunk cool. I wondered how she liked being identified as an 'Osney Man', since Osney had been co-ed since 1918. Sure enough, her lips were tight shut. She wasn't saying it. It was the first little shred of rebellion I'd detected in her. I tipped back as Mr Llewellyn shouted, 'Is there a Quarters Man?'

Loam stepped forward. 'I am a Quarters Man!' he barked.

'Who is the Toppers Man?'

The school chorused, 'Loam is the Toppers Man!'

Then Loam marched to the middle of the quad, and took off his top hat and threw it into the air as high as he could. This was Loam, so that was pretty high. I didn't even hear it come down again. Then old Llewellyn, I'm not kidding, *crowned* him with the lid of the dumb trophy. There was no other word for it. It was a fricking *coronation*.

Then Loam turned around, all proud and triumphant, with a face that said *Winning*, even though he looked like a dick with this pointy silver roof on his head. Then the rest of the school – with the exception of me – threw their top hats in the air. It looked like the rich kids' version of graduation day, all those black hats flying around. I had a surreal moment at that point. I caught Flora's eye, the hats falling all around us like in slo-mo, and saw that she was still wearing her hat too.

Then, in the chaos of falling top hats, all the Ones sort of rushed Loam and picked him up. He was carried to the grand archway and then literally passed around the whole quad, all four sides of it, from the Ones to the Elevens, as if he was crowd-surfing. Everyone cheered hysterically as Loam came all the way round to me, the only Twelve, and the Elevens let him down and he landed painfully on my feet. I could smell his familiar sweat and aftershave combo, as he fell heavily against me. But he didn't say sorry or even look at me; he just ran off round the quad, jogging easily, not sprinting, holding the silver trophy lid to his head with one hand and waving with the other. Someone had brought out a school flag from somewhere, with the tree and the island on it, and wrapped it round his shoulders like he'd won the frickin' *Olympics* or something. Old Loam was really milking his moment.

As I watched, the only one in the school apart from Flora who was not cheering, I could see Miss Hardy smiling and clapping and jumping up and down, and Mr Adamson doing that really loud two-fingered whistle that everyone wishes they could do but few people can. And then I saw something that shattered all my hopes. Mr Errington – Mr *Errington* – wiped away a tear.

Really.

He did that thing people do in movies when they're overcome with emotion, just a little swipe with the forefinger, the tear glittering in the sun like a diamond. And that single tear told me it was no good. Despite my academic smarts, they'd always come down on the side of Loam, the Champion of the School, the Sir Frickin' Lancelot of this little island of Camelot.

10

The Camel's Back

I had to endure two more Toppers ceremonies at Osney School – both won by Loam – before I got the hell out of there.

It's fair to say that my time at the school got progressively worse. What, you say, worse than poop running down your legs on the playing field? Worse than watching your phone in fear until the grey small hours of the morning?

Yes, I say. As we got older, the bullying got more, well, *grown up* too. Before I tell you about the dark stuff, one of the most significant aspects of getting older was that we were getting nearer our exams – the GCSEs that you do aged sixteen in England.

I was still doing the usual errands. I said very little at school for three years except the word that America gave to the world and has since become the most popular word on the planet: OK. That one little obliging word became my mantra, my catchphrase.

'Selkirk. Go and get me a violin string. I need an A. There's a music shop called Caswell's on Banbury Road. And get me steel, not nylon.'

'OK.'

'Selkirk, get me a mango Bubble Tea with strawberry boba. No apple jelly or I'll send you back.'

'OK.'

'Selkirk, my G! Get me twenty-four paracetamols. Man's gonna need that shit as soon *as*, cuz. So ten-toes down to Boots, fam.'

'OK.'

If you were thinking that I escaped my slavery in the run up to the exams you'd be wrong. Loam had me running out for bottles of water and Red Bull and energy bars and all the crap he mistakenly thought would make his brain work after sixteen years of dormancy. But as well as the usual menial errands, the terms of my service at this time became somewhat more . . . scholarly. None of the sporty kids gave a crap about academic subjects, but even Osney School had to scrape their students through their exams. I started writing essays, revision notes, mind maps. I wrote bespoke flash cards, even on subjects I wasn't taking. The only benefit of this was that I knew every subject backwards. I became – like the great Abraham Lincoln himself – something of a polymath; aka a know-it-all. And that gave me an idea. If I turned all this extra learning to my advantage I could ace my own GCSEs. I could lay ten level nines at my parents' feet, like a knight delivering a dragon's head in days of old, and then tell them that I was leaving school.

Once I'd had the idea I became obsessed with it. I began to count the days until I could tell my folks, and even had a chart in my room, tallying the days until I could leave: four strokes and a diagonal cross stroke to make five, like rows of

little gates. I'd pretend I was Edmond Dantes, [cut off]
favourite book, locked up in the Château d'If, [cut off]
prison, counting the days until he could escape an[cut off]
the Count of Monte Cristo. But just like Dantes, I di[cut off]
anyone any clues as to what I was planning to do. Edmond
Dantes ate all the bread and water that was shoved through
his door. Edmond Dantes acted the same as ever in front of
the guards. Edmond Dantes did not once betray, by a gesture,
by so much as a flicker of an eyelash, that he was planning to
escape, and that he had an accomplice in the next cell and a
fricking great tunnel dug out beneath him.

I ate everything that was put in front of me at home, and I
studied for my exams. I went through the motions of choosing
my A levels. I even signed up for this Osney summer camp
overseas called 'Preparation for Life' that my parents said I
should go on. It sounded pretty lame but they were teaching a
summer school in the long vacation and thought I'd be bored.

And if I hadn't been sure enough that it was time to escape
Osney Island, something else made my mind up for me.

OK, now for the slightly icky stuff. Leave the room if you're
of a sensitive disposition.

The torments at Osney School got darker, and more, well . . .
sexual.

Loam got taller, I got taller. Loam got wider, I got skinnier.
I suspected that my extreme thinness possibly made me even
weirder-looking than before. I certainly never got any female
attention, (not positive anyway) unless you count from my

ɔm. I caught her looking at me speculatively one day – after my growth spurt, this was.

'What?' I said.

'You know, honey, underneath that tragic haircut and those glasses you are really a very good-looking boy.'

'All mothers say that.'

'Not all,' said my dad from behind his *New Scientist* magazine. He hated his mom.

'I'm not speaking as your mother but as a scientist,' said Mom. 'Scientists aren't in the habit of bending data. I'm not talking about opinion. As a matter of empirical fact, you are attractive.'

'Shucks, Mom.' I blew it off but I immediately went to the bathroom and studied myself in the mirror. My eyes were this sorta sludgy green, and I had new angles to my face and jaw. My lips were kinda fat and girly. I was too thin, but I was at least tall now – I could look Loam in his stupid face if only I dared. My hair was a bit crazy as ever. I didn't exactly *hate* my reflection, but I certainly didn't look anything like Loam, and Loam was my benchmark for a good-looking guy. He and I looked like the before and after pictures for an ad for going to the gym. If I was Dr David Banner, Loam was the Hulk.

All the boys at Osney had gone through changes at least as dramatic as the Hulk's. Sure, we didn't turn green, but we got taller (me), broader (Loam) and our voices got deeper (all of us). Hair grew on faces and armpits and balls.

And the girls had their own equally startling transformations – they started growing boobs to fill out their Osney School jumpers and presumably also grew hair in places that I never saw. Thinking about the places girls might have hair made me feel hot and weird and not totally in control, a feeling I both liked and hated. Most potent of all, girls began to *smell* different. On hot days or after games, their own smells, their REAL smells, gross and exciting at the same time, would surface above all the flowery perfumes and sickly-sweet body sprays they covered themselves in, which emanated from the changing rooms in a choking cloud.

Miranda Pencroft became even more beautiful, and, in the least surprising development ever, started going out with Loam. Just as in the States the most beautiful cheerleader would go out with the biggest jock, who was almost always also the biggest jerk. It was expected. They were fulfilling their roles as much as I was fulfilling mine. I don't know how much Miranda actually liked Loam – yes, he was a good-looking sonofabitch, but he was dumb as a box of hair, and I couldn't imagine that he was very good company. Still, they seemed pretty hot and heavy – everywhere I looked they seemed to be twined around each other, kissing and grooming each other like a couple of chimps.

I became desperate, as I grew into my gangly limbs, to not be a total doofus around Pencroft. God knows why I still liked her – she'd been nothing but a bitch-on-wheels to me via social media for years. But I really wanted her to think I was cool. And, of course, the more cool I tried to appear, the less cool I actually was. People have long memories at school and no one had forgotten my little diarrhoea incident, but added to that, with puberty Loam's cruelties became a bit more focused.

They became what my parents would call 'gender oriented'. My parents had jargon for everything.

I'm pretty sure Loam saw me looking at Pencroft, and it pleased him. It pleased him that I was looking at something which he regarded as his. Loam was no feminist – Pencroft was his girl, his property. He would devise little humiliations for me to do with her, like making me give her intimate messages about what they'd be doing that evening, or telling her that she'd left her bra at his house, gross cringey stuff like that. Even though Loam was pretty dumb, he'd construct these messages as if *I* was saying them to her, in the first person. I'd have to say 'I want to kiss you all over', not 'Loam says he wants to kiss you all over'. Super-mature of him, but designed to make me squirm and I did squirm. Loam knew that I wanted to say those things to her, do those things to her, and it was just one more way, as if he needed it, to keep me down. When I talked to Miranda I could barely meet her eye – and when I did – I saw triumph there – she was pleased, I could tell, to be able to reduce a kid who was taller than her to jelly just by her very goddess-like presence. Li would watch me sharply like an attack dog, while I talked to her BFF. But she couldn't stop me giving the messages – they were on Loam's orders, and Loam was King.

I'm quite intuitive – geeks tend to be, as we spend a lot of time watching and listening and thinking, and being outside of things. For the first time I got the feeling that Loam was insecure. And, more than that, that he was somehow insecure about ME.

I know.

I can almost hear you laughing.

Why, you are no doubt saying, would someone like Sebastian Loam be insecure about a long streak of shit like *you*? The answer is, I don't know. Despite my terminal lack of cool, I just got the feeling that he was, and I was proved right by the punch.

11

The First Punch and the Last Straw

We all have our tipping point, and the punch was mine. The run up to it was the nastiest and most humiliating episode of all the nasty and humiliating episodes at Osney School.

Sports Day. Osney School wasn't about to let a little thing like exams interfere with Sports Day. At other schools, once you've done your exams that's it. Not at Osney. We all had to make a comeback for Sports Day and Toppers. So after a month of blissful gaming in my room, and trips up to London with my folks, and visits to Stratford for swans 'n' Shakespeare, I found myself back at Osney. I *almost* didn't mind. On my Edmond-Dantes-tally-chart-countdown before I could escape from Osney Island, this was my penultimate day. My folks didn't know it yet but I only had Sports Day that day, and Toppers the next, before I would leave Osney forever. Without being a total wise-ass I knew I had aced my exams – probably thanks to all the extra revision I did for the Ones – so I would be able to present my results to my folks as part of my exit plan.

But on that final Sports Day, the final-straw day, Loam went too far, and he issued the order that broke the camel's back. He summoned me at lunch and said: 'Selkirk, I want you to go to Boots.'

I was puzzled – anything medical or chemical was usually Turk's remit.

'OK,' I said as I always did, waiting for more. It came. 'Miranda needs tampons. I want you to get her some.'

Now, I knew what tampons were – just about. We'd had sex ed., and my mom kept some in our bathroom pedestal, and when I was younger I took one out of its packet, bemused by the little white creature of soft cotton with a mouse-tail string. But I had no idea about *buying* them. Did they come in different sizes? Would I have to *ask*? My face grew hot just at the thought of it. I just said OK again, and walked through the gateway, over the drawbridge and into town. I knew Boots on the High pretty well, from buying stuff for Turk, but the mysterious aisle of women's products signposted 'Feminine Hygiene' was not one where I'd ever ventured before. My eyes passed over the bewildering array of brightly coloured packaging, all designed to look pretty and girly and doing a pretty good job of disguising what they were actually FOR. Swiftly, trying to give the air of a metrosexual dude doing a favour for his girlfriend, rather than a creepy pervert poring over sanitary products, I grabbed the biggest packet I could find, with words like 'super' on it. I glanced at the three blue raindrops on the side (they were obviously not allowed to use red – too gory) and headed for the checkout and the curious eye of the shop assistant.

Back at school I handed the box, shrouded in a Boots carrier, to Loam. He looked at it, then at me, and said: 'What am I supposed to do with this? They're for Miranda, not me.'

Turk, lolling next to his boss in his gangsta stance, yukked it up like a hyena. 'What's he meant to do with them, cuz? Man can't use 'em hisself. We ain't *all* gay, fam.'

'OK,' I said, my catchphrase. 'Where is . . . er . . . Pencroft?'

Loam turned his wrist to check his state-of-the-art, most-expensive-one-you-can-get Fitbit.

'She'll be in the girls' changing room, changing for the swimming events. She'll need them before then. Get a wriggle on.'

Turk sucked his teeth. 'Better ten-toes, cuz.'

I turned away and ten-toesed to the pool and the changing rooms. In that part of the school you left behind the oak-panelled walls hung with silverware and switched to state-of-the-art white-and-blue changing rooms giving onto a state-of-the-art white-and-blue swimming pool. For some reason, Loam and Turk followed me. I didn't exactly need a tour guide, because, without sounding like the perv I'd resembled in Boots, I knew where the girls changed. I thought then that they were helping me find her. That's before I realised what was going on.

The door had one of those stick figures in a skirt on it. I knocked and waited. There was no answer. The sharp smell of swimming pools – of Miranda Pencroft – came from within. Loam and Turk were at my back. I twisted around, looking for a passing girl to take the package in for me. The passage seemed suddenly full of people but they were all boys. Turk sucked his teeth again in that particularly annoying way that he had. 'No one in, cuz, innit? Nooooobody at the inn, fam.'

I turned away to find Loam standing beside me, arms crossed like a bouncer on the door of a nightclub. 'Just have to take them to her yourself, won't you, Selkirk?'

Then three things happened at once. Loam pushed the door open and propelled me through it, while Turk took hold of my pants and pulled them down to my knees. I don't just mean pants in the American sense, as in trousers. I mean pants in the English sense too. I mean underwear. I lurched through the door of the girls' changing room, effectively hobbled, clutching a box of Tampax and naked from the waist down. It was literally as if someone had broken into my psyche, written down my worst nightmare and re-enacted it with me as the star of the show. I dropped the box on the floor and covered myself up, but not before every single girl in Year Twelve, including Miranda Pencroft, had seen my junk.

Suddenly there was a circle of girls screaming at me, calling me a pervert – of course – and worse. Li was the shrillest and loudest, moving Pencroft away from me as if she was her bodyguard. I could see Flora's shocked face, mouth gaping open. I was jostled out of the door. My face was burning with what they'd seen, but also with what I'd seen, those secret undergarments, the hidden parts of girls' bodies, the straps, the lace, the hair. And the smells – a hundred body sprays and deodorants and perfumes and under it all that indefinable, elemental female smell. Oh God.

Back in the oak-panelled passageway the boys who had clearly gathered to watch the show were all laughing and chanting. Turk opened the tampons and emptied them all over me. Then the boys got hold of them and started shooting them out of their packets like bullets, and swinging them around by their strings. It had obviously been their last chance to get me before summer, and they were going to go big. A phalanx of smartphones surrounded me, unblinkingly recording. I'd be viral before home time. And if that was the case, I was going to give them something worth watching. I neatly caught one of the flying tampons in my hand – ironically the only time I've neatly caught anything – and I rounded on Loam, coldly furious. I held the cotton between two fingers, tiny, mouse-like.

'Better keep one,' I said. 'She might need something that's a bit bigger than you.'

The crowd did that half-laughing, half-shocked *Oooooooo* thing, and even Turk, Loam's vice-president, said, 'Get *wrecked*!'

I don't know where the words came from. That wasn't like me at all – a crude, gross thing to say. It was the second time in my life I'd blurted an insult at Loam and I'd come a long way since the Sockdologiser. I hadn't seen it coming.

I didn't see the punch coming either.

I felt it connecting. I heard a girl's voice cry out: *No!* I saw everything brighten and then darken in my vision, and I felt an excruciating pain in my tooth. I hit the deck and just lay there for a moment, staying down. I turned over onto my front, tasting the metal tang of blood in my mouth. Then, like Frankenstein's monster, I slowly rose from the floor, the curve of my back first. No one moved. I could see white blobs of shocked faces; even the Ones thought Loam had gone too far. I could hear Turk breathing, 'Oh my *days* . . .' I didn't look at anyone. Least of all Loam. My tongue touched the jagged edge of a broken back tooth – it must have chipped against my top teeth at the impact. I blinked once, twice, straightened up. Everyone was watching me to see what I would do, wary, unsure, as if for once I had the power. But I didn't do anything. I turned and walked right out of the school, across the bridge and off Osney Island. I didn't care that it was Toppers tomorrow, that Loam would be crowned with silver and carried around the quad, top hats raining on him from above. It would have to happen without me.

I was going, leaving for good, and I'd never have to see that asshole again.

12

The Deal

'I want to leave school.'

I'd waited until dinnertime. We ate late, when my parents got back from the faculty – well, it was Europe – and despite my broken tooth I'd savoured my food for the first time in three years.

. My mom put her knife and fork down carefully, lining them up precisely like she was laying uranium rods. My dad pushed his aviator glasses up his nose a little, as he always did when he was perturbed. 'You want to *what* now?'

I swallowed. 'Leave school. I want to leave school.'

My mom placed a hand on my dad's forearm. 'Now hold on a minute, honey. What would you do? You've got to get your A levels, surely. Go to university.'

I knew from their faces then that it wouldn't fly. I'd buried myself with those predicted grades – grades I'd been predicted partly thanks to all the revision I'd done for Loam and those lazy-ass Ones. Two years of A levels seemed like a prison sentence, and I imagined university, certainly Oxbridge, which is where they would surely want me to go, would just be exactly like Osney. I took a breath. 'I could learn to do a bunch of things. I could be a mechanic. A coder. Or tech support.'

My dad clasped his hands together, as if he was going to pray. 'Son, we've got no objection to you getting a job like that. But just do it after college, so you've got a fallback.'

'And besides,' put in my mom, wearing a strangely pleading expression, 'you've always said . . . *we've* always said . . .' She stopped and pressed her un-lipsticked lips together, not quite meeting my eyes. I knew that look. I'd *invented* that look. My mom had my Wi-Fi forehead. She was almost crying, and when I figured out why I was pretty incredulous.

'Is this about me being *president?*'

She didn't say anything.

'It is, isn't it?'

'No, honey, of *course* not. That would be ridiculous.'

This was unbelievable. 'I'm pretty sure you can be president without a degree, Mom. Look at Trump. I'd be surprised if he graduated *high school.*'

My mom stacked the plates together, really carefully, as if any sudden moves would break them, break everything.

This discussion – the raised voices, my mom's tears, was the first of many. They explored every option. They would get me a car, a vacation, a new phone. Would I agree to doing the sixth form at another school? A technical college? I refused all the bribes and all the alternatives. I'd figured out by now that I just wasn't good around people. I couldn't get along with them. I needed a job where I could have minimal human contact. Machines were fine, just fine. I needed a job a boy who was an island could do. *Fix my computer. Here you go, ma'am. Fix my car. Here you go, sir.* That last week of term was the only time I ever really disagreed with my parents. At the end of it they called me into their study as though I was about to be fired and sat me down.

I looked at them both sitting in their leather chairs, with the wall of books behind them. Floating above my mother's head was the leather-bound Bible, the one I'd cried over on my very first day at Osney, the very first time Loam had broken my glasses. The first of numerous times. The bullying had been going on for *three years*. It was time for an ending.

'OK, honey,' said my mom, letting out her breath in a long sigh. 'We're going to cut you a deal.'

This was good, as for the last week they'd been absolutely immovable. I leaned forward.

It was my dad's turn next. 'We're going to agree to you leaving school and getting a job.'

I punched the air like a champion sportsman might. 'Yeeeerrrrsssss!'

'But,' said my mom, 'your dad and I have a condition.'

I sat back again. 'What is it?' I thought I would pretty much agree to anything as long as I never had to go to Osney School again.

'This Preparation for Life summer school that you signed up for,' said Dad, 'we want you to go.'

I'd almost forgotten. In the run-up to exams I'd agreed to go on this bullshit summer school, somewhere overseas. I'd agreed to everything, knowing I was planning to leave, but I never planned on actually *going*. My dad must've seen my face.

'We've already paid for it, and they're expecting you. And we think it might help you see things differently. It's teambuilding, mindfulness, cooperative games.'

'Your dad and I aren't blind,' added Mom. 'We know things haven't been easy for you.' It was the first indication she'd given me that they might have an inkling of what had been going on. I could feel my Wi-Fi forehead coming on. I had to be flip about it or I would cry.

'Understatement of the year.'

'So we want you to go, try to reach out to these guys, give them a chance.'

I rejected the idea of stating that these people did not deserve a chance, that they were fiends not friends, but instead I said, 'And if I do?'

'Then Dad and I will meet you in LA, in two weeks. Our summer school will be over and we'll have a vacation, *all* of us, together, back in the States. We'll go back to Palo Alto.'

I barely remembered Palo Alto, but I would take the vacation. God knows I needed one. 'And I don't have to go to school in September?'

Dad said, 'Not if you don't want to, no. If it really doesn't work, and you haven't made any friends, well, *then* we'll let you leave.' He pushed at his glasses again. 'Two weeks, Link. That's all we're asking.'

I could barely process what they were saying; that I'd got my own way. 'I don't have to put on that uniform, or cross that drawbridge, or walk through those gates again?'

'Not unless you *choose* to go back.'

I considered. Two weeks of camp, if I could then leave school forever, was nothing. I'd endured three years. Camp would be supervised – there'd be camp counsellors; I could stay away from those jocks, keep my head down, and then I was done.

I put out my hand. 'Deal,' I said.

They looked at each other and solemnly shook my hand in turn. I felt like I'd won, so I couldn't really understand why they looked so . . . well . . . *relieved*.

I spent the next few days packing. I hadn't actually paid attention to any of the letters or meetings about summer camp, because I hadn't thought I was going. It would've been like Edmond Dantes being told they were going to do a fancy new extension to the Château d'If, and would he like to see the blueprints? But now I had to pay attention. Apparently we were to fly to LA and then take a light aircraft to some Pacific island where there was a 'sports and leisure' camp. I was pretty sure I'd be taking more advantage of the leisure than the sports – I didn't mind water slides and massages. Beach volleyball in the sun though – forget it. It did sound a bit more evolved than most of Osney's school trips – there was mindfulness, as my mom had said, and fishing in glass-bottomed boats and stuff. It really sounded OK. So I duly packed my shorts and some crazy seventies Hawaiian shirts of my dad's which were the nearest I got to beachwear. I packed my phone and my iPad and, most importantly, my Kindle. However bad things got, that baby had a hundred novels on it so I'd be OK.

I smiled when my parents waved me off at Heathrow, and I smiled all the way to LAX. In LA, when I saw exactly who was going to camp, even then I smiled. *Of course* Loam was there, and Egan, and Li and Turk, and Flora too (complete with a new nose stud), and Pencroft. All the people who had seen me at my lowest ebb, and seemed only too ready to remind me that they had seen everything I had in my pants as well. I wondered, briefly, why Flora's bosom buddies Smith and Fry hadn't come – she was in for just as uncomfortable a two weeks as me. I wasn't about to make it easier for her – she hadn't made things easier for me. I smiled while I thought this. I even smiled while they taunted me about my genitalia. If this was my parents' price, that was just fiiiiiine.

I got on the light aircraft with Loam and his gang quite happily. We were all given these dumb polo shirts, in the bottle-green and gold Osney colours, with **Osney School Preparation for Life Summer Camp** emblazoned on the back. I shoved mine in my holdall. I wouldn't be seen dead wearing it. Loam, though, who wasn't comfortable outside of a sports strip, put his on straight away. And then, of course, Egan did too. They looked like twin toddlers going to church. I smiled again. Nothing could faze me, everything amused me. I could even smile as the big lunk handed me his bags, knowing what I knew, that after these fourteen days I'd never have to carry them again.

The plane was really great – a carrier I'd never heard of before called Oceanic Airlines. The interior was all creamy leather seats and wooden finishing. I pretended I really *was* the president – this was Air Force One and these losers were all on *my* plane. I can remember tiny details of the flight. The spirit level of the surface of the water in Flora's bottle of

Evian water at take-off. Loam fiddling with his Fitbit. Pencroft crossing her tanned legs under this amazing suede miniskirt the colour of a baby mouse. I was content. I ordered a Coke from the stewardess, tipped back my seat and slotted in my headphones. I selected 'Nowhere Man' and pressed the little triangle. I could listen to it now without pain. Because soon I was going to be a Somewhere Man.

I remember getting out my Kindle and beginning to reread the Count of Monte Cristo, a book that always gave me comfort. I remember reading the first lines, lines I almost knew word for word:

On the 24th of February, 1815, the look-out at Notre-Dame de la Garde signalled the three-master, the Pharaon *from Smyrna, Trieste and Naples. As usual, a pilot put off immediately* . . .

And then I don't remember anything else.

DISC THREE

Survivor – Destiny's Child

Anthony Dent, Beyoncé Knowles,
Mathew Knowles (2000)

13

Monarch of All He Surveys

I don't know what it is about being a castaway that gives you a biblical frame of mind. But I was Adam on the first day in Eden, the world created just for me. I was a colonist, and this island was mine. Americans have a long inglorious tradition of colonising, and I was going to colonise the ass out of this place.

Being a colonist, I figured I had naming rights. I thought I would call the island Lincoln Island. In Jules Verne's *The Mysterious Island* the castaways called their island Lincoln Island too, but that was different. For one thing, those guys escaped the American Civil War in a hot-air balloon *Fortnite* battle-bus style. For another, they called their island after the actual Lincoln, as Commander-in-chief of the Union. This island was going to be called after *me*.

After I'd done with my little victory dance, and my Glee-club-of-one rendering of the school song, I wandered around for a bit on my beach. The beach would need a name too, but that could wait. I paddled my feet in the warm water, picked up a few shells and bits of seaweed and pitched them into my sea. I looked both ways down my coast as far as I could see through my steamy glasses. The smooth golden shore rounded a point in each direction. I was in some sort of bay. I wasn't really sure what to do next. The books never tell you this, but I will: there's quite a bit of confusion when you find yourself cast away on a desert island. Not fear though. I still didn't feel that.

I turned my back on the ocean and looked inland and the answer became clear. There was a fricking great mountain in the middle of the island, with verdant slopes and a blue misty summit. One thing most castaways did in books was to establish that they were actually on an island. I think it was St Brendan, or one of those old saints, who got off his boat onto an island and found out it was the back of a whale. I didn't exactly think I was on a whale but I might well have been on some sorta peninsula thing, and to establish that I had to get up high. I decided to go for a climb.

I walked inland, encountering a tangled little jungle before the ground started to rise. At that point I really wished I had my sneakers, because all the brushwood and twigs underfoot were pretty spiky. Put it this way – I couldn't have run very fast if anything came after me, like a tiger or a crocodile or something. But just then it didn't seem to me that this was an island that was populated, or had ever been discovered before. And, like the man said in *The Count of Monte Cristo*, two-legged tigers and crocodiles are more dangerous than the others, and so long as I was rid of my classmates I was happy. I was sure, convinced, that mine was the only heart that beat here, the only lungs that breathed, and I loved it. There was never any doubt in my mind that I'd be rescued eventually. Even a light aircraft, I knew, had a black box recorder. People would be looking for me right now. Until then, I was gloriously, blissfully alone. This way I didn't have to spend two weeks doing dumbass teambuilding games with people I hated. The people I hated were dead.

My stomach started to growl – I'd had nothing to eat since LAX, and had only had one of those mini airline Cokes on the light aircraft before it had, presumably, crashed. I looked around for some of those green coconuts – if they grew on the trees there should be some on the ground, right? But I couldn't seem to see any. Instead I found some fat berries growing in the blackthorn, which were a sort of chocolatey colour. I picked one and even though I was starving I only ate a fraction of the berry at a time, and walked for about half an hour before I had another minuscule bite. I was like old Charlie Bucket gnawing away at his annual chocolate bar in tiny increments. But I wanted to be safe. Now I had my own country I didn't want to lose everything by poisoning myself with one of my own berries on Day One. I wasn't about to get caught that way. Once I figured they weren't poisonous, I ate some more. The Bucket berries, as I dubbed them, weren't nice at all – they sure didn't taste of chocolate. They sorta tasted of mud, but they shut my stomach up.

The hike was tough, but I loved every step. The vegetation changed as I climbed. There were bushes clinging to the slopes with glossy leaves and this fragrant blossom, there were rock roses growing up the stone, and unseen crickety-type insects were chirping this happy little Jiminy Cricket song. I named the mountain as I climbed. It was a no-brainer. I was gonna call it Monte Cristo. This was the island that had changed my life for the better – the way that Monte Cristo had changed Edmond Dantes's life. He'd found something: a butt-load of treasure. I'd lost something: my classmates. And that made me just as happy.

At last I was at the summit and the view was a knockout. It also answered the big question: I was indeed on an island. The island – Lincoln Island – was shaped roughly like a Pac-Man. It was pretty round, with a V-shaped sandy bay for the mouth. An enclosed lake made the eye of the Pac-Man, good news because this would be fresh water. I made a mental note to take a trip to it first thing in the morning. There was a green forest covering most of the inland, with birds rising above it on the warm evening thermals. Around the island an indigo sea nibbled at the coasts, the waves from this distance no more than frills of white lace. Over all of it lay a lovely silvery mist like a bride's veil waiting to be lifted, waiting to be discovered. By me. Who else was there?

'I'M A SURVIVOR!' I shouted, holding out my arms. They were the first words I uttered on the island. And by some accident of topography the words echoed back to me from my bays, my lake, my streams, my forest.

I wanted to do something momentous to mark my colonisation of the island. If I'd had a flag I woulda planted it. But I didn't so I built a little cairn of rocks to mark the highest point of Lincoln Island.

After that I didn't really know what to do. The sun was

going down, and I knew I should find someplace to sleep, but it was so pretty I decided to watch for a while. Even at the very summit there was one of the massively tall palm trees with the two green coconuts hanging below the leaves. God knows how it grew up there. Nature's a wonderful thing, I guess. I sat with my back to the smooth trunk, looking warily up at the two green coconuts in case they decided to fall on me.

The whole sky turned this kinda rose gold and instinctively I reached for my phone to take a picture, before I realised what a dumb idea this was. Who was I going to show? Why didn't I just enjoy the fricking sunset? I didn't take the picture, but now I didn't look at the view either. I was staring at the bashed and blameless glass screen of the phone.

I remembered how many times I had thought about smashing in the face of my tormentor, with its beeps and tings and swooshes and innocent little emojis and icons all denoting another stab in the back or a knife to the side. Now the face was ruined, a beautiful snowflake smash radiating out in silver lines. What I'd never dared to do had been done by the plane crash, and I was glad. The phone did not look so clever now. I could no longer see my mascot – Link from *Zelda* – on the home screen in his jaunty green outfit. I could just about see the time: 18:15, and the little icons at the top of the screen telling me that I had seven per cent battery and absolutely no signal. This was not a surprise to me. I lost signal when I went to the basement of Blackwell's bookshop in Oxford so I wasn't exactly shocked that there was zero signal on a desert island. So instead of watching the sunset I sat there on the promontory watching my phone die, and it was beautiful. It finally gave up and the screen went black, showing an empty white battery with a red line, which is usually so annoying but to me was the most lovely graphic I'd ever seen in my life. 'Goodbye, you absolute asshole,' I said aloud. Then I stood up, and as hard as I could, I whipped the phone out to sea. I know it was crazy to trash a smartphone, knew I could've charged it up when I got rescued, and got the screen mended, but I didn't give a shit. Without charge it was just a hunk of nickel and glass, and no one needed to know it had survived the crash in the first place. I turned away before I could even hear it fall. Now I was totally alone. Just me and my island. Even though I knew I'd be rescued, it occurred to me that I wouldn't actually bum too hard if they took their sweet time. I wouldn't mind a few days or even weeks here on my island. These past three years had been so full – full of unhappiness, and nasty comments, and errands, and pings and whooshes of texts and emails, and just general *feelings*. I felt like I wouldn't mind a bit of respite. A bit of emptiness, a bit of space, feeling nothing. But my psyche wasn't going for that. An unfamiliar feeling bubbled up in me and swelled in my chest. This must be happiness. I was finally happy for the first time in three years. I galumphed down the mountain as skippy as a mountain goat.

I headed back to the original beach where I'd woken up – for the first night I figured it would be wise to be somewhere familiar. Hopefully there'd be plenty of time to explore the rest of my island before the cavalry came. The sun got lower, and everything got even prettier, the sky blood red now, the palm trees silhouetted against the sky. I knew I should find somewhere to sleep.

I was pretty hungry and thirsty but not enough to worry me. I wasn't about to go poking around in the dark. Finding a place to sleep had to be the priority. Starting tomorrow I would get organised – find the castaway's holy trinity of food, water and proper shelter, and start building stuff. Ya know, the whole Robinson Crusoe 101. But I still did a bit of calculating. From what I'd seen from Monte Cristo there were two beaches making up the V of the bay. The rest of the island seemed to be cliffs or rocks where the land met the sea. I figured that I'd first woken up on the bottom jaw of the Pac-Man, as it were, so I decided to wander up to the other beach. There was a keen wind picking up from the west and I figured it would be more sheltered. I walked towards the sunset, remembering the other beach was westerly, and that the sun sets in the west. Soon I was across the tussocked grass of the dune and sinking into powdery sand, and then the wetter flats of the shoreline. All the time I was thinking that, if you had spent three years wanting to be alone, that there was no greater pleasure than walking on virgin sand where no other human foot had ever trodden. But as it wouldn't be very smart to make my bed where the tide would come in, I was about to turn back when I saw something that made my feet stutter and my heart thud painfully.

A single solitary marking, no bigger than a sneaker but big enough to ruin all my happiness.

A footprint.

14

The Possibility of a Polar Bear

I walked forward in the dying sunlight, pulse thumping in my ears, and fitted my foot into the print.

It sure as hell wasn't mine. It was bigger for one thing, and wider. For a moment I had visions of a friendly native, some sort of Man Friday. Straight after that I had visions of an *un*friendly native – perhaps the original Bigfoot. Even that would've been preferable to the most likely theory, which was that someone else had survived the crash.

I looked for a second print and I found it – heading for an outcrop of rocks like a little peninsula. I followed the second print, and the third, and the fourth.

As I rounded the cape I realised the terrible truth. They'd *all* survived. All of them.

I'd never understood until that moment what people meant when they said their heart sank. But right then mine felt like it was going down in an elevator in my chest. There was a little knot of people, some sitting, some standing. They weren't much more than silhouettes but after three years I could recognise my tormentors even in the half-dark. And of course the tallest standing one, towering over everybody like the chief fricking meerkat, was Loam. When I saw him my tongue subconsciously sought the sharp edge of the tooth he had broken, the tooth I hadn't gotten fixed before I left. I hadn't had that reflex since I first woke up on the island. Now it was back.

I walked over, legs as new-foal wobbly as they had been when I first woke up on the sand. The figure on the floor was Egan, nursing what looked to me like a pretty superficial graze on his knee. My heart bled for him.

My eyes strayed, as they always did, to Miranda Pencroft. Understandably for someone who had just survived a plane crash, she didn't look as good as usual. It occurred to me for the first time that she might have the kind of looks that needed a lot of maintenance. A lot could be forgiven, though, for the fact that she was still wearing the Amazing Skirt, the crazily short mushroom suede number she'd had on on the plane. It had survived unscathed, unlike its owner. Li, too, looked bedraggled – her usually mirror-shiny black hair was everywhere, and she was already angrily engaged in taming it into its regulation plait. Loam and Egan looked like Tweedledumb and Tweedledumber in their Osney-School-Preparation-for-Life-Summer-Camp polo shirts. And Turk, in his branded rapper gear, just looked faintly ridiculous in this setting.

And then there was Flora. Flora looked strangely at home. She'd always had a slightly tough, ruffled edge to her. Already in ripped cut-off denim shorts and a faded black Motörhead vest, she looked pretty much exactly as she'd looked on the plane. In contrast to the fragile Miranda she appeared sturdy and ready for anything. But her expression was unsure – she stood uncertainly on the edge of the group. I remembered she was an Eleven, and didn't know these people at all except for fellow Eleven Egan. She wasn't in their orbit; as an Eleven, she wasn't important enough for them to know nor lowly enough for them to victimise, once there was a Twelve in the school. I was glad about Flora – glad she felt uncomfortable, I mean. At school I'd almost felt more betrayed by her than by anyone. I felt like we could have been friends but she didn't make the effort after that first day when she'd been nice about my glasses getting broken. But it had seemed afterwards that the gulf between Elevens and Twelves was just as great as that between Ones and Twelves. She didn't want to know me. Well, now, without her buddies Smith and Fry, she looked like I'd always felt. I wondered then why they hadn't come on the camp if Flora was coming. But of all the reasons that flitted through my brain, I could never in a million years have come up with the right one.

'Ah,' said Loam. 'Room service has arrived.' I sidled up to the group, instantly reduced to my shy, reticent self, no longer King of the Castle, reverting to my stooped, concave posture, trying to fold my long body into itself, to take up as little room as possible. Through lowered lashes I collected the expressions that greeted me: Loam curiously chipper, as if he was glad to see his slave. Li rolled her eyes. Flora looked relieved and Egan looked downright pleased to see me – presumably glad that he was no longer the lowliest creature on the island. Turk sucked his teeth and said, 'My G! True what they say 'bout cockroaches, am I right, cuz?' Pencroft looked at the sand – anywhere but at me. Presumably she was bummed that I wasn't, apparently, too ugly to live as she'd once suggested. I looked around. In this company I wanted, badly, to revert to my normal invisible self, but there was something I just had to know, so somewhere I found the nuts to speak up.

'Did you see anyone else?' I asked the group at large, my voice coming out too loud.

'Who else would there be?' asked Egan.

'Well, the pilot? The stewardess?' It was suddenly desperately important to me that one of them had survived. Now I wasn't on my own I needed an adult, any adult, and I didn't mind if it was the guy who flew the plane or the lady who'd served me a Coke. I'd read *Lord of the Flies*. I knew how this went. Things had been bad enough at Osney; I was only really safe under the eye of the teachers. On a desert island without an adult, who knew what would happen?

'Nope. Just us.'

'Were you all together? Or scattered about?'

Pencroft, looking at the sky, said boredly, 'Me and Loam woke up close together. Turk was a little way off, on the dunes. Egan on the beach.'

'I was in that sort of brush land over there,' said Flora, pointing. 'And I saw Li almost at once.' Li shrugged grudgingly in confirmation.

'Any wreckage?'

'Of what?' said Li rudely.

'Of the plane,' I said patiently. 'Did you see any wreckage?'

'Just bits,' said Flora. 'Like that bit.' She pointed to a small piece of battered metal on the sand. It was white, with the red and blue stripe of the light aircraft. I'd seen pieces like it myself, on the beach where I'd woken. 'But not the fuselage?' I dumbed it down a bit. 'The main cabin section? Wings?'

Blank faces, shaken heads.

'It must have broken up pretty low over the island,' I mused, 'if we all survived with not much more than a scratch.'

'What do you call this?' bleated Egan, indicating his knee with both hands.

'A scratch,' I said wryly. I wasn't afraid of him. 'But really, it's kinda odd. In fact . . . it's almost . . . *miraculous*.' This plane conversation was the most words I'd ever spoken to any of them.

'Selkirk,' put in Loam.

'Yes?'

'Zip it.'

'OK.' It slipped out – my old catchphrase. I'd been about to say that at first light we needed to track down that plane. But after Loam's reprimand I shut the hell up. It occurred to me suddenly that I didn't necessarily need to tell them everything I was planning to do. On an island of limited resources, I didn't need to share with everyone. This wasn't grade school.

'We should make camp,' said Loam. Even he could see that it was getting pretty dark. 'Let's find somewhere in those trees.' He pointed to the jungly bit behind us. I looked doubtfully at the dark tangle of branches hiding God-knows-what. With the discovery of the others and the coming dark, all that 'mine is the only heart that beats on the island' stuff went away, and fear replaced it. I thought of wild animals coming out of the forest to devour us in our sleep. When I was little my folks were really into this TV show called *Lost*. They would box-set the hell out of it, watching multiple episodes at once, and because they didn't believe in bedtimes or boundaries I caught quite a lot of it. It was about a plane that had crashed on a desert island and all the survivors were led by this hero dude called Jack Shephard. Anyway, one of the only things I remember was that there was supposed to be a polar bear in the woods (even though it was a tropical island – I never really got that), because for a kid that's much more interesting than all the other relationships on the island and sex and stuff. I never actually found out if there was a polar bear or not, or whether it was what my parents would call *a psychological manifestation of the inner psyche*, but you know what I mean: something scary and monstrous in the woods. (Side note: parents can really screw with you, because when I did eventually go to bed after watching stuff like *Lost* they would read me fairy stories where bad things live in the woods to threaten kids. Fairy tales should come with a health warning.) So although I was afraid of Loam, I was afraid of the woods more. I steeled myself to say a word I'd only ever said once to him before.

'No,' I said. 'I'm going to sleep in the dunes, high up as I can, out in the open.' I looked again at the black tangle of jungle. 'Just in case.'

'In case of *what?*'

'Ya know. In case.'

I didn't want to verbalise my fears about a polar bear in the woods, because I would sound like a fruitloop.

Then Flora spoke up. 'Selkirk's got a point.'

'Yeah,' agreed Turk of all people, 'that jungle is bare *booky*, fam.'

'I think so too,' said Pencroft, weaving her fingers around Loam's. 'C'mon, Seb. I don't fancy being in the jungle in the dark. Maybe tomorrow when we've scoped things out a bit.'

No man on earth could've resisted her appeal. 'All right,' he said begrudgingly. 'Dunes it is.'

So, unbelievably, everyone followed *me* to the dunes, instead of following Loam into the forest. Yes, he'd had to give the command, but it was my idea, and everyone trailed after me like a bunch of ducklings to the high ground where the bitter grass blew in an unexpectedly keen breeze. Not entirely sure what had just happened, I settled everybody down in a ring, facing outwards, close enough for safety, but ranged around the compass points so we could see anything approaching.

I didn't sleep for a while, lying on my sandy pillow. For one thing, it was unexpectedly cold. Tomorrow we'd have to figure out how to make a fire. For another, my eyes were mapping the unfamiliar stars, incredibly bright and close. I could recognise enough of them to know we were in the southern hemisphere; the Pole star and the Big Dipper had been replaced by the Southern Cross, moving slowly overhead like the changing backdrop of a stage set. I thought about the stars, and what had just happened. Wherever the hell we were, the world had been turned on its head.

15

The Breakfast Club

My first morning on the island resembled my first moments there – sand in extreme close-up, reaching for my glasses, putting them on. Trying to get up, wobbly as a foal again. But that morning there was no sense of euphoria.

I stood up and stretched aching limbs. The night had been bitterly cold for a desert island, and my arms and legs felt like they had frozen solid. I shook them out, slowly waking up, feeling the blood circulate, taking stock. Pencroft and Loam were still asleep, tangled together turned towards each other, like some Calvin Klein advert. If only they could stay asleep. They were only evil when wakeful. Then I shivered again. To stay asleep was to be dead.

The sun was rising over the horizon, and looking seawards I could see Egan on the frill of the shore, paddling his feet in the surf. Turk sat high on a dune, sucking on a seagrass straw and looking out to the ocean, his dumb curtain hair blowing in the breeze. Li was standing close by him, throwing pebbles moodily into the surf. And Flora was wandering on the yellow sand, stooping now and again to pick up a shell and discard it again, her pink and purple hair shrouding her face.

I felt a knot of anger in my stomach. Turk was munching on my seagrass. Li was skimming my pebbles, Flora was collecting my shells, and Egan was paddling his pale feet in my surf. Lincoln Island was no longer mine; it was polluted. There was a whole bunch of serpents in my paradise, and if it couldn't be mine I just wanted off this rock. In fact I wanted out of there so badly that the need to be rescued even overrode the gnawing hunger pangs in my stomach. Jazzed by my success of getting everyone to sleep where I suggested, I decided to try to call a meeting. In the absence of a conch shell to blow, I just shouted, 'Hey!'

Everyone turned to look at me. I gestured in a beckoning, embracing motion, the opposite of what I felt. I wanted everyone to go away. But if I had to work with these people in order to get rescued, I would do it.

'I just figured we should have a bit of a meeting, ya know, figure out what we're gonna do.'

To my surprise, they all stopped what they were doing and wandered over, not exactly enthusiastically, but they all came nonetheless. We sat in a circle and Li shook Pencroft officiously, like a mom trying to wake a kid for school, even though she and Loam had already started stirring when I'd shouted.

Loam's first waking comment, animal that he was, was, 'I'm hungry.' Everyone else murmured in agreement. *Yeah. Me too. Starving.* I imagined what they must eat for breakfast at home, all these sporty types; mountains of protein and fruit and cereals to fuel their athletic endeavours – the most important meal of the day. But I didn't have to imagine because they all started talking about it.

'What I wouldn't give for a full English,' said Loam.

'Me too,' said Egan dreamily.

'Croissants and hot chocolate,' said Li, her face softening.

'Sausage and Egg McMuffin,' said Turk predictably.

'Buttermilk pancakes, crispy bacon and maple syrup,' said Pencroft more surprisingly – she looked like she'd never been near a carb in her life. They all fantasised in turn about what they'd be eating right now; everyone but Flora, who started to laugh in these cute little snorts.

'What?' I said, curious.

'*The Breakfast Club*,' she said. 'You know: the movie.' She pointed to everyone in turn. 'Loam is the Jock. Pencroft is the Cheerleader. Li is the Prodigy. I'm the Emo. And you, Selkirk, are the Nerd. And all we can talk about is breakfast.'

I saw what she meant. All of us corresponded to a classic high-school type. I was too interested in her theory to mind her identifying me as the Nerd – I mean it was self-evident, everyone knew it. I actually thought it was pretty clever of old Flora to see the Breakfast Club thing. I was kinda relieved that not everyone I was stuck here with was a moron. But I wasn't about to let her off the hook – not yet. 'Great,' I said. 'Hereafter known as the Breakfast Club. Very good. But where does it get us? We have to get organised. The only food source we know of for sure is the plane, right?'

Loam challenged me at once, ever the alpha male. 'What about *them*?'

We all followed his finger, craning upwards. He was pointing to the top of one of the tall smooth palm trunks, to where two enormous green coconuts hung beneath the glossy leaves.

'They look like nuts,' said Loam.

'They are nuts, you nut,' said Flora scathingly.

'Nah, fam,' said Turk, 'he means *nuts*.' He grabbed at his crotch like a rapper.

I sorta smiled despite the gross gesture. I was trying to keep everyone on side. 'He's right,' I admitted. 'Green gonads. But I don't know how we could get them down. Those trunks are smooth as glass.' This, at least, was indisputable. Instead of having those ridged trunks sectioned like a pineapple skin and handy for climbing, these trees were incredibly tall and had no bark you could hang onto at all. I suppose it was nature's way of protecting the fruit. 'As I was *saying*,' I said, 'if we can find the crash site, we can at least recover all the drinks and snacks. There may even be aircraft meals that they never got a chance to serve before we went down. Yesterday I found some berries but they were pretty rank. We should take a look while it's light and before it gets too hot. If we're lucky, there will be food, drink, and also,' I said, 'our luggage. The least we can do is make ourselves comfortable before we're rescued.'

'D'you think we really will be rescued?' asked Li. She still looked hostile, but, however she looked, she was at least asking my opinion. It felt good.

'Yes,' I said. I wasn't particularly trying to comfort them, I still hated their guts, but I needed to reassure myself. *I* needed to get out of here. 'Bigger light aircraft have black box recorders. Two- or three-seaters don't because of the weight.' That was true, as far as I knew. 'But this one was a ten-seater. They're probably looking for us right now. Besides, it's possible that if the pilot knew there was something going wrong, he may have radioed in a Mayday signal before we went down.' I looked around. 'Does anyone actually *remember* the crash? Because I don't.'

They all looked at one another and shook their heads.

'We can't *all* have been asleep,' said Flora.

'Well, we may all have lost consciousness if there was a sudden drop in cabin pressure. We must've been pretty relaxed when we fell – hardly any injuries.'

Flora shrugged, not convinced.

'Anyway, it's kinda pointless guessing. Let's do something practical.'

I walked over to the flat expanse of silver sand above the tideline and looked around for something to write with. Lying right in my path was a piece of driftwood, round and smooth as a club, whitened with salt and as tall as me. It was a perfect staff. This will sound quite US-West-Coast spiritual, but it didn't feel like I found the staff, it felt like the staff found me. I picked it up and weighed it in my hand, then started to drag it through the sand.

They all stood up and wandered over to watch. The letters were so big – I meant them to be seen from high above – that it must have been difficult at first to see what I was writing. The sun was climbing up the sky, so by the time I'd finished the three enormous letters with a period in between each, I was sweating.

'Soss,' said Loam, as if it was a word.

105

'Not *soss*,' I said, breathing heavily from the exertion. 'S.O.S.' I pronounced it Ess-Oh-Ess – surely even he would get the point.

'What's that stand for? Something about Osney School?' He pointed to the breast pocket of his green polo shirt, which carried the same logo as the school blazer I'd never have to wear again, the little gold tree on the island and the letters O.S. below. But really, did he honestly not know? Had he really never read, or even seen on TV, any of those Castaway-on-a-Desert-Island stories, the grand tradition that began with *Robinson Crusoe*? 'You never come across any Robinsonade?' I asked.

'Sure,' he said, surprising me. But then he said, 'It's that fruit squash they drink at Wimbledon.'

I stared at him, and had another experience they have in books. The scales fell from my eyes, and I saw him at last for what he was. The realisation freed me, as surely as a slave whose shackles are struck off at a sparking anvil.

Loam was stupid. Outside of the school hierarchy, and the familiar language of sports, he was clueless.

And once I'd made that earth-shattering discovery I began to be a little bit less afraid of him.

'S.O.S. means Save Our Souls.' I said patiently, as if to a child.

He snorted. 'Save Arseholes?'

'Yes,' I shot back, almost without thinking. 'I wanted to make sure you were rescued first.'

Then something weird happened. They laughed. The whole of the Breakfast Club laughed. Sure, they didn't laugh for long, and sure, they all stopped soon enough when they saw Loam's furious face, but it was too late by then. I'd seen. They'd laughed. There had been a small, but significant, sea change. Was I *funny*?

Growing in confidence, I said, 'All right. We've written our S.O.S. It'll help our rescuers find us, and passing aircraft might spot it too. It's above the tideline so it should stay there. Let's try to make sure no one treads through it.' I shoved the staff into the sand decisively. 'Now let's get organised and pool our resources.' I was met with blank faces. 'I mean: let's assess what we all brought with us from the crash. What are our possessions? What do we have?' I sat down on the sand, cross-legged, and amazingly they all followed suit, until we were once again in a circle. I noticed something straight away. 'No one's got shoes on,' I said. 'Did you all take them off on the plane?'

'Nah, fam,' said Turk, shaking his head. 'There's no way I was taking those babies off. They were some fresh creps, cuz.'

Some had, some hadn't. 'But we wouldn't have taken off our socks too,' said Flora. A fair point.

'I was on the beach,' I said, 'so maybe I kicked mine off to swim. Anyway, what's gone is gone. Let's not worry about what we don't have. What *do* we have?'

Slowly they all emptied their hands and pockets, laying their precious objects in front of them on the sand like we were about to do an incantation. Most of them had the latest state-of-the-art phones. 'Any charge in any of them?'

'No,' said Li. 'It's the first thing we tried, to call someone.' I looked at the circle of phones. They just looked like a bunch of ornamental garden tiles. Which is pretty much exactly what they now were. 'All right. Let's see what else we have that might be useful.' My eyes went where they always did. 'Pencroft?'

She indicated the Amazing Skirt, which was barely covering her thighs. 'This skirt,' she said.

Flora cackled. 'What? How is *that* useful?'

'Shut up, Flora. It's a genuine Missoni, made of Italian calf suede.'

'Well, unless it's made of chicken wings,' drawled Flora, 'it ain't much use here.' Evidently Flora was braver on the island too. Turk noticed it. 'Spicy,' he said, to no one in particular.

'Turk, what about you?'

Rather sheepishly, he held up a small stone bowl and a tiny stone baseball bat. I actually had to look at it for a few seconds before I realised what it was. It was a pestle and mortar. 'How in the Sam Hill did that get here?'

He shrugged. 'It was in my pocket. Always is. You never know when you need to cook something up, cuz.'

Flora began to laugh again.

'What, fam?'

'Well,' she said, 'it's just so . . . so *you*, Turk.'

He didn't look unpleased. 'Man's gotta deal,' he said. 'When you live round my ends, you gotta be equipped.'

I rejected the idea of stating that Turk's 'ends' were actually my 'ends'; a pretty WASPy part of Jericho. It wasn't exactly Compton. I moved on. 'Egan?'

Egan just had a ballpoint pen, in his top pocket. He waved it in a slightly shamefaced way as if it outed him as a dork next to Turk's drug paraphernalia, and then put it in the strange circle of objects.

Loam had his Fitbit. He declined to take it off his wrist but he held his arm out straight like a kid at Christmas. 'Fitbit Surge. Brand new. Exclusive tangerine strap,' he said proudly. 'It's got an activity tracker and a heart-rate monitor.'

'That's just terrific, Loam,' I said, 'But all we need is for it to tell the time. Does it tell the time?'

'Of course.'

'It's on England time?'

'Yes,' he said.

'All right, cool. More of that later. Li?'

'I've got my violin,' she said. 'She's in the trees. I covered her in leaves for safety.'

'What, you fell out holding it?' I asked, mind-blown.

'No, not that,' she said, reddening. 'I found her. Not far from where I woke up. She was in the cabin, not the hold, in the seat next to mine. My mum always buys an extra seat so she can travel with me.' I didn't know what was more remarkable, that the violin got its own seat or that Li called it 'she'. She spread her long fingers. 'So I suppose when the plane broke up she came down where I did.'

'But why did you bring it? Her? Wasn't the camp supposed to be teambuilding and stuff? "Preparation for Life"?'

'I never go anywhere without her,' she said shortly. 'And she *is* going to be my life I've got a Royal College of Music audition in September, and my mum ...' She checked herself. '*I* want to practise every day.' She turned the tables. 'What about you?'

'Nothing.' I said. 'I had my phone, but it got smashed in the crash.' I didn't admit that I'd tossed it. I was starting to think that my grand gesture had been sorta dumb – there might have been something in it we could've used.

'Not nothing,' said Flora. She reached out and I thought she was going to poke me in the eye with one of her black-lacquered

109

fingernails, but her nail met glass with a sharp *tap tap*. 'You've got your glasses.'

I'd forgotten them. I was so used to wearing them they were a part of my face. I shrugged. 'No use to anyone else though, are they?'

'I s'pose not,' she said. 'But at least they stayed on your face. I wasn't quite so lucky.'

I studied her. 'I didn't even know you wore glasses.'

'I don't,' she replied. 'But I lost something which you would have thought would be *literally* fixed to my face.' She tapped the side of her nose, as if she had a secret. 'My nose stud.'

Along with all the rest, I peered at the side of her neat nose. Sure enough there was a tiny hole just above the flare of the nostril, with a little redness around it. 'What, you mean it just fell out?' I asked.

'Well, that's just it. They can't really fall out. It doesn't have a back to it like an earring. It's a little spiral – it screws in like a mini corkscrew.'

Pencroft screwed up her perfect face, put her fingers in her ears and started going, 'Lalalalalalala.'

Over the din, Li said pointedly, 'Was it valuable? Like a diamond or something?'

'No, Kim Kardashian,' said Flora. 'It was just a tiny diamanté stud. But I only had it done three days ago, after a lot of sneaking around my parents. Now I'll have to get it done again when we get rescued.'

'*If* we get rescued,' said Pencroft, breaking off her song.

'On that note,' said Flora, 'I did manage to keep something

110

with me that will benefit *all* of us.' She held up an empty Evian bottle, with its screw cap still on.

'Be more use if it still had water in it,' said Pencroft, Flora's crack about her skirt clearly not forgotten.

'Sure,' I said. 'But we can fill it when we find a water source.'

'I was thinking more of a message in a bottle.'

'That's not a bad idea either,' I mused. 'But first we have to have something to write in it.'

Loam pointed to the enormous letters on the sand. 'What about that?'

'Perfect,' I said. 'If someone in Japan, or New Zealand, or wherever the hell we're nearest to, gets a message in a bottle saying "S.O.S.", what are they going to do?'

Loam looked puzzled. It was as if I was a teacher suddenly, asking him a question he couldn't answer. 'Send help?'

'Where to?' I flung out my hands, indicating the island, the sea stretching to the distant horizon 'How will they know where we are?'

I could see the problem dawning on Loam.

'We don't exactly got GPS, cuz,' said Turk unhelpfully. 'We can't exactly find out, true?'

'We can actually,' I said. 'But that's for later.' Once again I held back from saying too much. Some instinct I didn't know I possessed was slowly prompting me to the power of knowledge, and, moreover, the power of withholding it. 'Loam, how much juice have you got in that Fitbit?'

He looked at the square face on his wrist. 'Three days?' he said.

'Cool. We've got time,' I said, no pun intended. 'We'll send the message tomorrow for sure. But we'll keep the bottle for now.' I jumped up, brushing my sandy ass. 'In fact, bring it with you, Flora, in case we find fresh water.'

'Bring it with me where?'

'To find the plane.'

They all stood too. 'Shall we split up?' asked Turk. He turned to me. 'Bruv?'

I registered, with a jag of pleasure, that Turk was deferring to me, not to Loam. I thought about his question. 'No,' I said. 'Not right now. We don't know the terrain well enough, and if people get lost we'll lose valuable time and energy looking for them, when none of us has eaten or drunk. Besides,' I said as a new thought struck me, 'there might be stuff to carry back. Stuff we can use. Let's stick together.' I looked around. I had no way of knowing where the plane might have crashed, but the most likely obstacle to flight was Monte Cristo itself. Most crashed light aircraft, I'd once read, went down through pilot error and were found on the side of a hill. I'd been up the foothills on the west side the day before and hadn't seen anything, so I pointed my staff in an easterly direction like a tour guide. 'Let's go.'

And so we set off to search for the plane, over the tough grass of the dunes and into the cover of the trees, and for the first time in my life, I was in the lead.

16

The Plane, the Plane

At first it was great. I had my stick with me – walking stick and staff of office. I used it to help me over difficult terrain and swish at the undergrowth like I'd seen in movies, like I was Dr Livingstone or something. A goat skipped across my path, nearly giving me a heart attack, but I was pretty pleased to see him. If this whole plane thing failed, we'd need something to eat beside Bucket berries.

My knowledge, long hidden, long abandoned, kicked in. I was identifying species like David fricking Attenborough. A red bird that flashed past was a Wilson's parakeet. I spotted a caucus lizard, a Cochineal beetle. Every name I uttered strengthened my reputation in the eyes of the Breakfast Club. In the forest I named deodars, Douglas firs, casuarinas, gum trees, eucalypti, hibiscus, cedar. And, most usefully: 'Bamboo,' I said. 'Great for irrigation, and good for building cos it's light and strong. We can chop it into cups for drinking, or cut it into laths for baskets. You can even make alcohol out of the pith.'

'XD,' said Turk.

Loam stopped, hands on hips, face red and sweating. 'Christ, Selkirk, you're *such* a nerd. How do you *know* all this shit?'

I didn't slow my pace. 'I read,' I said. 'Books. Not just my phone when I'm in the can.'

Turk gave a little shout of laughter, and I grew another couple of inches. Humiliating Loam could easily become a habit. And God knows, I was entitled. But as I walked away my back prickled with sweat, almost expecting Loam to deal me a blow from behind. At that moment Egan shouted and dropped to the ground. He came up holding an aerofoil, a white wedge-shaped piece of metal with a red and blue stripe.

After that it was like an Easter-egg hunt, and the Breakfast Club cried out excitedly whenever they found a piece of the plane. My first thought was that we should collect every bit of plane debris we found, and use it for our shelter or tools. But we found a surprising amount of bits, and in the end it became impossible and we set the pieces down. The sun got higher, and hotter, and we still hadn't found anything apart from odd fragments. My mouth was dry as dust, my glasses had begun to steam up and I was beginning to doubt the whole mission. Should I have split the party up? Should we have climbed Monte Cristo and looked for the crash site from above? But eventually we began to find more and more bits – we were undoubtedly on the right track. As we climbed higher up the eastern slope of the mountain Egan piped up again. 'Look!'

I looked in the direction of his pointing finger. My stomach gave a sick lurch as I saw what he'd seen. A dome of bright metal, a white wing sticking crazily into the sky, and a long scar of broken branches and fallen trees behind it, the pale wood beneath the rough bark splintered and exposed like bone.

The crash site.

The plane was pretty well spread about, bits on the ground, bits in trees; one wing section separated from the main fuselage and flung metres away. It looked exactly as you'd expect a crash site to look, everything artfully spread about just as you see on the movies. It gave me a shiver to look at it; I couldn't believe we had survived this. But the Breakfast Club were happily clambering over it, into the hollow cabin and over the shredded leather seats like it was a woodland adventure playground. I had to organise them. 'Food and drink first and foremost.' I called. 'Then luggage. Also look for sharp things, tools and weapons.'

There was absolutely no luggage to be seen. 'Maybe the hold bit is somewhere else,' said Li.

'Yes, but we should still find our handbags,' said Pencroft in a voice of keen disappointment. 'Mine had my make-up in it.'

The search wasn't totally fruitless though. Egan found a sheaf of A5 cards, with *Oceanic Airlines* printed at the top in gold relief, and a delicious menu printed below. 'Well, that seems hopeful,' I said. 'Let's find where they keep all that food.'

Then I heard a distant voice – Flora's voice, yelling something from a way off, outside the cabin. It sounded like 'Ukit!' Thinking she was in trouble I scrambled out of the cabin, leaving the others hunter-gathering, and ran through the trees to her side. She stood in a little clearing pointing. 'Cockpit,' she said. Sure enough, the cockpit section was suspended a little way up in a tree.

She began to walk forward, as if in a dream. I put my arm

out across her chest, as if she was crossing a busy intersection. 'No,' I said.

She turned to look at me. 'What?'

'The pilot,' I said. 'However we managed to fall from the sky, and I'm still not sure how that happened – I'm pretty sure the pilot is strapped into his seat. Which means –' I couldn't look at her – 'he might still be there.'

I watched realisation dawn.

'Oh,' she said in a small voice.

'Yes. So let me look first, OK?' My catchphrase slipped out.

She licked her lips nervously. 'OK.' It was about the first time anyone had ever said it to *me*.

I walked across the clearing, my stomach churning. There was no reason why I should've been more able to cope with seeing a dead body than Flora – in fact, I'm sure I wasn't. Most probably her Gothic, Death-Metal-loving little head would more readily handle a corpse than mine, but somehow I just couldn't do it. For a feminist, my mom was very hot on chivalry and had no problem with my dad and me holding doors open and carrying suitcases. She always said that the 'two concepts were not incompatible'. And it was some sorta chivalry, I guess, which made me climb the twisted tree and clamber into the cabin, to potentially meet a dead pilot.

I could see at once that there was no one there though, and I gotta admit I breathed a huge sigh of relief. There were two empty seats, a radio dangling on a curly wire, a bewildering array of switches and long-dead dashboard lights. Something furry with a long tail scuttled across the dash and out the open window and scared the shit out of me. I cried out.

'Selkirk? You all right?' Flora called from below.

'Yes,' I shouted, heart racing. 'You can come up.'

Heart slowing to normal levels, I traced the path of the small creature. It had gone clean out the open window.

The open window.

'That's weird,' I said aloud.

'What's weird?' asked Flora, clambering breathlessly into the cabin.

'There's no glass.' I put my hand through to show her.

She put her hand through too, and wiggled it around like she was doing a magic trick, an impression that was assisted by the fact that she had that ace-of-spades tattoo on her wrist.

'Must've fallen out when it crashed.'

'But there are no shards.' I ran my finger around the frame where the windshield had been. 'No jaggedy bits like when you smash a window. It's almost like . . . like there was *never* any glass.'

'Well,' she said, 'maybe it's designed to blow out in one piece if you lose altitude. You know, so it doesn't injure the pilot.'

'It's not though,' I said. 'It's designed to craze – ya know, get all the zigzaggy cracks all over it, but not break at all.'

'Selkirk, you're such a know-it-all. No wonder . . .' She stopped.

'No wonder what?'

But before she could reply, there was another shout from below. We scrambled out of the cockpit and down the tree, and ran back in the direction of the sound.

We found the others surrounding a large metal cube like hunters with the carcass of a fallen deer. It was the cart of drinks and snacks, and the Breakfast Club were already raiding it. The cart was only small, and the drinks were only mini cans, like you get on most airlines, and there were no gourmet meals as the menus had promised, just salty snacks like crisps and pretzels. But at that moment we didn't care. I grabbed with the rest, found a Coke and poured it down my throat in one go. It was the most beautiful moment of my life. Looking around, I could see the others felt the same. Miranda Pencroft looked like a Coke ad, but for once there was a more beautiful sight than her to be seen. A drawer full of packets of chips. Fancy-ass artisanal chips called Swiss Crisps. I pulled the packet apart and crammed the chips into my face. As I ate I saw Loam – had to be him, didn't it – reaching for another pack. 'One each,' I said, like a nagging mom. 'We take the rest with us, and divide them up equally. We don't know how long they've got to last.'

Loam regarded me, his dark brows drawn together. 'Kiss my arse, Selkirk. Maybe you're forgetting I'm a *Quarters* Man. A *Toppers* Man. I'll eat what I want.' He reached out and deliberately opened another bag of Swiss Crisps, emptying the lot down his throat. Then he opened another Coke can and poured that down his gullet too. Then he actually crushed the can on his forehead like you see in movies and tossed it over his shoulder. Then he gave a massive belch that practically shook the palm trees. I looked to where the can had fallen. Funnily enough, it was the Coke can lying red and crumpled in the undergrowth that made my Wi-Fi forehead crinkle up. Loam was littering my lovely island. It was a dumb thing to get upset about – there was so much crumpled metal hereabouts anyway, from the plane. What difference did a stupid Coke can make? But it did. It made *all* the difference.

I swallowed down my useless rage and said no more. Loam continued to help himself from the cart, picking through the flavours to find the ones he liked. Furiously, I looked at the others. None of them, even Pencroft, looked too happy, but no one even here was going to argue with a Quarters Man. No one would gainsay a Toppers Man. Only when Loam had had his fill did we share out the sloppy seconds. The cart was too heavy to carry and we could never have wheeled it through that terrain. Instead we found those puke bags in the seat backs to carry our shares of the (much-depleted) provisions, along with all the bits and pieces we'd thought were useful from the plane.

Loam led the way back down. He didn't carry anything except an armful of crisps for himself. It was left to the rest of us to carry the booty we'd found – a window blind, a torn-off hatch handle, a seat arm, the menus (just so we had some paper) – all spoils from the downed metal beast. The sound of Loam's munching kept time with our footsteps and grated on my nerves – every crunch was a reminder that he was still the King of the Castle.

Then it occurred to me. I'd already won. Loam was defeating himself with every salty little snack he munched. I smiled to myself. Let him eat as much as he wanted. He was doing me a favour. Yes, those snacks were food, but they'd only serve to make him thirstier. That's why you get peanuts and crisps in bars; if you're thirsty you buy more drinks. In this heat, he'd be panting like a hound dog in an hour or two.

My footsteps became lighter and sorta *skippy*. But I wasn't going to say nuthin'. No, sir. When you're playing a game of poker, which is what Loam and I were evidently doing, you don't show all your cards. I was the only one who knew about the lake, you see. The freshwater eye of the Pac-Man I'd seen from the top of Monte Cristo. That was the winning card I held up my sleeve; because if Sebastian Loam wanted to drink ever again, then sooner or later he'd have to follow *me*.

17

Orange Is the New Black

It was Li who found the golden egg of the Easter-egg hunt. On our way back down the mountain she all but tripped over whole tail section of the plane. It lay in the undergrowth like a beached white shark, with the plane registration number – a huge black ED-34 as long as my arm – stencilled across it. But I barely looked at the painted characters. I was too excited. 'The tail!' I exclaimed. 'This is where the flight recorder will be.'

'What are we looking for, cuz?' asked Turk. 'Just a black box, true?'

'It's actually painted orange,' I said, 'so it can be spotted. It's made of titanium to withstand impact, and has a thermal core to withstand heat.' From the edge of my vision I could see Flora rolling her eyes, but Pencroft looked at me with something *almost* approaching respect. I could feel my concave little pigeon chest expanding and ballooning into a magnificent scarlet breast of feathers, like the parakeet we'd seen on the way up the hill. All my showing-off was for her, and maybe it was working. She'd never, ever come so close to meeting my eyes before.

Using the sharp pieces we'd already found, we attempted to tear the tail section apart. Soon we were hammering away like a bunch of blacksmiths. Even under the leaf canopy it was pretty tough work in the midday sun, and soon we were all sweating, but at that moment, for the first time, we were a team. And even I had to admit that the Most Valuable Player was Loam, the big lunk. Hopped up on sugar and carbs, he used one of the seat struts as a crowbar to prise away the side panel like it was the lid of a can of beans. When the metal separated everyone cheered him and I saw his handsome face lighten for a moment, as he remembered what applause was like. My bird-of-paradise chest deflated, and my heart shrivelled within it. I had to regain the ascendancy. The box had to be there, or else I'd lose face again. But there was something else too. I wanted to be the one to actually pull it out.

Here I was assisted by Loam's Hulk-like dimensions. He physically couldn't get his shoulders through the hole. 'Let me,' I said, before anyone else could try. He studied me, his face purple and dripping with exertion. 'All right,' he panted, standing back. 'You are pretty puny.'

I crawled in, blinded by the sudden dark, almost gagging on the stench of aviation fuel and choking on glass fibres. I scrabbled around for a few panicked seconds like an outsize rat, then my searching hands found something and pulled. I backed out of the hole into the light and studied the something, blinking. It was a bright orange rectangular box, with two white lines striped diagonally across it, a canister with a black wire attached to it at one end, and the words FLIGHT RECORDER DO NOT OPEN stencilled in that army writing you see on

122

tanks and bombs. I held it high like the baby Lion King, and now everyone cheered *me*. My puffy scarlet-feathered chest inflated once more like a life jacket.

I lowered the thing and looked at it, cradling it tenderly as if it was a baby. 'Orange is the new black,' I said.

'Now what?' demanded Egan. He sounded pissy, but still, he was deferring to me, not Loam.

'Now we take it back with us,' I said. 'It has a sensor and will be sending out sonar beeps. Now rescuers can trace us right to our camp, instead of just finding the crash site.'

Loam, emboldened by the success of his brute force, asked belligerently, 'Why don't we just stay here? We could make a shelter back there in the main bit of the plane. It could be our house. It's ready-made. And I'm tired of walking.'

Everyone looked at him, and I could see they all thought this was a pretty cool idea. Pencroft was drooping in the heat and twining around him like poison ivy round an oak tree.

'No,' I said. 'We know it's here, and we can plunder it for materials bit by bit. But we need to be near a water source. And once the Cokes run out, this isn't one.'

This hit home. Loam, as predicted, was panting from his exertions, and when he spoke his mouth had that gross dry 'click' to it that you get when you're thirsty. It was really hard to listen to. I didn't know how Pencroft could stand him. I glanced up at the sun overhead and pointed downhill. 'There's a *lake* just to the south of here. A *freshwater* lake with a *waterfall*.' I hit all the wow words hard, like a used-car salesman.

'How do you know?' challenged Loam, eyes narrowed against the sun.

'I saw it yesterday. From the slopes of Monte Cristo.' It just popped out. 'I mean, from the mountain.'

Loam eyed me. But this wasn't Osney School. I eyed him back. Time to play my winning card. 'I don't know about you guys, but I could sure do with a swim.'

That did it. The Breakfast Club started babbling about jumping into cool water, and drinking the whole lake dry, and they all began to follow me again with fresh energy. Before we left the tail though, I grabbed the side panel Loam had torn off. 'This'd be a good roof for a shelter,' I said, by way of explanation.

That wasn't entirely true. Like a college kid stealing a highway sign to put in his dorm, the plane number was a trophy. When we were off this rock – and now we'd found the recorder I was confident we would be soon – I wanted a souvenir to remember the adventure. Some proof that we – I – had cheated death.

It was now the hottest part of the day, and as we trudged what I thought was lakewards I prayed I'd remembered the way. We seemed to be walking for miles and I could hear mutinous whisperings behind me from Loam, Turk and even Egan, and tired moanings from Pencroft and Li. Only Flora trudged on without complaint, carrying the orange-is-the-new-black box recorder. As I swished through the undergrowth with my staff, the panel I carried got heavier and heavier and the sharp metal bit into my underarms and fingertips. I began to despair of ever finding the lake. And then, like a mirage, it appeared.

'Oh my *days*,' said Turk.

It was so pretty it was hard to believe it was real. We just sorta rounded this corner and there it was, like blue glass reflecting the green mountain. The jungly forest stopped a little way out from the water and there was this mini beach – rocky though, not sandy – dotted with the omnipresent palm trees.

It was so hot that we all dumped our booty on the shore and rushed and tumbled into the water like otters. Miranda Pencroft shed the Amazing Skirt like a skin on the shingle, and – sue me – I watched her as she splashed into the water in her underwear. If you'd observed us you'd have thought we were all best friends, laughing and splashing. We drank as much as we swam because we were all intensely thirsty after our hike. Flora filled her Evian bottle for later and left it with our bits of plane.

After a while of blissful floating I thought I would find a quiet corner and rinse out my shirt and shorts and underwear, which were all pretty rank after two days of sweat. It won't surprise you to learn that I'm not the world's greatest swimmer, so I half waded, half breaststroked towards the falls I'd seen from Monte Cristo. They formed a crystal cascade tumbling down from the mountains, and like one of those floaty net curtains they masked a pale cliff face riddled with caves, and tumbled and played down stones studded with wild rock roses. The falls were heartbreakingly beautiful. And what made the scene even more beautiful was the incredibly gorgeous water nymph bathing underneath.

Miranda Pencroft had beaten me to it. She stood in her underwear, which looked basically like a white bikini, letting the spray pound on her face and shoulders, and – sweet Jesus – all of her *curves*. She played with the water, dodging back so the curtain of water hid her completely, and then lurching forward so the stream closed behind her back. Despite her teenage body, she was as laughing and carefree as a child. It was a side to her I'd never seen before, and it made me like her for the first time.

I tried to creep away but I was too close – I made a clumsy sloshing sound as I moved, praying that she might not hear over the roar of the falls. But her eye must've been caught by the off-white of my shirt or the glare from my dumbass glasses. Anyway she saw me. I had to stop and try to look nonchalant, as if I'd meant to be discovered here, staring at a half-naked classmate, waist deep in lake water, glasses steaming up in the sun.

She waded towards me, looking like a mermaid, blonde hair streaming, bronzed flesh glossy with water, until she was close enough for me to see her lashes splayed like starfish.

I stood in the water; fortunately it was waist deep. Miranda's breath was coming fast, from the exertion of her play. She said, 'I see you looking at me. You always look at me.'

I could feel myself going scarlet and looked down at the water. There, broken by ripples and eddies, I could see the reflection of a pale, skinny kid in a dirty white short-sleeved shirt, with weird hair and weird glasses. Glasses. We'd rushed into the water so fast I'd forgotten about them. Who wears glasses to swim? A nerd. It was a real moment: it brought me back to my old self, Lincoln the nerd. What right had a nerd to look at a goddess? My new-found confidence ebbed away. 'I'm sorry,' I mumbled.

'OMG,' she said. 'You don't have to apologise.' She didn't sound pissed at me. She sounded – flattered. Then something miraculous happened, as miraculous as seven teens walking away unscathed from a light aircraft crash, as miraculous as the Breakfast Club laughing at my jokes. Miranda Pencroft put one single finger under my chin and lifted up my face. She looked me in the eye and smiled her perfect white smile.

DISC FOUR

Light My Fire – The Doors

John Densmore, Ray Manzarek, Jim Morrison,
Robbie Krieger (1967)

18

Catching Fire

I never did get to wash my clothes. But I didn't care. I'd followed Miranda Pencroft out of the Blue Lagoon and back to the others feeling ten feet tall. I was sure she'd changed her opinion of me because of how I'd acted that morning on the beach and at the plane. I think Pencroft liked someone who was in charge and, for the moment, that was me. I was determined not to let my new role slip through my fingers. I was consumed with a desire to show off – If I'd been a peacock I'd've been spreading my tail right then. And I thought I knew how to big up my supremacy even more. The most elemental fricking caveman thing I could possibly do. I was going to make fire.

When we got back to the OG beach we all sorta scattered. A couple of people napped in the shade of the palms, some of them paddled, and Pencroft, who drew my eyes as ever, amused herself drawing emojis on the sand with her finger. By tonight she'd be warming her long coffee-coloured limbs in front of my fire, the golden light playing on the planes of her perfect face.

I went off into the dunes. I was left to myself, and that's exactly how I wanted it. My idea had been to find a window from the plane, and use it to concentrate the sun like a magnifying glass. That hadn't exactly worked out, since all the glass in the plane had mysteriously disappeared, and there wasn't so much as a plastic cup on board. I'd read online that you could make fire with the bottom of a Coke can – apparently the parabola of the bottom of the can, if you polish it, is just the right angle to concentrate sun rays in on itself and make a flame. But I was pretty sure it wouldn't work on those mini airline cans, and that was all we had. We'd have enough crisps and peanuts to feed us for another day – two if we rationed ourselves – but after that we needed to hunt something and cook meat, unless we wanted to survive on those stomach-ache-inducing Bucket berries. I had to find a way of making fire, not just for food and heat but for my own position.

The answer, of course, was literally right in front of my eyes. I'd read *Lord of the Flies*, and although it wasn't my top Robinsonade title (I preferred the stories where one person was isolated, my ultimate fantasy), I did remember the part where they made a fire using Piggy's glasses. The method comes from an invention from the olden days called a 'burning glass', and if there's a cooler name for a firelighter I've yet to hear it.

Well, I'm here to tell you that using a burning glass ain't as easy as it might seem. I sat on the top of those dunes for the rest of the afternoon, in direct sunlight, trying to direct the fricking sun's rays through the right lens of my glasses onto some dry seagrass. The grass got warm, but there was no spark – nothing was happening. William Golding was clearly full of shit. I guessed Piggy's glasses had been thicker than mine – mine were so weak (on account of my not actually needing them) and so thin (as they were a minus-one prescription), they seemed to have absolutely zero magnification. I sat there for a long time just looking at the glasses in my hand, turning them this way and that, the sea roaring gently at my back and the sun baking my scalp. Nice that it wouldn't light the grass but had noooo problem at all frying my skin. Then I remembered something from those copious GCSE revision notes I'd written out for the Ones at Osney. Something about water and magnification and the refraction of light.

I went down to the sea. The tide was flooding back in, swallowing all of Pencroft's emojis. A smiley face with hearts for eyes, some kissy lips and a Snapchat ghost were washed away as I watched. The tide was rising and the night was coming. I didn't have much time. First I dipped my face in the sea to literally cool my head, and dashed my hair out of my eyes. Then, standing there ankle deep in the surf, looking out to the infinite sea, I steeled myself to do something that felt pretty damn symbolic. I took one lens in each hand and snapped my own glasses.

It felt so different doing it myself. Kinda empowering. I popped the lenses out of the broken black frame and dipped them in the salt sea, which made them grab at the light. Then I sandwiched the lenses together and a thin layer of water between them shone out like a crystal line. I took the glass sandwich, no bigger than the palm of my hand, back to the dunes, with my salty hair whispering at my ears, *Hurry, hurry.*

I tried again – this time with a mantra. *C'mon, baby, light. C'mon, baby, light.* I don't know whether it was my wheedling words, or the sun dropping to a nice low angle, the optimum angle for firelighting, or the fact that I'd doubled down on the lens power, but the burning glass suddenly decided to work. When I hit the sweet spot a tiny gold circle illuminated my little pile of seagrass, concentrated to a pinprick, then began to smoulder. Heart thudding, I blew on the smoke gently, until the spark became a gilded worm, consuming the seagrass as it fattened. Suddenly I was ten feet tall again. Fire was the one thing that set man above the beasts, that made him King of the Jungle. And it had kindled at my command.

Then I panicked a bit. Only when the spark smoked and spread and the flame started to crackle merrily did I realise that I hadn't actually expected it to work. I'd got no fuel. I cast about for the nearest kindling and lighted on a bamboo crop at the edge of the dune grass and started pulling at the dry pale sticks, tearing and snapping them free. The live green ones, I knew, wouldn't catch as they'd be too wet. Running back and forth I fed the greedy golden monster until the pyre was so high the others came running, crowing with glee.

The Breakfast Club whooped and capered like savages, dancing round the sacred flame. 'It's lit!' exclaimed Turk, and for once his dumb roadman-speak was right on the money. Then it got to be like camp, as we all sat and allowed ourselves another packet of chips and pretzels around the fire, hopeful now that they wouldn't have to last us until rescue, that the next day we would eat like kings. The chat was standard for the Breakfast Club, in that it was all about food.

'Man's getting cooked munch.'

'We can hunt that goat we saw.'

'Or that bird, remember?'

'I bet there's fish in that lake. We could cook fish.'

'Well, we'd have to catch them first,' I said. I felt like I had to put the brakes on a bit. 'We'll have to find something to be a line. Since our shoes all mysteriously disappeared, we have no shoelaces.'

'What about vines or some shit?' said Turk. 'Like Tarzan.'

'I didn't see any today,' I said. 'Maybe we could strip some bamboo for thread. It's quite fibrous. But it'll be tricky. Or we could unravel some cotton from our clothes, but it's so weak when wet. Also we only have one outfit each, since the luggage is lost.'

We were all silent for a bit, looking at the hypnotic miracle of flame. All too soon though, the flames began to dwindle, and the fire that I'd hoped would burn brightly all night was turning to an ashy orange glow, giving merely light, not heat. 'C'mon, baby,' said Loam, speaking to Miranda as I'd spoken to the flame, coaxing her, kindling her, hauling her to her feet. They walked into the night, wrapped around each other. It made me sick to think about what they'd be doing out there in the dark.

Then everyone else began to drift away to settle down in the dunes. This wasn't what I'd planned. I wanted them all to be lying around my fire, not exactly singing camping songs and baking s'mores, but at least basking in the glory of Link, the Fire God. I could feel my power failing. I'd run out of kindling. I'd taken all the dry bamboo from the frill of the forest. The palm leaves were too high to reach, and to gather hardwood from the jungle would take too long – the fire would be out by the time I got back. I'd screwed up. Bamboo was a bad choice – it might have been good for building and making cups and irrigation and all that shit, but as firewood it was a bust. It was full of flammable spongy crap which just burned right up in five minutes. Tomorrow I'd get hardwood, maybe chop down one of the palms, but I still had to worry about tonight. The fire gave me my power and when it dwindled my power did too. Outside the circle of its light, in the dark, who knows what would happen? Would they revert to their old, bullying selves, gang up and rise out of the night to attack me?

Then I saw a feminine silhouette before the fire. For a moment I thought it was Miranda, come back again to worship at the flame. But the figure who crossed the firelight and plumped down cross-legged next to me was Jun Am Li.

She didn't say anything, but something dark crashed onto the dying flame, sending sparks skyward. For a moment I thought she was trying to sabotage the fire and felt myself heat with anger where the flames had let me down. But then the fire began to lick and rise around an unmistakable shape. The glossy mahogany curves of a violin.

'Wha . . . ?'

I turned to her. Her dark eyes and dead-straight glossy hair reflected the flames, and her face looked more relaxed and contented than I'd ever seen it. 'Li? What the hell? Your *violin*?'

'Doesn't matter,' she said simply. 'I *hate* her.' Her savage tone reminded me of how I'd said goodbye to my phone. 'When I get home from school, she's waiting. When I get up in the morning, she's waiting. My mum makes me practise before school, after school. Four hours a day I have to play her.' She humped her knees and rested her chin on them, watching the merry flames. 'Then at the weekend it's tennis coaching with my dad, both days, all day, except for violin practice before I go and then again in the evening when I get back. And that's my life. My mum wants me to be a violinist and my dad wants me to be a tennis player. They pull me both ways and I'm so stretched and taut that I feel like I might snap.' I could hear the tension in her voice and her tone tuning higher and higher. 'I thought this was what I was supposed to be, you know? Asian, achieving. But I can't do it any more.'

I wasn't very used to conversation, but I knew I had to make a joke now, calm her back down. 'Well,' I said, nodding at the fire, 'I guess you're not going to be a violinist *now*.'

She shook her head and her black hair fell about her face. I thought, out of nowhere, that she looked really sorta pretty. 'No. Not a tennis player either. If I had my tennis racket here I'd burn that too.'

'Won't your parents bum really hard?'

She shrugged, beneath the shiny cloak of her hair. 'How will they know my violin even survived the crash? She might have gone down with the plane for all they know.'

'I didn't mean that so much as the career thing.'

She was silent.

'What *do* you want to be?'

She took a long breath. 'I'd like to have children. I'd like to have a daughter. I'd like to make a home for her. I'd like to bring her up to make mud pies, and eat candy, and climb trees.

135

I wouldn't make her learn a musical instrument, or play a single sport. I'd let her be a kid.'

I thought about that. I thought too about how she looked out for Miranda. She wasn't being a bodyguard after all. She was being a mom. 'Sounds great,' I said.

She yawned hugely. 'I'm going to sleep,' She took my hand and put something in it. 'For tomorrow,' she said. I opened my hand. There were four violin strings in my palm, twisted neatly into little figures of 8. 'Fishing lines.'

I poked them with my finger. Strong coiled strings, one of them almost invisibly fine. It could've *been* a fishing line. 'You *beauty*,' I said.

'Good night,' she said in reply. But she didn't move and she and I watched the violin burn together, the flames licking through those little S-shaped holes on the belly.

'Li,' I said, 'what kind of music *do* you like?'

'How d'you mean?'

'Well, if you were stuck on a desert island –'

'I *am* stuck on a desert island.'

'– what tracks would you bring with you? You know – what would you be listening to if your phone was charged?'

'Classical stuff mostly. Bach's a big favourite. Concerto for two violins in D.' She looked back at the burning violin. 'I do love *listening* to music. I just don't ever want to *play* it again.'

I nodded, and we sat in companionable silence, something that would have been difficult to contemplate only a day ago.

I don't know if it was the hard cherry wood of the violin, or the varnish or what, but that sucker burned all night. Everyone gravitated back to the fire and settled down just as I'd imagined, even Loam and Pencroft. My last thought before sleep was that maybe, just maybe, the island could be mine again after all. I had treasure in my pockets, treasure that would be garbage anywhere else in the world but here on the island was more precious than the gold coins of the missionaries, stamped with the faces of strange kings. I had four fishing lines in one pocket, and in the other, cold now and sleeping, lay the jewels in my crown – two spectacle lenses.

And no one knew how to use them but me.

19

Hunters and Gatherers

I woke to the sound of a female voice, speaking in a low, musical tone.

It was like an incantation to greet the sun, and it was working. The bright gold disc peeped over the horizon. I could see Li, sitting cross-legged, facing the sunrise. To start with I thought she was meditating, but then I heard the words.

'*Pan-seared Filet Mignon*
red-wine jus.
Grilled Lamb Chops
minted lamb jus.
Pan-seared Colorado Rack of Lamb
mustard-grain sauce.
Veal Scallopini
tomato tapenade.
Grilled Pork Tenderloin
mustard onion jus.
Herb-roasted Chicken

lemon sage sauce.'

I got up and stumbled over to her, drunk with sleep. Looking over her shoulder I could see that Li was reading from a card, one of the menus we'd found on the plane.

'Pan-seared Colorado Striped Bass
green-pea pesto & white-wine sauce.
Grilled Scottish Salmon
Sancerre & leek sauce.
Almond-crusted Mahi-mahi
lemon herb sauce.
Poached Whole Maine Lobster
in a Thai seafood sauce.'

I couldn't listen to any more. It was torture, pure food porn. I stepped over the ashy skeleton of Li's violin, walked out to the peninsula and peed into the blue sea, looking out at the horizon. From the corner of my eye I saw Loam along the cape doing the same, like we were peeing at urinals in the most stunning men's room in the world. The mere sight of him still made me feel afraid, and I hated myself for that. I was King of the Hill, Link-the-maker-of-fire. A Heath Robinson Crusoe. But I knew that in order to consolidate my position I needed to bring Loam to heel. It wasn't enough for me to be raised high. Loam had to be brought low.

Once everyone was awake I convened a meeting of the Breakfast Club. As they groggily collected in a circle on the dunes, I noticed that Miranda had changed out of the Amazing Skirt. She must have folded it away somewhere safe, because she was now wearing a pair of khaki boxer briefs as shorts. They were short and tight on her but I couldn't find them at all alluring because

I was as sure as I could be that they were Loam's underwear.

I stood at the centre of them, this circle-jerk of bullies. But I felt pretty pumped and determined to lay down my new constitution. We were still living under Osney rules. But this wasn't Osney. This was Lincoln Island. 'I'm going to make a few changes around here,' I said. 'First up, names. We're not having any more of this superannuated surname bullshit.'

Loam looked blank.

'We're not on a football pitch. First names only from here on in. You call me Lincoln.' I'd thought about my name quite a bit. I called myself Link in my own head, but Link was for people I liked – the *only* people I liked, i.e. my parents. Besides, I thought my full name gave me more authority than Link, was more presidential. And it was the name of the island, so there was a brand at play here.

And if I was to have my full name, Loam's name, Sebastian, should be shortened. 'Loam, you are Seb. Egan, you're Gil. Pencroft, you are now Miranda. Li, you're Jun, and Turk, you're Ralph. And Flora, you're still . . . Flora. Agreed?'

No one looked too happy. But no one dared to disagree. I was the keeper of the flame.

'While we're on names,' I said, 'let's get our geography right. The mountain –' I pointed to the looming mass, slate-grey in the young light – 'is called Monte Cristo. Goddit? The jungle is the Emerald Forest, and the lake is called the Blue Lagoon.' And, because I couldn't be hard-ass all the time, I said, 'Today we'll hunt, so tonight we'll have hot food.' That menu reading of Jun's had really got me going, and I knew hot food would do good things for my polls.

They cheered weakly, back on side. But then it all went wrong.

'Right. Hunting. This is where we take over,' said Seb.

'But . . .' I protested.

'No, Selkirk.'

'It's Lincoln,' I said. 'Didn't I *just* . . .'

'*Whatever* your name is.' He talked over me. '*You're* going to chase one of those goats down? Really? You're a *Twelve*. I'm a Quarters Man, remember? I won Toppers three years running.'

A small seed of panic rose in my chest. Seb had used my surname – he was reasserting Osney rules and it seemed to work. As soon as he'd mentioned my status as a Twelve, and his as a Quarters Man, everyone sort of snapped to attention. I realised how institutionalised they'd been – the very mention of the Osney rules had placed them back in their hierarchy.

'We'll head towards the big mountain,' Seb announced.

He wasn't using the name. He had to use the name.

'Monte Cristo,' I murmured.

'The big mountain,' he said, looking at me defiantly. I dropped my eyes first. 'Light your little fire, sweetheart,' he said, like I was a wife in the fifties. 'We'll bring back something for you to cook.' And then he walked off into the forest.

They all went with him. All of them. 'Jun?' I appealed to her. I felt we'd made a breakthrough last night. But she just shrugged and followed the others. Even Flora, who'd never had anything to do with the Ones before, skipped off with them like they were poker buddies. They were literally singing as they went, and my stomach plunged as I recognised the song.

141

The tune was 'Ode to Joy', Beethoven's Ninth, and the words floated back to me:

Run on, run on, you're an Osney Man
Run on, run on, run as fast as you can.
If your goal is wealth and fame
There's a game to play, so play the game

I sat there by the ashes of Jun's cremated violin, which was spookily holding together, a grey ghost of its former self. I don't know how long I sat there. For a while anyway, alone again, feeling all the dreadful Osney feelings come rushing back. It was unbearable.

I couldn't just stay there, wondering how they'd got on. Logically, I knew I still had power over them. They'd have to come back. Seb could call it a 'little fire' all he liked, but they still needed my little fire to cook whatever they killed. But I couldn't bear the thought of Seb as the supreme hunter, Seb getting admiration, Seb standing over the body of some huge lion and wearing a pith helmet like those old prints of Colonial England.

I got up and followed them at a distance, as quietly as I could. My feet were already hardening at the soles, my tread already easier, as if I'd never worn shoes at all. They'd gone, as I'd advised, to the slopes of Monte Cristo, and it was easy to follow their tracks through the undergrowth and even easier to follow their shouts and laughter. *Some hunters*, I thought. Not exactly silent and deadly – surely they would scare the goats away? But then it occurred to me they might have a pretty easy mission, even if they didn't shut the hell up. If these goats had never seen a human being before, they might not have learned to be afraid. Was fear something you were born with, or something you learned? I could only speak from my own experience. I wasn't afraid of other kids as a concept. All the time I was home-schooled it didn't occur to me that when I mixed with other kids they would come after me. I didn't learn to fear them until I met some. But in the animal kingdom? I really didn't know.

I soon got my answer. Half a dozen goats streaked past me, hurtling at speed, bouncing through the undergrowth. I don't know whether they were afraid, or just loving life, but they were goddamn fast. This wasn't going to be easy.

And it wasn't. I climbed a little way up the mountain so I could see the hunt.

It was beautiful. I watched them for about an hour and it was like the best movie ever. I was just sorry I didn't have popcorn. They all ran around, purple-faced in the midday heat. Gil and Flora, the poor Elevens, soon collapsed on the ground, but even the elite Ones had to stop eventually, hands on hips, bent double and panting. I watched Seb wiping his streaming face, his beloved Fitbit Surge still on his wrist. I wondered what it was saying. *You have been chasing a goat for one hour. Your heart rate is through the roof. Ground covered: a zillion kilometres. Calories burned: shit-loads. Goats caught: zero.*

Eventually, reluctantly, I left my eyrie and headed into the undergrowth. I had to search around for a while before I found what I needed – a natural deep crevasse between one rock and another, cut into a forest pathway. I stood there and looked down into the dark crack for a few moments. It must have been two metres deep, easy. It would do. I set to work, snapping down bamboo branches and leaves, nothing too solid, as delicate as basketwork.

My task took me a good couple of hours. I could hear, nearby, raised voices. I didn't care now. They could make all the noise they wanted. It would only help me. As I worked I could hear that the nature of their chatter had changed. This was no longer the joking and camaraderie of folks going on a jolly hunt. They were bickering, hot and tired. I wasn't afraid now. I knew they wouldn't catch a goat in a million years. I just hoped that I would. I climbed the nearest tree and waited.

It took an amazingly short time. A bunch of goats ran by, startled by the noisy arguing of the Breakfast Club. Some of them skipped over the delicate lattice of leaves and bamboo I'd built over the crevasse, playing the-floor-is-lava. But one of them, poor sucker, fell right in.

I leaped down from my tree. The goat was deep down in the rock, bleating and struggling, his tough little hooves clattering on the stone as he scrabbled. I put my hand down and stroked his hairy greasy head, feeling the skull hard beneath the skin. He quieted and looked up at me, unafraid, with his slabbed yellow eyes. I knew then that I'd been right; I was the first human he'd seen, and he didn't know to be afraid of me. For quite a few seconds the goat looked up at me and I looked down at the goat, before the others came up and broke the moment. They were still trailing after the herd and had followed them to me. Grabbing my staff I jumped into the crevasse with the goat. He was *my* trophy: not a cup or a silver plate, and with

144

fur and teeth, not ribbons and rosettes, but he was mine. The Breakfast Club, shiny with sweat, gathered round the pit and looked down at us.

'*Damn*,' exclaimed Ralph in admiration. 'He got one. My *man*.'

Seb crouched down on his haunches. 'Well, well,' he said. He was above my head but my position was unassailable. Now *I* was the guy in the pith helmet standing over the lion. But Seb still didn't get it. 'Hand him up,' he said. 'I'll kill him for you.' The goat, trustingly, nudged his hard little head into my hand. The Breakfast Club were all watching. 'C'mon, Selkirk. What are you going to do? You going to kill him yourself? You haven't got the *nuts*, Selkirk.'

Looking back on the horror of what happened next, I can see now that it wasn't the insult that bothered me. I'd had worse, and in the last three years Seb had called me most things. What bothered me most just then was the use of my surname. I can't remember much of the next few moments except that I raised my staff and brought it down on the goat's head in a frenzy, not just once but ten, twenty, thirty times. I was beating Seb, and Ralph, and Miranda, and all of them. This was my reply for all the insults and texts and Instagrams and Snapchats. Three years of misery and fear boiled over and I didn't stop until I realised the goat was no longer moving. Then I looked up. Miranda and Jun had their hands clamped to their mouths and even Gil had turned away. Ralph and Flora watched me, open-mouthed. I stooped, a little dazed, suddenly feeling I might vomit, but instead I picked the goat up and threw him at Seb's feet. A little bit of blood splashed his toes and he jumped back. 'Jesus *Christ*!' The fear the goat had never felt was written in his eyes.

I scrambled out after the body, with the help of the bloody staff. I stood facing Seb, the goat between us lying on the forest floor with a red head. I pointed down. 'Pick it up,' I said, breathing heavily, my heart thumping with murder. I met his eyes for the second time that day. Suddenly we were back at Osney, his enormous kit bag between us, my hands hovering at the handles, my back stooping to lift it. But this time I was powerful, shored up by death. I had death sitting on my shoulder, I had death shining out of my eyes, I had death pulsing through my veins.

It was enough.

Seb dropped his eyes first, then bent and gathered the goat in his arms like a child. He straightened up. And then he said, humbly, 'Which way, Lincoln?'

20

Gutted

I led the Breakfast Club to the lake on the way home. They drank and swam and I washed the goat in the shallows, like a baptism in the bayou. The red blood smoked away from the ruined head in the water, the yellow eyes still stared. 'Why weren't you afraid of me?' I asked him, sorry now. 'You should've been afraid.' But no answer came.

We all drank our fill, and bathed, as sober today as we'd been drunk with joy the day before. Then I led everyone back to the dunes, and the site of the fire. Seb laid the goat tenderly next to the violin ashes.

There, in the place we were already thinking of as home, the spell of horror was broken and the practicalities of real life took over.

'Can we cook it now?' Seb asked, speaking for all of them, almost politely, the hunger plain in his voice.

'Well, not *yet*,' I said patiently and gently, trying to rehabilitate myself by being extra-civilised. 'It needs to be prepared. You can't just shove it on the fire like that. It's got all this shit inside it. *Literally* it has actual shit inside it. Bowels and stomach and everything. The meat would be inedible.'

Everyone just accepted that. Everyone expected that the new Lincoln would know exactly what to do, that the new Lincoln would take care of it. Thing is, I *didn't* really know what to do. I'd read in *Robinson Crusoe* about him eating goats, but Daniel Defoe didn't exactly go into detail about taking the guts out. What I wouldn't give for my hated phone now, a quick but bizarre Google search: *How to gut a goat*. But I didn't let on. They believed in me now, and I wasn't about to mess with that. 'You guys go and take a break,' I said, magnanimous as hell. 'You can finish the snacks from the plane. We'll eat tonight. Just chill on the beach. I got this.' I thought I would need *some* help though, and I knew just the guy. The gangsta, big talker, the guy who thought he knew his way around a knife.

'Ralph, come back when you've eaten. You can help me with this.'

The others looked at him. He shrugged and sucked his teeth. 'Sure, big man.'

I retrieved my sick bag from where I'd hidden it in the undergrowth. I was starving so I ate my last bag of pretzels and drained my last Coke in one go. Then, taking care not to cut myself, I punctured the Coke can with a rock and tore it carefully into a wicked, crescent-shaped blade.

When Ralph returned I handed him the Coke-can scalpel and turned the goat on its back. It was now stiff, which made things easier. 'I'll hold the legs. I think you just cut him all the way down the belly. The guts are connected at the throat

148

and the ass. If we make two cuts, top and bottom, we should be good.'

He licked his lips. 'You mean, just shank him, yeah? Right down the front?'

I knew I'd been right to choose him. 'Yes. I think that would be best.'

I waited a long moment. Time stretched out and I could hear the others on the beach, talking calmly and happily, cracking the ring-pulls on the last mini cans, pulling open their final pretzels and chips, safe in the knowledge there would be hot food tonight. I thought: *I did that*. Then I realised Ralph had not moved in a while.

His hand, hovering above the goat's hairy belly, holding the knife, was shaking. I looked at him and, with astonishment, I saw his forehead crease in a way that was all too familiar to me. It looked exactly like my Wi-Fi forehead. Ralph Turk was about to cry.

'Lincoln,' he choked, 'I can't do it. Please, *please* don't make me.'

It was quite a different voice to the street-smart, wise-ass tones he usually used. There was no slang, just a desperate, sincere appeal. My heart swelled with cruelty. I remembered the day Ralph had spiked me, the Lucozade laxative, the rugby field, the shit as runny as pee running down my leg, the stomach cramps I'd endured all that afternoon. Now it was *my* turn. I could make him stay there, make him gut the goat, watch him cry and puke and completely crush him. But there was something far more powerful I could do to him.

'I got this, pumpkin,' I said. Then his own phrase came back to me. 'You ten-toes. I'll take it from here.'

I watched him scramble away, to go back to the Breakfast Club, to style it out and start using his roadman slang again. But the damage had been done.

I knew who he was now.

And now I knew him, he was mine.

Like most things you dread, gutting the goat was easier than I thought. Once I'd made the incision in the belly, the guts just slid out obligingly in one slippery mass, like they were all conveniently packed in a plastic bag. The skin came off like a jumper. It turned out that being a savage was easy. I looked at the goat's dark heart and seriously thought about eating it, but decided that might be a bit much, a bit Mr Kurtz. I walked to the headland instead and tossed the guts into the sea. It felt like a primal, savage act, strangely satisfying, giving nature back to nature, a sort of sacrifice. The wind blew a stripe of blood across my sun-bleached white shirt in return. I didn't mind. In fact I kinda liked it.

I saw the Breakfast Club watching me from the beach, me and the sergeant's stripe of blood that I'd earned. As I walked back to light the fire, Miranda's eyes followed me, like mine used to follow her.

DISC FIVE

Gimme Shelter – The Rolling Stones

Mick Jagger, Keith Richards (1969)

21

Night on Bare Mountain

That night I watched everyone munching my goat, cooked on my fire, seasoned with my sea salt and sprinkled with some of my mountain thyme. It was the nicest thing I had ever tasted.

The next morning, I decided it was time to complete the rout of Sebastian Loam. I would make him my assistant when I calculated the longitude and latitude of the island, the two sets of numbers that would give me our location. This was the information we'd need to put on our message in the bottle. True, we now had the plane's black box recorder, sheltered from the weather in the undergrowth at the edge of the beach, so the search for us had probably already started, but I'd always intended to send a message as soon as the crucial business of finding food and water and fire was behind us. Actually, now it didn't seem so urgent that we were rescued; but if I wanted to make the calculation there was literally a ticking clock. Seb's Fitbit.

At our morning meeting I asked, 'How's the Fitbit, Seb?'
He checked it obediently enough. ''Bout a day left.'

'Good.'

I stood inside the circle, and clapped smartly before I realised that was what loathsome Sports Nazi and Osney principal Mr Llewellyn did. I shoved my hands firmly in my pockets so I wouldn't do it again. 'Right. Goat steaks for breakfast.' (I'd stripped the carcass of last night's feast and wrapped the remaining meat in leaves for morning.) 'Then we'll hunt. Then the lake for a wash and a drink. Then back here for noon.'

I took my staff with me. It helped with walking, but who was I kidding? It helped more with my self-esteem. It was my staff of office and it marked me out as a leader.

We caught another goat and I killed and gutted it. It was much easier the second time, more of a pain in the ass really. I thought I might delegate the whole killing and gutting thing down the line. But not the fire, never the fire. So long as the Breakfast Club didn't learn how to light the fire, they couldn't do without me.

We had another delicious swim and drank the lake dry. In a private pool I washed my clothes. The stripe of blood would not completely come out, and I was not at all bummed about that. I looked down at my reflection and saw that I was already starting to change. My skin was lightly tanned, my hair fluffier and lighter from the sun, and boy-band shaggy. Of course my glasses were gone, now hanging around my neck on one of Jun's violin strings like glass dog tags in the tanned V of my open white shirt. Without their frames my eyes were green as olives. I'd always been pretty baby-faced, and only had to shave about once a month, but now I had an ashy shadow of stubble on my jaw, which looked stronger and squarer. I studied the person in the water and felt like I was looking at someone else. Suddenly self-conscious, I broke the skin of the reflection with my hand. I noted as we headed back to camp that Seb put his arm around Miranda's wet shoulders, but she saw me looking and shrugged it off. I smiled to myself. *Interesting.*

Back at camp, basking in sunshine and triumph, I climbed to the hearth and lit the fire, making sure as always that I wasn't overlooked. Since I planned to climb the mountain with Seb I'd toyed with the idea of deliberately not lighting the fire before I left. One cold night, without cooked food, would underline just how much they needed me. But I had to keep my people happy.

I remembered the warnings from history. French queen Marie Antoinette kept her people hungry. During the French Revolution they turned up at the palace gates starving and protesting that there was no bread. Old Marie Antoinette, totally misreading the situation, said, 'Let them eat cake.' Weeks later they chopped her head off. I didn't need a revolution, so I took myself off to the undergrowth to collect some hardwood from the forest for the fire. I'd sharpened one of the tailfins that we'd wrenched from the plane to make an axe; there was no handle but it was heavy in the hand and had a good edge, so I could hack off branches pretty easily. I even had a go at cutting down one of the palm trees, but the trunk was too damn tough, almost like it wasn't even made of wood.

155

I lit the fire and gutted today's goat. Then I collected all the bits I needed for the calculation – some straight sticks, some shreds of Coke can, a huge scallop shell which I marked up as a makeshift protractor, my staff and one of Jun's violin strings. Then I went to get Seb.

'Ready?'

He looked up mutinously, the incident with the goat clearly forgotten. He'd ceased to be afraid of me, now that I was providing food for him. I was less of a killer now than a supermarket. 'For what?'

'We're going to figure out where we are.'

'Why do I need to come?'

The truth was I wanted him to see how much cleverer I was than him, but I couldn't tell him that.

'I need your Fitbit. Unless you want to lend it to me?'

He looked at his wrist and back at me. I could see what was going through his tiny mind. The Fitbit was to him what the fire was to me. 'All right,' he said, getting to his feet grudgingly.

I walked with him out onto the salt flats, to the most level bit of beach. I talked as I went. 'To pinpoint our position on the Earth,' I said, 'we have to work out our longitude and latitude. Then we'll have something we can actually put into the bottle, some fairly accurate coordinates for someone to rescue us.'

Seb looked blank.

'We're going to calculate longitude using what's called a "noon sight".'

I walked Seb through the whole thing, feeling a bit like a science teacher. Under the eye of the sun, high and hot, I constructed a rough quadrant out of two pieces of wood,

156

binding them together with the violin string. Then I drove two sharp shards of Coke can into the cross-beam to give me two sightlines. I aligned the two makeshift nails with the sun, and waited and watched while the two long shadows on the sand crawled towards each other. Seb did too, but he mostly watched me, like I was some sort of magician or something. Slowly, so slowly, the two shadow-lines merged together to make one. The sun was at its highest point in the sky.

'Now!' I said. 'What does your Fitbit say?'

Seb checked the time. 'Seventeen hundred hours.'

'Noon here, five o'clock at home.' I did some quick mental math. 'We're at 60 degrees longitude, as near as dammit,' I said.

'How the *hell* do you figure that?'

'The Earth rotates one full turn in a day, that's 360 degrees. Because one day is twenty-four hours long, you can use time to calculate longitude. One hour of time difference corresponds to 15 degrees of longitude, because 360 degrees divided by twenty-four hours is 15 degrees per hour. If your Fitbit was on British Summer Time (which it was) and it travels a great distance (which it has) to a place where the sun is highest in the sky at 5 p.m. BST (which it is), then we know that we are at longitude 60 degrees west.'

He shook his head, like he could shake himself clever.

'How?'

'Because BST is an hour ahead of Greenwich Mean Time, and four hours times 15 degrees an hour equals 60 degrees.' This was pure dick-swinging, to make Seb feel dumb, and when I looked up from the Fitbit he was staring at me as if I'd just walked on water. It was working.

'Can I go now?'

'Yeah, you can go. You can go up there. With me.' I pointed up to the summit of Monte Cristo.

'What the hell for?'

'We've figured out our longitude. We need latitude too in order to find our actual position.'

'*Christ.*'

But he couldn't exactly say no, with all the others watching us. And so, after I'd lit the fire and made sure that the others had everything they needed for the night, Sebastian Loam and I set off for a night on the bare mountain.

22

Monte Cristo

Climbing Monte Cristo I discovered that what I'd noted on the first day on the island held true. With my wiry frame, I wasn't half bad at long distance and endurance. Seb suffered more, being all muscle and speed and bulk, and he was soon huffing and puffing and begging to rest. If he was Usain Bolt, I was Mo Farah. If the Osney Dash had been 1,600 metres, I might have had a shot. I enjoyed the climb. I enjoyed Seb being behind me. I have to admit I had a little fun with him.

'Come on, Seb,' I said, then broke into song. *'Run on, run on, You're an Osney Man. Run on, run on, run as fast as you can.'*

Purple-faced, he shot me a murderous look.

The sun was setting behind us as we climbed, and finally there was a dip in the relentless heat. Yielding, I let Seb rest. We sat for a moment on the warm, thyme-scented rocks and looked at the view. The sea was turning a deep mauve colour and the sky was a sorta deep rose. We could see the lake below and the falls in the low light held a rainbow in their spray.

'Jesus. Look at that! It's beautiful.'

Seb bristled. 'God, you're not going to try to put your arm round me, are you? You're so *gay*.' He was hopeless. Just a jackass. But then I remembered the last time he'd tried to put his arm round Miranda, and her shrugging it off. So I just smiled to myself and pushed on up the mountain.

Once the sun had started to dip it got dark rapidly – still we climbed until we could no longer see the pinprick of light that was our campfire. Going up Monte Cristo in the dark was pretty different to when I climbed it in the daylight on my first day on the island. Strange noises came from the heart of the darkness, and I wondered, then, what we were walking into. Night-time noises, sightless creatures, nocturnal things that slept the day away. The whisk of tails, the flash of night-seeing eyes, the chirrup and scratch of insects and arachnids. This was their time, and night was their kingdom. But I wasn't afraid. If this was my island again, these were my creatures, and I had dominion over them.

The noises clearly bothered Seb more than they bothered me, because he was the one who grudgingly started a conversation.

'Why did you give it that homo name anyway?' he asked, breathing heavily as he climbed.

'Huh?'

'Monte Cristo,' huffed Seb. 'What's it mean?'

There were several answers to this. I picked one. 'Monte Cristo is a mountainous island off the coast of Tuscany. It's in my favourite book, *The Count of Monte Cristo*.'

Seb was silent for a bit as we climbed. I could tell the mention of an actual *book* had turned him off. But he must've been bored, because he said, 'What happens in it?'

'So,' I said, 'it's the year 1815. This guy Edmond Dantes is falsely accused of a crime. He's framed by a bunch of people he thought were his best friends. He's stuck on this prison island called the Château d'If, for years and years and years. This island has the reputation of being inescapable.'

'And?'

'Well, Dantes does escape.'

'How?'

'He swaps places with a dead body, gets sewn into a sack and is thrown into the sea by the guards. But he cuts his way out using a knife he's made.'

'Then what?' Seb was starting to sound grudgingly interested. I wondered then if he'd ever had anyone to tell him stories, or if his rich folks had been so busy training their little sportsman with energy drinks and early bedtimes that they'd neglected to do it.

'He gets rescued by a merchant boat and joins the crew. Then he goes off to find this island his cellmate told him about, the island of Monte Cristo. Word is this island is stuffed with treasure that this Italian cardinal buried there in the olden days.' The story was a bit more nuanced than that, but I kept it simple for him.

Then I didn't say anything else. I wanted to see if he'd ask. And he did.

'And did he find the treasure?'

'And then some. By the time he leaves the island he's richer than ... than ... Scrooge McDuck.'

Seb let this sink in. 'Then what?'

'Then he recreates himself as an entirely new person, the Count of Monte Cristo. Handsome, fabulously wealthy. He's changed, you see, on the prison island; hardened, grown up, got an education. Everyone thinks Edmond Dantes is dead anyway. He can start again.'

Seb took a beat to think about this. It was so dark I couldn't see his expression. At length he spoke. 'And at the end, when he's got all the power, does he go after the people that framed him?'

'Oh yes,' I said in the darkness. 'He gets his revenge on *everyone* who wronged him.'

Seb thought for a moment. 'Cool,' he said.

The climb got a little harder after that, so we didn't say anything more till we got to the top of the mountain. I put down my stuff and looked up at the gazillion stars. They seemed close enough to touch. 'At home we'd calculate latitude using the North star,' I said to Seb. 'That's the easiest way to find the Prime Meridian, the imaginary line which runs from the North Pole to the South. But of course we can't do that here.'

'Why not?'

'Because we're in the southern hemisphere. Literally the far side of the world.'

'So what now?'

'There are some stars we can use. The Southern Cross – the constellation that's on the Australian flag – and two guide stars called the Southern Pointers.' I knew the theory, but I was bullshitting a bit here. I really didn't know the southern stars at all. Fortunately, before I lost face, I found the quartet stars, incredibly bright and close, hanging above us in a handy celestial square, and two other satellite stars shearing off at an angle. 'All righty.' I got out my makeshift protractor for the second time that day. 'Latitude is calculated by the angle of the Southern Cross relative to the horizon.' I held out my thumb as a guide to sea level. 'The angle that the Southern Cross sits above the horizon is the angle our line of sight to the Southern Pointers forms with the line that is tangent to the Earth; that is, our line of sight towards the horizon.'

'I've got no idea what you just said,' Seb spat crossly.

I smiled to myself and held up my protractor in the moonlight, closing one eye so I could triangulate the pinpoints of light.

'That looks like 30 degrees to me.'

Seb shrugged. 'If you say so.' Luckily he was too befuddled to ask me why I didn't use his Fitbit. The truth was, I didn't need it on the mountain. I'd needed him for no other reason than to blind him with science.

'C'mon, Seb,' I said. 'Where's your childlike sense of wonder?'

'Can we go now?' he said, by way of a reply.

'In the morning,' I said. 'It's gonna be safer to sleep up here than try to get down in the pitch dark. Do *you* know what other animals live here? Could be anything. Could be polar bears.'

It didn't occur to Seb to remark that if we were in the wrong hemisphere for a polar star, we'd be unlikely to see a polar bear. So we lay down, reasonably near each other, close enough for conversation, so this time I started one.

'What kind of music d'you like, Seb?'

163

He was silent for a bit. 'What kind of *music* do I like?'

'Yeah. If you were stuck on a desert island –'

'I *am* stuck on a desert island.'

'– what kind of music would you bring with you? If you could choose your favourite tracks?'

He sighed. 'Selkirk, are you trying to chat me up? I'm not interested in your homo small talk.'

He moved away, turned his back to me a little and rolled himself into a fetal ball, but not far enough, I noted, to get devoured by wild animals. Nor did he storm off and attempt to make it down the mountain by himself. He must have known that without my guidance he'd get himself lost.

I wrapped myself in the knowledge like a blanket: he needed me.

But. He'd used my surname. Again. He'd insulted Monte Cristo. And he'd insulted *me*. And that might fly at Osney School, but here, on my island, it was definitely *not* OK. Old Seb still needed a bit more taming, and I thought I knew exactly how to do it.

23

S.O.S.

At first light Seb and I set off down the mountain, and the heavens opened. It was the first rain since we'd been on the island, and it wasn't polite Oxford rain but a real knock-you-off-your-feet deluge. We'd all done Shakespeare's *The Tempest* for GCSE – or rather *I* had, on the Breakfast Club's behalf – and this storm was a bit like the one that kicked off that play, a ship-wrecking, tree-flattening doozy. Seb and I couldn't have heard each other even if we'd had anything to talk about. We could barely see each other for the rain even when we were two metres apart. By the time we got back to camp the sun was breaking through the grim clouds with golden streams of God-light, but we still found the others sodden and utterly fed up. 'We've *got* to build a shelter,' said Miranda, before she even said hello to Seb. She did not look as good as usual, as if the rain shower had rinsed away some of her beauty. Under the waterfall she'd looked like the goddess she was, but this morning she was bedraggled, her hair frizzy and half dried, grey circles shadowing her eyes.

'That was my plan for today anyway,' I lied glibly. I actually hadn't thought a shelter necessary now I knew how to make a fire and warm us at night. But the rain had been a warning – for all I knew we might be entering a rainy season where we'd be flattened by more monsoons. 'Colonials always build on their new territories,' I said. 'You Brits should know that.'

'And you Americans,' Flora shot back.

She was getting way too sassy. Time to blind her with science, just like I'd done with Seb. 'Flora, where's the Evian bottle?'

'I caught some rainwater in it.' She picked it up from the ground and it was half full. That just showed you how heavy that downpour was, because the hole at the top was pretty damn small, but that sucker had still filled up.

'Good thinking,' I said. You had to give the little guy something. 'Let's share that now.'

'Shouldn't we keep it for later?' she asked, hesitating. 'In case we don't go to the lake today?'

It hadn't taken everyone long to get into the desert island mentality of saving stuff up.

'No,' I said. 'We need to send the S.O.S., so let's get rid of the water now.'

Then Flora did an odd thing. She came over and brought the bottle to me, to drink from first. Gratified, I took a swig, then handed it to Miranda. Then it went to Jun, and back to Flora, before going through the boys, again in their order: Seb, then Ralph. Poor Gil got a tiny dribble in the bottom.

'OK,' I said, shaking the last drops out. The bottle was already steaming up in the extreme heat of the rising sun. 'Gil, I need your pen. And someone find me a menu.' Luckily someone had had the presence of mind to move the treasures from the plane, along with our stock of firewood, under the tree cover once the rain started. Jun brought me the menu she'd read out so poetically the morning before.

I sat on the warm sand and wrote resting on my knee. Carefully I etched two sets of numbers onto the paper. Latitude first: 20 degrees south. Then longitude: 60 degrees west.

Then, below my calculations, I wrote:

S.O.S.

I went over the numbers and letters twice, so they wouldn't be washed away by the sea.

The Breakfast Club stood around me, casting long morning shadows like a sundial. Time stopped as they watched me appeal for their salvation. I felt their hopes pinned on me, but I wasn't afraid. I *wanted* them to depend on me, even though, in this case, I was planning to let them down.

I rolled the paper small as a cigarette and popped it into the bottle. I screwed the light blue plastic cap on tight, then stood up. 'Come on,' I said. We all proceeded to the headland, everyone solemn, no one talking, like it was some sorta ceremony. When my toes met the edge of the cliff, I crooked back the arm that held the bottle, ready to throw.

A hand caught at my wrist.

'Wait,' said Gil. It was his hand. 'Shouldn't it be Seb?'

It was like I'd been punched again. My stomach sorta dropped at the impact of his question. I looked around at the faces of the Breakfast Club. None of them would look directly at me, except Flora, who gave the tiniest of nods. Seb held out his massive paw and I reluctantly put the bottle in it, like the baton of a relay. As his fingers closed around it he looked me in the face, his dark eyes challenging me. Suddenly the bottle seemed enormously important, and my fingers closed around it too. I didn't want to let it go. It had been my idea to find our longitude and latitude, my calculations. It was my island. Seb hadn't even known what S.O.S. *meant* for Chrissake. The moment stretched out forever and I had to talk to myself firmly. Great men delegated. If Napoleon had needed something thrown, and he'd had a big lunk handy who could throw further than him, then he would've let the lunk throw it.

But as I let go of the bottle and Seb grasped it, it felt like I'd lost something. He arced his arm right back, and then Seb, champion fast-bowler, all-round slugger and Toppers Man, pitched the bottle out to sea, so far that it practically flew out of sight. We couldn't even hear the splash when it fell.

He turned and looked me right in the eye again. 'Howzat?' he said.

24

Bikini Bottom

I felt sick as we walked back to camp from the headland. Seb was in the lead, and I was bringing up the rear.

I had to control the panic that was rising in my chest. Gil's question had blown a hole in me, punching in the walls of my leadership. The Breakfast Club were still planning to build a shelter, but now they were asking *Seb* what to do. Luckily, he didn't seem to have a clue. 'Just collect some branches and stuff, I s'pose,' he said, shrugging, '*I* don't know, do I?'

With a vast feeling of relief, I noted people starting to defer to me again. Slowly, slowly, throughout the morning, I regained the ascendancy. We took the tools we'd collected from the plane wreck into the jungly forest and began to hack and carry logs and branches until we had a pile the size of a fourth-of-July bonfire on our beach. On my advice we also collected thinner, more pliable strips of young green bamboo for holding together the bigger bits of wood.

I noticed Seb, though, becoming more and more distant,

until he physically detached himself from the group. I could have actually done with his brute force, to tear some of the more stubborn branches from the trees and carry them back. But for most of the morning he was nowhere to be seen, and Gil had vanished with him.

By noon, when the heat forced us to stop and seek the shade and the cool of the Blue Lagoon, we left a pretty neat skeleton of a shelter behind us. But when we came back from the lake in the late afternoon, having bagged a goat and brought it back, there was still no sign of Seb. 'Where d'you think he is, Miranda?'

She shrugged. 'How should I know?' she said, in a way that was both perplexing and satisfying. They were clearly no longer joined at the hip, but on the other hand it was unsettling to have two members of the Breakfast Club gone rogue. 'Ralph?'

'Dunno, bruv.'

'Well, we could really do with him for this bit. We need a bit of brute strength,' I said, carefully reducing him to dumb muscle in the others' eyes. I wasn't kidding though – we were ready to put the roof on our structure and we needed him. I went to find them.

As I rounded the headland I saw them at once, way out on the sand, far beyond the still-intact S.O.S. I'd written in huge letters on the first day.

Seb was bent over like a croquet hoop, holding my staff in both hands at one end, the other end touching the beach. Behind him three sticks of roughly the same length stuck into the sand. Gil was about twenty metres from him, and as I watched he ran towards Seb and bowled something overarm to

170

him. The something – it looked like a pine cone – flew towards Seb. Seb stepped out, opened up his shoulders and smacked the pine cone sweet and true, and so hard that it sailed right over Gil's head.

They were playing cricket.

Cricket.

For a moment I was transfixed; Seb was such a talented, natural player, and beautiful to watch. It was as if, having thrown the Evian bottle to sea, something had been ignited in him, as surely as the fire had been lit on the dunes the night before, the spark glowing and spreading to become a flame. He'd remembered where he'd excelled.

He'd remembered that he was a sportsman.

A sudden, frightening fury took hold of me. 'Hey!' I started to run. 'Hey!' I ran down the beach, faster than I'd ever run, way faster than I'd done the Osney Dash, scattering the herring gulls that were strutting cockily on the beach. I ran right through my huge S.O.S. letters on the flats, scattering sand, making them illegible. Both cricketers stopped and looked at me as I approached. Gil stopped chasing the ball like a little doggy and Seb straightened up, the staff dangling from his hand. I pointed at the stick. 'That's Lincoln's staff!'

I have no idea where that came from. I mean – I have no idea why I spoke of myself in the third person like that. 'I mean, it's *mine*.'

The bat-eared Gil spotted it, and, just as he used to, jumped on me. 'Jesus, it's not a holy relic. Who are you, Thomas à Becket?'

I ignored him. 'No sports on the island!' I ordered, almost

171

crying with rage. I could feel my Wi-Fi forehead crinkling up dangerously. I knew my command must sound crazy and quickly searched for a justification for my ban. 'There's no *time* for games. We're busting our asses building a shelter over there. *All* of us.' I turned round and gestured to the rest of the Breakfast Club, who'd gathered at a polite distance to watch. 'You should be helping. You'll be the first ones cowering under it if it rains again. Seb, we need to put the roof on. Get over here.'

He squared up to me. 'Make me.'

I was already a lot musclier than I had been at Osney, but Seb was still a good bit broader than me. There was no way I could drag him over to the shelter, and we both knew it. But I wasn't scared of him any more, and I held all the cards.

'Well, it's this simple. If you don't help, you don't eat tonight.'

Gil stepped in. 'I think you've forgotten that Loam is the Toppers Man. You're a Twelve.' He was defending Seb like an attorney, but his defence made no sense here; not on this island. I didn't even look at Gil, but turned and started walking away. I'd given my ultimatum; there was nothing else to say.

'Good luck enforcing that one!' Gil shouted after me.

'Hey,' I said, turning round to walk backwards as I answered him, 'thanks.'

Still shaking with rage, I went back to the others where they stood in an anxious little semicircle.

'Well?' said Miranda.

I shrugged. 'Seb won't help. I guess he's just not a *team player*.'

The rest of us worked together all afternoon. Now and again, tiring, I'd straighten up and look out to the beach, where Seb and Gil were sporting together.

Once Flora caught me, and stood next to me, looking out too, hands on hips. 'What are you going to do to him?' she asked wryly. 'Make him walk the plank?'

Quickly I turned back to the joists I was lashing together. 'Actually, that never happened.'

'What didn't?'

'Walking the plank.'

'You're kidding,' she said. 'I've seen it in about fifty movies.'

'That's exactly it,' I said. 'Movies. It's a myth sold by Hollywood. Never happened on the pirate ships.'

'Ha,' she said. 'Every day's a school day around you, isn't it?' and went back to work.

By the time the sun went down we had a little house and I had to admit it was amazing what a team could do. I was never a fan of teamwork, had always been a solitary dude, although I never heard the end of the concept of teamwork when I was at Osney School. For a school that set such store by individual achievement, they sure went on about teams when there was some silverware at stake. We all stood back in the setting sun, muscles aching but feeling proud. We had a good-sized shelter, with a sturdy wooden frame, woven bamboo-wattle walls and a roof covered with palm leaves we'd gathered. In pride of place, as a porch roof above the door, was the side panel from the plane, bearing the legend ED-34.

'We should name it,' said Jun.

'One hundred per cent, cuz,' said Ralph.

I opened my mouth to suggest something worthy from

literature – maybe Granite House from *The Mysterious Island*, or the Summer Residence from *Robinson Crusoe*.

Then Flora piped up. 'Since we're clearly on the island from SpongeBob,' she said, 'what about No. 1 Bikini Bottom?'

They all started to smile. Morale, I was learning, was an important part of leadership. I already had the seeds of a revolution to deal with, so I had to keep these guys on my side. I abandoned all my literary names and agreed. 'Why not?' I said. 'No. 1 Bikini Bottom it is.' I even scratched a number one into one of the doorposts with our seat-arm chisel, and Flora did a passable carving of SpongeBob, Squidward and Patrick underneath it with one of the fishhooks we'd made. She worked concentratedly, hunched over the door frame, like the tattoo artist she'd probably be some day.

While she did that I went back to the hearth to light the fire. I'd almost left it too late, as the sun was quite low and the dune grasses were a little wet from the downpour. But soon the fire was smoking, today's goat was gutted and spitted and glorious cooking smells began to waft down the dunes.

The builders – Jun, Miranda, Flora, Ralph and me – gathered for dinner. At first there was no sign of the cricketers, but soon enough Seb and Gil wandered up. I eyed them over my goat steak, my appetite suddenly gone. Seb loomed over us and I could almost hear his stomach rumbling. 'Give us some meat,' he said, like he was a fricking caveman.

'Pretty tiring, an afternoon of cricket, huh?' I said. 'Really takes it outta ya.' My heart was thumping, but I fixed my gaze on my meal. 'But it's a lot more tiring building a house, I can tell you. *They* can tell you.' I nodded to the other builders.

This was the moment of truth. No one looked up from their food. He'd really pissed them off by not helping. At Osney he'd looked after them all but now, on the island, he'd neglected to do that, and it was costing him.

'Miranda?' he said. 'Come on, babe?' A last pathetic appeal. I looked at her. If she caved now and gave him some food, I'd lost the high ground. My ban would be meaningless, my rule finished. He could play cricket all day; hell, he could play fricking *tiddlywinks* if he wanted, if his gal pal was just going to feed him every night anyway. But Miranda encircled her food with her arms, the way you do when you don't want anyone to copy your test paper. 'Maybe help tomorrow, eh, *babe*?' she said.

Seb looked around at us furiously, and now we all met his eye with identical blank stares. My heart warmed within me. They were on my side. 'Screw you,' said Seb, far too loud, like a toddler. He'd completely lost the power. 'Screw *all* of you.' Then he stormed off down the path into the undergrowth, slashing the leaves viciously with my staff.

Gil hesitated for just a second, hovering, undecided, before he turned on his heel and followed Seb.

Only Flora seemed to have any misgivings as she watched them go. 'What are they going to eat?' she said, as they disappeared into the dark.

'Let them eat cake,' I said.

25

The Loam Mutiny

Seb and Gil didn't come back. In the morning there was no sign of them. I didn't know where they'd made camp, but it wasn't nearby. I had no idea what they intended. The only thing I did know is that they would have to eat Bucket berries – they were the only things on the island we'd yet found that you could safely eat uncooked. And I was the keeper of the flame. Bucket berries tasted of dirt and if you ate too many you got a crippling stomach ache, but that would be all they'd have. I was sure that after a day or two of the Bucket-berry diet they'd be back. Unless they somehow managed to get hold of one of the green gonads. The thought made me feel physically sick.

Despite my confidence that the mutineers would return, the fact that they'd mutinied in the first place represented a seeping loss of control. When old Fletcher Christian led that mutiny on *The Bounty*, and took the ship from Captain Bligh, it wasn't Christian's fault. A mutiny was *always* the captain's fault. A mutiny meant the captain had lost the loyalty of his men. That whole screw-up was on Captain Bligh, if you ask me.

I started to worry about Gil more than I worried about Seb. I was pretty sure Gil was egging Seb on. Gil could become a leader, the little guy with the muscle working for him. Gil was nearly as bad at sports as I was, but I was starting to think he might be quite clever. I thought about the Thomas à Becket comment. Most people didn't even know who Thomas à Becket was. Most people, seeing a guy with a staff, would've said Gandalf. Not Gil. Gil referenced a twelfth-century saint with a pretty hot line in holy relics, including staffs for pilgrims. At Osney I, like everybody else, had written Gil off because he was no sportsman; it'd never occurred to me that he might be clever. But then, everyone had written *me* off because *I* was no sportsman. And I was damn sure *I* was clever. So. What if Gil was manipulating *Seb*? What if *Gil* was Fletcher Christian?

It was a pretty depressing breakfast. The remaining members of the Breakfast Club ate the leaf-wrapped meat in silence. There was unease among the ranks, and the goat steaks didn't taste quite as good as usual. When we'd finished I wiped my fingers on the sand and said, 'Right. Let's go hunting.'

All their shoulders dropped. '*Again?*'

'I am soooooo sick of it,' said Jun, dragging the syllable out.

'We *have* to go every day,' I said. 'We have no refrigeration. This is a desert island, not Sainsbury's.'

'Yeah, cuz,' said Ralph. 'But it really gets my goat.'

They laughed, but at his joke, not mine. 'LOL,' said Miranda.

I could tell that there was a change. They were dispirited. I wondered how many of them were thinking of Seb and Gil – without them here it was easy to imagine they were dining on Subway and KFC, that they'd found greener grass elsewhere.

I had to think of something to keep my troops happy. 'OK,' I said, 'let's do something different. Let's go fishing instead.'

We set off for the Blue Lagoon. I felt naked without my staff, but didn't bother to find another one. It was that one or nothing. It had become symbolic – Gil had been right when he'd invoked old Thomas à Becket. Even though it was just an old stick it had become sorta sacred, a symbol of leadership on the island. Without it I felt like there was something missing from my hand. Seb was probably playing hockey today, or fencing with the damn thing, and that made my blood boil.

Going to the Blue Lagoon always cheered me up though – it cheered all of us up. It was exactly the right thing to do. I gave everyone some downtime – we had a delicious swim and a long drink and an opportunity to wash our clothes after the sweaty building work of yesterday. Miranda didn't laze around like the rest of us but powered up and down the lake, her athlete's muscles remembering their skill. It was crazy beautiful watching her swim, her strong tanned limbs cleaving through the water. She was in her element like the mermaid I'd thought her. As she pulled herself out of the water, glowing, I closed my mouth and wished I could hand her a towel or something.

She sat on the shingle, drying in the sun, squeezing her silvery mermaid hair out over one shoulder. I sat next to her, something I'd never have had the nuts to do at Osney.

'Do you miss it?' I meant the swimming, and it was the most

178

obvious question ever. She'd just answered it by powering up and down for quarter of an hour.

'Yes,' she said. Then her wet hand flew to her mouth. 'But, that is . . . I mean to say . . . OMG . . . I forgot. I'm *so* sorry, Lincoln.'

She looked at me nervously through her wet starfish lashes, as I wondered what on earth she was apologising for. 'Why are you sorry?'

'You know. The no-sports-on-the-island rule. The we've-got-no-time-for-games thing.' I'd forgotten the Breakfast Club had heard me yelling at Seb over the beach cricket. The ban now seemed like the act of a crazy dictator. 'I know we're here to fish, and I'm ready to help now.'

I studied her, her humble demeanour, blue eyes all anxious, and realised. She was a little bit afraid of me. Miranda Pencroft, who had tortured me for three years with her social media snarkiness, was afraid of what I, Lincoln Selkirk, would do to her for breaking the laws of my land. It weirded me out, but it also felt kinda good. I needed to reassure her, let her know that I wasn't the bad guy. Keep it light. I looked out at the peerless lake, blue as her eyes, with the others splashing around in it, no one really a proper swimmer like Miranda. We were sitting alone, hunched side by side on the beach, our knees so nearly touching I could feel the warmth radiating from her drying skin. The view, the opportunity; it was a real moment, and I spent it trying to figure out how you talked to a girl like Miranda Pencroft. I had nothing. But I had to say *something*.

'What kind of music d'you like?'

'What?' She looked at me, all spiky again.

'You know, what are your favourite tracks? If you were stuck on a desert island –'

'I *am* stuck on a desert island.'

'– what would you bring with you?'

'Oh . . .' She looked out again at the view. 'Ariana Grande. Justin Bieber. Zara Larsson. You know.'

Just as I'd thought. 'Yes,' I said, looking at her and smiling, 'I do know.'

She smiled back, like we'd made a connection, and of course, that was the moment the others decided to get out of the water and join us.

I'd decided that before we fished we'd take a little look around the lagoon. Once we'd caught the fish we'd have to get them back right away, cos the sun was hot and we didn't want them going bad before they were cooked. But I thought the lake might have some other resources that a good colonist might plunder, so we should at least take a look-see. The trees at the edge of the foreshore were slightly different from the ones in the forest proper; they were shorter and their leaves spread like umbrellas. They also had a loose layer of pliable bark around them like a baggy jacket, which felt like canvas to the touch. 'Let's strip some of this,' I said. 'It would be good for blankets, or drapes for Bikini Bottom.' It was a bit of a trick to get the bark all off in one good big piece, sorta like peeling an orange in one go, but we managed to get the hang of it. We each got one blanket for ourselves and everyone was ready to move on when I said, 'Hold it. We need two more.' I didn't need to explain. We needed them for Seb and Gil. No one said anything, but turned back to the trees with blank faces. I could tell they didn't think Seb and Gil were coming back. I had to believe they would.

We walked back through the trees and found ourselves on the edge of the waterfall pool where Miranda had bathed on the first day, the cascade thundering down from above. Behind the curtain of water were a series of caves carved into the white rock.

'Man-made or natural?' called Flora above the din of the water.

I hadn't thought of that. I'd assumed the caves were just here. I looked doubtful. 'Carved out by some ancient civilisation, you mean?'

'Yes,' she said grimly, 'or a *not*-so-ancient-one. I'm saying they could be inhabited.'

I'd been so busy colonising the place it hadn't occurred to me that there might be people already on the island, but it sure as hell occurred to me now. Because of course they wouldn't be civilised, have-a-cup-of-tea British colonials, they would be as the Robinsonade always had it: savages.

'Well,' I said, far more glibly than I felt, 'only one way to find out.' And, as any good leader would, I led the way.

It was pretty difficult to see once we were inside the caves, but there was some light coming from somewhere – I imagine the water had, over millennia, made natural little skylights where the sun would come in. We spent probably an hour trooping in and out of the cave system. Some holes were passageways, some were just dead ends; little chambers entire of themselves, but there were no cave paintings, and no scary locals. The caves were uninhabited. The last one we found was a pretty big white chamber, just behind the waterfall, so the cascade fell past the entrance like those bead curtains old people have in Florida. The cave was dry, with a flat floor and a bit of leaf-dappled light filtering in from somewhere above. Ralph summed up what we were all thinking: '*Cool.*'

'We could *so* live here,' said Jun, turning around like she was on a music box.

'And build furniture!' put in Flora excitedly. 'Like chairs and a table and things.'

'And proper beds!' said Miranda, hugging herself.

They were all chiming in, getting excited.

'It's not a bad idea,' I said. 'Certainly if there's a hard winter here. It's a bit more solid than Bikini Bottom.' I collected their downcast expressions. 'But I'm sure we won't be here *that* long. We've got the orange-is-the-new-black box, remember?'

We all trooped out of the waterfall cavern. Bringing up the rear I had a brief fantasy of living there in the caves, just me, with Miranda bathing outside my door every day, singing like a mermaid. The white cave could be my palace, and Miranda could be at my side. Napoleon had his Josephine and Caesar his Cleopatra. All great leaders needed their consorts – Miranda could be mine.

26

Plenty of Fish

Outside the caves the sun was already sinking, and if we were to be back for fire-lighting time, we'd need to get on with the main mission of the day – fishing.

I'd planned this to be another triumph, another isn't-Lincoln-great experience. I knew there were fish in the Blue Lagoon, as I'd seen their silvery shapes slipping below the surface when we'd plunged in on the first day; but I'd no clue if we'd actually be able to catch any. Suddenly it seemed pretty important for what remained of the shreds of my leadership that we did.

I had all the gear ready – I'd made some pretty sharp hooks from the mini Coke cans that would slice your finger right open if you weren't careful. As we gathered on the foreshore I got the hooks carefully out of my pockets together with the four violin strings Jun had given me.

'Better use the E string,' she said.

'Why?'

'It's the thinnest.' She smiled, a sight I still couldn't get used to. 'They won't see it coming.'

We then dug around for some grubs or worms and found some particularly meaty ones under a nearby rock. Ralph seemed to have the biggest problem with this part of the process, jumping to his feet and whooping with distaste. 'Dat shit is bare *disgusting*, cuz.'

So I transfixed the wriggling worms on the hooks myself, and we all went to sit on a rock overhang while I dangled the thinnest line in the water.

The fishing turned out to be as easy as the hunting had been. It seemed the fish just couldn't wait to nibble on the bait, and within minutes I'd whipped a big silvery feller onto the bank. He wriggled for a bit; then, as if he really couldn't be bothered any more, lay still. It was so easy I let everyone else have a go, and in the end we used all the violin strings. Even the thickest – the G – was apparently invisible enough to fool the fishes. Evidently they were as green as the goats.

Flora said what I was thinking. 'Well, all I can say is that the fish on Lincoln Island must be awfully stupid,' she remarked. 'They're just gobbling up the bait – they don't even seem afraid of us.'

I was pleased that she'd used the island's proper name. 'Likely as it's uninhabited no one has tried to catch them before,' I said. 'They're obviously not very wary. When they see a lovely meaty grub just dangling in the water in front of them they just think it's Christmas.' The dumber they were, the smarter I looked. By lunchtime we had a ton of fish, which

I tied together on a string with one of the fishing lines and carried back to camp triumphant.

'I'll light the fire as soon as we get back and we can cook them,' I said. Flora, Miranda and Jun gave a weak cheer. But Ralph looked at the silvery corpses swinging on the fishing line and turned up his nose.

'That is *rank*, fam,' he said. 'Miss me with that.'

I smiled. 'You'll see. You can find us some herbs to stuff them with. That will make them delicious.' At that he seemed to perk up, and positively skipped ahead, zigzagging here and there like a sniffer dog, looking for wild garlic. I looked at him meditatively.

As we approached camp I suddenly began to fear for our shelter, convinced that we'd find No. 1 Bikini Bottom reduced to a pile of sticks, like the windmill in *Animal Farm*, trampled on by a vengeful Seb. But there the house still stood, proudly on the beach.

While the others scattered I lit the fire with the help of the low sun, and soon had the fish baking in sea salt and the wild garlic Ralph had found. The smell was delicious and quickly got the Breakfast Club gathering like hungry cats. I handed the fish out, one each, on the broad leaves we'd found to use as plates.

As we ate we all looked at Ralph, the anti-fish brigade, to see what he thought. It was like one of those shows on TV with a cooking segment, where the guest has to taste what the TV chef has cooked.

Ralph said nothing for a moment as he chewed. Then he closed his eyes before he spoke. 'No doubt, cuz,' he pronounced. 'That is the *pengest* munch.'

I had no idea what he'd said but it suddenly seemed the funniest thing we'd ever heard. We all laughed. We ate our fill around the warm circle of the fire, before wrapping up the remaining fish in leaves for morning and wrapping ourselves up in our new bark matting for sleep.

I'd have been completely happy, were it not for the hole in our circle where Seb and Gil should have been – obvious as a missing tooth.

27

The Hand of the King

I slept badly, with a nagging toothache, so when I convened the Breakfast Club the next morning I was already in a bad mood. We all collected in a circle, this time with no gaps. The circle seemed much smaller.

'No Seb and Gil.' It was a statement, not a question.

No one said anything, but I had my answer. They weren't coming.

I gave everyone their briefing for the day but my mind was elsewhere. I had to face the fact that there was a splitting of the gang.

It was to be expected – it happened in *Lord of the Flies*, when two guys both thought they were boss. It happened in *Swallow and Amazons*. I looked around me at the faces of the remaining Breakfast Club. I had to make sure of my troops. I thought the girls were cool – Miranda seemed totally on team Lincoln after our swimming convo yesterday, and Jun had been with me since the first night when she'd ceremoniously burned her violin and confided in me. Flora, always sardonic, never afraid to criticise my rule, was a problem for me to deal with later. She could wait, as she had no associations with Seb and hated him almost as much as I did – there was no chance she was going to join his team. But Ralph? Ralph I had my doubts about.

He wasn't quite meeting my eye and I saw him casting longing glances at the undergrowth where Seb and Gil were last seen. I thought again that when you can't see someone it's easy to assume they are having the time of their lives, that they've found bluer skies. Heck, I was doing it myself. I could see that he thought that old Seb and Gil had found a branch of McDonald's on the other side of the bay, while Roadman Ralph himself was stuck here with an uber-nerd and a bunch of women.

And there was another enemy to fight alongside Ralph's FOMO – his loyalty. Old habits die hard, and he'd been the Hand of the King for so long it must have been hard to see *Gil* go off with Seb like that. I had to get Ralph on side. Ralph's support, I thought, was the crucial makeweight, like the boom of a sail swinging one way or another to determine the course of the whole ship. I was convinced now that Ralph's banter and his innate sense of cool had had a lot to do with Seb's power at school for the last three years. Being a sports champion was one thing – and sure, it inspired admiration and devotion at a place like Osney – but Ralph had been in charge of the fear factor. His street persona, however bogus, made everyone scared – made them think that Seb's crew were the cool kids. Ralph was the kingmaker, and if he went to join Seb and Gil now, his presence would power up their outfit. If this island was an open-world video game, which it sorta was, I still had the power of fire, and that meant the power of food, but the three boys could easily OP me. They could tie me up. Torture me, force me to make fire for them. I had to secure Ralph. I had to make him *my* Hand, and I thought I knew exactly how.

I decided to do something I suspected no one had ever done to Ralph before, and that was pick his brain. And in order to do that I had to pick my own. My mom used to say *feed your head*, it was a lyric from some song she liked, and she made me read a whole bunch of stuff besides my home-school work, and if I didn't know stuff she'd make me run-and-find-out. In those years of being a boy island – those three lost *Nowhere Man* years at Osney – I'd become a bit obsessed with Robinsonade, that is to say books (and shows and movies) about desert islands. One of them, *The Mysterious Island*, had this kid in it who liked plants and stuff, a naturalist, and he started to medicate all the other fellows.

All the best ideas produce more than one benefit. A pretty major side effect of this one was that it was hopefully going to solve another major problem I had. The problem of my tooth.

The tooth that old Seb had cracked the day he punched me had been bothering me ever since I got to the island. The break was really sharp and my tongue kept finding it in my mouth, constantly seeking it and running along the crack, testing the edge. When it had first broken it hadn't really hurt – I mean the punch hurt but not the tooth, and that's why I didn't bother to go to the dentist despite my mom

189

dogging me. But on the island it started to hurt and now, a week in, it *really* hurt. During the day I could kinda ignore it; the pain would just make me a bit crabby sometimes. But at night it was awful. I would lie awake looking up at the strange southern stars, my tooth throbbing, the pain taking over the whole of my consciousness. When I slept, pretty fitfully to be honest, I would have strange, broken dreams about my head swelling up to three times its usual size, until it felt like it was way too big for my body, like one of those Pop figures. It was way worse when I lay down, my whole skull beating like a drum with pain. So I would half sit, half loll on this little pile of rocks I'd made and covered with brushwood, and you can imagine how comfortable *that* was. And then of course I didn't sleep, and lack of sleep made me even more crabby, and less likely to be able to do what I had to do for everyone every day, like the hunting, or the fishing, or the fire-lighting.

Two things about that. One: a crabby ruler does not make a happy ruler. You can bet your ass that old Hitler had toothache the whole time, or at least he acted like he did. You know those teachers who are constantly in a bad mood? It doesn't make you want to do what they say when they bark at you. You're far more likely to obey a cuddly smiley teacher.

Two – and two was way more serious – there was a good chance that my tooth was infected, and that was dangerous. I remembered going to the orthodontist and seeing those white models of a tooth that were a sorta cross-section showing a whole mess of crap inside, dentine and nerves and stuff. I figured that when Seb had punched me, he had cracked away that outer white layer and just left a thin layer of outer stuff covering all that inner stuff. Then as the days had gone by (because there weren't exactly toothbrushes on the island), the last outer covering had decayed and now the rot was burrowing down into my nerve endings. And if I was right, and it was becoming infected, I could get seriously ill, or even die. (Side note: if I died, everyone else would too, because our rescuers seemed to be taking their sweet time. I didn't really care too much about that but it's just an observation. I guess they could live on Bucket berries and water for a while, but it was possible this island had seasons we didn't know about yet, and would get a lot colder or wetter, and there'd be no fire. Unless I did one of those deathbed confessions. I pictured myself all green and puffed up with the infection, croaking out the precious knowledge of how to light a fire, putting the lenses in Flora's palm and closing her fingers around them with my own blackened swollen digits. I don't know why Flora – she just seemed the most competent. Plus she'd given me my glasses way back that day at school, so there was some poetry to it. But I wasn't about to let that whole scenario happen when I'd just got me an island. No siree.)

So I had to find some sort of cure, or else my battle for supremacy would all have been for nothing. I wouldn't be King of the Island any more; I'd be right down the bottom of the heap like I'd been at Osney. I'd be the weakest of the herd, the sickest, the one the other buffalos leave behind while the lions watch greedily from the long grass. But I wasn't about to give up yet. I looked out on the Emerald Forest, the green bowl of vegetation under Monte Cristo. The island was a drugstore. Somewhere at its green heart there was a cure and I figured Ralph was the guy to find it.

28

Ship's Doctor

'Ralph. C'm here a minute.'

Ralph sauntered along the beach – all loose limbs and shredded rapper gear. 'Yeah, cuz?'

'It's Lincoln.'

He shrugged. 'Sorr-ee, big man.'

'My tooth hurts.'

'So?'

'Go and get me something to help it.' I decided to downplay my three-in-the-morning fears – I didn't want him to know I was weak. 'A painkiller first cos this thing is killing me. And also,' I added nonchalantly, as if it didn't matter much, 'something that will act as an antibiotic, in case it's infected.'

Ralph squinted against the sun. 'What sort of something?'

'*I* don't know. You're the Walter White of the party. Like bark or something. Aspirin's the bark of a pine, isn't it?'

'White willow.'

'What's that now?'

'Aspirin,' he said. 'It's from the bark of the white willow, innit, fam?'

'There you go. Try to find a white willow.'

He rubbed the back of his hair and shifted his feet in the sand. 'Er, yeah. Yeah, cool.' He wasn't going to do it.

'Ralph,' I said, 'in my opinion this island is giving us an opportunity to be who we *could be*. Our better selves. At home you were a bit of a chemist, right?'

He shrugged again but I could see he was flattered. 'I got some people some tings. Cooked up some shit. *You* know.'

'Well, then. Here you could be . . .' I thought for a moment, 'Stephen Maturin.'

'Who he?'

'Didn't you ever read any Patrick O'Brian books?'

Ralph sucked his teeth in that dumb 'street' way he had. 'Nah, fam,' he said. 'Not gonna lie. Don't read *no* kind of books.'

I looked him with fresh eyes. That explained a lot. 'Stephen Maturin was a naturalist and a medic. He was the captain's best friend, and when they went to an island he logged all the new species and found new medicines and stuff. That could be *you*, Ralph. You have your pestle and mortar. Those are the tools of your profession.'

'You what, cuz?'

'*You* could be the ship's doctor.'

'Ship's doctor.' He started to smile. 'Sounds pretty safe, G.'

'And, Ralph – let's drop the roadman speak. You're not really fooling anyone.'

He took a beat, looking at me the whole time. Then he straightened up. 'If you say so.'

'So off you go.'

'All right, Lincoln.'

'What do we say? Ralph?'

It took him a moment. 'OK.'

Ralph was gone for the whole afternoon. I fiddled about making futile little improvements to Bikini Bottom, but the pain made it hard to concentrate. Every minute I wanted Ralph to come back with something to take the pain away. As I lit the fire at sundown, and there was still no sign of him, I had to admit I'd screwed up. I'd given him leave to go off on his own, I'd even sent him off into the goddamn forest. He'd met up with Seb and Gil and joined up with them.

The fire was lit and the fish was cooked and Ralph still didn't come. My heart sank and my tooth throbbed. I could hardly eat, not just with the pain, but with the disappointment. What now? I stayed up, feeding the fire as one by one the girls dropped off to sleep under their bark blankets. We were rapidly running out of firewood and would need to do a big gather tomorrow. It would be that much harder without any of the boys – not because girls were weak or any of that crap, but just because our numbers were now cut in half. As my spirits sank to rock bottom, the stars rose in their comfortless beauty.

'Lincoln?'

A shape kindled out of the dark. 'You awake?'

Ralph. Thank God.

He sat beside me, heavily, tiredly. 'Hold out your hand.'

He shook a little stream of powder into my palm from the mortar he carried.

194

I regarded the powder in the firelight. It could've been any colour. It could've been anything. It struck me then that he could be spiking me, under orders from Seb and Gil. He could wait till I was dead and take the lenses that were hanging inside my shirt, and the fishing lines from my pocket.

'It's not poison, is it?' Like he would tell me.

I could hear a smile in his voice. 'You've got to take your chances, Lincoln. First do no harm, right? Isn't that what doctors say?'

The pain was so bad I almost wouldn't have cared if it was poison. At least the agony would be over. I lifted my hand to my mouth and knocked it all back, whatever it was. I even licked the residue off my palm. It was bitter and grainy, with a woody taste. 'What is it?'

'White willow,' he said. 'There was one by the Blue Lagoon. I scraped the bark, washed it, sundried it on a rock, then powdered it up. It was the drying that took the time.' He held both healing hands out to the fire. 'Give it a minute. Let's just talk, take your mind off it.' He said it gently, with a perfect bedside manner.

I was pretty bad at making conversation, through sheer lack of practice. But as we sat side by side watching the fire just like I had with Jun, it was suddenly easier. I don't know what it is about fire that helps people open up, but it really does. I think it's because you feel like you're talking to the fire, not the other person. And I found that there was, suddenly, something I was able to ask.

'How did you spike me that day, back at Osney?'

I half expected him to deny it. But he felt the lure of the

fire too, and talked to it, not me. 'I watched you buy that blue Lucozade every day. I just got the same one, put some laxatives in it. Then when I shoved up next to you on the bench, I knocked yours off the table, and put mine back on.'

I nodded. 'Clever.'

'Thanks.'

There was no bitterness on my part, no guilt on his. It was like we were talking about somebody else. The gradual easing of the pain in my jaw meant I'd forgive him anything.

'Ralph?'

'Yes?'

'If you were stuck on a desert island –'

'I *am* stuck on a desert island.'

'– what music would you bring with you? If you could, I mean. If you had a phone.'

'Wretch 32,' he said without hesitation. 'Dizzee Rascal. Skepta. Onyx Stone.'

His answer was exactly what I'd expected; but it didn't seem to fit, somehow, with this new ship's doctor Ralph. 'You really like that stuff? It's not just . . . part of the persona?'

He laughed, but not his usual crowing street laugh. This was a pleasant sound. 'No, I really like it. Grime has all these . . . layers.' He wasn't used to expressing himself, but it was a start. 'You should check it out sometime.'

'Maybe I will,' I said, looking at him now, not the fire. 'Maybe I will.'

29

23b

The night of the white willow I slept properly for the first time in days. In fact, I overslept – my body was most likely catching up on all the sleep I'd lost.

When I woke up, the fierce sun was already climbing, my tooth was a dull ache and I felt a bit groggy. The light made it difficult to see, so when I set off down the dunes for a pee in the ocean I didn't see the pile of kindling that had been left just below the fire hill, and I tripped right over it.

'Wha . . . ?'

I picked myself up and regarded the woodpile. There was tons of it, all good hardwood. We could have about three fires tonight.

I looked around. Jun and Miranda were paddling in the surf. Flora was sitting on the headland. Ralph was stooped over on the beach, no doubt picking up some interesting seaweed. So who had collected the wood?

The answer walked out of the forest, another pile of kindling in his arms. It was Seb. You could barely see his face for logs. Gil followed him, carrying a few sticks. They both came over to the wood, over to me, and dumped their burdens in the pile. As if drawn, the others gathered too, cautiously greeting the home-comers.

Miranda did no more than nod coolly to Seb. Seb, meantime, seemed to have eyes for no one but me. He looked at me sheepishly, indicating the pile of wood with the staff he still carried. 'Can we have something to eat now?'

What with the night's sleep, and the nearest thing I was going to get to an apology from Sebastian Loam, I felt the warmth of triumph spread through me. It was all I could do not to let it show on my face. 'Sure,' I said. 'We wrapped up some fish from last night. I'll get it.'

I started to walk to the shelter where we'd made our primitive refrigerator, stopped, turned back. 'I just need one more piece of wood.' I knew I was being a dick, knew I was pushing it, but I didn't want there to be any doubt about my authority. 'The staff.'

I held out my hand. Seb put the staff into it, and I felt right again.

'Thank you. Welcome back, both of you. Now, just to be clear, everyone hunts, everyone builds, everyone gathers firewood. All right?'

Silence. Gil and Seb stood like sulky schoolboys.

'Seb? Gil? What do we say?'

They got it. 'OK,' they chorused grudgingly.

After that everything was cool. Ralph made me more aspirin

powder to manage the pain in my tooth and was now turning his attention seriously to finding something that would fight the infection. I don't think he was doing it just for me, even though we were much friendlier than before. I think he was doing it for some intellectual satisfaction of his own. He was doing it for science. He would go off for hours. He made a shoulder sling from one of the plane seat covers instead of his old Adidas pouch, and collected plants and herbs and roots to crush in his pestle and mortar. He even started to catch these little shrew-like rodents to experiment on. They were way too small to bother eating but they made great lab rats for Ralph. He started to act, and look, halfway normal. His curtain hair was growing out and he wore it twisted up in a little man-bun, and no longer spoke like he lived in the projects. He looked, and sounded, about a thousand per cent better.

Everyone seemed to settle down, even Seb and Gil. Seb still wore his Fitbit with pride, despite the fact it had long since run out of charge, but he didn't attempt to play any sports again. We kept working on Bikini Bottom. The house now had a table, and I'd figured out how to make fish-oil lamps from conch shells, which we lit every night with tapers from the fire. They weren't the best-smelling things in the world, but they gave light for a good few hours. I built a couple more things, like a water butt to catch rainfall and a toilet with a seat overhanging the cliffs. We'd swim every day, fish or hunt every other. Things were going pretty well.

Until the night my tooth took a turn for the worse.

I woke in the dark, in agony. My whole head was a ball of pain. I knew, now, that it was definitely infected, and imagined that if I had a mirror I'd see my head enormous and green, and glossy with sweat like one of the green gonads. The others were sleeping around me but I twisted in pain. If I lay down, the tooth throbbed unbearably. I could actually feel my heartbeat in the infected root. But if I stayed upright I'd never sleep. I was in trouble. The infection, unchecked, could spread throughout my body and kill me. In vain I tried to chew the latest of Ralph's willow bark powder but I couldn't even do that, it hurt so bad. I remembered the movie *Castaway*: when Tom Hanks's character smashed out a bad tooth with an ice-skate. I must've seen that film a hundred times in my Robinsonade phase, but I'd never once been able to watch that bit, when the metal skate connects with the tooth. Right now though, if I'd had an ice-skate I would have smashed my own tooth out in a heartbeat.

I wandered the island for a time in the blue moonlight, looking at the silver sea and watching the blackly waving palms. But nothing could calm the tide of panic. I was gonna die here, and Seb had won after all. That dumb parlour game of pick-up-sticks we'd been playing was nothing. This was the real game, where the stakes were life and death. And it was a long game too – he'd punched me weeks ago, and only now was the infection leaching into my bloodstream and travelling to my organs, corroding them, choking them. I hated him with every beat of my green heart.

There was no one to help me. I had told no one except Ralph of the toothache, not wanting to appear weak. Eventually, exhausted, I lay down again, probably for the last time, I thought. I must have fallen into some sort of delirium, because a ghostly white-clad shape interrupted the view overhead, blocking out the stars. At last the mysterious inhabitant of the island had shown his face. I thought then of *Heart of Darkness*, of climbing Monte Cristo with the eyes of strange creatures twinkling out of the night like stars, the strange chirps and cries emanating from the black jungle. Did these creatures have a dark lord; was there a settler here already who was watching us with evil intent? 'Mr Kurtz?' I said. But I couldn't see his face – he seemed to be masked and I could only see a pair of eyes.

Gloved hands prised my jaws apart, and the squeak of rubber was on my teeth. A light shone in my eyes, brighter than any star. Then I knew no more.

When I woke it was morning and the sun was already high. Flora sat beside me, arms around her knees. 'We let you sleep,' she said. 'You were making some pretty weird noises.'

My mouth was dry as dust, as dry as when they suck out your saliva at the orthodontist. 'Nightmare,' I mumbled, the image of Mr Kurtz leaning over me, dressed in white, masked, rapidly receding in the daylight, as all dreams do, I could hardly talk. The side of my face felt strangely numb, as if I couldn't move it properly. Jesus, had my tooth given me a stroke? I sat bolt upright and pressed my fingers into my cheek. It didn't hurt any more – I must've lost the feeling in my face. My heart started to thump with fear – I swallowed and I noticed a chemical tang at the back of my throat. And there was something else. My tooth was gone.

My tongue prodded frantically at the place where the tooth had been. The gum was smooth, empty, a clean hole with the faintly metallic taste of blood. I shoved my finger in there – probably a mistake as it was none too clean, but I had to know.

No tooth.

A tender, tooth-sized gap.

The feeling was returning to my face, a tingly, not unpleasant sensation. I waggled my jaw, helping the blood return.

Flora watched me closely all the way through this pantomime. 'What's wrong? You look like you've seen a ghost.'

The ghost, the white-clad figure of my fever-dream – should I tell Flora? I thought it would make me sound crazy, and I didn't want to sound crazy. As I knew from Osney's founder, old King George III, crazy was not a good look for a leader. So I kept things as casual as I could. 'I had a bad tooth. But I think it fell out in the night.'

'Goals,' she said. 'You had a problem. Now you don't.'

'I guess.'

She caught my tone. 'What's the new problem? Tooth fairy didn't come?'

'No.' I shook my head; it didn't hurt any more. It was hard to get used to feeling normal again, well again. 'Everything's fine. Everything's better than fine.'

She gave me an odd look. 'Good then.'

Flora watched me for the rest of the day, but I didn't care. I was King of the Island. Whatever had happened in the night, and however my tooth had fallen out, I didn't care. I was, well, invincible. I'd been given a second chance, and I was determined to enjoy all the benefits of my premiership. I felt like doing something symbolic.

After our morning hunt and swim I went through Seb's woodpile and chose the straightest, strongest pieces of wood. I carried them inside No. 1 Bikini Bottom. The shelter was really taking shape. Although we all still slept around the fire each night, because for the most part it was warmer, Bikini Bottom provided refuge from bad weather, and we'd begun to take pride in it.

Jun was there, making a shelf for the orange-is-the-new-black box, so the flight recorder could have pride of place on the wall, almost like some strangely shaped deity that was going to save us all. Flora was occupied in making a hinged door, to protect us from the wind and rain if there was another tempest.

'Those for me?' she said, nodding at the wood.

'No,' I said. 'I'm making a chair.'

'What do we need a chair for?'

'We don't,' I said. 'That's the point.'

'How d'you mean?'

'A chair is a symbol of civilisation,' I said.

'*How* is it?'

'Because we don't need it. We can sit on the floor. It's a luxury. And if we're at the point of making luxuries, we're becoming a civilisation.'

She shrugged. 'It's your time you're wasting.'

I hated the way she disrespected my authority. I needed to deal with her. But I wasn't going to let her harsh my day. 'Well, that's the one thing we got plenty of.'

I spent the next few hours making some little stools, binding sticks together with bamboo straps and making a lattice of twigs for the seat. Then I got ambitious and made a bigger chair with a back. When I was done I stood back and looked

203

at it, pretty happy with my creation. Four sturdy legs, four branches bowed and bound to make a back.

Flora stood at my shoulder. 'That's not a chair,' she said. 'That's a throne. For a king.'

Busted. 'I never said so.'

'You never *said* it, no.'

I had a sudden thought. 'Can you put a number on it?'

'Sure,' she said, selecting her plane-fuselage chisel. 'Let me guessa – number one?'

'No,' I said. I didn't want to be that obvious. 'I think I'll call it 23b.'

'How completely random,' Flora said.

'Not at all,' I said a bit huffily. I didn't like being questioned. 'It has great significance to me.'

'Why not?'

'It was my seat on the plane.'

'London to LAX?'

'No,' I said. 'The little one. The one that crashed. Oceanic Airlines.'

She laughed at that. 'It can't have been.'

'Why?'

'It was a ten-seater plane.'

That set me back on my heels. I echoed her. 'It can't have been.'

'It was, you know.' She counted on her fingers. 'Seb. Gil. Jun. Miranda. Ralph. Me. You. Two seats for my friends Smith and Fry, who didn't make it to LAX. And the pilot. Ten.' She smiled, but not unpleasantly. 'I think you must have had a knock on the head.'

I didn't want to lose authority in front of her – she respected me little enough as it was. 'Just carve,' I ordered.

I left her carving *23b* on the back of my new throne – seat – and went outside. It was getting to late afternoon and I'd have to take advantage of the lowering sun to light the fire. I walked away and waded into the surf to wet the lenses of my glasses. I always did that alone because I didn't want anyone to learn my fire-lighting tricks, but today I also wanted to think. The warm waves pounded the sand and the lacy foam swirled around my legs and I thought about what Flora had said. *A ten-seater plane.* I was *sure* my seat had been 23b. It had been on my ticket, and on my boarding pass at LAX. Oceanic Airlines, flight ED-34, seat 23b. More than that, the number had been etched in a little gilt circle set into the plush creamy leather of the seat. I'd seen it when I'd got on board, and I'd seen it again, the seat tattered and ripped, when we'd visited the wreck on Day One.

I walked back to the fire circle and lit the fire, watching the concentrated sunbeam igniting the seagrass, as I'd done almost every day for nearly six weeks. But this time, and this time only, I didn't feel the usual matching spark of satisfaction in my belly. Had I been wrong? You couldn't argue with what Flora had said. Eight people, two empty seats. Was I going mad, like old George Three?

I spitted the goat over the flames and called Jun to watch it – she'd gotten to be a pretty good cook and liked looking after the others. I guess the mothering instinct she'd talked about that first night had kicked in. Then I set off, in the early evening sun. I had to go back to the plane.

30

Those who mourn

The crash site was pretty creepy at night. Although it wasn't really dark, more twilight, and the sky was this pretty rose colour, I still didn't really want to be there.

As I approached the fuselage the plane looked like a big sleeping beast. The white curve of the cabin could've been a polar bear lying down, the one from *Lost*. I approached it exactly as I would approach a sleeping bear, carefully, silently, and trying not to break any twigs. Another thing that was messing with my head was the thought that it might be a graveyard, even though we hadn't found any bodies last time. But before the light disappeared altogether I wanted to see if Flora was right – had I confused my seat number?

The plane, when I got right up to it, was a little bit worse for wear. Six weeks of weather had taken the gloss off the Air-Force-One-style luxury finish. Inside the cabin, plants had started to grow through the cracks in the fuselage and little suckers and leaves were twining over the seat backs, as if nature was trying to claim this intruder, a giant high-tech Gulliver pinned down by nature's Lilliputians.

I looked around the cabin and found my seat. There was the table of four that I'd shared with Miranda and Seb, when I'd first seen Miranda in the Amazing Skirt. I'd had to tear my eyes away from the skirt and fix them instead on the Kindle and the adventures of the Count of Monte Cristo. There was now, conveniently, a hole above the table which let in the last of the daylight and shone on the little brass circle set into the leather, turning it to a bright coin.

The seat number, neatly etched on it, was perfectly visible. 23b.

'I was right,' I said, as if it was not enough to think it.

'I know,' said a voice from along the cabin.

I nearly jumped out of my skin. Flora was almost a silhouette in the dying light, sitting way down the cabin in a shredded leather seat. All she needed was a white cat.

'I knew you'd come here, as soon as I said what I said.' She got up and came along to me. 'You love to be right, don't you?' She reached out her hand and ran a grubby fingertip across the number on my seatback, as if it was written in Braille.

'What are you doing here?'

'Same as you,' she said. 'I guess we *both* like to be right.'

'Well,' I said, and I couldn't help sounding a little smug, '*one* of us was.'

'Actually we *both* were.'

I looked at her. I wasn't used, by now, to hearing backchat.

'You about the seat number. Me about the plane. It was – *is* – a ten-seater.'

'Interesting, isn't it?' I said, the understatement of the year.

'I'll tell you what's *more* interesting: all the other seats are numbered normally. Look.' She pointed to the seat she'd been sitting in, and its neighbour. 'Three and four. They're numbered in the usual way, one to ten.'

I looked. 'Well, one number must be missing.'

'How d'you mean?'

'Well, one must have been replaced to become number 23b. Let's find out which.'

'Does it matter?'

'It might.'

We looked at the remaining seats, shouting out numbers. 'Seven,' she said. 'Seven is replaced. It jumps from six to eight.'

'That's weird. I've heard of seat number thirteen being missed out on aircraft, even *row* thirteen in bigger ones. Because of superstition – people think they're going to crash. In China it's number four that is considered unlucky because the word for "four" sounds like the word for "death". There's no fourth floor in some skyscrapers in Hong Kong.' Flora was looking at me consideringly. 'I've never heard of seven being unlucky though. Seventeen, yes. Friday the seventeenth is considered the unluckiest day in Italy. It's because an anagram of the Roman numerals for seventeen, VIXI, spells out, "I have lived", i.e. I am now dead.'

Flora listened to this speech and said, 'You do that a lot, you know.'

'What?'

'Tell people facts they haven't asked about. You did it about walking the plank.'

208

'Oh.' I wasn't sure what to do with that information.

'It can be a *little* bit annoying. Now I come to think about it, maybe that's why . . .'

'Why what?'

She was silent.

'Why what, Flora? Maybe that's why they *bullied* me? Because *I* was annoying?'

She looked slightly shamefaced. 'No, I didn't mean that. I just meant . . .' She took a deep breath. 'People that are bullied aren't necessarily nice people, just because they're victims. That's all I meant. OK?'

'OK,' I said. The two letters I'd sworn never to say again slipped out. Was she saying I wasn't a nice person? I'd never been liked, but to be *dis*liked was another deal entirely. Suddenly I was back at Osney. I felt cowed, picked on all over again.

I made my way down the aisle. I didn't need this. Then I got to the place where the cockpit had broken off, an abrupt breach and a mess of wires and metal. The fate of our pilot, and our stewardess, pulled things into perspective. My bullying, versus dying in a plane crash. *I have lived. And now I do not.*

Then Flora exclaimed, 'Hey, what's this?'

I turned. She held up a rectangle of oxblood leather. For a moment I thought it was my Kindle – it had had a red case like that. But what she held wasn't an eBook reader. It was an actual book. This was better for me than a whole chest full of treasure. I hadn't realised until that moment how much I'd missed them.

'Excellent. Let me see.'

She passed it over. 'Not yours then?'

'No. I had a Kindle.'

'Curiouser and curiouser.'

I recognised the *Alice in Wonderland* quote. 'Oh, so *you* read then?'

'Yes, of course. Knowledge is power. Remember what the Dormouse said? Feed your head.'

That was exactly what my mom used to say to me. 'So is it yours?'

'Nope,' she said. 'Someone else must have brought it.'

'One of that lot?' I thought of the Breakfast Club. 'Are you kidding? They don't read. I did all their GCSE revision notes, so I was the one who read all the set texts. That was back when I did everything for them.'

'You *still* do everything for them.'

'Huh?'

'You think things have turned around from Osney. But they haven't. You're still doing everything for them, every little *thing*. You practically wipe their arses for them,' she said in her cut-glass voice. 'They've got you running round just as much as they ever did. They still don't *like* you. They just *need* you.' I thought about that, and it suddenly seemed so true, and so uncomfortable, that I had to change the subject.

'Well, they wouldn't read *this*,' I looked at the title page. 'It's the Bible.'

'Oh,' she said with disappointment. 'Who the hell brought *that*?'

'Maybe no one. Maybe it was here to start with.'

'What *can* you mean?'

'Maybe they have Bibles on planes like they do in hotel

rooms. Ya know, those Gideon guys who put them in bedside drawers. Maybe they rolled it out, I don't know.'

'I thought you knew everything.'

'Not this.' I flicked through it, and it made a little breeze on my face – a dusty breath that recalled the safe smell of libraries.

'Shall we take it?'

'*Hell* yeah.'

We clambered out of the plane and through the clearing, blue in the twilight, the shape of the Bible solid in my hand. 'Hey,' I said suddenly, 'now we have the Bible, d'you think we should say something?'

'To the others, you mean? About the plane seat?'

'No. No. I mean, say something *here*.'

'What sort of something?'

'Like . . . a prayer.'

'A *prayer*?'

'*I* don't know. It just feels like, if people died here, we should. I mean, last time we practically looted it. It was a bit *Lord of the Flies* to be honest. I just feel, I dunno, that we should show some respect.'

Flora shrugged. 'OK. D'you know a good bit?'

'It just so happens I do.' I held the Good Book to the dying light and flicked through the pages until I found what I was looking for. I knew exactly one bit of the Bible, and that was the line my mom had told me on my first day at Osney, about the geek inheriting the earth. I'd since found out that it was in the bit that people called the Sermon on the Mount, when Jesus preached to a whole bunch of people. Anyway, I thought it was fitting now. We faced the white arc of the wrecked plane and Flora stood beside me, head down, hands clasped, and I began.

'Blessed are those who mourn,
for they will be comforted.
Blessed are the meek,
for they will inherit the earth.
Blessed are those who hunger and thirst for righteousness,
for they will be filled.
Blessed are the merciful,
for they will be shown mercy.
Blessed are the pure in heart,
for they will see God.
Blessed are the peacemakers,
for they will be called children of God.
Blessed are those who are persecuted because of righteousness,
for theirs is the kingdom of heaven.

Blessed are you when people insult you, persecute you and falsely say all kinds of evil against you because of me. Rejoice and be glad, because great is your reward in heaven, for in the same way they persecuted the prophets who were before you.'

At the beginning I was thinking about the pilot, who had, briefly, given me the best flying experience of my life. Then I thought about the stewardess, one of the only women, apart from my mom, who'd ever bothered to smile at me. But by the end I was thinking of myself. That bit about being blessed when people insult you, and having your reward in heaven, that seemed to be all about me. At the end I felt sorta awkward and said *Amen*, and Flora, who had been standing beside me, head bowed, said it too, which made me feel a bit better. We looked at each other.

'Now you.'

'I can't say anything,' she said. 'I can sing though.'

'Sing then.'

I expected something hard and shouty and metally, and my toes had already begun to curl up inside of my sneakers like when someone really bad, but very earnest, comes on *The X Factor*. But my toes needn't have worried. When she began to sing, her voice was sweet and true and soared up to the stars. The song was a bit country, and it had these really great lyrics. Something about not being able to keep your feet on the ground when you were born to fly. It was exactly the right elegy for a downed plane. I must've let my mouth fall open because she didn't say *Amen* at the end but, 'What?'

I shut my mouth. 'I dunno – just, well, that wasn't what I expected. I didn't think that was the kind of music you'd choose.'

'What kind of music *did* you expect me to choose?' She was all spiky again.

'Well, I mean . . .' I was floundering. 'If you were stuck on a desert island –'

It was then that Flora said something interesting. She was the only person, out of the whole of the Breakfast Club, not to say, *I am stuck on a desert island*. Instead she said, 'You mean, like *Desert Island Discs*?'

'Yes!' I said, kinda pleased. 'My parents are obsessed with it.'

'Then I think we have the same parents.'

'Did you know they did a fake castaway in 1963? They did

213

a whole show on this guy called Sir Harry Whitlohn. He was supposed to be this great explorer, but he was played by an actor, and all his song choices were made up.'

'How very British.'

'How d'you mean?'

'Well, you like presidents. In the same year that JFK was shot in the US, with all the fakery and conspiracy surrounding that, the BBC faked a genteel little radio show.'

'Huh.' I never thought of it that way. 'So? What would you choose for your music?'

It was pretty dark by now, but I could still sense Flora turning to look at me as we walked. 'What do *you* think I'd choose?'

I thought for a minute. 'Twenty One Pilots. The Cure. Green Day. Fall Out Boy. My Chemical Romance. The Damned. Oh –' I pointed to her vest – 'and Motörhead.'

'Metal and Emo bands then.'

'I guess. You're just . . . well, you're that *type*, aren't you?'

'That's right.' She swished angrily through the undergrowth. 'And I hang around graveyards on weekends, and train ravens, and when I leave school I'll probably be a tattoo artist or something.'

I was silent. I actually had thought that very thing, when she'd been etching SpongeBob and Squidward on the doorjamb of Bikini Bottom.

'You've got me all worked out, haven't you, Lincoln?'

I shrugged in the dark. I actually thought I *was* a pretty good judge of character – from all the waiting and watching and being outside of conversations and friendships. But I wasn't enough of a dick – at that point – to say it. My true dickishness on the island came later. But even though I reined myself back, Flora still stalked ahead of me all the way back to Bikini Bottom. I wasn't quite sure why she'd gotten her panties in such a bunch but I felt like there was something vaguely wrong. As leader I really should have been in front, but she seemed pretty mad at me for some reason. So just this once I let it slide, and followed her in silence.

31

The Green Gonads

We entered a strange phase on the island, a period of limbo. I'd kept a calendar by marking the days on a flat rock at the headland, which quickly became known as the 'Clock Rock'. I made a daily tally, just as Edmond Dantes (the Count of Monte Cristo) had on his prison island, just as I'd done in my bedroom when I'd been crossing off the days until I could leave school. After fourteen marks, Jun had remarked, 'We'd all have been going home today.' And that got us all thinking about home. The orange-is-the-new-black box recorder sat in the corner of Bikini Bottom, orange paint glowing, presumably doing its thing, sending out its unseen sonic signals. But in those fourteen days we hadn't seen a single ship or aircraft, no notion of civilisation in any part of this ocean. The S.O.S. in the Evian bottle presumably floated somewhere at sea, helpless, useless, no human hand to pluck it out.

As the weeks went on, the Breakfast Club began to talk less about food and more about their parents, their home lives, and

I, for the first time really, thought about mine. I knew they'd be moving heaven and earth to get me back. I was so confident I'd be back with them soon that I hadn't been worried about them, hadn't really missed them. I'd been so busy trying to fix everything here, filling my new role as a leader, and yes, as Flora had said, still doing everything for everyone. Sure, I thought of my mom's hugs and my dad's bad jokes, but beyond a momentary pang I had to get on with the job in hand. I had to lift the Breakfast Club out of the funk they were in. There was now just routine, none of the adrenaline that had fuelled those early days, the bid for survival. We'd achieved the holy trinity of the castaway: food, shelter, fire. I felt eyes watching me, hopes pinned on me. *What next?*

The green gonads watched me too. The huge green glossy nuts which hung in pairs from every palm tree glowered at me like eyes, goading me. They even had three little holes like those gourds do, around the bottom, and they looked like eyes too. Eyes on top of eyes. I became slightly obsessed with the green gonads. I *needed* to get at them. I thought they would be just what the Breakfast Club needed. We had everything for our survival; now what they needed was a treat, a luxury. We alternated fish and goat, fish and goat, fish and goat, everyone heartily sick of the flavours no matter what Ralph brought us to season them. Every mouthful we'd eaten for nearly seven weeks had been savoury. We needed something sweet and I was convinced the green gonads held that in their secret insides. In my mind their juice would be as creamy as a five-dollar shake, their flesh as sugary, coconutty and chocolaty as a Bounty bar.

217

I wasn't the only one eyeing the green gonads. I caught Seb
shinning up one of the palm trees on the beach.

'Get down here right now!' My rage, out of all proportion,
frightened me. It sent my heart racing. 'Whaddya think you're
doing?'

Seb must've felt the heat of my fury, even from halfway up
the tree. He slid down, stood to attention and looked at the
floor. 'Sorry, Lincoln.'

'What were you doing?'

'I want to get one of the green gonads down.'

'Why?'

He shrugged. 'I dunno. They just bug me.'

I knew exactly what he meant. The green gonads bugged
me too. They hung in front of me in my dreams like emeralds,
just out of reach. They gazed at me throughout my waking
moments, like green eyes. They were everywhere on the island,
dotted all the way up the mountain, ringing the lake, but we
never once found any on the ground. You were never out of
their gaze. They were a prize, the nearest thing to a trophy
on the island, and I was damned if I was going to let Seb win
this one.

'Why *not* let him get one?' said Flora later. 'I've seen him
shinning up there. He hasn't made it yet but he will soon, if
you only let him. He's pretty strong. Let someone do something
for *you* for a change.'

She must've seen my face.

'Oh, Lincoln. What does it matter, so long as *someone* gets
one?'

I couldn't explain why it mattered. I couldn't admit the years of humiliation I'd suffered at not being a winner, of never having my name etched on any of the silverware at Osney, not even so much as a rosette. Of the three years of Seb being crowned as a Toppers Man. We were gonna get one of the green gonads down all right. But it was gonna be me who achieved it.

I didn't have long. The one thing Seb understood was training, and from what Flora said he'd been in training for this, the island's ultimate prize. I had to get my head in the game, and quick. Seb's skill – if you could call it that – was blunt, brutal muscle memory. If he climbed the slippery trunk enough times, he would eventually achieve his goal through sheer repetition. My skill was my brainpower, my cunning. Building the furniture for Bikini Bottom had given me confidence. I'd been building stuff since I was a little kid, crazy Heath Robinson inventions for delivering marbles or parking toy cars. It was time to build something again.

Of course, the easiest solution would have been to chop one of the palm trees down, but we'd tried that when we'd been gathering wood for the fire, and the trunks were just too tough for our makeshift axes. Besides, it didn't feel quite right just trying to bash one down; it was a bit brutal, a bit *Seb*. I needed something with nuance, something elegant.

I thought about lassoing one of them, Wild-West style; but the only thing was we hadn't found any vines on our various excursions. The fibres inside the bamboo, while good for furniture making, were too sticky and short to be of use. In fact, the only thread of any kind on the island was Jun's violin strings, and, even strung together they wouldn't be nearly long enough.

The answer, as usually happens with me, came from literature, of a sort. After we'd found the Bible in the plane I'd decided to read the whole thing. After all, more people in the world have read the Bible than Harry Potter so I thought I should be one of them. The first section was plenty boring, pages and pages of family tree, all who begat whom. But then it got good and there were some pretty neat stories. My plan for the green gonads came from a little story called David and Goliath. David, as you must know, was a weedy boy who killed a huge giant called Goliath with a single stone from a catapult. And as I was also in the business of giant killing, I was going to make a slingshot.

I didn't tell anyone what I was doing. Seb was making his own attempt on the tree nearest to Bikini Bottom, in full sight of the Breakfast Club, and his popularity was growing every day. Even Miranda seemed re-captivated by the sight of him, shirt off, muscles straining, climbing the tree like a great ape. They were all, I knew, willing him on. Judases. No, wait: Judi.

I decided to skulk away and achieve in secret. It's what we nerds do. Our kingdom is generally our bedroom. All those FANG guys – you know, the MDs of Facebook, Amazon, Netflix and Google (nerds to a man) – started their empires in their bedrooms. So I found the nearest thing: a little clearing bang in the middle of the Emerald Forest with a high palm right in the centre, and two great green gonads hanging from it. None of the trees roundabout were high enough to get to the nuts, but I didn't worry about that. I was gonna shoot that sucker down from the ground up.

I set about making my war machine, hoping against hope that I'd get it done before Seb made a successful attempt. The first green gonad to be downed, I knew, would be a game changer, and I couldn't let Seb have the credit. If they were as good to eat as I suspected they would be, Seb would have provided the camp with a food source without fire, and that could seriously damage my position. I worked for days, only stopping to hunt and light fires. I had no idea how the others were getting on, how their different relationships were healing, or rotting. I couldn't worry about that. I was busy making my contraption. It was man against nature, nerd against nut.

My idea was to make a kind of crossbow/slingshot hybrid. I found two pieces of straight bamboo for the shaft, and a more pliable piece of hardwood for the bow part. I used the strong fibres from inside the bamboo to bind the whole thing together, in the same fashion we'd used for the chairs, wetting the short fibres first so they dried solid. I decided the thing would have more power, and I'd suffer less kickback from the shot, if it was fixed to the ground, so I anchored it with a little pile of stones, so I could dictate the angle of flight. I did my math, using the same triangulation principles I'd used to calculate longitude. My calculations told me the angle would have to be pretty steep to aim right up at the green gonads, and that meant I had to work out the loading of the shot – I didn't want my missiles to reach the top of their parabola and start arcing down before they'd reached the treetop. There would have to be quite a bit of poundage on my bowstring.

My plan was not to shoot at the nuts themselves, because

if they were filled with sweet Bounty-flavoured 7-Up as I'd fantasised, I didn't want to smash the things to pieces. I was aiming at the tough hairy stalks which connected the gonads to the tree – I figured if I shot them enough times, they would fray and break. Equally I didn't want the nut to split in two when it fell, so I collected blanket bark and made a comfy heap to catch one of the gonads if I was successful. I had to get one of those babies down whole.

I had exactly four options for my bowstring – Jun's four violin strings. Those strings gave me control over fishing rights, in the same way as my lenses made me King of fire. I got them out and examined them. The slingshot would be the exact opposite of the fishing – there we'd chosen the thinnest, the most invisible in the water, to fool the fish. Here I needed the fattest, the sturdy G string. I fitted it to the 'bow', knotting it as tense as I dared. I spent the whole morning sharpening the flattest sharpest stones I could find, so they had a wicked edge, using a bigger rock as a whetstone.

Then I began my siege.

The first shots, as you'd expect, went absolutely nowhere near my target. At the end of the morning I was in despair. I thought I'd have a better shot at killing a parakeet by accident than getting one of those damn nuts down. But I wasn't about to give up. I sat down and did my math again, calling up all the garbage about angles and trajectories I'd learned for GCSE and thought I'd never need again. By the end of my second session, I was getting closer – a couple of my stone missiles actually scarred the nuts themselves, but I was no nearer to severing a stalk.

Whenever I'd go back to camp I'd hang about in the trees before I announced myself, watching. Most of the Breakfast Club would be working on Bikini Bottom, or chilling on the dunes, but Seb would always be halfway up his chosen palm tree, with Gil at the roots egging him on. They were defying me. Seb was obviously loving that he'd found a way to make his sporting prowess count on the island. His faithful muscles, unused for so long, were in training again, remembering what they were created for. I could see them working, straining, the definition growing in his tanned limbs and torso every day. He seemed to be growing even more, a giant indeed. Gil would watch admiringly as Seb climbed. He was close, getting higher and higher with every attempt. When I'd come crashing though the undergrowth, making my final approach deliberately loud, Seb would slide down guiltily and pretend he was just hanging with Gil.

This went on for days. I spent hours shooting at those tough, hairy stalks until at last one of them began to fray. It was not lost on me that Jun and the rest would probably have better hand–eye coordination than me, since they were future Wimbledon champions and Lord's cricketers and all that. But where I had the advantage was in all those shoot-em-up games I'd played in my bedroom. All those hours on *Overwatch* blasting the bad guys away had really paid off; I was actually a pretty good shot. Maybe if they'd had archery or sharpshooting at Osney I'd have gotten some respect. I had the slingshot lined up perfectly, but every rock I shot was, of course, a different size and shape. I decided then to collect the same rock each time from wherever it fell, and use that. This, of course, took a helluva lot longer, because sometimes my chosen missile would fall into the undergrowth and I might spend five or ten minutes looking for it.

I might have gone on like this forever, trying and failing, watching the stalk of the nut fray to a thread, but for the fact that one day I witnessed Seb climbing so high up his chosen palm as to be almost in touching distance, grazing the huge glossy green nut with his fingertips, before gravity beat him and he slid, huffing and puffing and purple-faced, down the trunk.

I knew that day had to be the day. It had become a desperate race. This time I went back to my glade after lighting the fire, leaving them all sitting around it. I worked into the evening, even though the light was failing. I began to talk to myself, *I am David, I am David*, I said to myself, like a mantra. The smells of cooking fish wafted from camp and made my stomach grumble, so I just talked louder. *I am David, I am David.* It was getting so dark I could hardly see, the slices of sky through the trees turning a rosy gold. But I wouldn't quit. Some instinct led me back to the fallen stone each time. The stalk of the green gonad was fraying more and more, the glossy green nut rocking with each impact. The same night creatures who had hugged the shadows of Monte Cristo woke and watched me from the dark through eyes bright as jewels, but they didn't scare me. They would just be witnesses to my triumph, a crowd on the bleachers cheering me to Olympic gold.

At last I knew I'd have to stop. I could barely see my hand in front of my face. Almost not looking, I let off one last shot, and turned to go.

An enormous thump behind me in the undergrowth stopped

me in my tracks, and I almost jumped out of my skin. I thought it was that fricking polar bear jumping out at me. I wanted to run but instead I turned back, and there, cradled on the blanket bark I'd laid down for it, lying in the last ray of sunlight like Long John Silver's treasure, was the green gonad.

I'd done it. I knelt beside it like I was at a shrine, and passed a hand over it. It was so smooth, and cold, and almost unreal. I could've taken my missile and smashed it open there and then, but I had other plans for it. Tenderly I picked it up.

When I walked into camp with the green gonad in my arms, heavy as a child, I saw a horrifying sight. In the firelight the Breakfast Club were all gathered round the roots of Seb's palm tree, They were all clapping their hands in unison, shouting, 'Loam, Loam, Loam,' just as they had when he'd raced me in the Osney Dash on my first day at school. Not Seb. Loam.

Seb himself was right at the top of the tree, his hand reaching for the hairy stalk of the nut. He'd done it. In a moment he'd have it down.

In desperation, I shouted. I could have said anything, but I said, 'Look!'

They all turned. Seb turned too, and lost his balance. His hand grazed the nut, and it swung gently like a bell, mocking him as he slid down the trunk and hit the deck. Only Gil waited to haul him to his feet, before they both joined the others in rushing over to me. Now I was in the centre of the circle again, and I carried the nut to the fireside. All the Breakfast Club knelt reverently, just as I had done.

'How the hell did you get it down?'

'Oh my days!'

'Is it heavy?'

'Did you climb up?'

'Can we open it?'

'Not yet,' I replied to this last. I looked round at the Breakfast Club, expectant, hopeful. You could see them almost tasting that sweet-ass Bounty juice.

You know when you buy a new game and it's in the cellophane, and you've wanted it for ages, maybe saving up your Christmas and birthday money, and then Amazon finally delivers it, and you don't open it right away? I read that's called delayed gratification. Well, I was going to delay the hell out of this gratification.

'Things are gonna change around here,' I declared. 'I'm moving into Bikini Bottom, and the green gonad is coming with me.'

I looked around at their firelit, frightened faces. Daddy was leaving them home alone. I was glad they were frightened. I wanted them to be afraid. I took a brand from the fire and walked down the dunes to the house we'd built. Inside I took the orange-is-the-new-black box recorder from its high shelf and put it on the floor, none too carefully. I put the green gonad in its place, and set the brand next to it. The flame burned like one of those candles you see in temples, illuminating the glossy green sheen of the nut. I could almost see my reflection in the surface, distorted but unmistakably me. It was beautiful.

Why would I split it open and share it?

It was mine.

DISC SIX

Rocket Man – Elton John

Elton John, Bernie Taupin (1972)

32

The Amazing Skirt

I woke the next morning in a new world. Flora was right. I'd been a schmuck. I'd run around after the Breakfast Club, doing everything for them, just as I had at Osney.

Well: no more. This was the era of Lincoln, the era of civilisation. Why would I sleep by a fire like a savage, when I could sleep in a house? Why would I be a slave for them, when they could be slaves for me? In future I would just do the thing that only I could do – light the fire. The rest I would delegate. My dad used to say you don't keep a dog and bark yourself, and he was right. I was the superior animal, the higher being, the top dog. I didn't really care if they learned to hunt and fish without me. They couldn't cook or warm themselves without my fire.

As for the gonad, sitting on its little shelf like the best trophy ever, I wouldn't open it yet. Maybe not ever. It only added to my power. If I opened it now and it was full of gross, pissy-tasting juice, then its allure had gone forever.

After a wonderful night's sleep inside the hut I went back

to the dunes and convened a meeting of the Breakfast Club. I took the green gonad with me – I don't really know why. I carried it in one hand and my staff in the other. I thought maybe it would give me a power-up for what I intended to say.

'All right,' I said. 'Here's how things are going to go down. I want you to be clear about the hierarchy on this island. Essentially, we're gonna flip the Osney system. I'm now a Quarters Man. Flora and Gil are now Twos.'

I had no love for Flora and Gil, but I'd figured out that they were the cleverest people on the island next to me. I'd worked this out from one little giveaway comment each. Gil had mentioned Thomas à Becket on the cricketing day and at the crash site Flora had quoted from *Alice in Wonderland*. Neither of those things were on the Osney syllabus and that told me that they both read books, outside of school. People who read books are clever and clever people are potential troublemakers. Promotion would be my insurance policy against any further mutinies.

'The rest of you are Twelves. Also,' I hurried on before there could be protests, 'I've been doing a lot of stuff for you guys. But now you're gonna do some stuff for me. Here are your tasks for today.' I pointed to each of them in turn. 'Gil – take Jun and go fishing.' I handed Jun two of her violin strings back – it felt weird letting go of them, but I wasn't afraid. Unless they wanted to eat sashimi, their fish would be no good without my fire. 'Flora – take Seb and go catch a goat like I showed you. Lead him back here and I'll kill and gut him.' Then I had a light-bulb moment. 'Actually, see if you can get a female too. We can keep her tied up here and milk her. I'm pretty sick of lake water.' I handed them the third string, the thickest, to use as a headcollar. The fourth was round my neck, strung with my precious lenses, and there it would stay. I wasn't about to give away all my treasures. I was satisfied with the pairings – they kept Flora and Gil apart, and separated Gil and Seb too. I was protecting myself. 'Ralph – you're gonna be my herbalist, my pharmacist, my doctor.' He was the only one who looked pleased with his task. 'I will continue to light the fire every day and cook for you all. I will also build and invent stuff, for as long as we are here. And it could be a while.' The thought no longer scared me.

'What am I going to do?' asked Miranda.

'You're going to help me at Bikini Bottom,' I said. Even I wasn't quite ready to say out loud what she would actually be doing. I meant she would be 'the help', in the American sense, like in *Mockingbird* times. I'd said help, but I meant serve.

They all went off to get on with their various tasks. None of them looked too pleased but I had them checkmated. There wasn't much they could say.

'Ralph.' I called him back.

He came to me. He didn't bounce now, like a rapper, but walked straight-backed, with purpose.

'I was just wondering,' I said, 'if you could get me a little somethin'-somethin' from the forest.'

'Are you still experiencing some pain?' he asked, just like a doctor.

'No,' I said. I'd forgotten only Flora knew my tooth had fallen out. 'No. Just something a bit . . . buzzy. Something to make a party go with a bang.'

Ralph stood back and looked at me, assessing. I stared back at him.

231

'I'll see what I can do,' he said, and turned to follow the others into the Emerald Forest.

That night was the best night ever on Lincoln Island. I'd lounged around all day, napping, bathing. I hadn't needed to get all sweaty running around the forest, or get my neck sunburned to hell while fishing in the lake. I took myself off to the waterfall pool and washed my clothes and my hair, admiring my new self in the pool. Muscles. Tan. Messy sun-bleached hair falling in layers around my brown face, eyes green and bright. The glittering lenses on the violin string still hung in the V of my open shirt like a couple of dog tags. My transformation was complete. Lowly Edmond Dantes had become the Count of Monte Cristo.

Back at camp I lit the fire when the sun started to lower, and gutted the tributes that my subjects brought me. Then, while the others cooked, I went to find Miranda.

She was paddling in the surf. The sea was all gold and peach in the sunset, and her silhouette was perfection. My heart damn near missed a beat.

'Miranda.'

She turned as if she was in slo-mo. She looked like a perfume ad. I wondered how to put what I had to say. 'You're on service tonight.'

'What does that mean?'

'You get my food from the fire, prepare it on a platter and bring it to me at Bikini Bottom. Then you wait at table.'

'And then?' She looked at me with her blue eyes, very directly.

'Then you get to eat.'

She shrugged. 'OK.'

The word – my slave word – was music to my ears. 'Oh, and Miranda.'

'Yeah?'

'Wear the skirt.'

'Huh?'

'You know. The Amazing Skirt.' It sounded odd saying it out loud like that. I'd been calling it that in my head since the plane. 'That . . . Missoni one. You wore it on the first day.'

'Are you crazy?'

'You wanna eat or not?'

I saw her get the point.

I don't know where she'd kept the skirt all that time, but when she came into Bikini Bottom, she was wearing it. She looked amazing, with her vest top and her blonde hair everywhere. She was carrying a broad leaf with my fish starter on it. I was sitting in my throne chair at the head of the table. Miranda set the fish down in front of me, then stood back.

'What now?'

'Just wait.'

She sorta stood by the wall while I ate, next to the altar where the green gonad sat, glowing powerfully in the light of the fish-oil lamps. It should've been uncomfortable but it felt incredibly powerful. I've never enjoyed a meal as much as that in my life. After my starter I sent her back to the fire for some goat, and I ate that too, again with her standing to attention by the door, hands on her hips, looking bored. She sighed and huffed a bit, but she did pretty good for a first-timer. We could work on her attitude later. When I'd finished she said, 'Now what?'

'*Now* you can sit and eat.'

'Here?'

'Sure.'

She went and fetched a plate. She sat further down the table, on one of the smaller chairs. I'd finished so now I watched *her*.

I was having dinner with a girl, actually having dinner with a girl. Not just any girl, but Miranda Pencroft. I didn't really know what to say, and it occurred to me that the fault wasn't all on my side. Miranda wasn't much of a conversationalist either. She talked in emojis, all OMG and LOL. If she wasn't so hot it would've been irritating. But I was learning. I'd learned that to get people to open up, you had to talk about what *they* liked. 'D'you think you'll be a swimmer? When you leave Osney, I mean?'

She looked at me properly. 'Yes. Like Rebecca Adlington.'

'Who?'

'She swam in the 2008 Olympics, when I was just a kid really. She was this really amazing British girl who won two gold medals.'

I remembered.

'That's when I knew I wanted to be a swimmer, just like her.'

'Not *just* like her.'

'Why not?' She looked suddenly hostile.

'Well, you don't exactly look . . . isn't she . . . she's not exactly . . .'

'She's brilliant,' she said defensively.

'Yes. But didn't she get a lot of shit online for being . . . being . . .'

234

'Ugly?' I'm glad she said it and not me. 'What do looks matter? She was an amazing swimmer.'

'Hey.' I held up both hands. 'I'm with you. I think it's . . .' I stopped.

'What?'

I took a breath. 'I think it's terrible when people troll you online. Call you stuff. Tell you you're too ugly to live.'

She looked at me through her lashes. I looked back at her, steadily.

'I'm sorry,' she said. 'I shouldn't have said it. You're not ugly. You're actually really good-looking.'

Of course I registered the compliment – my first ever from a female I wasn't related to. But I wanted to know more. 'Why *did* you do it?'

She looked at her hands and didn't answer. I answered for her.

'You did it to me because you didn't want people to do it to *you*.' I couldn't keep the surprise from my voice. 'Because despite looking like an angel you're a mess of insecurities.'

She half shrugged. 'I s'pose so.'

I could've gone further. I could've torn her apart for what she'd done to me. But I still, despite everything, really wanted to be with her, so I left the dangerous subject of the Real World for something hypothetical.

'What would you rather be: an Olympic champion swimmer, or fabulously beautiful?'

I could see she wasn't used to being asked philosophical questions. She thought about it. 'I don't know.'

'Well, *you* don't have to choose.'

She smiled at me and put a hand over mine. 'Thanks.'

235

So I'd learned something else. She liked a compliment too. I tried another. 'I'm sure you'll make it.'

'Maybe,' she said, taking her hand away. 'I'm a little out of practice.'

I sat up straight. 'You can swim now if you like.'

She sat up too. 'Really?'

'Sure.' I could be magnanimous now.

Miranda smiled this big beaming smile and practically ran outside onto the silver moonlit sand. Before I could catch up with her she'd wriggled out of the Amazing Skirt and left it on the shore like a skin. She peeled off her vest top and dived through the waves in just her underwear. For a bit she swam up and down the shore, incredibly strong and fast, cleaving the path of moonlight that joined me to the horizon. After a while I waved at her.

'Hey,' I called. 'Not just crawl.'

She came into the shallows and stood up, half in, half out of the water, her body as glossy as a seal's. 'What?'

I didn't just want to see her thrashing up and down. I wanted more of a . . . show. 'Try that thing they do in the Olympics when they stick their arms and legs out of the water.'

She waggled a finger in her ear, as if she hadn't heard properly. 'That's synchronised swimming. That's not my event. I'm freestyle.'

'Try it.' I said it pleasantly but there was an edge to my voice. It was an order.

She hesitated for a moment, then fell backwards and floated on her back. She turned and turned like the mermaid she was, somersaulting, spinning. In the path of light I'd see her strong, graceful arm, or a long lithe leg with a pointed toe poking out of the water, a show just for me.

'OMG. I feel so stupid.'

'Keep going,' I called. 'It's lovely.'

I felt a presence at my elbow.

'Lincoln.'

'Not now, Ralph.'

But he pressed something into my hand. I looked at my palm – a large leaf lay in it. It was impossible to tell what colour it was but it had frilly edges, kinda like rocket.

'I think they contain something similar to caffeine. Should do something.'

I crumpled the leaf in my hand, as if it was something illicit, rather than totally natural. 'Thanks,' I said. 'Now go get something to eat.'

'OK, Lincoln.'

As Ralph walked firewards I opened my hand and looked at the luscious leaf uncurling in my palm. *Eat Me*, it seemed to invite. I hesitated just a moment, wondering how, or if, it would change me. Then, slowly, I nibbled the leaf, and waited. It gave me a pleasant, buzzy feeling in my head, like when you get up too fast. I chewed the rest as I watched Miranda. She seemed to be swimming in a beautiful Disney haze of starshine. And suddenly I felt sorry for Robinson Crusoe, the Tom Hanks castaway, those guys from *The Mysterious Island*, *Treasure Island*, *The Coral Island*. All those *Lord of the Flies* dudes, and even poor Edmond Dantes. I had one thing on my island none of those schmucks had.

Girls.

33

The Amazing Skirt (II)

We were in the age of Lincoln, and it was fricking beautiful.

The next morning I gave the Breakfast Club their morning briefing. 'Flora – you and Seb go hunting again.' They'd done as they were told yesterday. True, they'd not managed to bring me a female goat – Flora had said they were all dudes, which was just plain crazy – but I saw no reason to change their pairing. I looked around the circle. 'Miranda.' I saw Miranda's face, angelic, hopeful. 'I want you to go fishing with Gil.' Her face fell.

'Jun – you'll be helping me today.'

She didn't look too bummed out – I wondered if she and Miranda had talked. 'Yes, Lincoln.'

'That's all.'

I caught up with her as she headed to the beach. 'Jun?'

'Yes, Lincoln?'

'I want you to wear Miranda's skirt tonight.'

'Pardon?'

'The suede one. The one she wore on the plane.'

'*Really?*' For a moment she looked almost as hostile as she'd looked back at Osney.

'It's sort of . . . a uniform thing,' I said, justifying it. 'You know how we had to wear uniform at school? Well, my server has to wear the skirt.'

'But . . . it's *hers.*'

'Well, she'd lend it to you, wouldn't she? Aren't you two besties?'

'Well . . . yes, but . . .'

'Good then. See you at sundown. Take the rest of the day off.'

Then I skipped off to find Ralph. 'Get me some more Rocket leaves, Ralph, old buddy, old pal,' I said. I made a little joke. 'Rocket for the Rocket Man.'

He gave me a long look. 'OK,' he said, then, 'It's pretty hard to find.'

'That's all right,' I said. 'You've got the whole day. I just need it in time for this evening.'

'What about the herbs for the cooking?'

'Oh, sure,' I said breezily, 'the herbs for the cooking, sure, sure, get them too. But prioritise the Rocket.' Ralph looked at me again, as if he wanted to say something else, then nodded once and set off for the forest.

I wasn't really sure what to expect from my evening with Jun. I wasn't looking forward to it as much as I'd been looking forward to the night with Miranda, but I was playing a game. The way I figured it, I had plenty of time on this rock to enjoy female company, and I was going to sample every dish on offer.

Never mind the desert-island guys, I'd been a guy *in* a desert. I'd never had any attention from girls and now I was going to enjoy it. *All* of it.

Once again I got myself ready for my date. I washed my clothes and hair in the lake, then came back and tidied Bikini Bottom. As I adjusted the green gonad on its trophy shelf my foot connected with something below it, abandoned, forgotten. I cursed and hopped on one foot rubbing my stubbed toe. Then I dropped to my knees and drew the offending object out. It was the orange-is-the-new-black box recorder.

I set it in front of me on the sandy floor and looked at it consideringly. Presumably it was sending inaudible sonic pulses from its mechanical heart out into space, telling those who sought us where we were. I looked at it with something akin to fear. It was a snitch, a tattletale. It sat there innocently enough, with its orange paint and its white army lettering: *FLIGHT RECORDER DO NOT OPEN*. Suddenly the lettering made me angry. No one was going to tell me what to do on my island. I took my staff and, in a sudden fury, beat it to death.

The box split and shattered surprisingly easily. I kept on spamming it with my staff until it was just a bunch of little pieces. When the red tide ebbed I surveyed the damage. I sifted through the blood and guts, expecting microchips, transponders, sensors. But I found nothing technical at all. I found only splintered balsa wood and a couple of zinc weights, and flakes of orange paint.

The flight recorder was a prop.

For a long time I sat looking at the wreckage. No one was coming for us, and I was glad. I threw the body and its false

240

innards into the sea. After all, I had to have the place looking nice for Jun.

Jun came in wearing the skirt, her olive T-shirt tied around her middle, and her curtain of shiny blue-black hair loose and hanging to her waist. While I ate she stood respectfully, head bowed, hands clasped neatly, eyes on the floor. She seemed to have a much better idea than Miranda of what was required. I was pleased with her and said so.

When I'd finished I let her sit and eat. And of course I engaged her with a subject that I knew would interest her – music.

'When would your audition have been? For the Royal College of Music?'

'September fourth,' she said. We knew from the Clock Rock that we were in mid-August. 'Three weeks' time.'

'Wow,' I said. 'Well, I guess you don't have to worry about it now.'

'No,' she said decidedly. 'You can't exactly play with just a bow, and that's all I have left. And even if we were rescued, I'd never have time to catch up on my practice. And once I've missed that chance, hopefully I'll never have to play, ever, ever again. I'm grown up now.' She sounded quite fierce, but there was something about her stating she was grown up that made her sound very much like a little girl. 'They can't make me,' she said unconvincingly. 'Nothing could make me play again.'

'*I* could make you.'

'Pardon?'

'I could make you play again.'

She looked at me with eyes so dark they were fathomless.

241

'How?'

'You said you still had the bow.'

'Yes, but . . .'

'Fetch it.'

'But . . .'

'Jun. Do you want to eat tomorrow?'

It was enough.

While she was gone, Ralph appeared as arranged with another Rocket leaf. I sent him to get food in exchange. As he left he crossed Jun in the doorway. I don't know where she'd hidden the bow, but she had it in her hand. She drew her thumb down the horsehair the colour of bone, and tightened it up in a practised way using the turnscrew at the end.

'Now what?' she said.

Tenderly, as if it was a Stradivarius, I handed her my staff.

I lifted her chin with my fingers and balanced the staff on her prominent collarbone, placing her long fingers around the length. Then I guided her bowing hand until the horsehair rested on the wood with a tiny rodent squeak.

I sat down again on my throne. 'What will you play?'

She looked at me with those dark eyes, impossible in the lamplight to see where her pupils ended and her irises began. Then, as if she was in her audition, she said, 'This is Bach, Concerto for two violins in D. Opus 236.'

I nodded graciously. Then I sat back and enjoyed the recital. She was beautiful when she played, eyes closed, fingers moving lyrically, instrument swaying from side to side. I chewed the Rocket leaf and listened carefully. I didn't know the piece but through some magic she conjured I could almost hear it. Bikini

Bottom was filled with music, the notes fluttering around my head like a cloud of iridescent butterflies.

I made her play eight pieces on my staff altogether. After the concert I let her go. I blew out the lamps and collapsed on the bed, content. *Almost* content. Tonight had been beautiful but it wasn't quite enough. I needed to *hear* the beauty. Tomorrow, when I got Flora to wear the Amazing Skirt, I would order her to sing.

34

The Amazing Skirt (III) . . . nearly

'No.'

'Flora.'

'Don't ask me again, Lincoln.'

'Yes. You're going to serve me tonight.'

'No way.'

'And you need to wear the Amazing Skirt.'

She'd been walking away from me, leaving the morning briefing before she'd been dismissed, marching down the beach. Now she stopped. 'The *what*?'

'Miranda's skirt. She'll lend it to you. She lent it to Jun.' I studied her. She was slimmer than she'd been at Osney; her limbs baked a dark coffee colour. Her eyes were a sort of orange-y amber, the colour of the sky on Lincoln Island at sunset, and they really stood out in her face now she was so tanned. Her hair was longer and all the purple and pink dye was fading from the sun. She was almost as blonde as Miranda. It struck me for the first time just how pretty she was. She'd look great in the Amazing Skirt. But, in the faded black Motörhead vest, she also looked faintly dangerous. I didn't think she'd be a pushover like the other two. And I was right.

'That's the most *ridiculous* thing I've ever heard.'

'You want the good dinner? Wear the skirt.'

'You've *got* to be shitting me.'

'I shit you not.'

I held her eyes long enough for her to know I was serious.

She didn't drop her gaze. 'Can I just ask one question, Lincoln?'

'Sure,' I said, ever the magnanimous ruler.

'Who made you King of the Island?'

Rage sang in my ears. I was so furious at her daring to question me that I couldn't actually think of a comeback. Unbelievably, in the pause, she turned on her heel and walked away.

By the time the wave of blood subsided and the tide of my fury washed out again, I had to admit her point. I was the rightful King. But I hadn't been crowned. I needed a coronation.

That night I didn't dine in No. 1 Bikini Bottom. It would be futile to sit around waiting for Flora *not* to appear. I had to assert my authority first. I fetched my throne from the head of the table, placed the green gonad and the staff on the seat and carried the lot right to the top of the dunes. I set the chair by the fire and sat in it, clutching my staff in one hand, and the green gonad, heavy as a bowling ball, in the other. The Breakfast Club collected around me, in a circle round the fire, all curiosity. Orb and sceptre in place, the stars shining above, I seemed, for the first time in my life, to be where I belonged in the universe. I addressed my subjects.

'Tonight,' I said, 'we are going to revive Toppers.'

For once I wanted to be at the centre of some sort of fricking *ceremony*, and for the Breakfast Club to celebrate, at last, my massive achievement of capturing a green gonad. My idea was that I'd cleave the nut in two, share whatever sweetness was inside – a literal and metaphorical Bounty, so to speak – and with the top bit, the bit with the stalk, I'd crown myself. I know I'd thought it looked dumb when Seb had been crowned at Osney with the silver lid of the All-Rounder trophy, but this was totally different. This Toppers hat wouldn't look too bad – I thought with my sun-bleached brown hair and that green hat I'd just look like my namesake: Link.

So I sat there on my chair, the green gonad in one hand and my staff in the other, and began to sing the Toppers song.

When you're th'eleventh man and there are six runs to get
When there's a score to draw and you're not even yet
When there's a furlong to run and your steed is tired
Or a duel to fight and your last shot's fired
When the whistle's raised and almost blown
Or you're out in front and on your own
Remember you're made of Osney stuff
Where only your best is good enough

Run on, run on, you're an Osney man
Run on, run on, run as fast as you can

If your goals are wealth and fame
There's a game to play, so play the game!

Run on, run on, through the quad of life
Run on, run on, through joy and strife
If your goals are wealth and fame
There's a game to play, so play the game!

One by one, they joined in and sang with me. First Ralph, my
VP. Then Seb, standing tall as if he was singing the national
anthem, with Gil, of course, following whatever he did. Soon
Jun and Miranda joined in too. There was no opposition. They
sang cheerfully and loudly, and the familiar song seemed a
comfort, a breath of home, a little corner of England on this
remote beach. It was like those old movies of straitlaced British
pith-helmeted colonials singing Christmas carols as they're
being boiled by cannibals.

Flora was the only one who didn't sing, and I watched her
from veiled eyes. I'd deal with her later. She'd sing for
her supper eventually. I was too busy enjoying my moment
to design my revenge. And the words of the song resounded
sweetly in my ears.

Because suddenly the Toppers song seemed to make all
kinds of sense. I'd always heard it from the loser's point of
view before – an outsider looking in. But when you were a
winner it sounded awfully sweet. I was in the club, not just
one of the gang but its leader. For once in my fricking life, I
was at the centre of universal adulation.

I laid the green gonad before the fire as if on an altar, with my staff beside it like the sacred knife. I'd prepared for the pivotal moment. I'd scored around the top of the green gonad first with one of our makeshift knives, so that when I cleaved it at the final moment with my staff the top circle with the stalk would come off cleanly. But that was for later. First we were going to celebrate. Ralph went around the group handing out Rocket leaves – one for each person. For tonight only, everyone was to join the party.

Ralph shouted: 'Is there a Quarters Man?'

They all (except Flora) shouted back: 'Lincoln is the Quarters Man!'

Ralph yelled: 'Who is the Toppers Man?'

The reply came: 'Lincoln is the Toppers Man!'

Suddenly I was being carried around the fire, shoulder high, the stars whirling above, the flames burning below. I deserved it. I'd done more than run round some shitty quadrangle. I'd saved their souls, all of them, with my intelligence and resourcefulness. They literally owed me their lives. And I drank in the adulation in what was the most perfect moment of my life.

Then they set me down and it got weird. Everybody was hugging everybody else; I even bumped jawbones with Seb at one point. Everybody started dancing around and whooping like savages. They all started shouting my name, and jumping up and down. I guess they were sorta letting off steam or something, but it was great because I was at the centre of it, and all the time they were calling my name, my first name as I'd never heard it, as a sports chant. *Lin-coln clap clap clap, Lin-coln clap clap clap.* It was awesome. The chant got louder and louder and louder, and the boys started jumping over the fire, and the girls started doing this kind of sexy dancing, which was seriously hot. Flora was wiggling her hips from side to side, eyes closed, throwing her hair about to the rhythm. She looked amazing, and I was determined that she would serve me as the other girls had. Miranda and Jun were kinda dancing with each other, and I swear at one point they were about to kiss. It occurred to me that if I asked them to, they would.

I would've let the dance go on forever but I wanted the climax of the moment, my ultimate moment of triumph. In the middle of the chaos I raised the staff above my head, like some sort of savage king. The green gonad lay below me, passive, already defeated, like a sacrifice.

Now I'd cleave it, and we'd drink the sweet innards and everyone would think I was marvellous. I'd put on the green Toppers hat and everyone would cheer me to the heavens. Then I'd announce what I'd been subconsciously planning since I'd landed on this rock, which was that everyone should call me *President* Lincoln. Looking at their firelit, savage, adoring faces, I knew they'd agree. At the peak of the frenzy, hearing the sweet music of my name, I raised my staff and brought it down on the green gonad. It split cleanly along the score I'd made and something rolled out.

Something almost unbelievable.

A video camera.

35

Love Island

We sat in a circle about the fire, completely sober now, with the green gonad occupying its own place like another member of the Breakfast Club. As the Toppers Man I held the camera in my hands. Heavy, black, small. It had a tiny, threatening light in one corner like a single red eye. It was completely wireless, and in some sort of weatherproof casing.

Everyone looked at me like the camera was the conch shell from *Lord of the Flies*, as if the camera itself gave me permission to speak. But I couldn't. It's amazing how the thought of everything you say being recorded makes you shut the hell up.

'OMG,' said Miranda softly. 'We're on a TV show.'

'A *reality* TV show,' said Jun.

'We can't be,' I said, eventually finding my voice. 'They'd have to have release forms and parental permission and all sorts of stuff. We didn't sign up for it.'

'We did, you know,' said Flora. 'Summer camp. We all signed the forms. So did our parents. You know how lots of school forms say to tick if you give permission to take pictures or film? I guess this –' she nodded at the camera – 'was in the small print.'

'Pretty small print,' I said. 'It was supposed to be a Preparation for Life camp.'

Gil said, 'If this is some sort of *Survivor*, what better preparation for life than that?'

'It's not *Survivor*.' We all turned to look at Miranda, who had spoken with such certainty. 'Look around,' she said. 'Seven sixteen-year-olds with tans. It's *Love Island*.'

'What the *hell*,' said Flora, 'is *Love Island*?'

'A bunch of teens on an island. They couple up and the most popular couple wins fifty grand.'

'Ugh,' said Flora. 'How utterly repugnant. That's the most empty-headed superficial concept for a TV show I've ever heard.'

Miranda tossed her hair. 'I'm not wrong though, am I?'

We all looked at each other, suddenly shy. My heart sank. If she was right, if this was some sort of dating show, then that was it for me. Everyone would couple up and I'd be left, the Irrelevant Man in the NFL draft once again. Miranda would just go back to Seb, Jun would probably pair up with Ralph, and Gil and Flora, who were already reasonably friendly because they were both now Twos, would probably make some sort of pact to win the show.

'Well, look,' said Gil. 'At least we know we're safe now.'

'*How* do we know?' asked Seb.

'We're being observed all the time. They're not going to let anything happen to us.'

Although that was true, I didn't take any comfort from the thought. In fact if anything it presented me with a problem. I didn't want a presidency that was under constant scrutiny. I'd had three days, *three lousy days*, to enjoy the Age of Lincoln. And in that time I'd given the cameras access all areas. Because I'd taken the green gonad *inside* the shelter, it had seen and recorded everything that had gone on in No. 1 Bikini Bottom. Miranda in the skirt, Jun in the skirt, Jun 'playing the violin'. I cringed at the thought. It wasn't that I was *ashamed* or anything. It wasn't exactly that I'd done anything *wrong*. But . . .

'This means we're going to be rescued,' said Jun definitely. 'Reality shows don't go on forever.'

This made me feel even worse. The last thing I wanted to do was to give up my newly won power. Presidents usually get at least four years. I hadn't even had four days. Well, if I only had limited tenure left, I was going to *carpe* the hell out of this *diem*. I got to my feet and approached the flames. 'What're you doing?' demanded Flora quickly, putting herself between me and the fire.

'Burning it,' I said. To be observed, to be under surveillance 24/7, was suddenly unbearable. I loved my power but I didn't want to be watched wielding it. The eye of the camera even watched me now, daring me, to see what I was going to do. I pictured it crackling and spitting on the fire until the red eye died. I held my victim over the flames.

'There's no point,' said Flora.

'Why?'

'Because they're everywhere. Don't you get it? There's not just *one* camera. You'd have to burn *all* of them.' She flung out her arms and turned 360 degrees. We were ringed with palm trees, each with two nuts. I remembered that even at places where palms would not usually grow, like on the top of Monte Cristo or right on the shingle of the lake, there were always two green gonads, always watching us. If each one had a camera inside, Flora was right. They were everywhere. I drew back my hand.

'Why two nuts?' mused Jun. 'What's the other one?'

'The support tech,' I said wearily. 'A Wi-Fi feed. A back-up camera. I don't know.'

It was too much. I passed the camera to Ralph, the Hand of the King, and took up my staff again, using it to lever myself to my feet. There was only one thing to do. 'Whatever this is, I can't live here and continue to provide for you all.'

They all looked bereft, like before, like when Daddy had left home.

'Where will you go?' asked Seb.

'To the caves,' I said, recalling the day we'd explored them. 'I'm going to take the big one as my residence.'

Before I'd known about the camera, I'd have named it the White House. Now that seemed a little too grand to say out loud. It was something to keep to myself. There was so much to keep to myself now.

'What about the fire? The food?' said Jun, a taut note of panic in her voice.

'Nothing's going to change. I'll just be at the caves instead of at Bikini Bottom. You'll be provided for. I'll come back every day and prepare the food and light the fire for you. I just can't be *watched.*' I was sure it was the right thing to do. I'd remove myself, and they could all couple up without me. I'd just stay right out of it. They'd still need me, for food and fire, but I didn't need the humiliation of being romantically rejected, and, worse than that, for my dating fails to be recorded. Thinking of the camera and what it had seen revealed the truth to me. I knew I'd bought dates with both those girls in exchange for food. There was no way they'd come just for *me*. I wanted to retire and lick my wounds and cling onto the shreds of my power for whatever time I had left. I now knew that my rule was coming to an end. Jun was right – the cameras meant that we wouldn't be here forever. Reality TV shows have a set running time, and once someone's won, that's it.

Nerds are not extroverts. We don't do well on reality shows. I was just channelling classic nerd behaviour when things get tough – returning to my bedroom. The cave – the White House – was going to be my bedroom from now on. I looked about me. And my room would need stuff. In the firelight the green gonad lay, flames reflected in it, like a severed head. It was still mine, the only trophy I'd ever won. I picked it up and held it under my arm where it nestled like a basketball. 'You can all come and visit me at the caves. Ralph –' he pricked up his ears like a dog who'd been told he was going to get a walk – 'you come now.' He scrambled to his feet.

'And bring that.' I pointed to the other thing I wasn't about to leave behind.

My throne.

36

The Complete Works

They always say on reality shows that people forget they are being filmed. I didn't forget, not for one single second.

In my cave I was safe, with only the green gonad for company. I called him Wilson, after the volleyball who was Tom Hanks's only friend in the *Castaway* movie. I even gave him a face, with a charcoal handprint. I gave him his own little stone niche, and he sat there quite happily. He watched me with his charcoal features, but now I didn't mind his scrutiny. His belly was hollow, the camera was gone, so he could look as much as he liked.

Ralph helped me bring the furniture from Bikini Bottom. I didn't bother with the table and the small chairs but I brought the bed, a rug, and the Bible from the plane. I also brought the section of fuselage, the bit with the number on it, ED-34. If the White House was going to be my nerd bedroom I needed my nerd trophies. I made myself pretty comfortable. And when I was moving in I discovered that I wasn't the first one who had thought that this cave would make a good home.

Someone had been there before me.

In the very back of the cave was a little antechamber with the natural skylight we'd seen when we all looked around. It let in green dappled daylight from the jungle above, and would make an ideal bedroom. As I cleared the leaves and rocks to level the floor I found something jammed into a niche – something firm and square and blood-coloured.

It was a book, with a maroon leather cover and gold-edged pages. I thought for a second it was another Bible, until I opened the title page and read:

THE COMPLETE WORKS OF SHAKESPEARE

I leafed through it, looking for a name, a bookplate or some annotations in the margins, anything that would give me a clue as to its owner, but there was nothing. Only a day ago this discovery would have been mind-blowing. It would've meant there was a settler on the island, a Mr Kurtz, a Captain Nemo. But now, of course, it could've just belonged to one of the technicians who'd set up the cameras before they'd deserted the island ready for our arrival. But it felt more significant than that somehow, like it could have belonged to some long-dead castaway. It looked pretty old – maybe valuable – but frankly I was just glad to have something else to read. I figured I was coming up on a pretty lonely period until the TV crew decided to get us out of there.

I knew a lot of Shakespeare plays, because of all those trips to Stratford-upon-Avon, but the only one I knew inside out was *The Tempest*. It was our set play for GCSE English Literature and I'd written about eight sets of revision notes for all the lazy Ones at Osney. Just for the familiarity really I started reading it of an evening, sometimes aloud for Wilson, my audience of one. I liked the Prospero bits. We had a lot in common, me and old Prospero. He was the leader of his own desert island. He had a cave and a staff and a couple of books. He had a bunch of servants to do his bidding. And he had a thirst for revenge. Like Edmond Dantes. Like me.

In the cave, with Wilson, I could be myself. But every time I set foot out the door and emerged from the other side of the waterfall, I was observed. I tried, as I moved about the island, to find blind spots, but the TV production team had done their job well before they'd abandoned the island – there was nowhere to hide. Flora had been right. Everywhere you went there were at least two green gonads overlooking you, like a pair of eyes.

Despite the scrutiny I still went back to Bikini Bottom every day. I couldn't stay away. I felt a burning need to know what was happening. Even if the Breakfast Club were all dating each other I couldn't bear the thought of them making a little society without me. It was FOMO again, and of the worst kind.

I watched them all from the edge of the forest, hidden, unseen. I found them all rather self-consciously making 'improvements' to No. 1 Bikini Bottom. It was a fake project, as the shelter didn't need any work beyond mending the hole in the roof where I'd taken the plane panel. No one was really doing anything much; it was all for the cameras. People were only doing things that made them look good. Bikini Bottom had become a film set. It was pretty interesting to note how the Breakfast Club changed for the cameras. The boys were all doing manly stuff like carrying the biggest log or chopping firewood. The girls had all made an effort with their hair, their teeth, their nails. Seb had his shirt off, Miranda had the Amazing Skirt on. Only Flora was exactly the same. Of the entire Breakfast Club, she was the only one who had either forgotten she was being filmed, or didn't care.

What *was* interesting, though, was that no one seemed to be coupling up. I'd fully expected Miranda to be back with Seb, using their past relationship as a piece of valuable TV drama. But they were nowhere near each other; Gil was hanging closer to Seb than she was. And the apathy didn't seem to be coming from the boys. Seb in particular was preening like a peacock, sending out all the signals. He was tanned, muscular, as good-looking as ever. But the girls just weren't showing an interest. What was going on?

That afternoon I went back to the White House to brood. I lay on the bed with my hands behind my head and Wilson watching me from his niche, and chewed on my last Rocket leaf. Rocket leaves always helped me to think. I had to get Ralph to find me some more.

A voice said, *What makes you think you can't win it?*

I sat bolt upright and looked about me. Was there someone at the door? Calling down from the skylight? But there was no one but Wilson. 'What did you say?' I asked.

What makes you think you can't win it? he asked again.

'What makes you think I can?' I said, looking at his impassive charcoal face.

It's already your island, he said. *Go back*, he urged. *Go back, and this time let them **see** you.*

258

The charcoal face suddenly took on a tribal significance. It looked like a totem, a symbol of power.

As if compelled I went out, dodged around the waterfall and waded into the lake. I had to see something. I looked, for the fourth time on the island, at my own reflection. Each time, it had changed. I looked again at the tumbling, sun-bleached hair, the green eyes, the tanned face. I looked at that face for a long, long time, just as I'd looked at old Wilson's charcoal features.

Then I went back to Bikini Bottom, and became, once again, the watcher in the forest. I just had to check something. The boys were still posturing for the girls as surely as peacocks opening their tails, pretending to do their 'strong-man' building, doing press-ups and sit-ups on the sand. The girls were all chilling on the Clock Rock, totally ignoring the boys, Jun and Miranda catching rays, Flora a little way off yeeting pebbles into the sea.

I walked over to the shelter, not hiding any more, but loudly greeting everyone, head high, smiling and waving.

And a weird thing happened. Miranda and Jun immediately got up from the rock, like sharks scenting blood, and came over to say hi, adjusting their clothing and shaking their hair into place.

It was a moment of revelation.

The boys were showing off for the girls.

But the girls weren't showing off for the cameras.

They were showing off for *me*.

Back at the White House, I sat on my throne, the waterfall at my doorway roaring and thundering, scoring my thoughts.

I'd turned the chair away from the door, just like in my bedroom at home, and faced the green gonad as if he were my computer screen. 'Here it is, Wilson,' I said. 'It seems we're in some sort of reality dating show. Miranda thinks it's a *Love Island* setup, and the casting of it, because it *is* casting, seems to bear this out. Three girls, four boys. That's three couples and one boy left over. They obviously hope that we'll couple up and then partner swap – there are too many boys so at least two boys would be fighting over any one girl. There would always be a spare. A loser.'

Wilson's charcoal face watched me passively. He sure was a good listener. 'Now, normally, In Real Life, *I* would be the loser. No contest. But it seems that's not the case here.' I was figuring it out as I went along. 'It's not so much the way I look now – although it's a giant improvement on how I looked in England – I think it's about what I can *do.*' He looked puzzled. 'Ya know – the fire, the hunting, the fishing, the building. The longitude and latitude and all the math, and the S.O.S. I sent.' I remembered about the S.O.S. and the secret I wouldn't even admit to Wilson, and skirted swiftly over it. 'All that stuff. I now think that, for the first time in my life, I am the alpha male. The girls don't want any of the other guys. And that means,' I said slowly, 'I'm the only boy who can win. I'm already the King of the Jungle. I even have the orb.' I nodded at Wilson. 'No offence. And the sceptre.' I twizzled my staff like a majorette's baton. 'But the position of *Queen* is up for grabs. And I get to decide who it's gonna be. Time to do some thinking.' I stood up. 'Wilson,' I said, chucking him on his charcoal cheek, 'you're one smart sonofabitch.'

Thanks, he said. *Good night, Lincoln.*

'Good night, Wilson.'

And I hunkered down on my bed, a big smile on my face, and I looked out at the stars through the natural skylight. I spoke aloud to them. 'Thou shalt be free, As mountain winds. But then exactly do, All points of my command.' You see, although I hadn't told Wilson, I'd already decided who my Queen would be.

Now I just had to get her to agree to it.

37

Versailles

I told Ralph to fetch Flora for an audience at the White House, and with very bad grace she came. She hovered at the doorway, but I made her come right inside. There were no cameras in the cave and I was sure you couldn't record sound because of the waterfall. Two things I loved about my new residence. What went on in the White House stayed in the White House. I sat on the throne and she stood before me.

'What?'

'Flora. I want you to serve me tonight. Here, in this cave.'

'Haven't you and I had this conversation?'

'Yes. But this time you're not taking turns with the others. I want *you* to do it. Don't you see?'

She gasped and her hands flew to her mouth. 'Me? Really and for true? Oh, Lincoln, that's . . . that's . . .' Her face changed. '. . . gross.'

'I don't think you understand. I've chosen *you*.'

'You don't *choose* women. We're not chocolate bars.'

'But I *want* you to come.'

'Oh, that's different then,' she said, flip as hell. 'See you about seven thirty.'

She had some sass, that girl. But I didn't mind. I liked it. It was part of the reason I'd chosen her for my Queen. I wasn't at all worried. I would bend her to my will one way or the other. I just would rather do it the easy way than the hard way. I wasn't a *monster*. 'Don't you *want* to win this thing?'

'You win some, lose some; it's all the same to me,' she said cryptically.

I tried another approach. 'I've always treated you well.' That was true. 'I warmed you, fed you.'

'The Lord giveth and the Lord taketh away,' she said.

'What's that supposed to mean?'

'Read your Bible.'

'I even made you a Two,' I said. 'At Osney you were an Eleven.'

She crossed her arms across her chest, so I could no longer see the word *Motörhead* on her vest. 'Utterly irrelevant,' she said. 'As irrelevant here as it was at Osney.'

'But you don't even have to *mean* it. Just come, and . . . go through the motions.'

'What motions?' She narrowed her amber eyes. 'What exactly did you have those other girls *do*?'

'Nothing like *that*,' I said. 'They just served my food. And . . . performed.'

'Performed?'

'Yeah?'

'In what way?'

263

'Well, Miranda swam for me and Jun . . . played a pretend violin.' It sounded way more durpy than it was.

'And exactly what would you be expecting *me* to do for your little cabaret?'

'Sing,' I said simply.

'Sing?' she brayed, incredulous. 'Forget it.'

'Flora,' I said, perfectly reasonably I thought, 'you come, and you serve me, in Miranda's skirt, and you sing; or you don't eat.'

She looked at me with utter contempt.

'Fine,' she said. And for a moment I thought she'd agreed. Then she said, 'I won't eat.'

Ralph came in as Flora went out.

'Anything else, Lincoln?'

'Yes,' I said, more sharply than I meant. It was Flora I was mad at, not him. 'Rocket leaves. I've run out.'

'Ah yes,' he said. He scratched the back of his neck, where his shaved haircut was growing out. 'Rocket. The others are asking for it too. Seems everyone had a pretty good time at Toppers.'

I was torn. Of course I was glad that my subjects had enjoyed my coronation. But I couldn't have them sharing my precious plant.

'Well, they can't have it. The supply is mine. I'm declaring a monopoly.' It seemed perfectly reasonable to me. Colonists did it all the time – they commandeered the crops of their territories.

Ralph looked at me again in that considering way he had. 'OK.'

When Flora turned me down I could've invited the others back to serve me again. But I didn't. I ate alone. Miranda, in particular, seemed put out. But I didn't care. I was consumed with the thought of Flora, of breaking her spirit, of bending her will to mine. Now that girls wanted to be with me for the first time in my life I wanted the only one who didn't.

I quickly adapted to my life as a recluse. I went out so rarely that I could practically hear the cameras whirring whenever I ventured out, their black gaze following me wherever I went. But I didn't feel like I had to give them anything to look at. Let them watch the others hunting for the tenth, the hundredth time. Because I was a geek I knew enough about editing to know that what would make the cut would be me figuring out how to catch the first goat, the first fish. They'd have my greatest hits – Jun burning her violin with me, Ralph failing to gut a goat, and me succeeding. My race with Seb to get the green gonad. Flora and I at the plane. I was all over this thing already. I didn't need to court the cameras.

And now – halfway through the broadcast – I'd done the most celebrity thing I could do: I'd disappeared. I'd become this elusive figure and I knew that footage of me would be gold. I was Howard fricking Hughes.

All I needed now was to bring the campfire into my lair. Then I wouldn't have to venture into the camera's gaze at all. And here, good ol' nature conspired with me to help me to hang onto my power. A precise beam of sunlight struck through the cave's skylight at a certain time in the afternoon and the fire ignited nicely. I feared to begin with that the fire would make the White House unbearably smoky, but the skylight acted as a flue and the smoke was drawn right out of the cave. Added to that, it was beautifully toasty at night. The only drawback was that a bit of the White House became the Black House from all the soot.

My perception of the White House had changed. It wasn't a nerd's bedroom any more; it was a palace. I wasn't a reclusive geek; I was Louis the XIV deciding that Paris was for losers and that he was going to build a fricking huge palace at Versailles and everyone could just suck it up and visit him there. I didn't have to hunt. I didn't have to fish. I made the others do it. I made them get fuel. I used one of the little caverns in the cave system to keep the goats and fish cool. I stayed in my cave, made fire and washed in the waterfall. I didn't go back to Bikini Bottom any more. And because I controlled all the food I could make sure Flora didn't get any. And I made the others eat where I could see them, to make sure that they didn't sneak any away for her.

Alongside the tributes of goats and fish from the others, Ralph, of course, brought me Rocket leaves, which I chewed every night in greater and greater numbers. One just didn't seem to cut it any more, but two or even three really got me buzzing. Even in my solitude they prompted some great conversations with Wilson, and gave some pizzazz to the little recitals I gave for him. I would stride around the cave with my staff in one hand and the Complete Works in the other, quoting *The Tempest* and pretending I was Prospero. I was just sorry I didn't have a swishy cloak.

All I needed now was my consort, a queen to install at Versailles, a First Lady for the White House. I had to break Flora. She would have no food until she paid me tribute. This wasn't as bad as it sounds; she had Bucket berries and all the water there was in the lake – I knew she wouldn't starve. I knew too that she wouldn't hold out for long. Seb had only lasted three days when he and Gil tried to make their stand. But day after day went by, and still Flora didn't venture behind the waterfall to the White House.

I didn't feel great about it. Of course I didn't. But it was for her own good. To make this a happy society, she had to learn to obey. It was like Wilson said: it was her own fault. *If she'd just done what you told her to, she wouldn't have forced you into this position, Lincoln.*

The whole thing was pretty unfair on me, when you came to think about it.

38

Chivalry Lives

The day that we would have gotten our GCSE results I got to sleep with Miranda Pencroft. In nerd terms that's bigger than winning Toppers, way bigger. But it wasn't quite how it sounds.

It was Jun, visiting to take my hunting orders, who'd informed me that, according to the tally marks on the Clock Rock, it was August 24th: GCSE results day. That set me thinking about what I had got in my exams. Now I knew we were being filmed, I had no doubt that we would be back home by the end of the summer. Even TV companies couldn't just spring kids from school. So our GCSEs, which had seemed irrelevant two months ago when we were just trying to figure out how to survive, now loomed large again. But I forgot all about my results when the second visitor that day came through the waterfall.

It was Flora.

I hadn't seen her for days and she looked much thinner – slimmer, now, than Miranda. Her cheekbones were prominent and her eyes enormous. With her black Motörhead vest and her cut-off denim shorts she could have been a Calvin Klein model. She didn't quite meet my eyes. 'I'll come,' she said.

'What's that now?' I cocked my ear forward with my index finger

She sighed. 'I'll come and serve you.'

'Why, that's just wonderful, Flora,' I said.

Not tonight though, said another voice.

It was Wilson. Sometimes he just chipped in.

Not tonight; tomorrow. You can't let her dictate when her punishment will end, Lincoln. Let her go hungry for one more day.

'Tomorrow,' I said. 'Come at sundown.' Then I'd feed her handsomely, let her know she was forgiven, allow her to show her gratitude.

Flora looked pretty bummed out at that, but there was nothing she could do.

'What do we say?'

'OK, Lincoln.'

Still she didn't look at me. I got it. She was ashamed. She'd given in. She'd lost, I'd won. But I was relieved. I didn't actually *want* her to starve. Tomorrow I would feed her, and everything would be cool.

When Ralph came with the catch of the day I had a special request for him. 'I need extra Rocket leaves for tomorrow, Ralphie. It's gonna be one hell of a night.'

I imagined watching Flora singing for her supper through the rainbow haze of well-being which the Rocket leaves always induced in me.

Ralph shifted his feet on the cave floor. 'Yeah. That's not going to happen, Lincoln.'

269

'What d'you mean? We can't have run out! It's a fricking jungle, for Chrissake.'

He looked at me in that doctor's way he'd adopted ever since I'd told him about Stephen Maturin. 'Lincoln. I *could* tell you that. It would certainly make *my* situation easier, to lie to you, to tell you that my stocks have run out. But the truth is, I'm cutting you off.'

'*What?*'

He drew himself up a little straighter. 'I'm cutting you off. No more Rocket Man.'

This was outrageous. 'I can stop whenever I like,' I shouted.

'Then stop.'

'I don't want to,' I said. 'Not yet.'

'You should,' he said. 'I don't really know what the constituents of the plant are, yet you're asking me for more and more leaves each day. It's time to stop, Lincoln. That's my professional opinion.'

'Your *professional opinion?*' I brayed.

'As ship's doctor.'

'Which *I* made you.'

'Yes,' he said calmly. 'You made me ship's doctor. And now I'm being one. First do no harm, Selkirk.' Then he turned on his heel and left.

The red tide of rage rose in my head once more, and I screamed after him, through the waterfall: 'Don't expect to eat anything any time soon! And it's *Lincoln*.'

It took me all day to calm down. I was *furious* with Ralph, furious. How *dare* he tell *me* what I could and couldn't eat on

270

my own island! He would know my revenge. I'd starved Flora, and she'd caved. I could starve Ralph too.

I contemplated going to look for Rocket myself, but I didn't want to be in the eye of the camera. I made a special effort with the cooking that day, angrily making it as nice as I could – the better it smelled, the more Ralph would suffer. As it cooked I paced around the White House like a tiger.

I only stopped when a slim, blonde-haired figure tentatively entered my cave at nightfall.

Flora was a day early – clearly the cooking smells were too much for her and she'd come to beg for meat. But as my eyes adjusted I saw that it wasn't Flora. It was Miranda, and she was wearing the Amazing Skirt.

'Miranda! What do you want?'

'To stay the night.'

Well, that was pretty frank. I took her hand and sat her down on the bed, sitting next to her. 'What's up?'

She half turned and took both my hands in both of hers. Our four hands rested in her lap, on the mouse-soft suede of the Amazing Skirt. '*Please* let me stay. We don't have to do anything.'

Then, before I could say anything else, she kissed me.

I wasn't really into Miranda any more, but she was offering herself to me on a plate, so I wasn't about to say no. I could practise on her as a starter before I got to Flora, the main meal. Now I had never, ever kissed a girl before, never mind one as hot as Miranda, but it wasn't exactly the fairy tale I'd expected. There were no starbursts over the towers of the Disney castle, as there had been when I'd watched her swim. It was an odd, bumpy, saliva-y combo of soft lips and hard teeth. Something was off. It just felt wrong. So I did something I never would've thought I'd do. If you'd asked me a year ago what would I do if a girl kissed me, I would've said, 'Are you nuts? I'd let it go on forever.' But I wasn't the me of a month ago. So I pulled back.

'What's wrong?' I asked.

'I guess I should ask you the same question.' She pursed her full lips.

'You're not really here for me, are you?'

She looked at her hands – our hands.

'It's the GCSEs,' she said. 'I know I'm not going to do well. In fact, I've got a horrible feeling I might not get any.'

'But . . . I did all those revision notes for you.' It seemed incredible now, that I'd used to be her slave.

'I know,' she said shamefacedly. 'But I didn't really revise. I didn't think I needed exams.'

'Well, you won't, will you? I mean, you're going to swim. Professionally, I mean.'

She looked down again, and something hot and wet fell on our clasped hands. Miranda Pencroft was *crying*. Actually crying. I suppose I should've been glad. She'd made me cry so many times, and now I'd seen her brought low. I should've been punching the air. But it was kinda horrible.

'I'm not going to swim. I'm not good enough.'

'What do you mean? You're amazing!'

'No.' She sniffed and looked at me. Her blue eyes were huge with tears. 'I had my trial for the Olympic team for Tokyo 2020 just before the end of term. I didn't qualify. My time wasn't fast enough.'

I put my arm round her, not in a creepy way, but in a comforting way.

'Shit, I'm sorry.' I was silent for a moment, letting her cry, then I said, 'But I don't get how coming here to me would help.'

She gave this huge sigh. 'I need other options, Lincoln. If I can stay the night, and it looks like we've done . . . stuff, then maybe I can win the show with you. We'd get the prize money. I'd get some TV exposure, get shit-loads of followers on Instagram and Twitter, and maybe that could lead to a career in TV. I've got to do *something*, Lincoln.'

I considered this. 'Why not Seb?'

She looked out of the cave entrance beyond the waterfall, as if she were seeing into the future. 'There's no chance for us after school. We're perfect on paper, but Seb doesn't function outside of Osney. I mean, you've seen him here. I just thought, you know, he was the top guy at school.'

'And on the island, it's me.'

'Yes. I feel I guess I kind of always felt – that I need to be with the leader, *whoever* that is. I sometimes think . . .' she paused, 'I sometimes think I'm not enough of a *person* to get through life on my own. And now I know I'm certainly not enough of a swimmer either.'

Again, I didn't feel what I should've felt. I should've felt hurt, or used, or maybe scornful that she was so puddle shallow. But I just felt pity. I, Lincoln Selkirk, felt sorry for Miranda Pencroft.

I let her sleep in the bed. I wasn't going to touch her. She'd never been safer in her life. She went to sleep really quickly, as if her confession had worn her out. I watched Miranda as

I had many times before, but now I wasn't yearning after her. In fact, I felt kinda *paternal*. She was still pretty, but not beautiful, not now, not to me. She looked like a little girl. I watched the sweep of her lashes, flickering on her cheek as she dreamed, her mouth pursed like a kiss, her hands clasped under her chin like a prayer. And I wondered how this angel could ever have sent all those evil texts to me. I wondered what had made her like that, and now I thought I knew.

Fear.

'You're very quiet,' I said to Wilson, who had watched the whole thing play out. I thought at least I'd get some kudos for my chivalry, but he didn't reply.

39

Swimming to Nowhere

I had rolled myself in the rug on the floor. So when in the first light of the day I had a visitor, I was woken by him pretty much tripping over me. I raised my head, and in the grey light of dawn watched a figure creeping into my cave.

One of the good things about the White House, security-wise, was that there was a fricking great waterfall right outside the door, and it was kinda difficult to get in without being detected. One of the bad things about the White House was that there was a fricking great waterfall right outside the door, so you couldn't hear yourself think. The very factor that would totally mess up any sound recording also totally messed up any chance of hearing an intruder coming into my lair.

And I had sure as hell missed this one. The dark shape crept stealthily across the floor. It stood over the bed, looking down for a long moment, then changed direction and went for my throne. The staff was leaning against the seat and the figure picked it up. Then it crossed to the niche where Wilson was sleeping. The intruder reached out its other hand and laid hold of him.

That did it. I sprang up, grabbed my bark-rug and dropped it over them like a fishing net. Wilson rolled away to safety and I twisted the staff from their grip and dragged the struggling creature to the floor of the cave. Neither of us made a sound – it was a curiously silent fight, as if there was some odd mutual understanding that we couldn't wake Miranda. I yanked off the rug, and in the half-dark, scrabbled for a face and a mouth, covering the dry gaping lips with my hand. Only when I'd torn away the bark matting did I see that it was Gil. I put my full weight on top of him, and both hands over his mouth. Eyes wide, nostrils flaring, he struggled to breathe.

'I'll let go,' I said softly, 'if you stop struggling. Agreed?'

Mute, he nodded under my hands.

I released him and he sat up. I sat opposite him, cross-legged, watching him warily. It was as if we were about to play chess, but there was no board between us.

'Now,' I said, 'what were you doing with Wilson?'

'Who the hell is *Wilson?*' he asked.

'The green gonad,' I said. 'You were stealing him, and the staff too.' He was silent, hunched, looking out at the waterfall. I knew I was right.

'You know,' I said slowly, searching for the right words, 'that those things are symbols. They don't *make* you the King of the Island.'

'Well, you certainly seemed to think they did.'

I breathed out. 'Seb sent you to get them for him, didn't he? Or did he send you to get Miranda back?' I thought about what

Miranda had said, about the two of them having no chance after school. Perhaps Seb thought differently.

Gil recoiled from the mention of Miranda. 'I don't know whether he wants her back or not,' he said sniffily, carefully avoiding the use of her name. 'But one thing I do know is: he didn't tell me to do this.'

'He didn't?'

'No. He doesn't know I'm here.'

'But you are doing it for him, right?'

'Yes.'

'But why . . . ?'

He looked at me then, a fleeting, angry glance, his expression a strange mixture of hurt and hate.

It all became clear. '*My God*,' I breathed. 'You're in *love* with him.'

He didn't give me an answer, but I had one. 'But he was a total *shit* to you for an entire year. You were his bitch before I came along.'

'I know,' he said. 'I expect it's like those people who fall for their kidnappers. Stockholm syndrome.'

'Jeeeesus.' I dropped my head, pushed my hands into my hair, then looked up again. 'After all that homophobic shit you gave *me*. You were totally in denial. All those things you called *me*, you were afraid people would call *you*.' It was Miranda and her anti-social media all over again. 'Why didn't you just come out? And take the power away from them all?'

'You're kidding, aren't you?' said Gil. 'In a sporty school like Osney? D'you know how many Premiership footballers are openly gay?' He shook his head hopelessly. 'Zero. Can you imagine what it would be like?'

277

'Yes,' I said, the red tide of rage resurging. 'Yes I *can* imagine, you absolute asshole, because you did it to me and everybody else did too.'

'I'm *sorry*, OK? I'm sorry. I was just afraid.'

He looked so wretched that I pedalled back a bit. 'Does Seb know?'

'Of *course* he doesn't know.' Then, '*You* won't tell him, will you?'

I hesitated. Gil had really put me through it, had got practically the whole school calling me a faggot. I wasn't going to tell anyone about him, but maybe the dark part of me, just for a second, just to punish him, made me want him to think that I would. That I would go running to Seb and blow the whole thing sky high.

That moment of hesitation was enough. In the few seconds I didn't speak, Gil scrambled to his feet and started to run.

I went after him, dodging the waterfall and plunging down the steep lake path in his wake. In the rosy light of dawn it was easy to see where he was going. He ran down to the beach and pounded to the shoreline. I followed him as fast as I could. I was much faster than I used to be but still was nowhere near catching Gil. If he'd been doing the Osney Dash now he'd be a Quarters Man. He plunged into the sea and just kept going, as if he was still running even in the water, ploughing deeper and deeper.

'Gil!' I shouted. 'Come back! It's OK!' I meant that I was never going to tell anyone, but I wasn't sure he could hear me. 'Gil,' I yelled, 'where are you going?' There was no land anywhere to be seen; believe me, I'd looked. Even from the

278

top of Monte Cristo there had been no tell-tale coastline on the horizon, not even a handy archipelago we could hop to. If there had been, we'd have been spending our time at Bikini Bottom making a boat instead of patio furniture. But as I yelled the question my mind answered it, and I was suddenly doused with a chill foreboding, as if the waves had washed back at me.

Gil wasn't going anywhere.

I wasted precious seconds dancing around in indecision on the sand. I knew there was nothing to be gained by me going after him. I was the original Duffer and could barely swim a stroke – we'd both drown. I acknowledged something I hadn't for all of my time on the island.

I needed help.

Miranda woke at once, like those people in movies who sleep with a gun under their pillow. I gasped out what was happening. 'Gil?' she said. 'He didn't even make the Elevens swim team.' She threw back the coverlet, all Wonder Woman, and raced ahead of me to the headland.

I was certain it was too late. Gil's head was a dot in the shiny path between us and the rising sun. He was thrashing now, bobbing and struggling. She'd never get to him in time. But Miranda didn't hesitate. She wriggled out of the Amazing Skirt and plunged in wearing only her underwear, just as she'd done the night when I'd made her swim for me. But this time she wasn't a sideshow. She was a heroine. I couldn't believe I'd made her do all that posturing in the water. She swam faster than an arrow, cleaving through the path of light. I saw her reach Gil incredibly quickly, despite his start, and saw their two heads merge, become one. Then she was dragging him back, and I could see them, as they drew closer, Gil turned on his back, Miranda's hands under his chin, like the proper lifesaver that she was.

She almost threw him onto the beach and together we pulled him above the high tide mark, turning him on his stomach. Panting, she doubled over with exhaustion. 'What the hell?' she gasped. She addressed the beached figure, sodden and spitting seawater. 'Gil, what the hell were you doing?' Her strong legs buckled and she fell to her knees beside him, raising her head to me. 'Do *you* know?'

I looked at Gil. He turned over on his back. He was breathing more easily now, but his bloodshot eyes held a plea. I gave him the tiniest nod of reassurance. My rage was gone, dissipated in those few minutes when I'd thought he was going to commit suicide. There was no way I was going to out him. Let him do it, when he was ready.

I turned back to Miranda. I'd loved her for years but now for the first time I *liked* her. 'All I know is,' I said, 'you were wrong. You're are one *magnificent* swimmer.'

40

An End to Dickishness

I didn't know what to do with myself after that. The shock of what Gil had done – what he'd *nearly* done – had shaken me out of my dickishness. In all the years I'd been bullied, I'd never once thought about ending it all. The enormity of it was overwhelming, and it had given me back my lost perspective. I was done being a dick. I was done with being President Lincoln. I was back to being Link.

I wanted to go back to camp, light the fire in its old hearth on the dunes and tell everyone that it was all over – the tributes, the numbering system, the concubines.

But I couldn't quite process everything. I felt sick, and shaky, and dizzy. I had to take a breath, be on my own for a bit. Miranda took Gil back to Bikini Bottom, but I wandered away, a bit dazed. Suddenly I was deathly tired. I hadn't slept the night before, as I'd spent half of it looking at Miranda and coming to terms with the reality of falling out of love, and the other half trying to get comfortable on the stone floor of the

White House. I went back and lit the fire in the chimney, as it was already laid there, and put a bunch of fishes on the grill. Despite the tempest going on in my brain, the sudden change in me, I was mindful of my responsibilities. When the fishes were cooked I set them aside in the larder. It was suddenly very important that everyone got to eat. Everyone, including Flora and Ralph. Then I suddenly felt deathly tired, wrung out by the emotion of the morning. I collapsed on the bed like a felled tree. I must've slept.

When I woke up the sun was going down, and Wilson was watching over me. His bland charcoal face regarded me, but now he said nothing, absolutely nothing. We sat there, in a bizarre stare-out contest, while the sky turned pink outside, until suddenly the room grew dark, not with night, but a shadow blocking the entrance.

It was Flora.

I'd totally forgotten about her, that yesterday she'd agreed to come and serve me and I'd sent her away.

She walked right into the cave and stood over me.

She was wearing her Motörhead vest, and on her bottom half she was wearing nothing but a pair of whitish underwear. She looked painfully thin now, and she had one of those thigh gaps that too-thin girls have. I was horrified. What had I done? What kind of monster starves a girl because she won't do what he wants? I wanted to offer her the food I'd cooked earlier right away, but before I could speak she said: 'I came to give you a message.'

She turned around like she was going to moon me, but on

the back of her underwear she'd written in Gil's biro: KISS
MY ARSE

Then she turned back. 'You know what? You've turned
into Seb, Seb how he was at Osney. And you're *worse*,
because you should know what it feels like to be *you*. I'd
rather eat Bucket berries for eternity than eat the fanciest
dinner in the world with *you*. Also –' Flora took a breath –
'BorntoFlyYourSongBeyondtheSeaNightswimmingSaveItfora
RainyDayWhiteRabbitNullainMundoPaxSincera.'

I was still a bit groggy, and genuinely didn't know what
she'd just said. 'What?'

'My eight favourite songs. My Desert Island Discs. You
thought you knew, but you didn't have a clue. You see? Not
one metal song, not one Emo song.' She put her hands on her
narrow hips. 'You thought you had me all figured out. But you
didn't know me at all. You made all your assumptions about
me because of the way I looked: the pink hair, the tattoo, the
nose ring. You thought you knew me, but you didn't. You were
wrong, and now you're wronger than ever, the wrongest person
on this island. You're all interested in me because I'm suddenly
slim and blonde and I fit some sort of Miranda Pencroft-clone
picture of what you find attractive. And instead of actually,
you know, *talking* to women to get them to like you, the only
way you can get them to hang out with you is to enslave them
in return for food. You're the original caveman, so you should
stay in here where you belong.'

She turned to go, but at the entrance of the cave she turned
back. The sun was setting so she was almost a silhouette. The
sky behind her was the same pink and purple as her hair

had once been. 'You know what? Abraham Lincoln would be *ashamed* of you.'

It was a blow, a blow as real as the punch Seb had thrown when he'd broken my tooth. When she'd gone my forehead started to crinkle up in a way that was strange yet familiar. My Wi-Fi forehead, the sure sign of tears. I hadn't had it since I'd taken control of the island.

I sat for a long, long time looking at Wilson. He looked back at me with a reproachful expression. It grew darker outside. Flora had articulated exactly what I'd been feeling all afternoon. She was right. I had turned into Seb. And for the first time ever, I understood him. Power was heady, seductive. I'd been drunk on it. The kicker had been what she'd said about Lincoln, my hero and namesake. She was right. He'd be ashamed of the kind of power I'd yielded. He was the freer of slaves, I was an enslaver. Eventually I said to Wilson, 'OK, OK.' I went to my larder, grabbed all the fishes I'd cooked and wrapped them in leaves.

Then I went to find Flora.

41

The View from the Middle of Nowhere

Flora was beyond the waterfall on the overhang above the lake, staring at the water as if she could will the fish out of the rapids and into her mouth. She was wearing her ripped denim shorts again. Through the faded black Motörhead vest you could see the knobbles of her spine. Her hair was longer and pale blonde, all traces of pink and purple now leached out by the sun. She'd been right. From the back she could have been Miranda now.

I went to sit down beside her. She didn't look at me. I laid the fishes-in-leaves across her ripped-denim thighs. The fish were dead-eyed, crispy-skinned and smelled deliciously of Ralph's mountain thyme. They were a truce, an apology and possibly the weirdest tribute in history.

She tore into the fishes and ate every scrap, like Gollum in *Lord of the Rings*, tail, eyes, everything. She must have been starving. I felt way worse than I've ever felt in my life.

'Parlay?' I said, like we were the Swallows and the Amazons.

She looked at me, all fishy-faced. Her cheeks were still full of food, there was fish all over her lips and juice running down her chin. She paused just long enough in her tearing and gobbling to flick me one long middle finger.

I deserved that – and more. I tried to explain. 'I'd been at the bottom of the pyramid for so long, that when I found myself at the top, I kinda . . . well, I went crazy with it.'

She carried on eating, as if I wasn't there.

'It's no excuse,' I said, making excuses, 'but I'd had three whole years of shit at Osney. From everyone.' I could hear myself whining – it was disgusting. 'Believe me, I hate myself right now more than you could ever hate me. I promise you, hand on . . .' I thought quickly, 'that Bible we found, that I will never, *ever*, treat anyone like that again, no matter what I do in life, no matter what my job is.'

She slowed her eating, stopped. She slid her eyes sideways to look at me. 'Promise?' she asked, mouth half full. There was all this shit in her teeth, but she looked drop-dead beautiful.

'Promise.'

She held out her hand. It was disgusting, covered in fish juice and scales. 'Shake on it.'

I took the hand and she ground all the mess into my palm. I deserved it. I started to smile too.

'I'm *really* sorry.'

'For the starvation?'

'Of course for that. I won't *ever* forgive myself for that.' It was true. I'd punished her for questioning me, for insurrection, for having a voice. 'But also for judging you. But you gotta admit – the tattoo, the vest. You were wearing all the signs.'

'So were you. The glasses et cetera. Now look at you – you're Harry Styles. I guess none of us are what we appear.'

I looked down, embarrassed by what I guessed was a compliment, and caught sight of her wrist, and her tattoo. I turned the hand over so I could see it properly. 'Why the ace of spades?'

'I had it done after I did the Osney Dash, when the school decided I was an Eleven. The elevens were the lowest of the low – until you came along.'

'You're welcome.'

She grinned. 'I didn't like that the school thought they could put a number on me, so I put one on myself. The ace of spades is the highest card of the pack. It even trumps all the other aces.'

I nodded. 'And your parents let you?'

'No. They didn't know about it, and when they found out they did their nut. They're pretty conventional. Which explains me, I suppose.'

'What do they do?'

'Both academics. History faculty. I wouldn't be anywhere near Osney School if it wasn't a freebie for the kids of the dons.'

'Me either. Mine are Behavioural Science.'

She nodded. 'Hey, don't you think it's weird that Osney admits the kids of academics when it's the least academic school ever?'

'Very weird. But it's historical, and exclusive, and prestigious, I guess.'

'Hmmm. I suppose we are supposed to be making those famous old school ties. But I can't imagine smoking a cigar in a London club with Seb in ten years' time. Can you?'

'*Christ* no.'

'I'd much rather go to Oxford High. Where I could just be Flora.'

'Me too.'

'And you could be Lincoln.'

'Actually,' I said, making a decision, 'it's Link.'

'As in Zelda?'

'Yes. It's what my parents call me.'

'And your friends?'

'Don't have any. Just my parents. They're the only ones who know that name.' I looked at her, and she was looking back at me with a half-smile, squinting against the sun. 'And now you of course.'

'Are we becoming friends?'

'Well, that's up to you. It's not the best start to a friendship, a week of starvation. It depends if you can forgive me.'

She looked serious. 'It was a shitty thing to do. But everyone deserves a second chance.'

'Good,' I said. 'But you have to bear with me. I'm not really sure how to talk to people. That is, I wasn't used to talking to people, on account of being home-schooled. That's why I bombarded you with trivia. It's the kind of thing I collect, but I don't really know how to process it. And as you said, it can be kinda annoying.'

'A *little* bit annoying,' she said. 'I only said that people who are bullied aren't necessarily nice people, just because they're victims.' I remembered when she'd first said that, in the plane at twilight, and how I'd thought her unfair. Now I couldn't fault her. Look how I'd turned out on the island.

'But I didn't mean to imply that it was *your fault* you were being bullied,' Flora went on. 'That was a dumb thing to say. Total victim shaming. They started on you at Osney before you even opened your mouth. Just for being different. But I should have had your back. Because I'm different too.'

She squeezed my hand, and that's when I realised a weird thing. All this time I'd been holding onto her hand. It felt nice, and right, like I could leave my hand lying in her fishy one forever, a million miles away from the awkward bumpy kiss I'd shared with Miranda. But I thought she might be beginning to feel uncomfortable, so it was me who pulled away. I made a joke of it. 'Better be careful,' I said, letting go her hand and jerking my head towards the nearest palm tree, where the inevitable pair of green gonads hung hiding their cameras. 'They'll think we're coupling up.'

She looked at them too and screwed up her face. 'Yeah. About that –' she looked back at me – 'I think you got it wrong.'

This hadn't been said to me for such a long time I was taken aback. President Lincoln would have devised some sort of punishment. Link took it better.

'How d'you mean?'

'I don't think it's *Love Island*. I think it's *Treasure Island*.'

'*Treasure Island*?'

'Yes. You've read every book about desert islands. You must know that one.'

She was teasing me, and I really didn't mind it. 'Of course.'

'So . . .' she made that winding-up motion with her hand that people make when they want you to catch up with them, 'a mysterious island, buried treasure, X marks the spot . . .'

'So the cameras . . .' I began.

'Oh, it's being filmed for sure,' she said. 'And probably televised. But I think the winners aren't the ones who couple up. The winners are the ones who find the treasure.'

It had honestly never occurred to me that that might be the deal on this island, and I felt dumber than I've ever felt in my life. I'd been so busy making president that I had missed the one thing you would associate with a mysterious island. Treasure. 'What makes you think that?'

'Clues,' she said. 'Weird stuff. It's not just a reality TV show, a documentary where they just let stuff play out naturally. We're being manipulated. For one thing, I'm sure we were . . . somehow . . . *selected*.'

'How d'you mean?'

'Well, look at us. I wasn't entirely joking when I named us the Breakfast Club. That's exactly what we are.'

I didn't know the movie well enough. 'I'm sorry, but you're gonna have to explain.'

'In *The Breakfast Club* this group of kids gets detention before school. But the thing about it is, there's *one* of each type: a Cheerleader, a Jock, a Rebel, an Emo and,' she said, looking at me pointedly, 'a Nerd. You're not telling me we are the *only* students from Osney who applied to summer camp.'

'I guess not.'

'I *know* not.'

'How d'you know?'

'Smith and Fry,' she said briefly.

For a moment I didn't know who she meant. Then I

290

remembered. Her two big buddies from Osney. Altounyan, Smith and Fry, the seventies folk band. They always went around together in a trio of Elevens, absolutely everywhere. The Three Amigos.

'Didn't they want to come?'

'That's just it. They *did* want to come. They signed up a year ago, when we first got the letters at school. They paid the deposit, they paid the balance. But when the rest of us got to LAX, they weren't there.'

I thought about this. 'Didn't you text them?'

'Yes. We've got a WhatsApp group.' Of course they did. 'And I emailed. And then I even called them, even though it murdered my minutes, because I thought they'd missed the flight.'

'And?'

'No replies at all. Nada. And voicemail.'

That did seem weird. 'They can't have *both* missed the flight.'

'No. I'm sure they didn't. I've been thinking about it. I think they were deselected at the last minute.'

'*Deselected?*'

'Yes. They were never meant to come.'

'But . . . *why?*'

'Firstly, they didn't need three of us. We are the same in our tastes, outlook, everything. They didn't need another one of me for this little game.'

I didn't know how to put this without seeming to diss her. 'But, why . . .'

'Why me and not them?' She was smiling, so I don't think she was mad at me.

'Well . . . yes.'

'I've been thinking about this. I think it's to do with health reasons. Smith is asthmatic, quite badly. She never goes anywhere without her inhaler. That thing is like crack to her.' I'd actually seen Smith, in the silver-lined halls of Osney, sucking on it like it was going out of fashion. 'And Fry?'

'Diabetic,' she said briefly. 'And not type two either. The hardcore one. He has an insulin pump attached to his stomach. He mainlines the stuff.' She shrugged. 'They're both absolutely fine of course. But not here. You can't exactly get refills, can you, however good a pharmacist Ralph is?'

She was right. If this was a video game Flora would have a big green bar full up with health. She was ready to play. Or she had been, until I drained her bar right to the bottom with my shitty starvation programme. But now wasn't the time for breast-beating. I felt we were getting somewhere.

'We've been chosen, like I said. Specifically *us*. To take part in this treasure hunt. And there's other stuff too.'

'Like what?'

'The goats,' she said. 'We've hunted every day, and we've only ever caught male goats. I've never even *seen* a female. I don't think there are any on the island. And that's impossible, because how would they breed? Maybe they are designed to run out after a finite time.'

I digested this for a moment.

'That's not all. Your seat number, remember? It was too high. That's why I went back to the plane. You did too.'

'Why didn't you tell me this that night?'

She looked at me directly in the light of the setting sun. 'We weren't friends then. I don't know what it means, but it means something. And I don't think we have long left. I think by the time term starts we'll be off this island. But I think if we can just put together all the clues we could find the treasure first.'

I looked out across the lake. The sun was an enormous gold coin sinking into a lake of molten gold. Treasure. My eyes filled with dollar signs. Money meant freedom. If I had money I wouldn't even have to work. I could write, invent, code computer games. I'd never have to talk to another person if I didn't choose to. I could stay in my room like Howard Hughes. Well, not quite like Howard Hughes; I didn't want to leave bottles of pee outside my door, but I could be as isolated as I wanted, as isolated as I was when I was home-schooled, just seeing my parents. But as the sun sank further and the gold disc melted away in the horizon, I had a revelation. I didn't want that. I wanted *this*. I wanted to sit shooting the breeze with a friend. I would help Flora win if she wanted to, possibly the first disinterested act of my life. I thought about what she'd said, that being bullied doesn't mean you're a nice person. I'd been selfish, probably all my life. I breathed out slowly.

'OK,' I said, a word I'd hardly used on the island. 'So what do we do?'

'Treasure Hunt page one,' she said. 'We make a map.'

'How?'

'I thought we'd go up the mountain and look down,' she grinned again. 'Sorry. Monte Cristo.'

She was taking the piss again; and again, I didn't mind. 'Shall we go up in the morning?'

She stood up. 'No. Let's go now.'

293

I stood up and followed her. I didn't want to say that we wouldn't see much from the mountaintop at this time in the evening. After all, she was in charge.

An hour, maybe two hours, later, we were at the top of Monte Cristo, at the cairn I'd made on my very first day, the place where I'd calculated the latitude and longitude of the island as a way to impress Seb. As I'd feared, it was way too dark to see anything below. Above, though, was a different matter.

We lay on our backs on the mountaintop, side by side. We stayed silent for a little while, feeling the sand on our backs, the warmth of our hands almost, *almost* touching, the cool of the night at our fronts. I wanted, so badly, to take Flora's hand again, but I didn't quite have the courage. It seemed an enormous step, something that I could never take back. The stars were super bright, and super close, and now more familiar. I could distinguish some shapes like the Big Dipper and the Bear.

'The view from the middle of nowhere,' Flora said.

After a little while I replied, 'You know, there actually *is* a middle of nowhere? It's the Oceanic Pole of Inaccessibility, and it's called Point Nemo.'

'Oh yeah?' Her voice sounded sleepy.

'It's the furthest point that man can get from any other human in the world. And at certain times of day on Point Nemo, you are closer to the astronauts in the International Space Station than to anyone else on earth.'

She let that sink in, and then she said, 'Can't quite break the habit of imparting knowledge, can you?' But she said it fondly, with a smile in her voice.

294

Now I could take it. Now I knew that banter was what friends did. 'Aw, come on. That's quite a good fact, you gotta admit. Those Rocket Men, way up there at the Final Frontier, might be our nearest neighbours.'

'OK. I'll give you that one. But that doesn't mean that –'

I sat up suddenly.

'What?' she said.

'Nemo,' I said. 'That's it!'

'What, the fish? From the movie?'

'No,' I said. 'Before that. *Captain* Nemo. From Jules Verne. *The Mysterious Island.*' I head-palmed myself. 'I'm an idiot.' I felt like the stars were rushing down on me, colliding in my head. 'The polar bear from *Lost*. Friday's footprint in the sand. Mr Kurtz in the heart of the darkness. I was on the wrong books all the time. It was Captain Nemo all along.'

Flora sat up too. 'What the hell are you talking about? Go back. *What* about Captain Nemo?'

'*Nemo* means nobody in Latin. On the Mysterious Island there was supposed to be nobody there, nobody but the castaways. But Captain Nemo was there all the time, and only revealed himself at the end. Who took my tooth out?' I remembered the shadowy white figure, the taste of rubber in my mouth, my numbed face in the morning.

'You're scaring me.'

'I'm kinda scaring myself.' I put a hand on my pounding heart. 'They didn't just leave the cameras and go. Someone else is on the island with us.'

42

X Marks the Spot

I woke first, with the dawn. The sleeping Flora looked beautiful, her hair pink again with the sunrise. I wondered what the hell I'd ever seen in Miranda.

Because we'd talked till pretty late, I let Flora sleep, but I thought I'd help by making a head start on the map. I took the folded menu from under her hand and found Gil's pen still in my pocket. I looked down at the island, Lincoln Island, in the rising sun. It was beautiful too.

I was reminded of the very first day I'd washed up here, when I'd thought I was on my own. Then, it was my island. Now, it belonged to all of us. Through the haze bright parakeets rose, and unseen creatures chattered in the jade green canopy of the trees. Above all the vegetation stood the tall palms, with the green gonads dangling beneath. Now I knew what they were I could see how unnatural they looked, like trees on a film set. What else had been created for our stay here? Perhaps drawing the map would tell me.

I smoothed out the menu, glancing at the front of it. *Oceanic Airlines*, printed in gold, and then a list of all the food we'd never gotten, the food that wasn't even in the wreckage. I turned the menu over to the blank side and began to draw.

I drew the familiar Pac-Man shape, round with a big triangular bay like an open mouth, and the Blue Lagoon as the eye. I drew where Monte Cristo would be, where I was standing now, then moved my eye to the forest area below me on the slopes. I'd never looked at the island from this vantage point at sunrise before. The morning after the night I'd been up here with Seb there had been that tempest and we'd run down in a mudslide in an attempt to stay ahead of the rain. I'd never had a chance to stand and stare, and that's probably why I'd missed it.

The rising sun crept over the canopy, and when it hit a certain height I saw it at last, something that had been there all the time, as plain as the nose on your face. Two golden pathways appeared, and brightened, leading through the trees and converging on each other at a crossroads. 'You've GOT to be kidding me,' I exclaimed.

Flora woke up at the sound. 'What's going on?' she said huskily.

I went to her, held out a hand and hauled her to her feet. Yawning, she stumbled over to the view with me. 'Look!'

She shielded her half-closed eyes with her free hand and followed my pointing finger with her gaze, towards the two sandy paths crossing through the woodland, intersecting at the middle in a huge golden X.

Flora's eyes snapped wide open. 'X marks the spot,' she breathed.

'Yup,' I said grimly. 'Let's go.'

We got down the mountain possibly even quicker than I'd done it with Seb. We scrambled headlong with very little regard for our own safety, desperate to get to the jungle. Very soon we were standing on one of the paths. It didn't look particularly man-made, it wasn't paved or tarmac'd – up close it was sandy and cobbled with pebbles and tussocks of tough seagrass. But it led straight into the tree cover and we walked into the dark until we met the other path coming the other way. The canopy was so dense there that we would never have seen the X in a million years without going up the mountain – there was no sense of perspective from the ground. The sun pierced through the leaves here and there like a knife strike.

At the clearing – right in the middle of the X – we stopped. Breathing hard, I turned around a full 360 degrees. There, towering above the tree cover, was a pair of palm trees, and below their glossy, too-green leaves, hung a single green gonad. Not two. One. 'No way.'

'What?'

'This is where I shot down the green gonad,' I said. 'Look.' At one end of the clearing was the makeshift crossbow I'd made, now worse for wear and a little overgrown.

'So you spent a good chunk of time here? Right in the middle of the X?' asked Flora.

'Yes. There's nothing here, I can tell you.' I thought of the hours I'd spent here, shooting at Wilson and picking up the rocks from the undergrowth. I knew this clearing pretty well, and there was absolutely nothing to get excited about.

'Well, of course,' she said, 'it's not going to be *above* ground, is it? Whoever heard of a treasure chest just sitting around in broad daylight? We have to dig.'

She was right. 'Where shall we start?'

She pointed to the very centre of the clearing. 'In the middle of the X of course.'

We walked over and crouched down, clearing the sand with our hands. The ground seemed pretty solid. 'We've nothing to dig with,' I said. 'We could go back to camp, get the axes.' I suggested it reluctantly.

'No,' said Flora. 'This is *our* thing.'

It felt good – the first time ever, for me, that I'd been a part of a joint enterprise.

'Why don't we use that?' she pointed. I was still carrying my staff. I hadn't even noticed that I'd brought it down the mountain – I was so used to carrying it now it had become a part of me. I looked from it to Flora and back again. It was my badge of office, the sceptre of this isle. But we needed something solid to break the ground. 'OK,' I said.

For the rest of the morning we dug, taking turns. One of us would break the impacted sand with the staff and the other would clear the loose sand away until a little mountain range of mounds stood sentinel around the deepening hole. We took turns. We didn't talk a lot. For one thing it was hard work, because the sand was pretty well damped down, and for another it was getting pretty hot as we got to the middle of the morning, even though we were under a lot of tree cover. The sand-clearing one would say 'Anything?' and the digging one would say, 'Not yet.' We were about a foot down when it began to occur to me that this might be a giant waste of time. Just because two pathways converged in the forest making an X shape, that didn't mean there would necessarily be anything here. What had seemed so magical at sunrise, the golden paths suddenly appearing in the undergrowth, now seemed totally ordinary. I began to feel pretty dumb. I was wondering if Flora felt the same, and whether I should suggest that we stop, when the worst happened. My staff snapped in two.

As I was leaning on it at the time, I ended up eating sand. I picked myself up out of the hole, half a staff in each hand, feeling more shaken than I liked to admit.

Flora looked at me, her mouth a round O. I realised then what a dictator I'd been – if someone had broken my staff two days ago, I'd've bust a gut. Her reaction was a reality check. I forced myself to smile. "'I'll break my staff. Bury it certain fathoms in the earth.'"

'If you say so, Prospero.' I guess she'd revised too.

'Yeah. Here.' I threw her one of the bits of staff, giving half of my power away without a thought. For a non-sporty person she caught it pretty neatly, and we both began to dig, side by side. The breaking of the staff made me want to go on, not give up. Otherwise it had broken for nothing.

The sun moved round, our digging slowed, and it looked as if we really would have to give up. Flora was tiring, and I thought again with a jag of guilt how weak she must be after I'd damned near starved her. I was about to call time of death on our dig when I struck something that was not sand.

There was a metallic clang and a hollow echo.

We looked at each other. Eyes wide. Tiredness and hunger

and heat were suddenly forgotten. I brought my half-staff downward again, like Gandalf.

Boom.

As one, we threw away our mini staffs and fell to our knees. Now we dug like bunnies, using our fingers, scrabbling and throwing the dirt out behind us. Sweeping and clearing the sand, we could make out a dull metal surface. I ran my nails along a long ridge, met a corner and another ridge. Then another. Then a fourth. I said, trying to keep my voice level, 'It's a hatch.'

43

Numbers and Letters

'*Cool*,' said Flora. 'Let's jimmy it up. Can we get the sticks under it?'

I tried to get my fingertips under the edge, but it was shut fast. 'Nah. But there might be a handle, ya know, like a ring?'

'Let's clear it off completely, and see what we're dealing with.'

Moving backwards, we swept all the sand from the hatch. The metal was a dull bronze colour, brushed and matt, not shiny, but quite new-looking. My leg, as I shuffled backwards, grazed something painfully. I sat back heavily, squeezing my injured knee as a little bead of dark blood bubbled out. I suddenly thought of Ralph, the Hand of the King, who had been cast aside when he'd refused to get me Rocket leaves. He'd have had something to put on my knee. I remembered his face when he'd left my cave, and the thought of it made my stomach twist oddly. He probably wouldn't help me now – would probably stand by while I got infected and my leg fell off. I was so struck by the thought that I didn't bother to look at what had hurt me. But Flora did.

'Link,' she said, pointing. And I forgot all about Ralph.

Right in the middle of the hatch was a numerical keypad, like you'd have on a payphone – twelve square metal buttons configured like this:

123

456

789

*0#

Flora and I both hunkered down on our stomachs, faces close together, peering at the keypad. 'No letters,' I said.

'There *are* some letters,' she said. She blew on the keypad and a little puff of sand rose up.

Etched into the corner of the keypad was a tiny monogram, like a logo. It was really small, so I got out of the way and let Flora look. However little I needed them, I did wear glasses, so her eyesight was bound to be better than mine.

'Can you make it out?'

'It looks like a T, a W and an R. No – a P.'

'TWP. What could it stand for?'

I thought of charades. T at the start of something was always the same word. '*The* something . . .'

'Wow, thanks. That really narrows it down.' She was teasing me again, but I was getting used to it.

'All right. Never mind that for now. We'll never guess it. Let's get started.'

'With what?'

'Cracking the code,' I said. 'There's obviously a numerical

entry code. And if we want to see what's below that hatch, then we have to figure out what it is.'

Flora put her chin on her hand. 'Better start tapping away,' she said. 'This could be a long old job.'

'No point,' I said. 'With a four-number pin, like you'd have at the ATM, there are ten thousand different combinations. It would take us a month to enter them.'

'We may have that long,' she said darkly.

'No,' I said, suddenly positive. 'This thing is coming to an end. I think we're meant to work it out. Everything on this island is by design, so the code is bound to be meaningful, not random. Look. We're even being watched right now.' I nodded up to the palm, where the remaining green gonad – Wilson's twin – observed us with its dark eye. 'This is all part of the entertainment.'

'No pressure,' said Flora through her teeth, waving at the green gonad with a fixed smile.

'All right. Where do we start?' I said, as much to myself as to her. 'Simon from *Alvin and the Chipmunks* always said that the first digit of a numerical code is likely to be a prime.'

'*Who* said *what* now?'

'Simon. From *Alvin and the Chipmunks*.'

'Was he the human?'

'No. Simon was, well, he was one of the chipmunks.' I smiled sheepishly. 'I always sorta liked Simon. He wore glasses. I identified. And,' I added, 'he was right. You got pin codes?'

'A few.'

'Do they start with prime numbers?'

'Actually, yes. And no disrespect to *Simon*, but I think we might be better off starting with a different nerd.'

'Who?'

'You,' she said simply.

'Me?'

'Yes. Whatever is weird about this place, it's to do with *you*.'

I wasn't expecting that. 'How d'you mean?'

Flora thought for a moment, struggling to express what she meant. 'If this was all a dream, it would be *your* dream,' she said. '23b was your seat; ours were all normal. So the number has to do with you. Try 23. That would be the obvious one.'

Fingers tingling with anticipation, I firmly pressed the 2 and the 3. We sat back expectantly. I don't know what I predicted, like some fanfare, or a blinding light around the edges of the hatch as it opened. But nothing happened.

'Hmm,' said Flora. 'Maybe you have to press another key. Like at the ATM when you have to press *enter*.'

I stared at the keypad. 'What would *enter* be? There's a star and a hash.'

'The hash,' she said. 'It tends to be the action key, like when you're topping up by phone.'

We both leaned in as I punched in 23#. Nothing.

'All right,' I said. 'Let's think about this logically. It was 23*b*. Maybe we need to include the letter somehow.'

'How?'

I remembered Mr Errington telling me about Pi, and numbers corresponding to letters. 'Ya know, like payphones have three letters on each number – ABC, DEF and so on. So maybe we have to press 23 and then 1, as that's where the **b** would be.'

'You mean 2,' she said.

'Huh?'

'2. 1 is blank. 2 is where the letters start.'

She tried it this time. Nothing.

'Oh,' I said. 'Except you'd have to press 2 twice, sorta scroll through the letters.'

She punched the numbers. I had much less hope that time. I knew we were reaching – knew it wouldn't work. And it didn't.

We sat back and looked at each other, bummed out but undefeated. 'Any other numbers that are significant to you?' Flora asked. 'Just to you?'

I thought right back, all the way back. I'd loved numbers since I was small. But I didn't think this was about toddler me, or grade school me. I thought this was about Osney. And on the very first day there I'd had chapter and verse, literally, from my mom. She'd told me to look in the Bible. *Blessed are the geek, for they shall inherit the earth.* Matthew, Chapter 5 verse 5.

'Try 55,' I said.

She did. 'Nothing.'

We put in 12, my number from the Osney Dash. 'Nope.'

'You talked to me about Lincoln,' prompted Flora, 'that first day.'

So we put in Lincoln's birthday, we put in 16 for the sixteenth president of the United States, and we put in 15/04/1865, the day he was shot at the Ford theatre, while everyone applauded the Sockdologiser and he literally died laughing. Then we put in Pi as far as I could remember it, using the trick Mr Errington had told me about.

'Hmmm,' said Flora, when all these had failed. 'Maybe it's

not about school. Maybe it's about the island. The Blue Lagoon, Bikini Bottom. Monte Cristo.'

Monte Cristo. My favourite book. The story of Edmond Dantes, a humble island prisoner who found priceless treasure on the island of Monte Cristo and became a count. Edmond Dantes, a prisoner who, for every day of his sentence on the Château d'If, was known not by name, but by a simple, two-digit number. 'I've got it,' I said suddenly. 'It's 34.'

Flora clapped her hands. 'The plane registration number,' she said. 'Good idea.'

'Wait, what?'

'The plane number. It was on the panel we salvaged.'

'God, you're absolutely right,' I said, going cold. 'Why didn't I see it before?'

'See what?'

'The plane. It was named after the initials and number of my favourite literary character. ED-34. Edmond Dantes, Prisoner 34, the hero of *The Count of Monte Cristo*. A guy who was stuck on an island. What the hell's going on here?' I asked, with a sudden shudder. 'I even brought the fricking book on the plane.'

'It can't be a coincidence,' said Flora. 'Punch it in.'

Shaking a little, sure this would work, I pressed the 3 and the 4 on the keypad. I was genuinely surprised when nothing happened.

Flora sat back. 'All right. If we accept it is a Monte Cristo reference, then are there other numbers in the book?'

'Yes,' I said slowly. 'Edmond Dantes has one friend in the world, when all the rest have abandoned and betrayed him, a friend who is a prisoner with him. The friend educates him and

307

shows him the ways of the island, and helps him escape and find the treasure.' I was struck, as I spoke, by the similarities in our situations.

'What's her number?'

'Him. He's an old priest, an Abbé.'

'Oh, thanks!'

I smiled. 'His cell is number twenty-seven.'

'Try it. Put them together.'

I punched in 3427, then 2734. Again, nothing.

I sat back on my ass, heavily. I'd been so convinced that the old Count of Monte Cristo was the answer. The coincidence of Edmond Dantes's prisoner number and the plane registration number had seemed so suggestive. My failure knocked the wind out of me. All my strength, all my leadership, melted away. I was fresh out of ideas. We'd tried everything. The sun was lowering and the dark of the jungle enveloped us, not sheltering now but forbidding. 'My mom used to watch this show when she was a kid in the States,' I said. 'It was called *Gilligan's Island*. You heard of it?'

Flora shook her head silently.

'It was about this boat that got shipwrecked and the passengers populated this island. It all centred round this goofball called Gilligan, who was the deck-hand on the ship. It was kinda funny, black and white, and it ran for three seasons. They were still showing reruns of it when I was a little kid.'

Flora wrapped her arms around her knees. 'What happened at the end?'

'They cancelled the show. So you never saw the characters getting off the island. In the world of the show, they're still there, stranded, frozen in TV limbo.'

I suddenly wanted my mom and dad very badly. Having hardly thought about my parents at all, in this *Lord of the Flies*, no-grown-ups universe we'd been living in, the thought that I might never see them again punched me in the stomach. It was unbearable. My Wi-Fi forehead began to crinkle up. 'What if it's not network TV? What if it's some horrible game on the dark net, and millions of people are watching us slowly die?' The idea of millions of nerds in bedrooms, somewhere beyond the sea, watching seven kids perish was a *Fortnite*-mare. Like in Neverland, we'd never grow up. 'What if we never get off here? What if the real treasure is being the last to survive?'

This was a true test of leadership. And it came. But it came from Flora. She stood up, tall and strong. She faced the green gonad squarely, raised her middle finger and flipped it off. Then she turned to me, hands on hips, all businesslike. 'Well, if that's the case, we just have to do the opposite of what they want. We have to believe we'll get off here. And I do believe it. I just think we need help.'

I looked up, squinting against the low sun. 'What kind of help?'

44

The Mission

The remains of the Breakfast Club were sitting around the empty fire pit, as if there was still a fire burning, a habit they couldn't break. With their matted caveman hair and tanned limbs they looked like those pictures of Early Man. They had clearly been attempting to light a fire, because in the middle of the charmed circle was a log, and a sharp stick, and a handful of seagrass. They'd been doing the old rubbing-sticks, the method I'd rejected on Day One. They all looked despondent, covered in ash, with paler stripes on their faces where they'd rubbed the sweat from their foreheads and cheeks. They were painted like savages. I suddenly felt paternal towards them, these Lost Boys and Girls. I'd given all of yesterday's food to Flora, and for all they knew she and I had disappeared. There had been no hunting and no fishing, and no fire. Some leader I was.

Suddenly unsure of my welcome, I walked into the middle of the circle and said, 'Hey, guys. Guess what.'

I got no further. Something barrelled into me and I was

thrown to the ground. Seb was on top of me, punching and kicking. Winded, I couldn't say anything else. I could hear Flora shouting *Stop! Listen, you have to listen.* But I wasn't at Osney any more. I was stronger – I had put on muscles on top of muscles on the island, and this time I could fight back. I fought furiously, pushing at Seb's bulk, rolling over and over in the smoky ash until we were covered. I don't know how it happened, but suddenly he was underneath me. But I hadn't counted on his fury. He put his knee to my chest and threw me off him – I flew through the fire circle and fell backwards. Seb was on top of me once more and he made a fist and held it high over my head, blotting out the fierce low sun. I'd been here before, and I knew this second punch would do far more than chip a tooth.

But a hand caught at his arm.

'No,' Gil said.

For a moment they looked at each other, Seb breathing heavily, Gil icy calm.

'Remember,' Gil said, 'you're being watched.' His voice had the strength of someone who didn't give a shit any more, someone who had been going to die and had then been rescued, and was damn well going to make the most of it. The feral light went out of Seb's eyes. He glanced up above Gil's head. The green gonads hung over the fire pit, watching every move. Seb uncurled his fist, Gil dropped his own hand, and suddenly there was a jumble of activity. The others crowded round.

'Where's our food?'

'Where's the fire?'

'Why did you leave us?'

I'd underestimated how much they needed me, how afraid they'd been. Adults had already been taken away from them, and I'd been the next best thing. I'd taken power, and with it had come a responsibility to them, a responsibility I'd now neglected.

'We thought you were dead.'

They all clung onto me, half embrace, half imprisonment. Ralph and Jun had my arms, and Miranda kept Flora, my only ally, at bay. Flora, in her weakened state, was not a match for Miranda's swimmer's body. Seb, still breathing heavily, paced in front of me like a tiger while Gil looked on.

I said, 'You need to come with us. We've found something. In the jungle, at the centre of the X.' I was making no sense.

'We aren't going anywhere with you,' said Seb. 'It's over.' I didn't need to ask what he meant.

'I have to go back there even if you don't,' I said, trying to keep my voice level.

'You're not going anywhere either. Not again. You'll stay right here, and hunt and fish, and light the fire, and . . . and . . . carry my bag!'

The atmosphere was so fraught, so dangerous, that no one laughed. No one pointed out that Seb didn't have a bag any more.

Miranda said exactly what Seb had been trying to say, with his punches and kicks and his clumsy words. 'We *need* you.'

I looked from one painted face to another. All that had separated them from savagery was hunger. The Breakfast Club indeed.

I had to turn them around. And I figured I knew how to

do it. Not with actions but with words. Words that were the hardest that I'd ever had to say. My thoughts flashed on all the petty humiliations: all the evil texts, all the bag-carrying and boot-cleaning and butt-licking I'd had to do at Osney. All the times I'd been picked last. All the times I'd had to say *OK*, that dreadful, submissive word, imported from America in the first place just like me, which had become my catchphrase.

I took a breath and said what I needed to say. 'But I need *you*.'

They all looked at me, hostile, savage, doubtful. No one believed me.

'It's a trick,' said Seb.

'No,' I said, 'I'll prove it.' I needed to give them a gift of good faith, just like the missionaries. When they discovered America they gave the natives gold and pearls. They were pretty useless gifts because the natives couldn't eat them or plant them, and they didn't know about trade or what treasure they held in their hands. But they were gifts of good faith.

'Let him go,' said Seb to Ralph and Jun. 'But watch him.'

Slowly, very slowly, like I was reaching for a gun, I took the lenses from around my neck, carefully lifting them, with the violin string they hung on. I stepped forward, very gently, as if the mere crack of a twig could break this fragile truce. Then I placed the string around Seb's bull-neck and centred the crystal lenses over his heart. It felt enormously symbolic. Seb, the Breaker of Glasses, was ceremoniously awarded the lenses. They hung round his neck like a mayoral chain.

'There.' I said. 'I have nothing. Now will you come?'

It was a giant gamble. I'd given away my staff, and now my glasses. I had neither the power of leadership, nor fire.

'Seb?'

I thought he was going to refuse, to stay here and set up camp with his lenses and his violin string, as useless in his hands as the pearls and sovereigns had been to the savages.

But then he said an amazing thing. 'OK.'

45

The Code

In the middle of the X, we all sat around the keypad as if it was the fire.

There'd been great excitement when Flora and I first showed the hatch to the Breakfast Club. They'd all gotten down on their knees as we had done, jostling each other, pressing multiple keys. I let them. If they cracked the code by accident, then so much the better. But I didn't think they would. I was beginning to see that nothing on this island was an accident. I let them play until they got bored, then I got them to sit down so we could get down to business.

'All right. Are there any numbers that you think might be significant, to you, to us as the Breakfast Club, to the island or the places on it, or to Osney School?'

'You could try all our Osney numbers,' suggested Miranda.

'Good,' I said, pointing at her like a teacher. 'What order?'

'Both ways. Top to bottom and bottom to top.' I did. We had a mini debate about how to express Seb's Quarters status, concluded that it would be a ¼, and punched the numbers. 14 1 1 1 11 11 12 descending from Seb to me, and 12 11 11 1 1 1 14 ascending from me to Seb. No dice.

'How about plane seat numbers?' This was Jun.

'Tried 'em.'

'No, we didn't,' said Flora. 'We only tried yours – 23b.'

This prompted lots of explanations about my unusual seat number, and Flora's and my secret expedition back to the plane. 'Let's try *all* the seat numbers,' said Gil.

'All right. That's 1 to 7, 23, 9 and 10. Was there a co-pilot?'

'No,' said Jun. 'Just a stewardess. She sat in a jump seat, remember?'

'Forget that one then. But we'd need the pilot's seat number. We didn't go in the cockpit the second time, did we?' I remembered the night, being afraid that a pilot's corpse, absent the time we'd looted the plane, would somehow have reappeared, rotting, to sit neatly and skeletally in his seat.

Flora shook her head. 'No. If the cockpit seats were numbered normally, he'd be number one.'

'Makes sense,' said Seb. 'He was in charge after all.'

'Yeah.' I agreed with him, anxious to keep the peace. 'But if the seats followed the numbering convention of *my* seat, he'd be number 21.'

'Ha,' said Miranda. 'Twenty One Pilots.'

Flora smiled at her. 'Link was convinced that was my favourite band,' she joked.

I checked suddenly. It wasn't her use of my private, friends-and-family-only name which had caught at my ear. It was something else. '*What* did you say?'

316

'I said you thought that Twenty One Pilots was my favourite band. When you asked me – you remember – what tracks I'd bring to a desert island.'

'You asked me about that too,' exclaimed Miranda.

'And me,' said Seb.

I started to tingle.

'Me too,' said Ralph.

'Me on the first night, by the violin fire,' said Jun.

'That's it,' I breathed. 'It's *music*.' The hairs rose on the back of my neck. 'It's *Desert Island Discs*. Your music choices – *our* music choices – will give us the numbers.'

'How do we get numbers from *music*?' asked Seb.

It was a reasonable question. 'Let's get a system going here,' I said. 'We're looking for numbers associated with all our tracks.'

The sun was sinking. Soon we wouldn't be able to see the keypad. I hadn't lit a fire; we'd be cold and hungry tonight. But no one seemed to care. We were all hanging on each other's words, taking turns to speak, working together. This, at last, was the teamwork we'd been so sorely missing till now.

'Let's take it in turns. Jun – you're the most musical; let's start with you. Any numbers connected with your tracks?' I smoothed out the menu with the Pac-Man map on it, ready, pen poised, to note down everyone's numbers.

'My issue might be that there are too many,' Jun said. 'If I was to choose eight tracks they'd all be classical, and classical music is often numbered. Bach, Beethoven, Haydn, all of them have what're called opus numbers. Mozart is all *K* then a number. Bach has got his own numbering system called BWV, Handel HWV and so on.'

'Just list them,' said Flora.

Jun screwed up her face. 'It's really tricky to think of eight,' she said. 'I'm trying to narrow it down . . . Well – there's Paganini Caprice, Opus No. 1.'

'That's easy,' said Flora, and I wrote down a 1.

'Then Tchaikovsky, Violin concerto in D Major. That's Opus 35. Concerto for two violins in D, Johann Sebastian Bach. Concerto in D Major, Ludwig van Beethoven. Concerto No. 5 in A Major, W.A. Mozart. Mendelssohn, Violin concerto in E Minor, Opus 64. The Bach Chaconne in D Minor . . . How many's that?'

I checked my list.

'Seven,' I said.

'Oh: and Vivaldi, Four Seasons.'

'Which bit?'

She half smiled and pointed up at the setting, but still fierce, sun. 'Summer of course.'

'Does it have a number?'

'Opus 8.'

I scribbled down 8, then stopped. 'All violin,' I said, surprised.

'I love listening to the music,' she said simply. 'I just didn't want to play her any more.'

'Didn't?' I remembered her performing Bach for me in Bikini Bottom by moonlight, playing a stick like it was a Stradivarius, eyes closed.

'Don't. I meant don't.'

'Never mind the therapy,' said Miranda. She turned to her friend. 'How do we narrow yours down?'

'Hold on,' Flora said. 'On *Desert Island Discs*, after the guest

318

has picked all their eight tracks, the host asks which one is their favourite, which one they couldn't live without.'

'That's true,' I said. 'They say, if a wave came and swept away seven of the records, which one would you run to save? They do it every single time. They even did it with the fake guy, Whitlohn.' Probably no one but Flora would know about Sir Harry Whitlohn, the fake castaway, with his own fake show and fake record choices, but there was no time to explain.

'Which one is your favourite? At least we know it has a number.'

'If I had to choose it would be the Vivaldi – Summer. It was one of my audition pieces for the Royal College of Music. I know every note backwards. I thought I'd never want to hear it again, but now I'd give anything to.'

Her eyes started to shimmer a bit the way people's eyes do when they're going to cry. I knew that look only too well so I circled the number 8 in Jun's column, and moved on quickly.

'What about you, Miranda? Give us just the song titles.'

Miranda didn't even have to think. She had her playlist all ready. '"Despacito". "Look at What You've Done". "Payphone". "Shake It Off". "There's Nothing Holdin' Me Back". "Attention". "Bang Bang". "Titanium".'

'No numbers,' I said.

We'd gone from one extreme to another – from too many numbers with Jun to none at all from Miranda. This was a pretty short-lived triumph as triumphs go. But I wasn't about to give up yet. I remembered what Flora had said about Twenty One Pilots. 'What about the bands?'

'Maroon 5,' said Miranda immediately. '"Payphone".'

319

'Of *course*.' I wrote down the number 5.

'How about you, Seb?'

He shrugged sulkily. 'I dunno.'

At first I thought he was pissed because he thought it was somehow not manly to like music – I remembered how aggressive he'd gotten when I'd asked him about music on the mountain. But then it dawned on me. He simply didn't know the names of anything he liked, and it was the fear of appearing stupid – the fear I'd played on so cruelly when we'd first got to the island and I'd blinded him with science – that was making him lash out. Once again, it was Gil who saved the day. He shut everyone up and sat with Seb patiently. He'd known what I had not – that there was nothing to be gained by being impatient with Seb. He understood enough of his friend's character to know that if he was prodded he would just flare up with anger or retreat into his shell, like a creature living in a conch. I thought, looking at Gil, *That's* leadership.

'Right,' said Gil gently, 'let's go through some. What do you remember hearing that you've liked? Think about films, ads, TV shows?'

Seb cleared his throat. 'I . . . I like that one from *The Champions League*. It sort of builds up.'

'Builds up how?' asked Miranda, rubbing his shoulder, kindly, fondly, like they'd never broken up.

Encouraged, Sebastian Loam actually broke into song – of a sort. 'It goes, duh-duh-duh-duh, duh-duh-duh-duh, duh-duh-duh-duh and then . . . Bang! There's suddenly lots of singing, which sounds like shouting.'

'I know it!' exclaimed Jun excitedly. 'It's "Zadok the Priest". George Frideric Handel.'

'Excellent.' I said. 'What's the number?' I looked at her, biro poised.

She shrugged '*I* don't know. I haven't committed *every* opus number ever to memory. I'm not some freaky genius. I only know the violin pieces because I kept seeing them on the music stand.'

It went on like that. We progressed from That One From *The Champions League* to That One From That Boxing Film ('Eye of the Tiger') That One From The Olympics ('Chariots of Fire') That One From *Match of the Day* ('Life of Riley') That Katy Perry One about Basketball ('Swish Swish') That One They Always Sing at Liverpool ('You'll Never Walk Alone') and That One From The Rugby ('Swing Low, Sweet Chariot'). None of them had a number.

'Any more?' I asked, heart sinking with the sun.

'There's one that I really like . . .'

We all leaned in expectantly.

'But I don't know the name of it.'

We all sat back.

'It's That One From FIFA.'

With immense patience, I said kindly: 'We're going to need a little more, champ.'

He looked at his hands. 'It goes woo-hoo,' he said shamefacedly.

I could barely hear him. 'What?'

He put his hands to his mouth and hollered through the jungle like Tarzan. 'WOO-HOO!'

The sound, savage but triumphant, echoed back and sent colourful birds scattering from the trees.

We all recognised it.

'I know it!'

'So do I!'

'Me too.'

'But what's it *called*?'

'I know,' said Gil quietly.

We all shut the hell up.

'It's my favourite too,' he said a little too loudly, defiant. 'It's by Blur.' He looked around. 'It's called "Song 2".'

We all fist-pumped. 'Yes!' I said. 'Terrific.' I wrote down the number 2. 'Gil?'

'Same for me,' said Gil quietly,

'Huh?' I looked up, pen poised. In the gloom it was kinda hard to see his expression.

'I'll have what he's having,' he said, making a joke of it. 'I told you, it's my favourite.'

I didn't question further – I didn't want to make him uncomfortable. It struck me then that Gil was the only one on the island whom I'd never asked about his Desert Island Discs. It turned out I hadn't needed to. He just wanted to like what Seb liked. I admired Gil's particular brand of devotion, and I had no wish to mock it. 'Well, that sure makes things faster,' I said, writing down another 2 before anyone could query it. 'So far we've got 8, 5, 2, 2. Ralph?'

'"Traktor". "Wot Do You Call It". "I Luv U". "P's & Q's". "Street Fighter". "Duppy". "On a Mission". "Man Don't Care".'

'No numbers again,' said Miranda.

'Wait,' said Ralph. 'Does it have to be just *one* number?'

'How d'you mean?'

'Like a *single* number. Or can it be two digits?'

I looked at Flora. We shrugged. 'I guess. There are no rules. We're making this stuff up as we go along.'

'Well, "Traktor" is by Wretch 32.'

'Good enough,' I said. 'Who's next?'

'What about you?' said Flora.

By now I knew mine very well. I'd lived them, subconsciously, all those days on the island. But there was one obvious contender which had the most relevance to our situation. We were all, after all from Osney School. 'It's the Toppers Song. It was the first sound I made on this island.'

Seb gave a short laugh, but it wasn't an unkind sound. 'I wouldn't have picked you for a fan of the Toppers Song,' he said, the nearest he'd ever come to acknowledging what I'd endured at Osney.

'I loved the tune before,' I said. 'I love it still, despite the words, not because of them.' I turned to Jun. 'It's "Ode to Joy", from Beethoven's Ninth Symphony, but I don't know the opus number.'

'Then 9 will have to do.'

I wrote down the number 9. 'Last but not least,' I said, 'Flora, I know you screamed them at me once.' Now I could joke about that night. 'But you're gonna have to run them past me again.'

She counted them out on her fingers, with no hesitation. '"Your Song". "Beyond the Sea". "Born to Fly". "Nightswimming". "Save it for a Rainy Day". "White Rabbit". And this Vivaldi thing –' she looked at Jun – 'called "Nulla in Mundo Pax Sincera".'

'That's only seven.'

'Yes.' She looked at her eighth finger. 'There was one, one I didn't tell you about when I yelled at you. I thought you'd be all smug, thinking you were right about me.' She smiled sheepishly. 'Number eight is "Ace of Spades", by Motörhead.'

'Hmm.' I read them back. 'No numbers.'

She shook her head. 'None.'

'Does any of that Latin mean numbers? The Vivaldi one?'

'No. It means there is no peace in this world without bitterness.'

I thought of our time on the island. 'You can say that again. What about the bands? Any numbers?'

'Elton John. Bobby Darin. Sara Evans. R.E.M. Motörhead. The Jayhawks. Jefferson Airplane. Vivaldi.'

'Damn.' We all sat there dejected.

Everyone except Seb.

He spoke up. 'You're kidding, aren't you? It's right under your noses.'

'Where?'

'There.' He crossed the sacred circle, grabbed Flora's hand and turned it wrist upward.

And there it was. Even in the dusk we could all see it. A number she identified with so strongly that she'd had it indelibly inked on her skin. The ace of spades.

One.

I could've kissed him. 'Seb, you're a *genius*,' I said, meaning it. He smiled, a really nice, shy smile, which told me he'd never been called that before. 'Right, now we're cooking with gas.' I added a 1 to the list. 'Let's put 'em in.'

'Wait,' said Flora. 'What order?'

I stopped in my tracks.

'You said there were ten thousand permutations of a four-digit pin code. Well, we've got seven numbers here. That's a hell of a lot more.'

I sat back. 'You're right. That's a lot of choices.'

'No,' Gil said slowly, 'only two. There are two ways of sorting ourselves. One our old leader decided. One our new leader decided.' He explained. 'Mr Llewellyn, via the Osney Dash, put us in an order. Then, on the island, Lincoln decided it. Our old island of Osney, Our new island of Lincoln. Old world or new?'

This was one decision that I really couldn't make. 'Up to you guys.'

'Well, we're on the island now,' said Ralph. 'New.'

Jun shrugged. 'Sure.'

Miranda nodded. 'New.'

'Seb?'

He gave a short nod.

'Gil?'

'Same.'

It was time. If the hatch didn't open now we had nothing. No fire and no food, and I would have no trust left in me. I'd given away my lenses and my fishing lines. We'd be in a chaos of different factions – our new-found camaraderie shattered by failure.

My hand was actually shaking as I keyed in the numbers, in the order I'd imposed on the island. Me, Ralph, Miranda, Jun, Flora, Gil and last of all Seb. 9 for me, 32 for Ralph, 5 for Miranda, 8 for Jun, 1 for Flora, 2 for Gil and 2 for Seb. 93258122.

I pushed in the last number, and sat back. We all did. For that one moment, we were a perfect team. We all stared at the hatch, afraid of something happening, then, as the seconds ticked past, afraid of nothing happening.

But something did happen.

A line of light appeared, bright as a knife-edge in the gloom, then another, then another, until three sides of the hatch were illuminated. Then the line of light became a slab, then a bar, then a rectangle, fattening to a square, as the hatch opened and a shaft of light reached up to the sky.

46

The Bunker

We stood up, one by one, and walked forward. For a time it was hard to see down the hatch as the light was so bright, and I hadn't fully realised how dark the forest had gotten. But after a couple of seconds shapes began to resolve below, and I could see the top few steps of one of those metal fire-escape staircases.

Now I was afraid, properly afraid. But I knew what I had to do. I'd held myself up as a leader for so long. I'd reaped all the rewards, now it was time to pay the price. A true leader had to be the first one in attack, the last one in retreat.

Very well then. I turned my back on the hatch and swung myself down onto the ladder.

Once I got down there it actually wasn't particularly bright. My eyes soon adjusted and I could see exactly where I was. It was a control room with a bank of monitors. And it was deserted. No backroom minions working away, no Wizard behind the curtain. No one. Beyond the monitors was a door. It was closed but from around the edges came not just more light, but a slight electrical humming of some sort of air con. It bore a sign with the same TWP icon that we'd seen on the metal hatch, but this time there were some words:

THE WHITLOHN PROJECT
AUTHORISED PERSONNEL ONLY

That's when I knew.

'Sonofabitch,' I breathed.

The others had followed, one by one. Miranda was craning over my shoulder. '"TWP",' she read. '"The Whitlohn Project". What does it mean?'

'It means,' I said grimly, 'that the whole thing is a fake.'

Flora gave a low whistle. 'Whitlohn,' she said. 'Cheeky bastards.'

'What the hell are you talking about?' asked Miranda testily.

I didn't answer. I put my hand out to open the door, ready to tear down the curtain and confront the Wizard. Then, from behind me, Seb shouted, 'Look!'

Starved of screens for a whole three months, he was staring at the monitors like a moth glued to a light bulb, and pointing.

I turned away from the door, from the immense practical joke that'd been played on us. I went over to the monitors and watched the cameras flicking between places, hunting us. There was even a camera trained at the top of Monte Cristo. As we watched, all the screens flicked onto the same picture. One by one, they all became the infrared image of a dark clearing at the crossroads of two paths. All were trained on the centre of the X, and the gaping square of light that was the hatch. On the screen a digital readout said: **Camera X, Whitlohn HQ.** I watched the monitors that were watching us. It was a thoroughly uncomfortable feeling.

'Lincoln,' said Jun, tugging my arm. I turned to look at her, but she didn't meet my gaze, her eyes fixed instead on what she'd seen.

I followed her gaze. She alone wasn't looking at the monitors, but down at the control console. There stood the most innocent and at the same time the most menacing thing in the world.

A cup of tea, freshly brewed, a strong red colour, steaming.

'They're coming back,' Jun said.

Then something weird happened. We all scattered, scrambling for the ladder. Not like there was anywhere we could go, or anyplace we could hide from the cameras or the person who had made the tea. But all that last-in-retreat stuff went plum out of my head as I ran with the others from that cup.

'Wait!' said Seb. He'd stayed till last, as I had not. 'They all have *names*.'

Only that could've stopped me hauling ass out of there. I stopped and turned, my foot already on the ladder. I went back to the bank of monitors. He was right. We'd been so busy looking at the content of the screens we hadn't focused on what was written around them. Each of the seven monitors was named, not with a Post-it, but with a word sorta stamped into the metal surround of the screen, in the same font as the TWP logo which was everywhere.

'Not just names,' said Gil, who had stayed by Seb's side as always. '*Our* names.'

'Here's mine!' Seb pointed, excited as a toddler, to the stamped letters that read SEBASTIAN.

'And mine,' said Gil, pointing to the monitor that was, appropriately, next to it.

His fingertips traced the letters: GILBERT.

I scanned the bank of monitors quickly, looking at the surrounds this time, not the screens. You know how your own name jumps out in print, just like it jumps out of conversation when someone says it on TV or in a coffee shop? Well, that didn't happen here. My eyes went past MIRANDA, JUN, RALPH and FLORA. For a moment I just couldn't see mine and thought, with a weirdly sinking feeling, that I was the only one without a monitor. Suddenly I was back at Osney, excluded, overlooked, picked last. But then I saw it; etched metal letters leaping out as if they were in relief, not stamped in.

I realised why I'd missed it.

I'd missed it because it was not the name I'd been looking for.

LINK

Not Lincoln. *Link*.

A cold tide of realisation washed over me, turning my blood to ice.

I turned my back on the monitor and this time I did climb back up the staircase. The warm night air wrapped around me like a blanket after the air con. For a moment I could see nothing. I went out into the dark and located, with my hands, the smooth fake wood of the palm tree. I'd knocked down one of the green gonads – Wilson – a fortnight ago but I knew there was one still up there, hanging high above my head, the camera in its belly humming with a tell-tale insect whirr, a red recording light somewhere in its insides like a little burning heart.

Loudly, and clearly, so they couldn't mistake my words, I said, 'Mom. Dad. I'd like to come home now.'

DISC SEVEN

Message in a Bottle – The Police

Sting (1979)

47

Debrief

The Behavioural Science faculty at Oxford University was all steel and glass. It was the complete opposite to the island, and a bit of a culture shock after being surrounded by nature for the best part of three months. I was now sitting under fluorescent strip lighting rather than sunlight and instead of the tide breathing in and out there was the low whirr of the air con. It looked like one of those Area 51 places that people are taken in movies after they've met aliens. Plus, in the room where I was sitting, as well as a table and two empty chairs, there was a dude at the doorway in a black suit and tie, just standing guard and saying nothing. I swear he had one of those little earpieces that bodyguards have.

When my mom and dad came in, they didn't hug me and cry like they had on the helicopter rescue day. They said *Hello, Link* and smiled and sat down, all strictly professional. They were dressed like they always were – Mom was in a tie-dye dress that brushed the floor, with little mirrors sewn into the hem. Dad was in a shirt with an enormous collar made of a material that looked as if it should be kept away from naked flame. Everyone else I'd seen in the facility either wore a suit or a lab coat. It struck me then that as the bosses of the whole Whitlohn Project, my parents could wear whatever the hell they liked. They looked exactly the same. It was me who had changed.

'When can I go home?'

'Soon,' said my mom. 'We just have to debrief you first. Don't you like it here?'

I did. It was like the best hotel. But I wanted to be in my house again, in my room. 'I like it fine.'

'I guess you have some questions,' prompted Mom gently.

I had a butt-load. But of all the things I could've asked, about the experiment, their part in it, the purpose of the Whitlohn Project, I started with something totally left-field.

'What happened to my tooth?'

'Dad and I talked about that for a long while,' Mom said. 'We thought about pulling you out of the whole experiment. You were otherwise completely healthy. Your student medical came back clear –you had one before your exams, if you remember.'

I did remember – every kid in the school had queued up outside the nurse's office at the beginning of the summer term. When it was my turn I'd found not just the school nurse inside but two doctors as well. I'd thought at the time it was a pretty elaborate medical – heart monitors and lots of paraphernalia – but I'd assumed it was just the norm for Osney as it was such a big sports school, as well as being uber-rich.

'Your tooth was the one question mark over your health. We tried, if you remember,' she said with a slight smile, 'to get you to go to the dentist.' I remembered that too – my mom had been dogging me for weeks. 'But you wouldn't cave. So when under observation we saw you'd had a few disturbed nights, we took it out.'

'*You* took it out.'

'Well, not actually *us*. Our dental team. They performed the extraction, and gave you novocaine and a universal antibiotic. Actually you had novocaine for seven days after that, administered while you slept. That was tricky, because at that point you were still in the camp. It would've been much easier if you'd already moved into the White House.'

I felt a bit squirmy that they knew – of *course* they knew – what I'd named my cave. I wanted to change the subject.

'You had a *dentist* down there? In the bunker?'

I thought about the white noise, and the white light, from beyond that door that said *The Whitlohn Project*.

'We had a whole hospital,' said my mom simply. 'Of course, we eliminated risk as much as we could. We even eliminated subjects who would have been too vulnerable.'

'Smith and Fry,' I said.

'As you say. Those with chronic conditions could not be considered as they needed constant care. Ruby Smith is an asthmatic, and Conrad Fry is a type-one diabetic. We couldn't take the risk.'

'And Flora's nose stud?'

'We took it out on the plane and swabbed her nose with antiseptic. We had to let it heal over – there's a lot of aftercare required with a new piercing and she couldn't have done it on the island. Her parents gave permission for us to remove it – turns out they were against the piercing in the first place. But as far as illnesses contracted on the island went, we were covered as far as we could be. All the food you ate was properly bred. The fish, the goats, the berries.'

'Really – everything?'

'Yes. But of course we couldn't fully protect you against injuries. You were all given jabs on the plane. But as far as things like bone breakages, from falling out of a palm tree while climbing up for a green gonad for instance –' she smiled – 'we had a very advanced medical facility.'

'What if things got serious? What about when Gil tried to drown himself?'

'We had a diver out just beyond him, ready to effect a rescue,' said my dad, pushing his aviator glasses up his nose. As simple as that.

'But what about the crash?' I asked. 'You can have all the medical personnel you want on the island. But what if we'd all died in the plane crash? What would you have done then?'

My mom and dad looked at each other, and then at me.

I answered my own question. 'There wasn't a plane crash,' I said quietly. 'It was staged.'

They said nothing.

'That's why . . .' I said, '. . . that's why there were no bodies. The pilot didn't die. Nor the stewardess.' That was a relief at least. 'How did you do it?'

My dad said, 'You were all sedated on the plane.'

I remembered the inflight hospitality. 'I had a Coke. It didn't taste any different to normal, but then it wouldn't, would it?'

He had the grace to look a bit awkward. 'No.'

'That's why we didn't remember anything.'

'Yes. You were given a perfectly safe sedative, just like a sleeping pill that anyone would take on a long-haul flight.'

'Dad, let's not rewrite history. You basically drugged me. And not just me. I guess I'm a minor, and your responsibility, but how the hell did you get permission to roofie the others?'

'You were over sixteen. You signed up for a Preparation for Life course, and that's what you got. And not only did we get your consent, but every child's parents gave their consent too.'

'*All* of them?'

'Yes. All of them – mostly dons, remember – had concerns about their children's development and/or progress at school.'

'Really? Like what?'

My mom hesitated. 'We can't tell you much of anyone else's story. But the short version is this. Seb's parents were worried that he had no social skills to fall back on after the relatively short life span of a sporting career, and Miranda's were concerned that she wouldn't even have that. Ralph's folks wanted to get him away, we understand, from some kids on the Blackbird Leys estate who they thought were a bad influence.' I said nothing but knew perfectly well Ralph had found a worse influence on the island. Me. 'They wanted him to bond with his school friends more. Flora's parents thought she was becoming a little wild. They thought she was rebelling for the sake of it, against a perfectly happy middle-class life. She was a rebel without a cause. On the island she found a cause – injustice.' She meant me. I'd become the villain of the island, not the hero I'd imagined. 'Gil's family wanted him to find some strength, to be less submissive. They felt he was in a toxic co-dependent relationship at school.'

'And what about Jun?' I couldn't believe that her parents would pack their precious daughter off to a desert island just weeks before the all-important audition for the Royal College of Music.

'Mr and Mrs Li were particularly keen that Jun should go. They thought she was in danger of burning out, of abandoning all the excellence she'd worked towards in both violin and tennis. They took the view that she needed a complete break, in a world where neither of her disciplines was important. They want her to decide on the direction her life should now take, without any influence from them.'

Huh. So Jun's parents deserved more credit than she'd given them. 'All right. So we got on Oceanic Airlines flight ED-34. We were all asleep in the air. Then what?'

'The plane landed safely, on the beach. Our operatives took you all off and laid you around the island. Then the plane took off again. We swept the sand flat, ready for you to write your S.O.S.'

I was confused. 'But we *found* the plane. It was in the woods.'

'A prop,' said Mom. 'If you'd taken it apart, you'd have found everything there, even an engine, but it could never have flown, never had. It was essentially a stage set. But everything was real, and mostly functional.'

'Not everything,' I said. 'There was no glass in the plane, not anywhere.'

'Yes. We were pretty impressed when you spotted that. We

338

thought you'd assume that it had blown out. But you were right. Plane glass wouldn't behave like that.'

'Why did you take it away? Were you afraid we'd cut ourselves?'

'No, not that. We wanted your spectacles to be the only glass on the island. That's why there were no drinking glasses.'

This had me beat. 'But why?'

'Because we wanted there to be only one effective way to make a fire. Your spectacles were burning glasses, as you discovered. We wanted to see what would happen when only one person had the power. We knew you, for one, would have a good idea how to make a fire, because you'd read so much Robinsonade. But still, there might have been a number of outcomes. You might have all cooperated to build a fire together. The others might have taken your glasses away. But as it turned out, the knowledge and the ability and the wherewithal were united in the same person – you.'

'And once you'd figured out how to make a fire,' said my dad, taking up the thread, 'we knew you'd be able to cook. But a fire has another use too.'

'Warmth?'

'Yes, that. But something else.'

I frowned.

My mom leaned forward. Her bodice was tied together with these strings with little sleigh bells on the end, and they jingled as she moved. 'You've read all the Robinsonade. What do *you* think?'

I already knew the answer. 'A signal fire.'

'You never attempted it.' It was a statement, not a question.

'Never sent a signal, never built a raft, never built a boat. Interesting.'

They studied me with expressions that were oddly alike. Suddenly I felt like not their son, but their subject.

Now I was on the back foot. 'We had the black box recorder.'

'Which you knew to be a prop. You took it apart.'

For a moment I'd forgotten they could see everything. 'Quite late in the day.'

'And yet you still didn't make a fire. Why not?'

'We knew by then we were being recorded, and so we knew we'd be rescued.'

'You didn't discover that for another few weeks. Why no signal fire in the meantime?'

I couldn't think of an answer. 'Why was the black box recorder a prop?' I countered. 'You could've made it look real inside, put in a transponder and some wires. We would never have known the difference.'

'As you say. That was designed to be found out. We wanted you to find other ways to help yourselves, not rely on rescue. That was really the point. You had to get yourselves out of there. And it worked,' said Dad, 'didn't it?'

'And you were never totally helpless,' said my mom. 'You all had what we called a "luxury".'

It clicked. On *Desert Island Discs*, as well as your eight songs, you were allowed to take a luxury, an item to make your time on the island easier.

'We did extensive interviews with the parents, and psychological profiling of their children. Each castaway had one thing left to them, besides the clothes they stood up in.

In each case, as far as possible, the item was connected with their particular personality.'

'What were the items? What was everyone's luxury?'

'You tell us.'

I thought for a moment. 'Seb had his Fitbit.' Standard issue for a jock. 'Jun had her violin.'

'Correct.'

'Ralph had the pestle and mortar. For his . . . pharmaceuticals.' I skated swiftly over the memory of Ralph's potions. 'What about Miranda?'

'Her skirt.'

The Amazing Skirt. 'That wasn't much use on an island,' I said.

My dad looked at me pointedly. 'Wasn't it?'

I felt my face going red and hurried on. 'How about Gil?'

'He had a pen. The one you used to draw the map and note down everyone's Desert Island Discs.'

'And Flora?'

'She had the water bottle.'

'And mine was my glasses.'

'Of course,' said my mom, 'your phones were left to you, but we knew they'd all run out in the first day, and there was no signal on the island anyway. The only functions they had were any in-app functions that didn't need data. You could have used a compass app, but that would only have told you which way was north, and you couldn't use a longitude/latitude or satnav app without data.'

'After the phones had run out,' my dad went on, 'it was up to you to use the luxuries, and you used them very effectively.'

'You used Sebastian's Fitbit to calculate longitude and latitude,' said Mom. 'And Jun's violin strings to fish with.'

'The bottle was interesting,' went on Dad. 'We thought you'd use it to collect water from the lake. But you sent the message in the bottle instead.'

I started to squirm. 'I thought that, since we had the lake for fresh water, it would be more useful. Ya know, to send for help . . . effect our rescue.' My voice tailed off guiltily. I wished they'd stop talking about the bottle. It was almost as if they knew what I'd done.

They both looked at me speculatively. 'Hmm.'

Thankfully, my mom changed tack. 'It was as much about what you *didn't* have with you as what you did. No glass in the plane, as you noticed. No shoes, so you couldn't use the laces for fishing or building. We did this to preserve the integrity of the luxuries. We wanted the resources to be limited, as they would be in a real castaway situation. Your spectacles were the only glass; Jun's strings were the only threads. But we still knew you'd be OK.'

'*How* did you know?'

'Because we designed the island. A human being can survive three minutes without air. Three days without water. Three weeks without food. We gave you enough food and drink for the first day – just what was on the trolley on the plane. The mini Cokes and snacks. You had the carcass of the plane to make tools and a shelter, and you did.'

'The trolley,' I said. 'Was that the only food in the plane?'

My dad nodded. 'There were never any hotboxes, as we wanted you to start hunting and foraging as soon as possible.'

So the menu, the food that we'd dreamed about, and that Jun had recited like a morning prayer, had never existed.

'There was a freshwater lake. We knew you'd find that on Day One and you did. The Bucket berries, as you called them, we'd planted. The goats we'd genetically bred on the island, disease-free and meat-rich. We stocked the lake too. The fish in the lake were genetically clean-bred too, to be easily caught and nutritious.'

'They were delicious,' I admitted. 'What were they?'

'They were *Clupea harengus rubeum*.'

'What does that mean?'

'Red herrings,' supplied my mom. 'A little joke.'

'Scientists can be fun too,' put in my dad.

'Oh yeah,' I said. 'They're a hoot.' I had a sudden thought. 'My seat,' I said, 'seat 23b – was that a joke too?'

Mom and Dad looked at each other. 'Yes,' admitted Mom. 'It was from the show *Lost*. 23b, Oceanic Airlines, was the seat number of the hero, Jack Shephard. We didn't expect you to remember that, as you were really little when that show was on. But we thought you'd probably recognise the flight number – ED-34, Edmond Dantes's prisoner number from *The Count of Monte Cristo*.'

'We wanted to scatter clues around the island that there was something off, something not real,' said Dad. 'Something that would get you thinking, and wondering, and enquiring about what was actually going on. We wanted to signal to you all that there was a mystery to be solved.'

'This experiment was finite,' said Mom. 'We knew we only had the three months of summer vacation. So we wanted to see if you all could figure it out.'

343

'So there were clues for *all* of us? Not just me?'

'Yes. We wanted a level playing field.'

'And did anyone else twig?'

'This is your debrief, Link, not anyone else's. But we can tell you that Flora figured out that we'd peopled the island with one of each high-school social group. We wanted to see how each stereotype would perform in a survival situation. Until, of course, we added you to the group. That meant we had a double.'

'And who did I double up with in this little cliché roulette of yours?' I asked, already knowing the answer.

'Gilbert Egan.'

At the beginning of the summer I'd have said, *Gee, thanks very much*. But now I had the utmost respect for Gil and didn't mind being grouped with him at all. 'I guess Flora didn't notice the nerd surplus.'

'No. But she did figure out that there were only male goats on the island.'

'So she was right?'

My mom and dad nodded, in perfect time with each other. 'Why? Were they s'posed to run out and then we go all *Hunger Games*?'

'No,' said Mom. 'We did that so we could control your food source. Those goats were genetically engineered to be disease-free, easy to catch, protein-rich, optimised for meat. Breeding would have introduced mutations, impurities. We wanted to control your nutrition as far as possible. Flora called it.'

'And,' said Dad, 'she spotted the anomaly of your seat number on the plane.'

'Huh.' I thought of the night Flora and I had been at the crash site together. 'What about the Bible we found under seat 23b? Was that a clue? Or just another oh-so-funny gag from Chuckles University?'

'The Bible was one of the clues.'

'To what?'

'Well,' said Dad, 'it wasn't the *only* book you found, was it?'

I head-palmed myself. Of *course*. 'The Bible and *Shakespeare*. On *Desert Island Discs*, they give you the Bible and Shakespeare to take to your desert island, along with your luxury and your own book choice. I shoulda known then.' Then another thought occurred. 'Did you want us to find out we were being filmed? Is that where all the clues led?'

My folks looked at each other. 'Originally the camera pairs were placed high so that the participants wouldn't be able to find out what they really were or reach them. And, of course, the palm trees could not be felled, as you found – they were made from a toughened fibreglass polymer, not wood. But when we saw that you and Sebastian had set yourselves the task of getting one of the gourds down, we let it play out. We figured it would be interesting to see how the subjects reacted to being filmed. Some changed their behaviour. Others hid theirs.'

They meant me of course. I'd retreated to the White House, in the knowledge that what I'd been doing was wrong. 'Why two nuts in each tree?'

'There was a camera in each gourd, so one would be a back-up if something happened to one of them. And something did happen to one of them, didn't it?'

345

They meant, of course, Wilson – I'd knocked him down and taken him home.

'And the palm trees that we couldn't cut down? I assume they were full of wires?'

'No. The cameras were wireless. They transmitted to the control room using satellite technology. That's how the one you took inside Bikini Bottom – Wilson, as you called him – continued to film.'

'So,' I said with a growing feeling of dread, 'you know about the Rocket.'

'The Rocket we didn't anticipate,' said my dad. 'Of course we tested the plants on the island as far as possible for toxicity, and removed anything deadly. But some plants inevitably had side effects we couldn't foresee. We have of course tested the Rocket, as you called it, since your rescue.' He spoke dispassionately, like a scientist, not a father.

'And?' I faked detachment as well.

My parents looked at each other. 'The leaves bear some relationship to the coca plant.'

I swallowed. 'Cocaine?' I whispered.

'Yes. But it also had hallucinogenic properties. You probably noticed, when Ralph cut you off, some changes in your perception?'

I had. No more crazy euphoria, no more rainbow clouds as Miranda swam or Jun played. And Wilson – Wilson had stopped talking to me, stopped telling me what to do.

'Don't worry, son.' My dad became a dad again. 'Your exit medical shows no remaining trace of the plant in your system. And you'll never touch anything like that again, will you?'

It was not a threat but a statement of fact.

'Never, never,' I said. 'I swear on my life.' And I meant it. Drugs. *Jesus*. Funnily enough I felt worse for Ralph than myself. 'Ralph was never a drug dealer in Oxford,' I said slowly. 'He wasn't one until *I* made him one.' *This thing of darkness I acknowledge mine.* It was what Prospero had said of his malign servant.

'Don't feel too bad for him,' said Mom. 'As soon as we saw what was happening we removed the supply, but as it happened Ralph had already refused to bring you any more. He regulated the situation himself. He's a good kid.'

Ralph was a good kid. And I was a bad one.

The thought was excruciating, and even worse was the fact that my parents had *seen* what I'd become. They'd seen *everything*. And worse, much worse than my Rocket abuse, was something I couldn't bring myself to mention even now. My horrible exploitation of Miranda and Jun in exchange for food, those two evenings in Bikini Bottom, and, most dreadful of all, the starvation of Flora when she wouldn't bend to my will. I could blame the Rocket, but I knew that wasn't it. Yes, it had made me kinda crazy, but it hadn't made me what I was not. It was me all along. *I'd* done it all. The island hadn't made me a president, or even a count, but a terrible person. And my parents had witnessed it all. It was like they had put a camera in my bedroom. Hell – that's *exactly* what they'd done. I was ashamed, and being ashamed made me angry. I looked at my parents like I didn't know them. This kindly, hippy bespectacled couple who had loved me, nurtured me, brought me up, then thrown me to the sharks and filmed me being devoured.

347

'How could you? How could you play this fricking giant practical joke on me? This was my *life*. You wasted my whole summer.'

'Are you sure that's what you think, Link?' said my mom gently. 'Because from our scientific observations we got the distinct impression that, well, you kinda liked it there.'

I snorted incredulously, a horrible sound. 'What made you think that?'

In answer my dad, very carefully, took an object from his battered briefcase and set it on the table.

It was mired with salt and caked with sand, but you could still see the blue shadows of some far-off French mountains on the label and the ghost of a scroll inside.

It was the message in an Evian bottle.

48

Wrong Number

We all looked at the bottle, sitting innocently on the table between us, under the bright fluorescent lighting.

Dad sat back in his chair. 'You know, son, when your mom was in high school she was a very popular date.' I felt faintly sick. That wasn't really something you wanted to know about your own mom. 'If a guy asked for her number and she didn't want him to call her, do you know what she did?'

I was very much afraid that I did know.

Mom took up the tale. 'I wrong-numbered him. I wrote down every digit of my phone number accurately except for one. Then I knew he could never call me, that I was safe.'

She unscrewed the top of the bottle and shook out the scroll. She unrolled the paper with her many-ringed fingers. 'At the top of the mountain you made a calculation. Can you remember what it was?'

'No.' I wasn't lying. I genuinely couldn't. So much had happened since then.

'We can. It was recorded. You calculated that the latitude of Lincoln Island was 30 degrees south.'

Of course. The green gonads hanging at the very top of the mountain, their cameras watching Seb and me, filming my calculations. 'And on the beach, using Sebastian's Fitbit, you calculated that the longitude of Lincoln Island was 60 degrees west.'

'If you say so.'

Mom handed me the flattened-out paper. There in my handwriting were the numbers 20 degrees south and 60 degrees west.

20, not 30.

I handed the paper back, my hand shaking a little. 'I made a mistake.' I couldn't quite meet her eyes.

'Did you? Because *we* think you wrong-numbered the coordinates deliberately.'

I said nothing.

'Why, honey?'

Dad leaned forward again. 'We think it's because you wanted to stay. Not forever, but for longer. This was Day Four, remember. We think you'd already figured out, even by then, that the island was a place where you could flourish, a place where you mattered, a place where you could *lead*.'

'All right,' I said, trying to turn the heat on them. 'Suppose I didn't totally hate it. You still *used* me. This project – the Whitlohn Project – is this why we came to England in the first place? To Oxford?'

'Yes. The University of Oxford agreed to a closed-island experiment ten years ago, when we moved.'

'And where exactly is it?' I asked. 'Where is Lincoln Island? Was I even close with those coordinates?'

My folks shared a look again. 'We can't tell you. You'd need security clearance at the highest level. All we can tell you is that it is the most expensive social experiment ever to be mounted in behavioural science.'

'But you didn't know about *Desert Island Discs* when we moved to England. Or about Harry Whitlohn.'

'The name came later. Once we'd fallen in love with BBC radio, and *Desert Island Discs*, we heard about Sir Harry Whitlohn, and the fake programme they'd done in 1963, with an actor playing Whitlohn and talking about his eight "favourite" records. We thought it would be a neat name for the project. Harry Whitlohn was a fake castaway, and so were you.'

'Was I always part of the plan?'

'No, of course not,' said Mom. 'You're not an experiment, you are our son, and we love you. Osney School was always a research partner with the University, that's why they let the kids of dons in for free, including you. But we didn't think about placing *you* in the Whitlohn Project until you said you wanted to leave school. Only then did we realise that you were in danger of misreading your place in the world, jeopardising your entire future because of a bogus hierarchy imposed by the school. We wanted to replace that hierarchy with a different one. We wanted you to be somewhere where you could discover your true worth.'

'You only get one chance at life, son,' said Dad, echoing loathsome Sports Nazi Principal Llewellyn. 'No do-overs. We wanted to set you on the right track. *We* knew, all along, you

351

could be a great man, that you had the brains to lead. And you did it. You got everybody off the island. You solved the mystery.'

'With help,' I admitted.

'Of course. All good leaders need help.'

I thought of the keypad at the centre of the X, and of us all crowding round with suggestions. 'That whole thing with *our* Desert Island Discs,' I said. 'How the hell did you figure out the number we would key in? I mean, it doesn't matter how much research you did with everyone's parents, there's no way they would know exactly what track their kids were going to pick. Or that everyone's favourite tracks would have a number in them somewhere. I mean, *you* guys wouldn't even know my choices. Hell, *I* didn't even know mine until I got to the island.'

'But we didn't know. And it didn't matter. There was no right number, no right answer. We were watching, and as soon as you all worked together to come up with a number, and you all made a contribution, we let you into the bunker.'

'It could have been anything,' said Dad. 'Your favourite numbers, your shoe sizes, your ages. We just wanted it to be a team effort. You all had to find out things about each other, to have a conversation. And you, Link, had to learn to finally delegate.'

At that moment I felt just how much I must've let them down. For so long on the island I was only out for myself. 'I was a shitty leader.'

My folks didn't even burn me for my language like they would've done at home. 'Not at first. Nor at the last. In between times, yes, you were corrupted by power. You abused your fellow man, and especially your fellow woman.' I hung my head.

352

'You even abused substances. But better to do these things at the age of sixteen than later. You learned some valuable lessons. And you won't make those mistakes again.'

No, I wouldn't.

'And, honey, you'd been brutalised for so long. I don't think we realised until you were on the island just how badly you'd been treated at Osney. And that's our bad, that's on us. So no wonder when you achieved power you went a bit crazy with it. That's one of the lessons we want you to learn *now*. There's no excuse for how you treated those girls, but we understand how it happened. You'd never had any interest from girls before, never been on any dates. And suddenly *two* girls wanted you. You were the alpha male. And you exploited that.'

Jeez. This was awful. What a conversation to have with your folks. Only the fact that they were being so damned scientific about it kept me from running from the room. I had to change the subject. 'So all the things I read growing up,' I said, 'all the Robinsonade – *The Count of Monte Cristo. The Mysterious Island. Treasure Island, Coral Island* . . .' All those islands. 'Even my video games, like *Myst*. All the things we watched on TV – *Lost, Castaway*. And *Desert Island* fricking *Discs*. Was that all part of this? Part of the Whitlohn Project?'

'Of course we had those references in the house – we were researching around our subject, and you picked them up from us, and embraced them. And why wouldn't you? They are great adventures. And whatever else happened on the island, you have to admit you had a great adventure too.'

I wasn't quite ready to give them kudos for that yet. 'So Oxford paid for the island.'

Mom and Dad exchanged a look. 'Not entirely. There was another pretty significant funder.'

'Who?'

'The US Government.'

Well, that was a record-scratch moment. 'Are you kidding? A specially designed island. A medical team, a dental team. Divers, helicopters. Paid for by the US Government for a bunch of British kids? That's an awful lot of expense to go to for a summer camp.'

They both looked at me. Then I got it. 'Oooooohhhh. It's *not* just for us.'

'No. You were the first. But we'll roll it out to other schools, and even corporate teambuilding, in return for their data. There's a bigger mission too though.'

'Quite literally,' said Dad. 'The ultimate mission.'

I got that hairs-rising-on-my-neck feeling again, the one I'd gotten when the hatch opened. 'Are you talking about . . . space?' I asked. I could hardly believe what I was hearing.

'Yes. We are working with NASA as a research partner. They are hoping to send up a mission to colonise Mars by 2024. They want us to collect data on how astronauts might socialise, and how their hierarchies develop, how societies establish themselves from the ground up.'

I remembered being with Flora on the top of Monte Cristo, our last night on the island, looking up at the stars and the middle of nowhere. That night I'd thought about a rocket man, on a forbidden planet, cast away in the ultimate solitude of the cosmos. But also, as Captain James T. Kirk famously said, space was the final frontier, the last place in the universe for the United States to colonise.

'But, Link . . .' Mom leaned across the table and took my hand, as if I was in prison. I kept expecting the guard guy at the door to leap forward and tell us that physical contact was not allowed. '*Dear* Link, you have to know that you were very, very far from being a guinea pig. This was the first, yes. But it will be the most important mission that the Whitlohn Project will *ever* carry out.'

'Why?' I asked.

'Honey,' my mom said. 'Because *you* were there.'

I let my hand lie in hers, but didn't return her pressure. 'Are you actually saying that this whole deal was constructed to make me stay on at school?'

'No, of *course* not,' she smiled. 'You heard what your dad said about the Mars landings. And that, like I said, we didn't ever intend for you to be a part of the Whitlohn Project, until the day you came home and said you were leaving school. Believe me, we thought – and fought – long and hard about whether or not you should go. The experiment was designed for six participants; you were the seventh. But we decided in the end it would teach you some valuable lessons, and as we knew you would be so closely monitored, not by dispassionate observers but by your own parents, we decided you should go. And if you staying on at school is a by-product, well, that's great.'

I thought about leaving to learn to be a mechanic, or a coder, or whatever jobs I'd promised myself while I counted down the days until I left Osney. Then I thought about everything I'd built and all the things I'd learned to do. Not just how to light a fire, but how to skin and gut a goat, how to catch a fish.

And more importantly what not to do. Don't treat people like shit. Don't make them your slaves. Don't make women your playthings. Don't do drugs. I'd made every mistake there was to make, some of them pretty serious, and in the real world, criminal. But eventually, pretty late in the day admittedly, I'd learned how to lead.

I'd learned something else too. That people can surprise you. I thought of Ralph and his medical ethics, Jun and her music. Miranda and her vulnerable heroism, Gil and his faithful version of love. And even Seb who, at the very end, had unlocked the mystery and the hatch with it. I'd learned, at last, that no man was an island, and that I couldn't've gotten off there without them all. Most of all I thought about Flora. If I didn't go back to Osney, would I ever see her again?

'*Are* you going to stay at school?' urged my mom. 'Now you know what you are, what you can do, what you can be?'

I looked at her and Dad, and uttered the magic word.

'OK,' I said. I stood up and picked up the bottle. 'Can I keep this?'

'Sure.'

I rolled up the lying message, popped it back in the bottle and screwed on the cap.

I shook it a little so the scroll bobbled about inside. 'I figure you owe me something, since there was no treasure.'

Then they both got up, came round the table and hugged me. My mom said into my hair, 'There *was* treasure. You found your own weaknesses. You found your own strengths. You found your capabilities.'

Then my dad said, 'You found yourself.'

You have to remember that my parents are from the west coast of America, so this didn't sound quite as cheesy as it might. But it still sounded pretty cheesy. As I sank into the hug, holding them hard, I was left wondering whether I had the worst parents in the world, or the best.

49

The Other Island

I walked back onto Osney Island wearing the bottle-green uniform of the sixth form. An island, three wavy lines of water and a tree were emblazoned on the breast pocket in gold thread. My shoes were uber-uncomfortable, not just because they were new, but because they were shoes. After three months of no footwear on the island, I could barely stand anything on my feet.

I crossed the little bridge across the moat, back onto my first island. As I passed under the stone archway I clocked the Latin inscription to George III chiselled into the architrave – the guy who had gone crazy but was still a leader – and wondered how things would be different now. I watched the other kids milling around and felt, vaguely, that they shouldn't be there. Surely it should just be us?

I hadn't seen anyone since our debriefing sessions at the faculty, when I'd seen the others fleetingly leaving medicals or interview rooms as I'd entered them, or buying soda from the vending machines. Ralph was the first one I met – he jostled into me just under the gateway.

'Hi, Ralph.'

Ralph said 'Sup,' before he could stop himself, then looked at the floor.

I studied him. 'How you doing?'

He shrugged loosely, not meeting my eyes. 'Safe, my doggie. Rolled and smoked.' He jiggled about, all street, just like he used to. 'Gotta ten-toes, cuz. Things to do. Man's cuttin'.'

I smiled thinly. 'All right, Ralph,' I said pleasantly. 'You "ten-toes".'

He bounced off, across the courtyard, doing his gangsta swagger. I was not really surprised.

I wasn't surprised when Miranda Pencroft went back to being Sebastian Loam's girlfriend faster than you could say 'Robinson Crusoe'. Nor that Jun Am Li asked me to buy some new violin strings to replace the ones that were once used to catch fish, or that Gilbert Egan still laughed along if someone said I was gay, or that Ralph Tuck went back to hanging out on the Blackbird Leys estate. They wanted to forget about the island. But I just watched them and smiled. Because I finally understood.

It didn't matter.

Let Ralph pretend he was a gangster. Let Seb play out his last few matches at school, pretending he was the great sporting hero. Let Miranda thrash up and down the pool until her hair turned silver again. Let them all pretend to be what they were not, before Real Life intervened. Because I knew, and they knew, who was who when the chips were down. I knew, now, where I stood in the pecking order.

I could smile.

John Donne had said no man was an island.

John Donne was one smart sonofabitch.

I could smile because I had someone to smile *at*, someone who did not want to forget, but had the most to forgive. I'd learned as much from what I'd done wrong on the island as from what I'd done right. Flora had forgiven me. She was the one who smiled back.

And as for Sebastian Loam? I waited for the confrontation I knew would come. And, one day, it did. Just like almost exactly three years before, I saw Seb as I was crossing the Great Court. We met at the centre of the quad, as if we were in a gunfight. We stopped on the very spot where we'd begun on the day of the Osney Dash.

He was carrying a familiar bag. It was made of navy waterproof material, with a red racing stripe, discreet Nike tick and rough Velcro handles. Loam held out the bag straight-armed in front of him and dropped it at my feet, narrowly missing the shiny toes of my new shoes. I looked at the bag, at the familiar Velcro handles.

Then I looked at Loam.

He looked back at me.

It was all about who would drop their eyes first.

DISC EIGHT

By the Sleepy Lagoon

(Signature tune to *Desert Island Discs*
BBC Radio
29th January 1942 – the present)

Eric Coates (1930)

Epilogue

'Mr President?'

I was jolted from my daydream by this new name of mine. I'd been staring out of the limo window at the streets of London. It was the first time I'd been in England for almost thirty years. We were headed to Buckingham Palace on a State visit, to meet the leader of this particular island.

I looked at the crowds of people wandering down The Mall, and I didn't think, as I used to, that everyone had their life sorted but me. I thought the same thing I'd thought when, my hand on the Bible I'd once found in the wreckage of a plane, I'd looked out across the Lincoln Memorial Reflecting Pool at the thousands of people who'd come to see my presidential inauguration. *A hundred million castaways, looking for a home.*

I thought now about the island, the island I had named. Of course I now knew exactly where it was, the precise longitude and latitude of that classified, US-owned Pacific atoll that would forever be, for me, Lincoln Island. Then I thought about the Breakfast Club and what they were all doing now. It was the kind of thing I could find out easily nowadays – I had people who could do it for me. Seb had become an international rugby player and retired due to injury, going into the remarkably similar world of politics as a Cabinet minister. Gil was his personal private secretary and, I was reliably informed, secret partner. I was happy for them. I just hoped one day they'd have the courage to come out. Gil, I suspected, already did – Seb, maybe not. Ralph, I knew, had become a doctor, and I liked to think that his pharmaceutical journey on the island had inspired him. Jun had gone on to the Royal College of Music and was playing in concert halls all over the world. I hoped she was happy, and that one day she'd have that little girl she longed for, and maybe let her play mud pies instead of violin. Miranda had given up swimming, or rather it gave her up. She went into TV, but after a sex scandal found herself on another island, in the *I'm a Celebrity* Jungle, by way of the *Big Brother* house. And Flora? Well, Flora had gone to Nashville and become a country singer. And that's where . . .

'President Selkirk? Can we just go over tomorrow's schedule while we have five minutes?' My chief of staff interrupted my daydreams. Jared Hollister was an efficient but humorous guy I'd had in my office since I was first a senator.

I gave him all my attention. 'Of course.' I was used to morning briefings. I used to do them myself, a long time ago, at the top of a distant sand dune.

'Chamber of Commerce, breakfast 9 a.m.. You're at No. 10 with the Prime Minister at 11 a.m. Lunch at the Guildhall at 12.30, then at 3 p.m. the BBC for *Desert Island Discs*.'

'Oh.'

Jared misread my expression as reluctance. 'You agreed to it some time ago.'

'Yes. Yes, of course, I remember.'

Jared scratched his nose with his pen. 'This is going to sound kinda trivial, considering where we're headed now, but can I just check your playlist? They need to line up the tracks for the broadcast.'

'Let's do it. It might calm the old nerves.' I listed my eight tracks for him without hesitation. I'd had them in my head for thirty years.

'Great,' said Jared, ticking off the final title. 'That tallies with my list from the BBC. Oh, and also I need a book. They give you the Bible and *The Complete Works of Shakespeare* on the island, but you can choose one more.'

'That's easy. *The Count of Monte Cristo*,' I said, 'by Alexandre Dumas.'

'And your luxury? You're allowed one luxury.'

'Hmmm,' I said, 'that's harder.'

'Hot tub?' said Jared. 'Grand piano?'

I laughed, but I was struggling. I really couldn't think of anything.

'I know,' said my wife from beside me. 'It's obvious.'

'It is?'

'Yes,' she said. 'A pair of glasses.'

I pushed my own up my nose. I still wore them, even though I didn't need them. I took my wife's hand and smiled. She smiled back, squeezing my fingers reassuringly. I carried her hand to my lips and kissed it. Then I turned it over and kissed the ace of spades on the soft skin inside her wrist. I was pretty sure she was the only tattooed First Lady in history.

She was right of course. She'd always been right, throughout the three years of dating and the ten years of marriage, keeping me honest, keeping me grounded, keeping me on the straight and narrow when the heady power of political office might have turned me from the right path. Flora had been what every castaway needs: a compass, on the island and ever since.

We drove through the gates of Buckingham Palace, and it occurred to me that, when my mom saw me tonight on the nightly news, watching me on a TV screen as she'd done for three months one summer long ago, she might very well say that the geek had inherited the earth.

THE END

Everyone's Desert Island Discs

Lincoln

1 *Ode to Joy* – Ludwig van Beethoven (1785)
2 *Nowhere Man* – The Beatles (1965)
3 *Survivor* – Destiny's Child (2001)
4 *Light My Fire* – The Doors (1967)
5 *Gimme Shelter* – The Rolling Stones (1969)
6 *Rocket Man* – Elton John (1972)
7 *Message in a Bottle* – The Police (1979)
8 *By the Sleepy Lagoon* – Eric Coates (1930)

Miranda

1 *Despacito* – Luis Fonsi and Daddy Yankee ft. Justin Bieber (2017)
2 *Look At What You've Done* – Drake (2011)
3 *Payphone* – Maroon 5 (2012)
4 *Shake It Off* – Taylor Swift (2014)

5 *There's Nothing Holdin' Me Back* – Shawn Mendes (2016)
6 *Attention* – Charlie Puth (2017)
7 *Bang Bang* – Ariana Grande, Nicki Minaj, Jessie J (2014)
8 *Titanium* – David Guetta ft. Sia (2011)

Ralph

1 *Traktor* – Wretch 32 (2011)
2 *Wot Do U Call It* – Wiley (2004)
3 *I Luv U* – Dizzee Rascal (2003)
4 *P's & Q's* – Kano (2005)
5 *Street Fighter Riddim* – D Double E (2010)
6 *Duppy (Doin' It Again)* – Skepta (2006)
7 *On a Mission* – Onyx Stone and DJ Bugzee (2018)
8 *Man Don't Care* – JME ft. Giggs (2015)

Jun

1 *Caprice No. 1 for solo violin* – Niccolo Paganini
(c1802–1817)
2 *Violin concerto in D Major* – Pyotr Ilyich Tchaikovsky
(1878)
3 *Concerto for two violins in D* – Johann Sebastian Bach
(c1717–1723)
4 *Concerto in D Major* – Ludwig van Beethoven (1806)
5 *Concerto No. 5 in A Major* – Wolfgang Amadeus Mozart
(1775)

6 *Violin concerto in E Minor* – Felix Mendelssohn (1845)
7 *Chaconne in D Minor* – Johann Sebastian Bach
(c1717–1720)
8 *Summer, Four Seasons* – Antonio Vivaldi (c1721)

Seb

1 That One From The Champions League
2 That One From That Boxing Film
3 That One From The Olympics
4 That One From *Match of the Day*
5 That Katy Perry One About Basketball
6 That One They Always Sing At Liverpool
7 That One From The Rugby
8 That One From FIFA

Gil

1 *Zadok the Priest* – George Frideric Handel (1727)
2 *Eye of the Tiger* – Survivor (1982)
3 *Chariots of Fire* – Vangelis (1981)
4 *Life of Riley* – The Lightning Seeds (1992)
5 *Swish Swish* – Katy Perry ft. Nicki Minaj (2017)
6 *You'll Never Walk Alone* – Richard Rodgers and Oscar
Hammerstein (1945)
7 *Swing Low, Sweet Chariot* – African American spiritual
8 *Song 2* – Blur (1997)

Flora

1 *Your Song* – Elton John (1970)
2 *Beyond the Sea* – Bobby Darin (1959)
3 *Born to Fly* – Sara Evans (2000)
4 *Nightswimming* – R.E.M. (1992)
5 *Save it for a Rainy Day* – The Jayhawks (2003)
6 *White Rabbit* – Jefferson Airplane (1967)
7 *Nulla in Mundo Pax Sincera* – Antonio Vivaldi (1735)
8 *Ace of Spades* – Motörhead (1980)

Acknowledgements

There are lots of friends and family to thank for *The Island*, which is nice as friends and family are very much what the book is about.

I'm indebted once again to the wonderful team at Hot Key Books, led by Jane Harris. Thank you to Emma Matthewson for her faultless editing and Talya Baker for her forensically thorough copy-editing. I'm also very grateful to Ruth Logan, Tina Mories and Ilaria Tarasconi for faithfully spreading the word about *The Island*.

Thanks as ever to my agent and friend Teresa Chris, who has been my own compass on the publishing seas.

Thank you to my son Conrad, inveterate gamer, for helping me to navigate Overwatch, Fortnite and the legend that is Zelda.

Thank you to my daughter Ruby, for being my invaluable social-media tech support.

Thanks to friend and MC Onyx Stone, for recommending Ralph's Grime tracks when I didn't have a clue.

Thank you to ace pilot and father-in-law Captain Colin Sharples, for giving me the lowdown on light aircraft.

Thanks to my sister-in-law Aurora Bennett, for talking me though teen piercings and tattoos.

Thank you to Sacha, whose schooldays gave me the inspiration for Link.

Thank you to that great British institution the BBC, for the wonder that is *Desert Island Discs*.

Many fictional works contributed to this book. *The Count of Monte Cristo*, by Alexandre Dumas (Père) is referenced throughout. Less obvious, but just as significant, is the influence of *The Admirable Crichton*, a play by J. M. Barrie, about a butler who is cast away on a desert island, where he quickly becomes the master.

In fact, thank you to *all* the fictional castaways, from Edmond Dantes to Chuck Noland, from Robinson Crusoe to Jack Shephard, who helped me to recreate what it might have been like for Link on The Island.

M. A. Bennett

M. A. Bennett is half Venetian and was born in Manchester, England, and raised in the Yorkshire Dales. She is a history graduate of Oxford University and the University of Venice, where she specialised in the study of Shakespeare's plays as a historical source. After university she studied art and has since worked as an illustrator, an actress and a film reviewer. She also designed tour visuals for rock bands, including U2 and the Rolling Stones. She was married on the Grand Canal in Venice and lives in north London with her husband, son and daughter.

Her first YA novel, S.T.A.G.S. was published in 2017 and was shortlisted for the YA Book Prize 2018. THE ISLAND is her second novel for young adults. Follow her at @MABennettAuthor on Twitter and at m.a.bennettauthor on Instagram.

Also from M.A. Bennett

There are some invitations you just shouldn't accept.

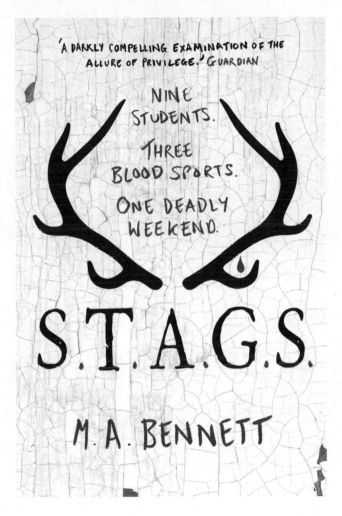

'A DARKLY COMPELLING EXAMINATION OF THE ALLURE OF PRIVILEGE.' GUARDIAN

NINE STUDENTS.

THREE BLOOD SPORTS.

ONE DEADLY WEEKEND.

S.T.A.G.S.

M.A. BENNETT

Turn the page to read an extract . . .

chapter one

I think I might be a murderer.

Although, as I didn't mean to kill, I suppose it was manslaughter, so technically I would be a 'manslaughterer', although I don't think that's a word. When I got my scholarship to STAGS, my old headmistress told me, 'You'll be the cleverest student in that school, Greer MacDonald.' I might be, I might not. But I'm clever enough to know that manslaughterer is not a word.

I should make it clear here, before you lose all sympathy for me, that I didn't kill with my own hands. There were a few of us. I helped to *cause* a death, but not alone. I'm a murderer in the way that foxhunters are murderers – they are each responsible for the fox's death, even though they hunt in a pack. No one ever knows which dog tore the fox apart, but all the dogs, and all those riders in their smart red coats, are part of it.

I just gave myself away. Did you spot it? Those coats – the coats that posh people wear out foxhunting – they are pink, not red; hunting pink. And the dogs are not dogs, they are hounds.

Every time I open my mouth I give myself away; Greer MacDonald, the Girl Who Doesn't Fit In. It's my northern accent, you see. I was born and raised in Manchester and went to Bewley Park Comprehensive School until this summer. In both those places I fitted in just fine. When I won my scholarship to STAGS I stopped fitting in.

I ought to tell you a bit about STAGS, because I now realise how connected the school is to the murder. STAGS stands for St Aidan the Great School and it is *literally* the oldest school in England. Not a single building in my comprehensive school, Bewley Park, was built before 1980. The earliest bit of STAGS, the chapel, was built back in 683, and it is covered in frescoes. *Frescoes*. Bewley Park was covered in graffiti.

STAGS was founded in the seventh century by the man himself: St Aidan the Great, I mean. Before the Church decided he was Great, he was just a plain old monk, and wandered around northern England telling anyone who would listen about Christianity. Then, presumably so he could stop wandering, he founded a school, where he told his pupils all about Christianity instead. You might assume that he'd been made a saint for all that telling people about Christianity, but apparently that's not how it works. In order to become a saint, you have to perform a miracle. Aidan's miracle was that he saved a stag from the hunt by turning him invisible. So the stag became Aidan's emblem, and the school's too. When I got my letter calling me for interview, the stag's antlers were the first thing I noticed, right at the top of the letter, like two little jagged black tears in the paper.

The first time I saw St Aidan the Great School was when I went for my interview. It was one of those sunny midwinter days, all glittering frosty fields and long, low shadows. Dad drove me through the gates and up this long driveway through lush green grounds in his ten-year-old Mini Cooper. At the end of the drive we got out and just stared and stared. We'd seen some pretty amazing scenery on the long trip from Manchester to Northumberland, but this was the best of all. It was a beautiful, vast medieval manor house, with a sort of moat and a little bridge to the entrance. It didn't look at all like the headquarters of a disturbing cult, which is what it actually is. The only clue, if I'd been looking for it, might have been the pair of antlers over the great door.

'*Another Country*,' I said shakily.

Dad didn't nod, or murmur, 'You can say that again.' He said, '*If.*'

My dad is a wildlife cameraman, and he loves films of all kinds, not just the nature documentaries that he mostly works on. We watch loads of films together, from obscure subtitled films to the stupidest brand-new blockbusters. I'm even named after Greer Garson, a film star from the black-and-white days. When Dad's travelling, or on night shoots, I watch films on my own, just to make up for the thirty-year head start he has on me. We have this game that we play; when something we see reminds us of a film, we say it out loud, and the other person has to name another film on the same theme. Now we were doing films featuring private schools. 'And,' he said, '*Zéro de Conduite.*'

'*Oh là là*' I said, 'a *French* film. The gloves are off.' I thought hard. '*Harry Potter*, films one to eight,' I said, a bit shakily. 'That's eight points.'

Dad could obviously hear the nerves in my voice. He knows

so many films he could have beaten me easily, but he must have decided that today wasn't the day. 'All right,' he said, giving me his lopsided grin. 'You win.' He looked up at the grand entrance, and the antlers over the door. 'Let's get this over with.'

And we did. I had the interview, I did the exam, I got in. And eight months later, at the beginning of autumn term, I was walking through the entrance of the school, under the antlers, as a sixth-form student.

I was soon to learn that antlers are, appropriately, a big thing at STAGS. Antlers bristle from every wall. There is also a stag on the school emblem, with the words *Festina Lente* embroidered underneath. (No, I didn't know either; it's Latin and it means 'Make Haste Slowly'.) In the chapel those frescoes that I mentioned show scenes from the 'miraculous' stag hunt, when St Aidan turned the stag invisible. There is also a really old stained-glass window in the chapel, of him holding one finger up in front of the face of a nervous-looking stag, as if he is trying to shush it. I've stared at those frescoes and that window a lot, because we have to go to chapel every morning, which is pretty boring.

As well as being boring, chapel is freezing cold. It's the only time I am glad to be wearing the STAGS uniform. The uniform consists of a long black Tudor coat of thick felt, all the way down to your knees, with gilt buttons down the front. At the neck we wear a white clerical tie, and at the waist a slim deer-leather belt which has to be knotted in a particular way. Under the coat we wear bright red stockings, the colour of arterial blood. It is pretty dumb as outfits go, but at least it keeps you warm on the borders of Northumberland.

STAGS, as you might imagine, is pretty religious. Me and my dad are not religious at all, but we kind of left that fact off the application form. In fact, we may have given the distinct impression that we were churchgoers. That was back when I actually *wanted* to go to the school. Dad was going to be mostly abroad for two years, making a wildlife documentary for the BBC, and if I hadn't come to STAGS I would have had to go to live with my Aunty Karen, and *believe* me, I didn't want to do that. My headmistress at Bewley thought I had the brains to get a scholarship to STAGS and it turned out she was right. I also happen to have a photographic memory, which didn't hurt either. I can't tell you how useful it was when I was sitting that entrance exam. But if I'd known what was going to happen that autumn half-term, I wouldn't have been such a try-hard. I would have gone to my Aunty Karen's without a word.

Apart from the incessant chapel-going there are loads of other differences between STAGS and a normal school. For one thing, they call autumn term 'Michaelmas', spring term 'Hilary' and summer term 'Trinity'. For another, the teachers are called Friars, not 'Miss' or 'Sir'. So our form master, Mr Whiteread, is Friar Whiteread; and, even stranger, our housemistress (Miss Petrie) is Friar Petrie. The headmaster, a really friendly Santa Claus-looking bloke who I met at interview, is called the Abbot. If that wasn't odd enough, the Friars wear a weird gown like a monk's habit over their suits, with knotted ropes at the waist. A lot of the Friars are ex-pupils and keep going on about when they were at STAGS in their day (which, by the sounds of it, was *exactly* the same – STAGS is so antiquated I'd be surprised if a single thing had changed). The Friars are practically antiques themselves – I'd have to guess they're all in their sixties. There's no doubt that this gives them loads of teaching experience, but I've also got a sneaking suspicion that oldies were employed so that no one would ever, *ever* fancy any of them. There's absolutely no danger of any of those teacher–pupil relationships you read about online.

The sports are strange at STAGS as well; we don't play ordinary games like netball and hockey and football but things like fives and real tennis, in Tudor wooden courts out beyond the playing fields. Those playing fields, known as Bede's Piece, are immense, but are not used for anything standard like athletics, only for sports like rugby ('rugger') and lacrosse. STAGS has its own theatre, but it doesn't have any fancy lighting or sets; it's a faithful Jacobean replica playhouse lit by candles. *Candles.* Instead of German and French we study Latin and Greek. The food too is different from normal school food, in that it is really nice. Actually it's amazing – it's the sort you would get in a really good restaurant, not at all like the slop we used to get at Bewley Park. Meals are served by women from the local village, who seem perfectly nice but are rewarded with the nickname 'dinnerbags'. But the major difference between STAGS and a normal school is, as you might have guessed, that it costs an absolute fortune. The STAGS parents pay the fees willingly, and it didn't take me long to figure out what they are paying for. They are not paying for their little darlings to benefit from the Jacobean theatre, or the Olympic-sized swimming pool, or for the incredible, knock-your-eyes-out beauty of the place. What they are paying for is for their children to be different too.

For the first thousand years or so there were just four houses at STAGS: Honorius, Bede, Oswald and Paulinus. Then a few decades ago they started to admit girls, so they founded a new girls' house called Lightfoot. I was told in my admissions letter that the Lightfoot dormitories were in one of the more 'modern' buildings, and I arrived expecting lots of pine and glass and central heating. It turned out that the Lightfoot building was built in 1550, and was all diamond-paned windows and crazy spiral chimneys. At STAGS 1550 was evidently considered 'modern'.

My room was on the third floor at the end of a panelled Tudor passageway. Through an immense oak door, the room itself was modern. It had chipboard furniture, office-blue carpets and a girl already in it. The habit of thinking in films was a hard one to break. If my first encounter with my roommate was in a film script, it would look like this.

GREER (smiling): I'm Greer. What's your name?

Greer's roommate looks her up and down in a snotty way.

ROOMMATE (rolling her eyes): *Jesus.*

After that first encounter I always called her 'Jesus' to myself, because it made me smile, and there was little enough for me to smile about at STAGS. I found out later that her name was actually Becca. She was a horse-mad girl, who had pictures of her ponies on her wall like I had pictures of my dad. Maybe she missed them as much as I missed him. I didn't see how. That's pretty much it for dialogue in this part of the story. There will be lots later, but the sad truth was no one talked to me much in that first half-term. Teachers asked me questions in lessons; the dinnerbags would say things like, 'Chips or mash, hinny?' (Their accents would make me homesick.) And Shafeen, this kid in my learning set, would occasionally murmur things at me like, 'The thermal stability of the nitrates follows the same trend as that of the carbonates.'

Despite sharing a room with me, Jesus did not talk to me until it was nearly half-term, and that was only because I got The Invitation. I now think that if I'd had more friends – or *any* friends – in that first half-term, I never would have accepted The Invitation. Maybe I accepted it because I was lonely. Or maybe, if I'm being honest, I accepted it because it came from the best-looking boy in the school.

chapter two

I mean, of course, Henry de Warlencourt.

You might have read about him online by now, on that creepy Facebook page they set up for him, or seen his picture on the news. But back then he wasn't famous – or infamous – outside of his own circle. They say you shouldn't speak ill of the dead so I'll just say you would never have known by looking at him what a terrible person he was.

I have to really struggle, now, to remember him as I first saw him; to be fair to that first impression, and try to forget what I know now. He was, quite simply, the most gorgeous boy I'd ever seen. Tall for seventeen, all blond hair, blue eyes and tanned skin. When people were around Henry de Warlencourt they watched him all the time, even though they pretended they weren't. Even the Friars seemed to be in awe of Henry. He never got punished for anything – and that's not because he didn't do anything wrong; it's because he got away with it. He was like one of those really cool frying pans that everything slides off. He thought he was invincible. But he wasn't.

Henry de Warlencourt was as British as they come, despite his foreign-sounding name. Apparently some distant ancestor had fought in the Frankish army on the Crusades, and had settled in England afterwards, conveniently marrying some noblewoman who owned half of northern England. The de Warlencourts had been fabulously rich ever since. Their house, Longcross Hall, is a beautiful manor house in the Lake District. I know it better than I ever would have wanted to, because Longcross was the scene of the crime.

Because I was in the top set for all my subjects I saw Henry de Warlencourt a lot; him and his five closest friends. The six of them were known as the Medievals. Everyone knew the Medievals, because it was the Medievals – not the Friars – who really ran STAGS.

The Medievals were the unofficial prefects of the school. You'd see them walking in the quad in their immaculate uniforms, long black coats fluttering in the autumn breeze. The Medievals were allowed to wear any colour stockings they wanted under their Tudor coats, and they emphasised this privilege by choosing crazy patterns like leopard print, or tartan, or chessboard checks. But it wasn't just the stockings that marked them out; it was a particular kind of confidence they had about them. They lolled about like expensive cats. That confidence, that comfort in their surroundings, told you that their houses were probably not that different to STAGS; that they probably had grounds too, rather than gardens, and houses with wings, instead of neighbours. And antlers too, houses with lots of antlers on the walls.

The Medievals were all tall, beautiful and clever, as if they were especially bred for the job. They held court in the Paulinus quad – a beautiful square of perfectly manicured grass, surrounded by four walkways of elegant arched cloisters, at the heart of Paulinus house.

Henry de Warlencourt was always at the centre of the group, his blond head visible, as if he was that king at Versailles, whichever one it was, one of those millions of Louis. Henry was the sun, and the rest revolved around him. They would hang out there in all weathers, talking, reading and, after dark, secretly smoking. There was a sort of ancient stone well in the middle of the quad, and if you ever got close enough to look down it, you could see that about a foot down a circle of chicken wire had been fixed for safety, and the chicken wire was stuffed with cigarette butts. I once dropped a coin through the holes, to see how deep it was. I listened for ages, but couldn't hear the splash of the coin hitting the water. I assumed that the bottom of the well was so full of fag butts that they were cushioning the coin's fall. The Paulinus well was just like the Medievals themselves. It looked pretty, but in its depths it was gross.

If Henry was the Medievals' leader, Cookson was his second-in command. Cookson was actually called Henry Cookson, but he was always known by his second name, as there could only be one Henry in the group. Cookson was good-looking too, as they all were, but he still looked like a bad photocopy of Henry. He was slightly smaller, slightly chubbier and his hair was a dirtier blond. His features were blunter, his skin paler, his voice more braying. But the two were inseparable, as close as the brothers they resembled.

The third boy in the group was Piers. Piers was elegant, and dark, and he had a monobrow that made him look like he was constantly annoyed. Piers added little details to his uniform, like a pocket watch, and a tooled leather belt instead of the regulation slim tan, and handmade shoes from his London bootmaker. Piers had been Henry's friend since they'd been shipped off to the junior bit of STAGS – the prep school – at the age of eight.

The three girls were pretty similar in appearance, all blonde-haired and blue-eyed. We'd been studying Homer in Greek that term and they reminded me of the Sirens: beautiful mermaids who looked gorgeous but would actually lure sailors to their deaths. Their names were Esme, Charlotte and Lara. They were all pretty, and slim, and they managed to make the strange ecclesiastical uniform look like something from the catwalks of Milan. Charlotte was some distant cousin of Henry's, Esme was minor royalty, and Lara, seemingly as British as the rest of them, was from a Russian family with an Oligarch-level fortune. They all had that hair that lifts at the hairline and falls over one eye, and they constantly flicked it from one side to the other as they talked. My hair (bobbed, black, heavy fringe) doesn't behave like that, but all the other girls at STAGS (including, tragically, my roommate Jesus) tried to copy their style. To begin with I made the mistake of mixing the Medieval girls up, dismissing them as all the same. If Dad was here to play our film game we'd be saying *Heathers* or *Mean Girls*, but those movies don't really do justice to the evil that lived behind the white smiles. They weren't dumb blondes, those girls, they were highly intelligent; you underestimated them at your peril, and that's exactly what I did.

All of the Medievals were incredibly rich – Henry's family had been coming here for centuries, and the school theatre was even called the De Warlencourt Playhouse. Lara's family, it was rumoured, paid for the pool. This made them behave as if they owned the place; because they kind of did.

There were only ever six Medievals, three boys and three girls from Six Two – the second year of sixth form. But beyond this hard core there were a whole bunch of hangers-on who idolised them, and did exactly what they wanted in the hope that in Six Two they would become Medievals themselves. Every year, six Medievals leave and a new pack is forged, so there are plenty of wannabes hanging around. Jesus is definitely one – she would die to be a Medieval.

All of the Medievals were OK individually; I was in a lot of their classes and they could be quite human. But when they were in a pack, like hounds, that's when you wanted to be invisible, like Aidan's stag. They mostly left me alone; occasionally the three girls would mimic my accent and snigger behind their hands once I'd walked past them in the quad. I'd feel like there was a cold stone of unhappiness lodged just below my ribs, and the feeling wouldn't subside until I'd gotten out of their eyeline. But I had it easy. Some people seemed to be in their crosshairs all the time. People like Shafeen.

Want to read
NEW BOOKS
before anyone else?

Like getting
FREE BOOKS?

Enjoy sharing your
OPINIONS?

Discover

READERS
FIRST

Read. Love. Share.

Get your first free book just by signing up at
readersfirst.co.uk

HOT KEY BOOKS

Thank you for choosing a Hot Key book.

If you want to know more about our authors and what we publish, you can find us online.

You can start at our website

www.hotkeybooks.com

And you can also find us on:

We hope to see you soon!